City of Ice

Scirye gave a jump when the bear reared up to his full height. There was so much of him! He had looked imposing enough when seen from above. Up close, he was downright terrifying. He towered over her like a white furry mountain. A growling furry mountain . . . with big claws.

Her legs suddenly turned to jelly, and she plopped backward onto the snow. As she sat on her rump gazing up at him, the bear seemed even more gigantic. When people saw bears in the zoo, it was easy to think that humans had tamed Nature, but they were only fooling themselves. Away from their cities, humans were lunches who very considerately delivered themselves to the animal diners.

"Why," the bear rumbled in a voice like boulders rumbling down a hill, "have you invaded my territory?"

STARSCAPE BOOKS BY LAURENCE YEP

City of Fire

City of Ice

City of Death
(forthcoming from Starscape)

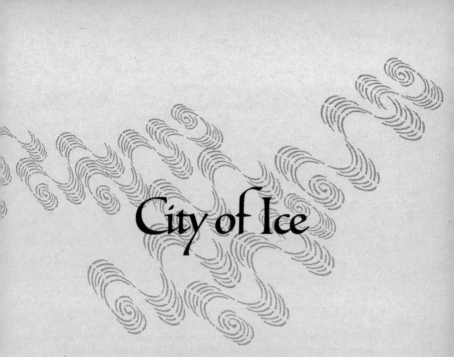

City of Ice

– CITY TRILOGY II –

Laurence Yep

A TOM DOHERTY ASSOCIATES BOOK
NEW YORK

This is a work of fiction. All of the characters, organizations, and events portrayed in this novel are either products of the author's imagination or are used fictitiously.

CITY OF ICE

Copyright © 2011 by Laurence Yep

City of Death excerpt copyright © 2011 by Laurence Yep

Reader's Guide copyright © 2011 by Tor Books

All rights reserved.

A Starscape Book
Published by Tom Doherty Associates, LLC
175 Fifth Avenue
New York, NY 10010

www.tor-forge.com

ISBN 978-0-7653-5880-6

First Edition: June 2011
First Mass Market Edition: June 2012

Printed in the United States of America

0 9 8 7 6 5 4 3 2 1

To Joanne, who dragged me up to Chena Hot Springs,
where I got to see the Aurora Borealis and
ride in a dogsled that hit a tree

Guide to Pronunciation
of Kushan Names

Ajumaq (Ah-yuh-mak). Arctic creature whose touch is deadly.

Amagjat (Ah-mahg-yat). A hag who preys on unwary travelers in the Far North.

Klestetstse (Klays-tayts-tsay). More often shortened to Kles (Klays). Scirye's lap griffin, a gift from Princess Maimantstse.

Koyn Encuwontse (Koin En-coo-wōn-tsay). Iron Beak.

Lady Miunai (Mee-oo-neye). Mother to Roxanna.

Lady Sudarshane (Soo-dar-sha-nay). Scirye's mother.

Lady Tabiti (Ta-bee-tee). A legendary Sarmatian warrior chief.

Lord Resak (Re-shak). An Arctic spirit.

Lord Tsirauñe (Tsee-rou-nay). Scirye's father.

Nana (Nah-nah). The Sogdian name of Nanaia.

Nanaia (Na-ni-ah). A goddess worshipped by the Kushans.

Nishke (Neesh-kay). Scirye's older sister.

Prince Etre (Ay-tray). Kushan Consul.

Prince Tarkhun (Tar-koon). A Sogdian prince and father to Roxanna.

Princess Maimantstse (My-man-tsuh-tsay). Cousin of Scirye's father.

Rapañne (Rah-pan-nay). Scirye's clan.

Riye Srukalleyis (Ree-yay Sroo-kal-lay-ees). City of Death.

Roxanna (Rok-sah-nah). The daughter of Prince Tarkhun and Lady Miunai who knows the Arctic like the back of her hand.

Sakre Menantse (Sa-kray May-nan-tsay). A name for the Kushan Empire, meaning "Blessed of the Moon."

Sakre Yapoy (Sa-kray Ya-poi). Another name for the Kushan Empire, meaning "the Blessed Land."

Scirye (Skeer-yay). Mistress of Kles.

Taqqiq (Tak-keek).

Tarkär (Tar-kir). Cloud.

Tizheruk (Tee-zer-ook). A serpent-like monster in the Arctic.

Upach (Oo-pak). An ifrit and servant to Roxanna.

City of Ice

1

Scirye

Scirye and her companions were thirty miles from
the city of Nova Hafnia, located near the Arctic
Circle, when they found the battle. Or rather, the
battle found them.

They had flown this far north in search of Roland, one of the
richest men in the world, and Badik, a malevolent dragon. Roland had ordered Badik to steal an antique archer's ring, a great
treasure of Scirye's Kushan people, from a San Francisco museum and killed Scirye's sister, Nishke, during the theft. Leech's
good friend and mentor, Primo, had also died during the theft.

Scirye, Leech, and their friends had set out in pursuit, the
chase taking them through a Hawaiian volcano where they had
fought by the side of the goddess Pele. When Roland had stolen
a second treasure from Pele, the goddess had summoned the

Cloud Folk to spin a wing out of straw, a triangle about thirty feet at its base and sixty feet long. Small triangles stuck up from its tail and belly like fins to make it more aerodynamic.

They had been flying for a week and, as usual, Naue was singing his own praises: "I am Naue, whose kindness dwarfs even his awesome strength."

Naue was one of the world's great winds, whom Pele had asked to carry the wing to the Arctic. Though he was as powerful as a hurricane, he had the mind, patience, and emotions of a three-year-old. "I outrace the sun and tickle the stars," he sang. There seemed to be no end to Naue's achievements—at least in Naue's mind.

"What's that?" Scirye asked, straining to hear over Naue's roaring.

"What's what, my lady?" Kles yawned. The griffin, only eight inches high, lay curled up on her lap like a napping kitten.

Scriye cradled her friend in the palms of her hands and deposited him on her shoulder. The lap griffin promptly curved around her neck so that his hindquarters remained on one of her shoulders while his head rested on the other as if he were a collar of tawny fur and feathers. Warm. Cozy. And very tickly.

Rising, she stepped carefully, because the matlike surface of the wing gave slightly beneath her feet, and got as close as she dared to the edge of the frame.

The frame was only four slender posts of straw united by crossbeams of the same material, and it sat within the center of the wing. The frame looked flimsy enough, like an unfinished house of straw, or a child's crude sketch of a house. But it shielded them against the winds and freezing cold.

This far north, Elios the Sun only lingered for four hours and even then his beams were weak. Scirye strained her eyes as she scanned the clouds below. They looked like the dirty stuffing of an old mattress that had been strewn about below from horizon to horizon. "It sounds like a motor."

Koko the tanuki was busy grooming his pepper-colored fur. The fastidious Japanese badger did that at least once a day. "All I can hear is that . . ." He mouthed the word "airbag" and waved his paw in an all-encompassing gesture to indicate Naue.

The wing lurched violently and then began to buck as Naue roared, "What did you say, Noisy Lumpling?" All ground dwellers were lumplings to Naue.

Scirye gripped the frame for support. For a creature without ears, Naue had very good hearing. "Oh, mighty Naue"—the wind ate up praise the way a child ate candy—"my friend is so full of admiration that he can think of nothing else but your magnificence."

The wing settled back into a smooth flight. "Well, of course," Naue said. "Am I not Naue, greatest of winds?"

Since Scirye's mother, Lady Sudarshane, was a diplomat, Scirye had heard more than her share of boring speeches at embassy functions. Out of sheer survival, Scirye had learned how to pretend polite interest in anything. "Yes, please, tell us more about your exploits."

As the wind started a booming, roisterous song about some race between himself and some Greek zephyrs, Scirye wondered how her father would have handled Naue. He was the imperial Griffin Master of her homeland, the Kushan Empire, which had grown rich and powerful controlling the trade between Asia and Europe for two thousand years. Scirye was sure her father, more at home in the sky than on the land and more comfortable with the creatures of the air than humans, would have Naue as eager to please him as a puppy.

Kles pointedly set a claw against his beak. "Don't hurt his

feelings," the griffin cautioned the badger softly, "unless you can sprout a pair of wings."

"Heads-up!" a boy cried.

Koko barely rolled onto his back in time as Koko's partner, the human boy Leech, buzzed low over the badger, the flying disks at the boy's ankles humming. They were metal circles that, when expanded to about a foot and a half in diameter, he was able to stand and fly about on—but he was still learning and practiced every chance he got.

In a second, though, he came up short against the frame and, crossing his legs, turned himself around in a neat maneuver.

Koko fluttered a paw at him as if Leech were an oversize mosquito. "Shoo! Go buzz that overgrown lizard."

An orphan, Leech had run away and joined forces with Koko, and they had survived in the mean streets of San Francisco with their wits. He had grown up thinking that he was gutter trash until he had met the man named Primo, who had begun educating him. He'd been devastated by Primo's death until he'd discovered how magical the disks were. Now they made him feel special and let him do what he loved the most: flying.

"What's up?" he asked Scirye.

"There's a kind of buzzing?" she asked.

Leech bobbed up and down a few inches while he listened intently. After a moment, he nodded. "I bet it's an airplane."

"I hear it too," Bayang the dragon said. She was sitting at the apex of the wing, holding on to the reinlike straw rope that guided their woven craft along. Though she could have flown them on her back, she would have been too worn-out for the battle that no doubt awaited them at the end of their journey. Not only could Roland hire an army of human and magical mercenaries, but Badik the dragon would also be there.

Bayang craned her long neck now and squinted, trying to

glimpse the source of the noise that Scirye had heard. At the same time, Scirye leaned against the frame, which was as strong as steel despite how flimsy it appeared. Leech flew over to the opposite side to check there.

Leech slapped the frame. "There's the airplane."

Scirye followed his pointing finger. She saw light wink off something flat and silvery below. "But is it Roland's?"

Scirye tensed, hoping that they were nearing the end of the chase. "I hope so."

"I'll go check it out," Leech said eagerly, and started to rise out of the frame.

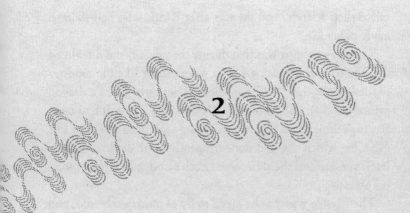

2

Bayang

The stupid little fool was making it so hard to keep him alive.

It was hard to believe that she had once thought of Leech as her prey, but then the idiot had the nerve to save her life. Even though she had been grateful, it had violated her professional standards as an assassin: Prey was supposed to be hunted, not helpful. It was just like a human not to respect his own place in the natural order of things.

And when she'd seen Badik stealing the Chinese archer's ring in the museum, she knew that her clan, the Dragons of the Moonglow, had worse problems than Leech. Badik and his clan, the Dragons of the Fire Rings, had almost destroyed her clan, so she'd joined Leech and Scirye. They were after Roland, who had killed their friends, and she was after Badik, who had slain so many of her kin.

The strange thing was that during the pursuit, she'd realized that the friendly, trusting Leech was nothing like the monster of the legends, Lee No Cha, who had not only killed a dragon prince but then had also made his skin into a belt. It had been Bayang's unpleasant task to assassinate each incarnation of Lee No Cha, which she had done diligently until she had met the latest version and she'd become Leech's bodyguard rather than his assassin.

The trouble was that he loved to fly as much as she did, and she remembered her own delight when she had first flown. However, that same eagerness made fledglings misjudge the level of their own skills and killed more of them than anything else.

Stretching out her tail, Bayang wrapped the tip around Leech's ankle. The disks were so powerful that she almost lost her grip, and she really had to haul at his leg to pull him back to safety.

"Stay in the frame, you little idiot! How many times do I have to warn you? You'll blow away if you stray outside it." She held on to him just to make sure he didn't try again.

Leech tried to tug himself free. "You're not my mother."

Bayang stiffened. "Don't be ridiculous! I'm a dragon and you're . . . a . . . a . . ." She caught her lip turning up in a sneer as she was about to say "human." Among dragons, that could be a deadly insult.

And yet his words, though true, hurt. She hadn't realized that the hatchling, her former enemy, had become so entwined with her life that she was vulnerable to his insults. When had that happened?

But he's right, Bayang admitted ruefully to herself. *No mother, dragon or human, would have done to him what you've done.*

I've killed all those earlier versions of him. And even if your sins could be erased, you're of two different species.

"True," she said. "So think of me as your bodyguard. In that capacity, I'm telling you that a human couldn't withstand the force. And even if you could, you'd freeze. If a dragon like me has trouble when I leave the frame to clear the ice from the wing, what hope does a human have?"

He still looked rebellious. "We'll never know unless you let me try."

She wondered if she had shown as much resentment when her flight instructor, Sergeant Pindai, had held her back. Probably. However, she hadn't dared talk back to the sergeant. The human hatchlings were the opposite, demanding reasons for orders that were actually just common sense.

"And what if Badik is in the airplane and comes out to attack you?" Kles asked.

Leech slapped his other armband. "I've got my weapon ring for that." The armband would expand into a metal ring, stronger than steel.

"You don't know enough yet," Bayang said.

"Whose fault is that?" Leech demanded. "You made me quit practicing."

Koko pointed to his forehead. "For all our sakes. You nearly beaned me on the noggin twice when you were swinging that thing."

"And what if you hit the airplane by accident?" Bayang pointed out. "If the airplane crashed, we'd lose the ring."

"Yes," Kles agreed. "From its heading, the airplane must be going to Nova Hafnia."

"A plane that size would need to re-fuel," Bayang reasoned. "When it lands, we'll see if it's Roland and Badik. And if it is, we strike."

"Okay, okay, gang up on me," Leech griped, and, folding his arms, he squatted a few inches above the mat.

"Now you're being sensible." She let go of his ankle and sat upright again. Beneath her, the airplane seemed to float along as serenely as a toy and then disappeared beneath a high layer of clouds.

Her shoulders ached and she was tired, for it was tricky to fly the wing within the turbulent sky currents. She'd been the only one to handle it all this time. Even though a dragon's power of endurance matched her strength, Bayang was nearing her limits. But she felt the excitement of the hunt surge through her.

Let's see if we can get close enough to check on the passengers, she thought. "Oh, mighty Naue, I've marveled at your skills. Great is your strength. Swift is your speed. And yet how delicate is your touch? Could you skim just above those clouds below without ripping them apart?"

"Is not Naue as tender as a moonbeam? As gentle as down?" Naue answered.

The wing angled downward as the wind began to descend until it was slipping over the top of the clouds, the mist barely rippling along the surface as it flew.

With gentle tugs, Bayang skillfully maneuvered the wing until they were as low as they could go and still be in Naue's embrace.

After a while, the clouds thinned until they seemed like gauze. They had flown close enough for her to see the airplane was a Ford Trimotor with engines on the wing and the nose. Instead of wheels, though, it had long skis for landing on snow or ice.

Kles made a hollow growling noise. "I smell falcon stench." The griffin's fur and feathers bristled at the scent of his rivals for the sky.

Scirye quickly reached her hand up to stroke his back. "Calm down, Kles. Calm. We don't want you going wild on us."

Peering over the edge of the wings, Bayang saw two giant falcons climbing toward the airplane. The Danish empire had used them as mounts for centuries and this species had been bred specially for the Arctic. Their bodies were the size of cars and their wings as wide as a small airplane's, but their great white feathers made them deceptively fluffy. Balls of down hid their eyes, their legs, and their claws and left their beaks half-covered so that they seemed shorter than they really were.

On their backs were human riders in heavy leather jackets padded with wool. One of them wore a helmet of the Nu Danmark colonial forces, but the other had a leather cap with flaps that covered his ears. Both of them wore leather boots that rose to mid-thigh.

"Bad luck for the airplane then," Bayang said. "They've run into some freebooters. The British and Danish empires fought a savage little war for the Arctic territories thirty years ago. Eventually, the Danes wound up ceding this area to the British in exchange for money, so Nu Danmark became the Cabot Territory. But the Danish colonial forces refused to surrender. They call themselves resistance fighters, but they're not much more than bandits."

The freebooters circled the airplane, their rifles trained on it. But then the airplane wagged its wings, the light flickering from one wingtip to another.

A door opened on the airplane fuselage and a human stepped out. Even as he began to drop, his outline blurred and he became the scarred dragon who had haunted Bayang's nightmares since she was a hatchling. Badik. Many years ago, he had attacked her clan.

Hatred swelled within Bayang and almost made her leap off

the wing and dive for her revenge. But the human hatchlings could never control the straw wing on their own, so she stayed, gnashing her fangs together with frustrated clacks.

"Wherever Badik is so's Roland," Leech said.

Bayang waited for the freebooters to shoot at Badik or flee, but instead Badik and the riders seemed to be talking. Then the humans actually saluted and banked away.

When Badik gripped the open doorway of the airplane, it dipped under the weight and then righted itself. As he still held on, his shape blurred until he was human again and could step inside and shut the door behind him.

Koko said, "So those big feather dusters are in cahoots with Roland."

"He probably hired them for whatever he's got planned," Bayang said. "I think we'll carry on with our original plan and catch them in Nova Hafnia."

The airplane suddenly increased its speed, pulling away from the freebooters. Bayang's paws tightened on the straw control loops of the wing. They were so near their goal now.

She was just about to coax Naue into going faster when something whistled past. A second and then a third followed immediately.

The badger put a claw through one of three neat little round holes in the wing. "Please tell me that it was big mosquitoes that made these and not bullets."

Worried, Bayang scanned the clouds ahead and underneath. Armored in scales, she had little to fear from bullets, but the human hatchlings were so fragile. The slightest thing could puncture them. It was a new sensation to feel this vulnerable, not for herself but because of others.

The freebooters were rising toward them, rifles aimed at the large target that was the wing.

"Hey, Naue," Koko yelled to the wind, "giddy-yap and take us out of here."

"No mere lumpling can command Naue," the wind declared haughtily.

Bayang had learned tactics from Sergeant Pindai as well as how to fly, and there was little that the wily old soldier didn't know. "If you can't beat an enemy, run," she had told Bayang. "But if you can't outrun them, outwit them."

Thinking fast, Bayang twisted her head around and warned the others to hold on to the straw loops woven into the wing. Then, lifting her head, she shouted to the wind, "Oh, mighty Naue, I know those lumplings below. They said they know a wind who's stronger and faster."

"They lie," the wind bellowed angrily.

The air currents around them grew turbulent and the wing bucked and danced, but still Bayang went on egging the proud gale.

"Lies, lies, lies!" With a deafening bellow, Naue dove, taking their wing with him.

It was like riding a raft down the rapids of a river and it was all Bayang could do to hang on to the loops.

The shocked freebooters never had time to fire as Naue barreled through them. They were knocked loose from their stirrups, and riders and birds screamed as they spun away to the sides, and then Naue was plunging into the thick bank of clouds himself, tearing the mist apart as if it were cotton matting.

For a moment, Bayang couldn't see, but fine drops sheeted against the invisible walls of the frame, thickening as they sank lower until it was like rain.

And then they broke through the clouds, mist hanging in tattered rags from the edges of the wing.

And—what was it the humans said? Bayang wondered. *Yes, it was out of the frying pan and into the fire.*

Literally.

Beneath them, a caravan of huge bargelike wind sleds slid along on runners, sails flapping from the sleds' masts as cannon boomed from their decks. Like wolves snapping at a herd of buffalo were small wind sleds carrying freebooters. Their rifles flashed with popping noises.

And Bayang and her friends were plunging straight toward them.

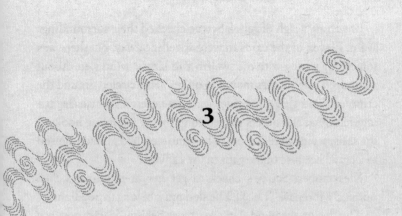

3

Scirye

"Pull up; pull up!" Koko screamed as they plummeted downward and the ground rose up toward them with alarming speed.

In front of Scirye, Bayang was digging her claws into the straw mat and hauling up at the control loops as she tried to free the wing from the wind's grip. It was amazing that the flimsy ropes didn't snap under the strain.

And suddenly they were whipping upward again as Naue leveled off fifty feet from the ground. As they soared parallel to the ground, the wind roared with laughter. "Ho, ho, ho, you lumplings screech like baby cave zephyrs."

Scirye didn't think it was a compliment, but Koko didn't care. "Zipper or zephyr, you can call me what you like. Just don't wear out my ticker." The badger wheezed.

Breathing a sigh of relief, Scirye checked their surroundings again. Eleven of the caravan were speeding away, but there was something wrong with the twelfth and largest wind sled. About a hundred freebooters mounted on reindeer circled around the crippled wind sled. One rider waved a tattered Danish flag triumphantly as the others darted in to throw grappling hooks at the sails, trying to tear them. The wind sled had already slowed to a crawl because of the gaps in the canvas.

Kles tapped Scirye's cheek to get her attention and then pointed a forepaw. "Look! The sled must belong to Sogdians."

The flag on the wind sled's mast was beginning to droop as it lost speed, but Scirye could just make out the red fire emblem on the field of yellow. She knew that symbol because her Sogdian nursemaid had worn a pin of it.

Just to the north of the Kushan Empire, the Sogdians had once been fierce warriors. But their wars with Alexander the Great and his Greek successors, then the nomads and the Chinese, had worn down their strength. So the survivors had poured their tremendous energy into trade instead of into fighting—though they could still put up a good fight, as the freebooters were finding out.

Riflemen in red coats and steel helmets fired from the sled's deck, and little cannon, mounted on swivels at the bow, the sides, and the stern, flashed and boomed at the attacking freebooters.

Scirye couldn't help remembering her nursemaid, fondly recalling the soft, warm voice singing Sogdian lullabies to her and how the plump woman had wept when she and her sister and mother had left for the Istanbul embassy. Her father had stayed behind in the empire because of his duties as the Griffin Master, for he not only oversaw the imperial eyrie—from lap griffins like Kles to the full-size racing and war griffins—but he also was in charge of the tricky relationship between all the griffins and humans in the empire. As strong and commanding a person as he was, he'd been crying too as he tried to comfort their old servant.

Scirye turned to Bayang. "We have to save them."

"I'm sorry for them," the dragon said, "but we're going after Roland and Badik. We can't risk wandering into a fight that isn't ours."

It was a hard choice, but Scirye had already made many difficult ones. "I don't expect you to help me," she said, trying to keep the frightened tremor from her voice, "but Kles and I have to help them. They're friends of the Kushans. So let us off and then go on ahead. We'll catch up with you somehow."

Scirye couldn't help feeling sad. She had spent most of her childhood moving from one consulate to another whenever her mother had changed posts, so she had never grown close to anyone except Kles. But in the short time that she'd been with her companions, she'd come to think of them as friends.

"Are you crazy?" Koko asked, but the look he gave them suggested he had already made his decision on that matter. "What're you going to do by yourselves? Do you even know these guys?"

"They could be kin to a person who was very important to me," Scirye said. *Since Sogdians have big clans and extended families, someone's probably related to Nanny.*

Leech studied her. "This is one of those Tumarg things, isn't it?" Tumarg was the Way of Light, the code of the warrior, and staying true to those laws, Scirye's sister, Nishke, had died defending her mother and sister and one of her people's greatest treasures.

Even though she knew she could never match her sister's example, Scirye nodded. "I have to do this."

"Then," Leech said, "I guess they're important to us too."

It was Scirye's turn to be surprised. "But Bayang is right. It's not your fight."

Bayang harrumphed. "You don't understand. If we're going to defeat Roland and Badik, we have to work as a team, and you're an important part of that team."

"So let's vote," Leech said, and lifted up his hand. "I say we help out."

Bayang nodded. "I second that."

"Well, I don't," Koko said, thumping his heels in frustration so that the wing shook slightly. "This is nuts."

"The 'ayes' have it," Bayang said. "Motion carried." Lifting her head, the dragon called to Naue again: "Oh, mighty Naue. Can you help the people below?"

"Pele only commanded me to help you," the willful wind replied. "Great Naue is not your puppet."

Bayang frowned. "Pele will be displeased."

"Pele is not here." Naue laughed. "So do not tell me what pleases her and what does not."

Scirye decided that if the strategy had worked for Bayang, it would work for her. "We understand, Naue," she wheedled. "You are too powerful to be anyone's servant. And anyway, a wind as strong as you could never touch such tiny sails without tearing them." As a precaution, she motioned her griffin inside her coveralls.

"I am Naue," the wind boasted. "I am the most delicate of winds. I can pick up a pebble without disturbing anything. A grain of sand. A tear from a baby's face. Sails are nothing."

The next moment the wind had swept lower and they were charging across the plain, raising sheets of snow in their wake. Naue bowled over the freebooters and their mounts like so many bowling pins.

The wind sled swelled in their view until they could see the Sogdian crew pointing at them.

"Hey, we're the good guys!" Koko cried in alarm as the Sogdians raised their rifles and swiveled their cannon to aim at them.

Scirye's nursemaid had taught her Sogdian, but that had been a simplistic toddler's vocabulary. From the dim recesses of her memory, she shouted hurriedly, "Friend! Friend!"

Kles had poked his head out of her coveralls and saw what was happening.

"Oh, warriors who travel like shadows across sand and snow," he shouted loudly in formal Sogdian. Even though Common Sogdian was used more often, the formal dialect was more polite and proper for a first encounter. "We have come to aid thee in thy hour of peril. Do not shoot your mighty weapons of death lest we perish!"

A big man in a hooded fur coat barked out a sharp command and the red-coated Sogdians lowered their rifles.

Naue puffed at the torn sails so they swelled like bubbles, and the wind sled shot forward as if it had rockets instead of runners.

"Ha, this is fun," Naue boomed.

The snowy plain had seemed so flat when seen from far above, but now Scirye could see how it was humped by small ridges. The wind sled's riders cried out as the sled bounced into the air and then banged down, sending crates and passengers sliding about the deck.

Still, the wind sled raced on until Scirye heard the sound of cloth tearing and saw the sled's sails were shredding. Strips whipped back and forth, and the sled's timbers creaked and groaned under the strain of a speed for which the sled was never designed.

"Mighty Naue, please stop," Scirye begged.

"Yes, I'm tired of this game." Naue laughed. "Let's play something else."

They veered to their right suddenly, circling back toward the freebooters.

Some of the raiders were searching for their lost weapons in the snow. Others were trying to round up their scattered mounts.

They seemed shocked to see the wing returning. A few tried to raise their guns and a submachine gun chattered briefly, but Naue twisted and curled back and forth like a snake, tumbling the freebooters onto their backs and sending the terrified reindeer bolting.

"Ho! I like this new game," Naue declared.

"Oog," Koko moaned. "I think I'm going to be sick."

Scirye was feeling dizzy herself from their wild ride, and even an experienced flier like Kles was clinging to her as if he, too, was feeling nauseous. She wound up shutting her eyes against the spinning world and gripping the straps for dear life

Just when she thought the nightmare would never end, she suddenly felt the wing straighten out.

"Ha, that was more fun than wrestling a typhoon," Naue exulted. "Now what else shall we do?"

Daring to open her eyes, she looked behind her and saw that the plain was littered with groaning freebooters lying in the snow. Beyond them the Sogdian wind sled was moving away, disappearing into the horizon as its momentum swept it on. It took her a moment to realize they were heading away from the mountains and Nova Hafnia and instead into the barren wilderness, away from Roland and Badik.

4

Leech

The others were pleading with Naue to turn around, but that only seemed to make the arrogant wind more determined to go on in the same direction.

Leech unfolded his legs cautiously, but Bayang was too distracted to notice. He still wasn't sure how much he could trust her. She'd told him that the original Leech—he didn't know how many lives ago that was—had killed a dragon prince and made a belt out of his hide and the dragons had never forgotten. Bayang had been hunting him down in all the lives after that.

He and Bayang had tried to form their own separate peace and had even fought side by side against common enemies. But she was still as arrogant as ever and kept limiting what he could do with his magical devices.

Stupid, she wants to keep you weak and helpless. She was

trying to kill you when you first met. Though she says she's changed her mind and swears she won't, she's having second thoughts. The whisper came from the back of his mind, from memories lost in shadow. He thought he'd heard it in that cellar in Honolulu when they had been following Roland and Badik to an island. He had no idea what the voice was, but he wished he could get rid of it. The best he seemed to be able to do was shove it back into the shadows and try to ignore it.

He shoved those notions away as quickly as they had come. *No, not Bayang,* he told himself. She was as dedicated to protecting his life now as she had once been determined to take it. *She's . . . she's just being overprotective.*

Oh yeah? the voice taunted. *Then show her you can handle yourself. When you leave the wing, crouch real low. You'll slice through the air like a knife.*

Leech wouldn't mind proving to Bayang that she was wrong about him. His friend Primo had always been telling him to have more confidence in himself. Leech felt a little twinge when he thought about Primo. He'd died in the museum with Scirye's sister, Nishke, trying to keep the ring from being stolen.

But this was no time to sit and mourn. As Leech began to hunch over, Koko glanced at him.

"Hey, where are you going?" the badger asked.

"I'm going to borrow a page from Bayang and Scirye's book on how to handle a windbag." As he rose within the frame, he called to the wind, "Great Naue, I dare you to race me now."

"Ho, Half Lumpling?" Naue said. Since Bayang and Leech could fly on their own, they'd been elevated to the status of half lumplings. "Yet another challenge? Didn't you see? A speeding arrow could not match Naue. How can you?"

"Scared?" Leech taunted.

"Come back!" Bayang shouted.

He ignored them, rising above the fragile-looking straw frame. He intended to turn Naue in the direction that Roland had gone. That way, they could resume the chase. However, as soon as Leech cleared the straw frame, Naue's powerful air currents caught him and he began to tumble backward like a rag doll, like a kite, like a leaf.

As he fell head over heels, he thought ruefully that Bayang had been right after all. The lower profile did not let him manage the force of Naue.

He didn't know which would be worse: her gloating or his breaking his neck.

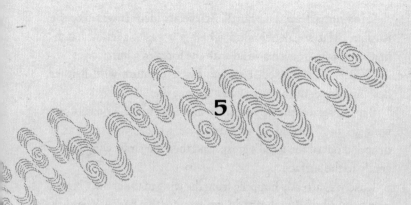

5

Bayang

As the little fool popped out of the wing's frame, it was all she could do not to go after him. *Because,* she assured herself, *I'm just trying to do my job as his bodyguard and not because I'm pretending to be his mother.*

But she had other passengers on the wing whom she could not abandon, so she stayed.

Then, to her amazement, Naue slowed and banked to the left, heading back along the huge gully left in his wake. "Fool of a half lumpling," the wind muttered. "Didn't he realize that he was no match for great Naue?"

As they returned, Bayang's stomach tightened. A dark figure lay still in the snow.

A few moments later, Naue slowed, circling leisurely like a breeze around the fallen Leech. "What a silly time to sleep!"

"He's not asleep, he's hurt!" Scirye scolded. It was like the Kushan girl to speak her mind, whether it was to a fellow hatchling, a dragon, or even a wind with the force of a hurricane.

"Hurt?" Naue asked, puzzled. For a creature with neither flesh nor bone, the concept was a strange one.

Bayang seized the opportunity and lowered the nose of the wing so they angled downward. The wing gave a jerk as it dropped out of the wind's grasp, and then the straw wing glided gently to the surface.

Koko was already hopping from the wing to the snow. "Here I come, buddy." But the padding around the badger's middle made him less than acrobatic and he wound up flopping on his belly.

Scirye followed a moment later. "Why don't you change into your human shape?" the girl inquired helpfully. "Longer legs would be better for the snow."

Koko straightened. "And give up my fur coat in this cold? Nothing doing."

"Is it really the temperature or your own clumsiness at transforming?" Bayang asked as she eased into the snow.

"Okay, okay, so I slept through some lessons," Koko said, the snow crunching under his paws as he floundered on.

Snow swirled about them as Naue kept circling and calling, "Get up, lumpling. Get up. There's races for us to run and sky to explore."

Koko had a head start, but Bayang's body had a better design that let her slither on her belly across the snow like a serpent. Her hind legs churned so that she plowed on, digging a furrow across the surface.

Reaching Leech first, she took his wrist. It seemed so thin and fragile in her paw. Gently, as if she were handling eggshells, she felt for a pulse. "He's alive."

"Good, good." Naue sounded relieved and made what was probably an apology for him: "I like his spirit if not his sense."

Koko slumped with relief. "That's Leech in a nutshell."

"Now if you'll just pick up the wing as soon as we all get back to it," Bayang began.

"Not now, not now," Naue boomed. The snow swirled as he whirled. "I hear my brothers and sisters. I think I will play them for a while."

"But we need to go after the Roland lumpling," Scirye protested.

"And we will," Naue said; his voice was already dwindling as he disappeared into the sky. "We will have lots more fun soon."

"When?" Bayang shouted after him.

They had to strain their ears to him.

"Call Naue, mightiest and swiftest of winds, and if he is ready, he will come," Naue said.

And then there was only silence, except for the whisper of snow being swept along by the slight breeze.

They were alone in the Arctic wilderness with Roland getting farther away with each passing moment.

"This," Koko groused, "is what we get for trusting someone with air for brains."

6

Scirye

Scirye gazed up at the sky helplessly. "What do we now?"

"If I grew larger," Bayang said, "I could lift the wing up high enough to catch a regular air current. The tricky part will be shrinking short enough to get onto the wing before it crashes."

"I'll pilot it," Scirye said.

"It's not that easy to fly," Bayang said, shaking her head. "That's why I haven't asked any of you to take a turn."

"Hey, if the debating society's finished, how about a little help here," Koko called. The badger was already kneeling by Leech.

"Yes, first things first," Bayang agreed, and twisting her lithe body around, she started to slither on her belly across the snow again.

As Scirye slogged through the snow after her, her toes felt like they were turning into icicles. Though immensely comfortable, her thin antelope-skin boots had never been meant for Arctic conditions.

Kles wriggled free from her coveralls. "I'll keep an eye out for more freebooters." He shoved himself away, dropping a few inches before he could spread his wings and flutter away.

By the time Scirye reached Leech, Koko and Bayang had already helped him sit up.

"Now I know how a sock feels in a washing machine," he said, rubbing the back of his neck. "I always wanted to see snow, but not from this close up."

The dragon arched her neck upward so that she loomed over him. "That was a reckless thing to do," she scolded. "Didn't I warn you?"

Leech let out his breath slowly in resignation. "Okay, I admit that you were right and I was wrong. So let's get the lecture over with."

The dragon seemed hurt. "I was worried about you."

"We all were," Koko said as he trudged up. "For once, I agree with the walking handbag."

Leech wriggled his shoulders as if there was a kink in his neck. "Well, Roland knows we're here."

"No, maybe not," Bayang said. "The airplane was out of sight by then and how could one of those aerial scouts carry a radio? The sets are pretty big. And when they met, the freebooters had to check the airplane out visually."

"So we still have a chance," Scirye said hopefully.

"The Sogdians are coming," Kles called down to them from where he circled in the sky.

"How did they repair that big wind sled this fast?" Bayang wondered.

They saw the small sail first. It came toward them at a leisurely pace in the faint breeze blowing now. It was a few moments more before they realized the sail was powering a small, narrower wind sled.

On it were two Sogdians. The one in the stern was the same man who had stopped the others from shooting. He was handling the sled's ropes, changing the angle of the sled so he could catch as much as he could of the slight wind in the single sail. The other in the bow was one of the warriors with his distinctive red-leather coat with fur lining, collar, and cuffs. He held a rifle as he scanned the terrain.

Suddenly, the Sogdian at the rear jumped up and lowered the sail quickly, and the sled coasted slowly toward them, coming to a stop a few yards away.

The rifleman remained in the bow, covering them with his gun. He continued to do that even when the other Sogdian got off and walked toward them at an angle that left his partner with a clear shot. Apparently, they were taking no chances.

When the Sogdian pulled back his hood, his gunpowder-grimed face and thick beard looked more suited for a pirate than a trader. "I wasn't imagining things the first time I saw you. I can understand why dragons aren't cold, because they're used to the chilly sea," he said in accented English, "but what about you children and your pet . . . ?" He studied Koko, perplexed. "Beaver?"

Koko stamped a paw in the snow. "Don't you lump me in with those bucktoothed rats. I'm a badger, badger, badger."

"A curious name that, but"—the Sogdian shrugged—"to each his own."

Scirye expected steam to puff from the exasperated Koko's ears. Bayang seemed to have the same suspicions and slapped a paw around Koko's muzzle so that all he could emit was squeals and grunts.

Smiling, Bayang explained. "We've come from Hawaii, where the goddess of volcanoes gave us each a magical charm that keeps us from freezing."

Even if the charms did not keep them warm in the coveralls they had borrowed from lockers at the seaplane terminal in San Francisco, the charms kept them from freezing.

"Astounding," the Sogdian said. "A straw mat that floats, a dragon, a badger-badger-badger, and..." He turned to Leech. "Did these eyes deceive me or did I glimpse this boy flying through the air just as we were coming here?"

"I'm Leech, sir," Leech said. "And yes, it was me."

"Astonishing," the Sogdian said.

Kles had spiraled downward so that he was hovering above Scirye. He bowed now as he flourished a paw gracefully. "A thousand and ten thousand greetings, O Mighty Lord," he said in formal Sogdian.

The big man gazed up at Kles with openmouthed delight. "Miracle upon miracle. O wondrous creature, are thou a real griffin or am I dreaming?"

"I assure thee that I am as real as thy boots, Lord," Kles said, and motioned a paw to Scirye. "I serve Lady Scirye of the mighty House of Rapaññe," he announced proudly.

When a Sogdian used it, formal Sogdian seemed as natural and graceful as the flourish and bow the man gave her. "A thousand and ten thousand greetings to thee, O Lady of the House of Rapaññe. This is a twice-blessed day. Not only hast thou graced me with thy company, but thou hast saved myself, my kinsmen, and my chattels. Know thou that I am Caravan Leader Tarkhun of the House of Urak. I and all mine are in thy debt until the sky shatters and the stars fall from the sky."

From the Sogdians she had met, Scirye knew that debt was as

important to Sogdians as it was to dragons. And *that* could be useful in their pursuit of Roland.

"And I, her humble servant," Kles went on grandly in a tone that was the opposite of his words, "hale from the Koyn Encuwontse of the Tarkär Eyrie."

The prince bowed again but not so deeply this time. "I am thrice blessed."

More Sogdian was coming back to Scirye now, for Sogdians had held many of the menial jobs in the Istanbul and Paris embassies, where they had cooked and gardened. Scirye had gotten along better with them than with her fellow Kushans. The Sogdian servants had polished her command of the language, so she had picked up some of the flowery phrases of the formal tongue—though she always felt self-conscious when she used it.

"And a thousand and ten thousand greetings, O Mighty Lord," Scirye said, also in formal Sogdian.

Straightening up, the prince clapped his hands in delight. "You speak Sogdian, Lady. I'm honored."

"Just enough to be misunderstood in it," Scirye said modestly. Now that she was close to him, she could see that the Sogdian's furs were of the richest and finest quality, which fit his title.

The prince tapped his chin. "If I remember right, the master of the Rapaññe is Lord Tsirauñe, the Griffin Master."

"You're very well informed, Your Highness," Kles said. "He's my lady's father."

"His reputation has reached even the top of the world," the prince said.

Scirye translated his Sogdian title into its English equivalent for the others. "This is Prince Tarkhun. His clan, the Urak, is the largest and noblest—"

"Don't forget wealthiest," the prince added smoothly in English. He had a twinkle in his eyes.

Scirye's head dipped in acknowledgment. "And the richest house of Sogdia."

Koko perked up at the mention of money and jerked free from Bayang's grasp. "Anytime you need saving, Prince Old Boy, just come to me," he said as if the rescue had been his idea.

Bayang bowed. "Your Highness," she said, "if you could help us on our journey, we would appreciate it."

The prince replied, extending his arms grandly, "But of course. Just name it and it will be done. And while you're in Nova Hafnia, I insist you be my guests. I must hear your tale."

Hovering in the air, Kles executed a bow so low it was almost a somersault. "We thank thee, Lord."

"But you must at least tell me what's brought you up here," the prince said, lowering his arms.

"We seek an evil man named Roland who sent a dragon to steal a precious ring from my lady's people," Kles explained. "And during the theft, my lady's sister was killed and so was Leech's friend."

The prince's head jerked up in surprise. "Roland? You mean the rich man?"

Scirye jumped on that: "You know him? He's flying in a Ford Trimotor."

"He comes up here sometimes." The prince frowned as if he had just found half of a bug in his sandwich. "We sell him fuel for his airplane as we do everyone, but otherwise I try to have as little to do with him as possible." He looked troubled. "I think I would rather wrestle a polar bear than tackle Roland, especially since he has a dragon."

"We can't ignore what he's done to us," Scirye said.

"Even so, My Lady, it would be wiser if you did." The prince sighed.

"And it might be in your best interest as well if we caught him," Bayang said. "We saw a pair of flying freebooters greet his airplane. They're probably working for him. We took care of them, but his plane got away. It was going to Nova Hafnia."

The prince rubbed his chin thoughtfully. "He's a ruthless man, but I didn't think even *he* would go that far. Why go to all that trouble to rob the caravans? They're rich enough for the likes of us, but he already has such great wealth."

"Perhaps he doesn't want anyone interfering in whatever he's got planned," Kles suggested. "The plunder is just a side bonus to the freebooters. I suspect they've also cut the telegraph and telephone lines to keep you isolated."

"We have no telephones here," the prince said, "but they've sabotaged the telegraph system." He nodded his head firmly. "You must tell the Mounties what you've just told me."

The Mounties were the Royal Canadian Mounted Police, who would maintain law and order in the area now that Canada controlled it. So it was logical to go to them, but Scirye remembered the trouble she and her friends had had at the seaplane terminal making the authorities believe them. If they went to the Mounties, it was Scirye and her friends who were more likely to wind up in jail.

The prince shrewdly considered their silence. "Or would the Mounties ask you awkward questions?"

"There could be a slight misunderstanding"—Kles gave a polite little cough—"that might cause delays."

"And any delay could be fatal, Your Highness." Bayang inclined her head respectfully. "We think Roland is re-assembling an ancient magical weapon. Have you heard of Yi?"

Prince Tarkhun drew his eyebrows together in thought. "I

remember a tale about an archer who shot down extra suns that were scorching the earth."

"That's him." Bayang nodded. "We think Roland is gathering together the parts of Yi's bow."

"There was an archer's ring that belonged to Yi before it was given to Lady Tabiti," Scirye said.

"And from the goddess Pele he got the bowstring which was disguised as a necklace," Kles added. "We think he's after a third part up here."

Prince Tarkhun stroked his beard. "Why would a man as rich and influential as him need an ancient weapon—even if it's so powerful?"

"Perhaps some country's paying him to do it," Kles suggested.

"Or he's planning to extort a fortune from some king or queen," Bayang said.

"Is all the money in the world worth angering a goddess?" Prince Tarkhun wondered.

"And he lost a fortune when he destroyed his own island just to get the necklace with the bowstring from Pele," Bayang admitted.

"If it was me," Koko said, "I'd have kept the island. Then I'd count the greenbacks while I sipped one of those drinks with the little umbrella in it."

"He must have some bigger goal in mind than mere gold," Prince Tarkhun said.

"Whatever his reason is, we know he's up here," Leech said. "So let's go after him."

Bayang looked skyward. "The launch will be tricky, but I guess there's no choice."

Prince Tarkhun cleared his throat. "Pardon me, Lady of the Sea, but the dragons' realms lie in more southern waters. If the Mounties see you flying on a magical wing, they will arrest you.

Since the war, the authorities have strictly limited magic in the area. Anyone with a magical object must have a license."

"I think we should take His Highness's advice," Kles suggested. "If we wait until dark, we might be able to sneak into the air unnoticed."

"More delays," Leech grumbled in frustration. "In the meantime, Primo's killer is still free."

Bayang shrugged. "I think your friend Primo would say that it can't be helped. If we get thrown into jail, we might be there longer than a few hours."

"The law also applies equally to magical creatures such as dragons and badger-badger-badgers." The prince paused and added shrewdly, "I have heard that dragons can change their noble shapes. Is this true?"

"Yes," Bayang said cautiously.

"And what of badger-badger-badgers?" the prince asked.

"Of course," Koko said, crossing his claws behind his back.

The prince spread his hands. "Then, since you must wait anyway, why not disguise yourselves and I will take you and the children on my sled into Nova Hafnia? There we can supply you with all you need for the chase."

"We thank thee," Kles said with a flourish of wings and forelegs, and then ended with a bow.

"We can alter our forms." Bayang indicated Scirye and Leech. "But I think the city would be just as curious about children wearing only coveralls in this weather. So, even though the children don't need them, would you have some furs their size?"

"Yes, the freebooters have made it too dangerous lately, but we used to take our families with us on trips and I never bothered to remove their furs from storage. I got some of them out and brought them along just in case you needed them." He gestured toward the rifleman. "Randian, bring some outfits for these heroes."

Slinging his rifle over his shoulder, Randian brought an arm-load of hooded coats, boots, and gloves over to them.

"This is my chakar," Prince Tarkhun said, introducing him. A chakar was a warrior pledged to serve a lord or lady.

When Leech had removed the rings from his ankle and re-duced them to disks that he slipped onto an armband, Prince Tarkhun observed, "I can't wait to hear your tale."

Randian helped the children into the clothing. Though the coat was a little big for her, Scirye was relieved to feel warm for the first time in days.

Bayang changed into a Sogdian woman in her thirties with dark skin and a nose like the prince's and furs as well.

Koko was having trouble, transforming into something that resembled a pink potato with fur along its sides.

Scirye fought to keep herself from grinning. "Maybe Bayang could give you some transformation lessons."

"That big lizard bosses me around enough," Koko said. "The spell worked smooth enough in Hawaii, so don't break my con-centration now." Muttering a charm, he waved his flipperlike limbs. The next moment he took on his human form as a plump, pear-shaped boy with round pink cheeks. He was also wearing a fur coat that imitated Leech's. "There, see? What did I tell you?"

Prince Tarkhun had been watching the transformations and studied Bayang's face. "You could be my kin," he said.

"Why, thank you, Your Highness," Bayang said as she began to fold the wing over and over until she had a neat square four inches on each side—just as the Cloud Folk had said she would.

By then, Kles had descended again and slipped inside Scir-ye's coat, pronouncing it much more comfortable than the cov-eralls.

Then, together, they headed back toward the wind sled. When Bayang saw a piece of oilcloth, she asked for it politely and the prince readily gave it to her. She wrapped the wing carefully and handed it to Scirye for safekeeping. "You and Kles can keep an eye on it."

After they had climbed onto the wind sled, Prince Tarkhun opened a pouch that hung around his neck. From it, he counted five small gold coins, all about the same size. Two had the Sogdian emblem, one had a Canadian maple leaf, and the other two had a picture of a king with some Danish lettering. "Here, each of you take one."

Bayang shook her head. "We can't take payment for saving you. We would have done it anyway."

"I owe you far more than this pittance, but if you take it, I can speak the truth when I say you're part of my crew. I suppose I should have asked you if you'd be willing to serve on board the wind sled for the short trip to Nova Hafnia." He held the coins out on his palm.

Koko's eyes glittered even more than the gold. "That's got to be at least sixteen karats."

"Eighteen if the mint is honest," Prince Tarkhun said.

Koko gave him a salute. "Then where I do sign on, sir?"

Prince Tarkhun chuckled. "It'll be enough if you just don't get in our way during the rest of the journey."

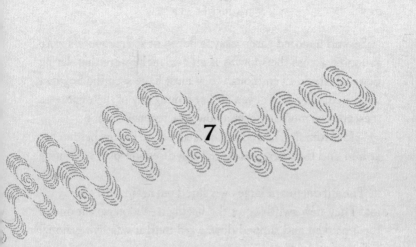

7

Scirye

The wind sled was more like a ship on a foamy sea than a vehicle lumbering over land, and though Scirye had traveled on boats, they had always been large passenger liners that were more like small cities than craft. So she watched the landscape drift by and listened to the orderly noise of a wind sled under sail: the crisp sounds the runners made as they glided over the snow, the thrumming of taut ropes, and the singing of the wind in the rigging.

Here and there, Scirye saw two-person tankettes and even part of a steel aircraft wing—ice-covered relics of the Arctic War.

The day was a mere sullen smear on the horizon when Randian, who was sitting at the bow of the wind sled, shouted a warning. "Freebooters!" Hurriedly he unslung his rifle.

Several hundred yards away, a dozen or so freebooters were galloping across the snow as if an avalanche were thundering down on them. Even though they must have seen the Sogdian wind sled, they didn't even bother aiming any of their guns—as if escape was more important now than revenge or loot.

"Ha, Mounties!" Randian shouted. Scirye looked behind her at him and then her eyes traced the direction of his pointing finger.

The silhouettes of large owls stood out against the setting Elios. They flew swiftly after the fleeing freebooters, but one of them banked and slipped downward until it was flying alongside the wind sled.

Scirye had never seen an owl so large or so snowy. It was about ten feet long, and in the clear moonlight each feather looked as if it had been chiseled from the finest, whitest marble. The down surrounded its large pupils so that its eyes seemed more like flowers.

Upon its back was a man in a coat and cap of black fur and blue trousers. A yellow stripe ran down the side of each leg into a fur-lined boot.

"Prince Tarkhun, I'm glad you're all right," the Mountie called. "We saw your signals and came as quickly as we could."

"Did you catch any of them, Captain Lefevre?" the prince asked.

The Mountie laughed. "Keep going and you'll find about eighty of them still left back there. A lot of them are still knocked out. And the ones who are conscious have lost their reindeer and can't get very far. The ones in that little bunch are the only ones who escaped. We'll have the whole lot rounded up soon."

"Wonderful news," the prince said. "But as we were making our escape, we saw two flying freebooters acknowledge a passing airplane. There may be some link."

"What sort of airplane?" Captain Lefevre asked intently.

"It was a long way off, but I believe it was a Ford Trimotor," the prince said. "It was heading for Nova Hafnia."

"I'll send on a messenger and have it held," the captain said.

The prince raised his hand. "One more thing; I thought I heard the freebooters shouting to one another that this raid would please their employer, Roland." It was a lie but a useful one.

"Roland?" the captain asked in surprise.

"You're not going to let him go, are you?" the prince asked.

"Not until I interrogate all the freebooters we capture," the captain said firmly. "And if he's the one behind all this banditry, we'll toss him into a jail cell just like all the others." His eyes turned to the wind sled's other occupants. "This has certainly been a day for curiosities. We passed by the caravan on our way here and they told me about some strange creatures who came to your aid."

"Yes, my saviors were very kind," the prince said.

"You know the Cabot Territory is still technically a combat zone. We can't allow any powerful magical beings in the city without government permits," Captain Lefevre said.

"I have only crew on my wind sled." The prince shrugged.

Scirye couldn't help thinking admiringly, *He really figures out all the possibilities and then takes care of them in advance.*

Captain Lefevre nodded shrewdly at Scirye. "I'm surprised to see children with you, Your Highness. I thought you were leaving your families behind?"

The prince smiled. "These rascals stowed away."

"Papa was always talking about his travels," Leech fibbed with well-practiced ease. "We wanted to see them for ourselves." He'd learned to be quick with stories while surviving San Francisco's mean streets with Koko.

"Well, we made them earn their passage," the prince said, equally glib. "But their inexperience showed when we were maneuvering during the battle. They fell overboard, you see, and I went back for them."

Captain Lefevre touched his cap. "You're crew too, ma'am?" he asked Bayang.

"I took the prince's money," Bayang said equitably.

The Mountie skillfully swung the owl even closer to them. "It's just that I don't remember you around town. And I make it my business to know everyone. Mind showing me your hands?"

"Really, Captain, we need to be getting on," the prince objected.

Captain Lefevre's eyes narrowed. "I hate to think that you're refusing to cooperate, Your Highness."

"Please, Lord, we can't have him think that," Bayang said. When she pulled off a glove, Scirye saw that her hand was calloused and leathery from years of hard work.

Captain Lefevre still looked suspicious but wasn't sure how to delay them any longer. "Thank you, ma'am." With a click of his tongue and a tug of the reins, his owl rose swiftly upward.

As they sped away, Prince Tarkhun sighed in relief. "I never saw you work magic before you took off your glove."

"My hands became like that when I transformed the first time. When I take on a disguise, I like to be thorough," Bayang said proudly.

So Bayang can plan ahead too, Scirye thought with equal admiration.

It was twilight when they reached the former battlefield. They discovered more Mounties were rounding up the dispirited freebooters and handcuffing them.

Overhead, Mounties riding owls flew back and forth either

on patrol or carrying messages—bearing out Prince Tarkhun's wisdom in not trying to use their wing.

Farther on, they reached the prince's main wind sled. By then, its crew had broken spare sails out of the hold and with the swift efficiency of sailors on a racing yacht they had replaced the old tattered sails with fresh new ones. They worked within a defensive circle that the red-coated chakar had formed.

After they climbed the rope ladder onto the deck of the bargelike wind sled, some of the Sogdians jumped down from the barge onto the snow and took apart the little wind sled. As soon as they had stowed it away, Prince Tarkhun ordered the new sails unfurled.

A strong wind was blowing and the canvas instantly bellied outward. The bargelike wind sled lurched forward, gathering speed as it slid over the surface. The long metal runners hissed over the snow, throwing up fine sprays on either side. Behind them, the dark ruts of their track stood out on the velvety whiteness as the wind sled raced home toward Nova Hafnia.

The booms of the mast could rotate a full circle, which allowed Prince Tarkhun to turn the sails in any direction and maneuver the wind sled along. Since he had no rudder to steer, he and his crew had to be skillful at handling the sails. He never needed more than a few words for each of his commands, but his crew almost seemed to read his mind.

Scirye moved toward the bow with the others, standing next to Randian at the swivel cannon.

"I suspect the prince and his crew have been together a long time," Kles observed approvingly. "And that speaks well of him. Only a good commander earns such loyalty."

"You couldn't find a fairer and more generous master," the chakar agreed, keeping his eyes on the landscape. He looked to be in his late twenties, with a closely cropped beard that could not quite hide the battle scars on his right cheek.

Leech came up beside Scirye and leaned against the rail. "What's a Sogdian prince doing here in the Arctic?"

"Sogdiana's in Central Asia north of the Kushan Empire," Scirye explained.

Kles cleared his throat. "It's made up of a number of city-states each ruled by a different clan, or House. And each tries to best the others in prestige and wealth."

"But we always unite when any foreigner invades," the chakar said, his white teeth flashing in the moonlight. "And we soon send the fools packing."

"The Sogdians are famous as warriors, but even more as merchants," Kles went on. "The clans have sent out groups around the world to establish a network of trade colonies."

"But Chach is the oldest, the loveliest, and the richest of all the cities of Sogdiana, and we can thank the House of Urak for that," the chakar said confidently. "And of the Urak, Prince Tarkhun is the greatest of the lords. So I've followed him into a place colder and harder than a landlord's heart because with him as my leader, I'll return home with money and prestige. Come to Chach after that and ask anyone for Randian and his inn."

"So you want to buy an inn," Scirye said.

Randian nodded. "There's a girl waiting for me," he said, "but in Chach I was only a guttersnipe and her parents wouldn't have me, so I joined the prince to make my fortune."

Scirye got Randian to teach her the words for different things on the ship. And after listening carefully to Prince Tarkhun, she pretended that she was commanding the wind sled herself.

Eventually the horizon became more irregular. The farther they went, Scirye could see what looked like gray and white lumps, which quickly became a low ridge of mountains with snow that clung to the peaks and shoulders but not to the steep sides. Prince Tarkhun seemed to be aiming for a steep gash in the side of the mountains that Scirye figured must be a pass.

Hills, white and humped and glistening with snow and ice, sat at the feet of the mountains. Prince Tarkhun roared out a command and signal flags ran up a line and another order sent the crew up the rigging to begin furling the sails and the wind sled started to slow down until it was barely moving ahead.

Finally, they saw the masts of the rest of the caravan. When the sails were furled, the masts stood up like a grove stripped of leaves.

The wind sleds had been drawn up into a defensive circle just outside a log fort where the Canadian flag proudly snapped on a flagpole.

Cheers greeted them from the caravan, and in a proud display of wind-sled handling, the prince's barge stopped about twenty feet away. People high-stepped through the snow toward them and the rope ladder had no sooner been dropped over the side than a small fur-clad figure clambered up it and onto the deck.

"Father, you're safe," a girl cried in Common Sogdian. And she flung herself into the prince's arms.

8

Scirye

With a laugh, the prince lifted the visitor from the deck and swung her around in a circle.

Scirye felt a small twinge at that. She was wondering what her own father was doing at this moment. He must have taken an airplane from Bactra, the Kushan capital, to San Francisco to tend her mother. She'd been injured during the same robbery that had killed Scirye's sister, Nishke.

Even now, Scirye felt a stab of pain when she thought of Nishke—Nishke so brave yet so kind. Because their mother was often so busy with her consular duties, Nishke had been a second mother to Scirye, playing with her, reading to her, and putting her to bed.

Not only had Scirye missed her sister's funeral, but she hadn't been there to nurse her mother either. Scirye fought back the wave of guilt. She'd made her choice and would have to live with it.

As soon as the prince had set the girl back on her booted feet, his grin changed to a frown. "What are you doing here, Roxanna?" he asked in Common.

"I knew I'd be safe as long as I didn't travel farther than the pass," the girl explained. She looked to be twelve, the same age as Scirye.

Roxanna's face was round, with the same sharp nose and lively, intelligent eyes as Prince Tarkhun.

He reached under her cap and pinched her ear so he could tug it playfully. "Humph, you went no farther because the Mounties wouldn't let you?"

Roxanna drew her eyebrows together in a stormy expression. "They weren't reasonable at all."

"Because they have more common sense than you." Prince Tarkhun let go with a chuckle.

Roxanna folded her arms in a huff. "I was worried when the caravan told me they'd left you behind."

"It was my order," Prince Tarkhun said.

"Well, you should have taken me along. You needed every gun you could get, and I can shoot as well as my brothers." She paused for breath and then spoke rapidly, driven by the injustice of it all. "And I beat them in dogsled races and navigation. Yet you take them."

"Because they don't give me half the arguments you do." Prince Tarkhun laughed and, wrapping his arm around her shoulder, turned her to face the companions. "And anyway. Who needs more rifles when heroes like these come to my rescue? These noble folk fell out of the sky and saved me and the caravan. I feel like a boy in a fairy tale. This is Lady Scirye of the noble Kushan House of Rapañṅe."

When Scirye greeted the prince's daughter in formal Sogdian, Roxanna bowed from the waist and replied in the same tongue, "I have never met a noble lady before."

"Don't let the fancy title fool you, kiddo. Her Ladyship's cute little schnozz snores just like us common folk," Koko commented.

Kles poked his head out of Scirye's coat. "Heed not the vermin," he said in formal Sogdian.

Koko scowled. "I don't know the lingo, but I know you said something nasty about me."

Roxanna gasped and then slipped into Common. "Is that really a griffin?"

"He's a lap griffin," Scirye explained, also in Common.

Kles lowered his voice to a seductive chirrup. "It's a pleasure to meet you, my dear."

Poor Roxanna was not able to resist any more than many other people and started to pet him. As she stroked his head, Kles let out a low series of even deeper chirrups and Roxanna smiled in pure contentment.

"Don't you have any shame, Kles?" Scirye scolded him.

"I have no idea what you mean," Kles said, blinking his eyes innocently, "for I am simply a humble worshiper of stars, for that's what 'Scirye' means in the Old Tongue and what 'Roxanna' means in Sogdian."

"If you get any oilier"—Scirye scowled—"I'll have to put you in a petrol can."

"Please, Lady," Roxanna begged. "This wonderful creature is only trying to be polite."

"Wait. The miracles do not end yet," Prince Tarkhun boasted. "This is Lady Bayang. I wish you could see her in her true form, but we were afraid that would attract too much attention." He dropped his voice: "She's a fearsome dragon."

Roxanna stared at the woman in front of her suspiciously, as if she thought her father was playing a prank, and only remembered to bow when her father tapped her on her shoulder and told her to mind her manners.

In turn, her forehead wrinkled in puzzlement when her father introduced the pudgy boy as "Koko, the badger-badger-badger." Prince Tarkhun tapped the side of his head as he grinned at Koko. "You see. I've a good memory for names. My brain is like a treasure chest. Once I hear a name, it never gets out."

Koko opened his mouth for a retort, but Leech gave him a pinch. "Iet-quay. E-way o-day ot-nay et-gay im-ay ad-may," Leech warned.

Koko rolled his eyes resignedly. "Just call me Three-B for short."

Prince Tarkhun had saved Leech for last. "And this is Lord Leech. Such a hero! He flies through the air faster than the wind. Whoosh!" And his hand shot out in illustration.

Roxanna didn't hear the derisive snort from both Bayang and Koko. Her eyes widened with excitement. "Show me how you soar through the sky like an eagle," she said in Common, speaking with the confidence of someone used to having others obey her—with the exception of the Mounties and her father.

"Sorry, I don't understand," Leech said.

Roxanna slipped easily into only slightly accented English. In her eagerness, she forgot her formal manners. "I said you must show me your skill." She seized his wrists in her hands. "In fact, please take me flying right now."

Prince Tarkhun laughed and, wrapping his arms around her, made her step back from the startled boy. "And this little savage is my daughter, Roxanna, the delight and curse of my life. And now if you'll excuse me, I must get the caravan ready for the last leg of our journey."

Bayang bowed politely. "With all due respect, Your Highness, is there any way we could go on ahead?"

The prince rolled his eyes skyward meaningfully as a Mountie passed overhead on an urgent mission to the city. Two more were coming from the city on their own errands. "I know you are in a hurry, but you would be noticed if you flew now."

Roxanna hooked her arm through Leech's. "Lord Leech, let me take you in my sled. And on the way, you can tell me all about your adventures."

Though she wanted to scream with impatience, Scirye said, "Yes, tell us, Lord Leech, about *your* adventures." The Sogdian girl's pushiness was rubbing her the wrong way.

Prince Tarkhun nodded to his guests. "Then I leave you to my daughter's capable hands. I just hope she doesn't wear out your ears with all her questions."

As he walked toward his caravan, several large wind sleds with Mounties on them were setting out, probably to pick up the prisoners. Scirye hoped the freebooters went to prison for a long time.

Roxanna gripped Leech tightly as she led them away. The Sogdian girl did not bother to check to see if the others were following.

"She's awfully pushy," Scirye whispered to Kles. "The sooner we get rid of her, the better."

"I think you just resent having to take orders from someone like yourself," the griffin commented.

"I am not bossy," Scirye hissed.

"You could have fooled me," Kles said with infuriating calm.

"You don't know a thing." Fuming, she stamped along through the snow.

"I lead such a humdrum life up here, Lord Leech, that I thirst for excitement. Simply thirst." Roxanna gave Leech a friendly little shake.

Leech's cheeks blushed a bright red. "It's just plain Leech actually," he said to Roxanna.

Koko shuddered. "Believe me, kiddo, adventures aren't all they're cracked up to be." He ticked off the items on his fingers. "So far, we've nearly been turned into hamburger, barbecued, and drowned. I'd rather be bored to death any day."

Roxanna waved her free hand breezily. "Your deeds have indeed proved you're a lord."

Leech told her about the attack at the museum by Badik the dragon and several monsters, the theft of the ring, and the death of his friend Primo. "We were friends as soon as we met," Leech said. "I felt like I'd known him all my life."

"How terrible to lose him," Roxanna sympathized.

"Scirye's mother got hurt and her sister died too," Leech said. Roxanna glanced over her shoulder at the other girl. "I'm sorry."

"Roland will be sorrier when we catch him," Leech insisted.

"Roland?" Roxanna was as worried at the mention of the rich man as her father had been. "Roland? What does he have to do with it?"

"Badik works for Roland," Leech said. "And he's probably behind the attacks by the freebooters."

"I'd like to get my hands on him myself," Roxanna said grimly. "His freebooters have kept everyone bottled up in the city. There are shortages of everything from food to fuel."

Her mouth dropped open when Leech went on to stowing away on the clipper to Hawaii, meeting Pele, traveling through the volcano, and then confronting Roland only to have him steal Pele's necklace and trap them. When Leech and his friends had helped her escape, she'd summoned the Cloud Folk to weave the flying wing for them and then Naue the wind to carry it to here.

"And then we saw your father was in trouble, so all of us"—Leech made a point of gesturing to his friends—"came to the rescue."

"You are too modest, Lord Leech," Roxanna said.

She stopped by a little wind sled the same size as the one Prince Tarkhun had used to pick them up. But the mast had been taken down and lay horizontally, tied to one side, and the sail rolled into a neat cylinder and stowed away.

A pair of musk oxen were hitched to the bow, with a short drover holding their reins. The shaggy beasts stood stoically, their breath rising in streamers from their nostrils and twining around the tips of their curved horns.

Curious, Koko strolled over toward them. "They look like hairy sofas with legs. And we'll be staring at their backsides. Not my idea of a scenic view."

The drover said something and Roxanna translated. " 'Please, Master Koko. Don't get so close.' "

"Yikes!" With a yelp, Koko hopped backward away from the gnashing teeth of one of the oxen. "I thought he'd be a vegetarian."

The drover laughed loudly and then spoke some more.

"The drover said that Old Pushtar bites," Roxanna explained. "And he's trying to keep his weight down."

Bayang beckoned impatiently to Koko. "If you're finished feeding yourself to Old Pushtar, come on."

As they climbed onto the sled with Roxanna, she pointed to a deep cleft ahead of them in the hills. "Beyond that pass is Nova Hafnia. The sails can't take the caravan any farther, so Father will hire oxen and haul the sleds the last few miles. And we'll do the same."

She said something to the drover, who clicked his tongue to the musk oxen. He had no whip but only a small stick with a tuft of fur on one end. He used it now to tickle their muzzles.

With loud snorts that sent steam spiraling upward like locomotives, the oxen lurched forward. The bells on the great team's harness chimed all along the red-leather straps and then the sled moved forward.

"He's a Laplander," Roxanna whispered. "They're said to have a magical way with animals. His people come from a long line of herders. The Danes brought them in centuries ago to tend the huge bands of reindeer here."

They passed by a corral for a small reindeer herd as well as the fenced-in kennels for dogsled teams. Next to the corral was a huge pen with posts as thick as telephone poles. From it, more Laplanders were leading teams of oxen down to the caravan, and their own drover spoke cheerfully to them in their own tongue.

"The pass hasn't seen so much business in a long time," Roxanna observed. "Father's caravan was one of the first to make a round-trip, so the city was getting short on everything. It's almost like we've been under siege."

At first the slope was so gentle that the musk oxen had no trouble, but as the path steepened they had to dig in their hooves and really pull, snorting and tossing their heads as if they would rather have thrown off the harness and rid themselves of the weight.

As they plodded along, Scirye missed the speed that the sails gave a wind sled. Suddenly, the sled's runners bit deep through the slush into a layer of ice below and the sled began to slide backward.

The drover was everywhere, tickling, scolding, urging his oxen forward, and Scirye and everyone else got off and pushed from behind until they were on a firm patch again and could climb back on.

Just before the mouth of the pass, Roxanna explained softly, "We have to be quiet from now on because of the danger of avalanches. The city tries to take care of any heavy accumulation of snow, but it's impossible to handle all of it promptly."

"Why is everyone looking at me?" Koko whispered in a grieved tone.

"Because the warning applies to you especially," Bayang snapped in a low voice.

The pass was a narrow valley where dark rock formed the steep sides. Snow pillowed on the ledges and crevices, but mostly it was dark stone walls that seemed to swallow up the moonlight. The wind forced into such a narrow channel whistled past them loudly.

As they entered the pass, Scirye felt as if she were entering a strange, hostile place where the rocks resented all life, where the earth was just as it had been when it and the stones had been the masters of the world. Knolls seemed like the heads of brooding giants, ready to crush them at the first excuse.

Salene the Moon was just rising when they reached the mouth of the pass. Roxanna pointed proudly. "Nova Hafnia. We call it the City of Diamonds."

Scirye gasped when she saw the city filling the little bowl between the mountains and the sea. City of Diamonds was a good name for Roxanna's home, for it did indeed glitter like a jeweled necklace laid on white velvet.

Every building was covered with icicles—belts of them fringed the roof edges and windowsills and band after band of icicles wound around the walls in several layers. With each frozen spike Mao's silvery rays sparkled and danced.

Glowing rectangles winked at them cheerfully from where

the light found its way around the edges of the shutters and through the layers of ice to the cold night outside. And the hard angles of walls had been rounded by a coat of frozen water so that the smaller cottages seemed more like the crystal mounds where fairy folk lived. Scirye wasn't surprised when she heard music floating up faintly.

Bayang squinted as she tried to make out the shape of the buildings better under their coating of ice. "I'd almost swear someone took an old town from Denmark and plopped it down right here."

"Nova Hafnia was founded by the great explorer Jens Munck, so most of Old Town dates back to his time in the seventeenth century," Roxanna said proudly, and then proceeded to point out the landmarks in Old Town. The walls and gates curtaining Old Town were of a rich brick red. Nearest the docks rose the tall watchtower, Jenstärn, which thrust into the sky like a spear, and Rosenborg Castle looked more like a fort than the governor's palace.

Old Town had grown up in the bowl-shaped area formed between the curving mountains and the sea, covering the flatlands. In the last century, New Town had sprung up outside the walls, spreading up over the foothills. The houses and other buildings here were of wood and stone and would not have looked out of place in San Francisco. There were compact houses, larger blocks of tenements, inns, and restaurants. Even some large hotels were going up to cater to the cruise ships that would come through when the Arctic Ocean thawed.

"It's lovely," Scirye said to Roxanna.

"Thank you." Roxanna beamed as happily as if she had built the city herself and pointed toward the broad white plain stretching beyond the city. "In the spring, the sea melts and the ships can come through. And planes land on pontoons. But in the winter, the planes switch to skis. Usually there are lots more aircraft."

"The freebooters must have been intercepting them," Bayang said grimly.

Scirye followed Roxanna's pointing finger and drew in her breath sharply. Out on the frozen ocean were three small planes with long skis instead of landing wheels. She would have liked to have smashed them all. Overhead Mounties were circling about on their owls as they kept watch from the air.

"Which is the Ford Trimotor?" Scirye asked Bayang.

The disguised dragon frowned. "It's not there. The most any airplane there has is two engines."

"I think," Scirye said, turning to her friends in disappointment, "that we better go down to the docks and see if we can find out what happened."

And the others nodded.

9

Scirye

The last part of the journey was the most difficult because Roxanna's sled had to be lowered down the seaward slope, which was steeper than the landward side and even more prone to avalanches.

The oxen were unhitched from the wind sled and led back to other side of the hills. Roxanna's sled was then attached to a capstan by cables thicker than Scirye's legs. A team of trolls and giants strained against the capstan as they lowered the sled.

There was a separate path for the sled's passengers with huge flagstones, but since they were icy and it was twilight, the humans had to walk down with care.

"The days are so short and cold in the winter," Roxanna explained, "that everyone's glad when spring finally comes. I just wished springtime lasted longer."

"Doesn't the opposite get a little hard, though?" Bayang asked. "I mean, the sun's out for almost twenty-four hours during the summer."

"It barely sets," Roxanna agreed. "And that's hard too. But the farms can grow huge crops with that much sunlight." She waved a hand behind her. "Part of the plain will be plowed up when enough soil thaws out."

Prince Tarkhun must have sent word to the city, because wheeled wagons, carts, and even huge drays were lumbering through the snowy streets to pick up the cargo for their impatient owners, but at the moment the result was a monumental traffic jam. And yet even though the vehicles were tangled together, everyone seemed to be in a cheerful mood at the pending arrival of the caravan.

Roxanna frowned. "Excuse me, Lord Leech. I know you're in a hurry, but if I don't set things right, everything will back up and then it will be chaos." Walking over to the nearest wagon, she climbed up the wheel and stood on the seat next to the surprised driver.

Shouting to get the wagoneers' attention, she began to direct them where to park their wagons and wait.

Roxanna carried herself with an easy authority that Scirye envied, expecting her orders to be carried out quickly and without question—which the tough-looking wagoneers did with respectful nods.

Clearly, she had handled this situation before, re-arranging the cursing drivers and their stubborn teams as calmly as another child might shift blocks around.

There were also several large drays with Sogdians at the reins. They were to take some of the cargo back to the caravanserai to be sold, picked up later, or shipped on by other means. These men she told to store her sled away with the other sleds.

Her task done, Roxanna jumped back down and returned to lead them down the slope through the slush.

"Who lives there?" Koko asked, pointing below them to a tavern doorway that was almost ten feet high. Lanterns had been lit against the growing gloom.

"That place caters to the frost giants," Roxanna explained. "The Danes brought in different races to work the mines."

At that moment, a tall creature stepped from the tavern into the street. His blond hair had been plaited in two braids as thick as ropes that hung down his back and his beard had been twined into a dozen little tails and tied with ribbons. He was dressed in regular boots and jacket, but on his head was a horned helmet.

He waved to Roxanna and said in stiffly accented English, "Caravan come?"

Roxanna smiled back. "Come to the caravanserai tomorrow and you'll have lots to buy."

He grinned broadly and punched his fists up as if in victory. "Good, good!"

A few buildings down was another tavern. It was the same height as the other, but the doorway was barely four feet high. Several squat gnomes lounged outside. Their noses were bulbous and they hardly had any torso but seemed to be all arms and legs. They seemed just as excited as the giant as they called something to her and Roxanna replied in what Scirye assumed was Gnomish.

As they walked down the broad avenue, people came out of their shops and houses. Apparently, it had been a while since a caravan had made it to the city, so Prince Tarkhun had caused quite a stir. The prospective buyers eagerly asked Roxanna when her father would be ready to sell his wares.

"Tomorrow," was Roxanna's stock reply in English and also

Danish, French, German, Trollese, and several other tongues—
the reply fitting the language in which the question was couched.
It seemed as if the whole world wanted to shop at Prince Tarkhun's the next morning.

But if she looked as thin as the humans, Scirye would have
been eager to buy food too. And she could understand the
carnival-like mood that seemed to be filling the city.

Roxanna was always friendly and polite, never letting anyone
stop them for long, but their progress slowed as they left the
straight streets of the newer part of Nova Hafnia and passed
through the gates into Old Town. Here the houses were jammed
together and their upper stories jutted out over the paths, reducing the sky to a narrow strip between the roofs of the opposite
buildings.

The roads, too, did not run straight but zigged and zagged
and curled like the path of a wriggling snake. Intersections came
up unexpectedly and side roads twisted off in surprising directions. They had barely gone three hundred yards before the
companions were hopelessly lost.

"Watch out for falling icicles," Roxanna warned.

Scirye scanned overhead. The icicles had looked so lovely
from a distance, but now that they were this close she could see
that they were as large and as sharp as daggers. She would not
like having one of those drop on her from thirty feet.

Koko covered his head with a hand. "I wish I'd packed a helmet."

However, Roxanna, who had grown up in the labyrinth, knew
exactly where she was and where she was going. The problem
was that the lanes became so narrow that it was difficult to step
around inquiring folk.

They emerged from an alley and into a street that ran down
to the docks themselves. They could see dozens of snow-covered

de-masted ships, hauled up out of the water, resting in the ship-yards with icicles hanging from the railings like frozen giant whales.

Before them stretched the glistening sheet of ice that was the bay. Hoping that she had made a mistake before, Scirye scanned the parked airplanes, but there was none with three motors.

However, there were a half-dozen Mounties on foot interrogating anyone on the dock. Two more patrolled up in the air on owls. Scirye assumed that Captain Lefevre's messenger had arrived with the warning.

Bayang gestured Scirye and the others into a doorway. "We'll wait here," Bayang said to Roxanna, "until you find out what happened."

She nodded at the wisdom of this. "Yes, we don't want to call any attention to you."

Leech fretted. "We should have flown after Roland after all."

"And have every Mountie trying to grab us as soon as they saw us flying?" Bayang squinted at the dockside as Roxanna went over to a gnome. "No, Prince Tarkhun was right. We'll wait until dark to sneak away. Don't worry. We'll pick up Roland's trail again."

The dragon spoke with a confident patience that made Scirye shiver a little—as if she were catching a glimpse of how relentless Bayang the assassin could be.

Roxanna returned apologetically a short while later. "People saw a Trimotor fly overhead a short while ago, but it didn't land. Roland must have fuel supplies out on the frozen ocean."

"Did you find out what direction it was going?" Bayang asked.

"That heading would take them straight to the Wastes," Roxanna said, "but they'll stop or turn long before they get there."

"How do you know that?" Scirye asked.

"Because no one goes into the Wastes," Roxanna explained. "As long as the Inuit can remember, hunters who went into the Wastes disappeared. And every now and then some strangers come up here because they've heard tales of treasure."

Koko perked up. "Oh yeah? What sort of treasure?"

Roxanna shrugged. "All kinds. We even had one pack of idiots hunting for the lost gold of Atlantis."

"What happened to them?" Scirye asked.

"They said there were invisible phantoms that tormented them day and night until they gave up and left," Roxanna explained. "And there are a lot of similar stories from over the centuries."

Leech nodded up at the Mounties on their owls. "What do we do? We can't take off with them out there."

Roxanna dipped her head respectfully. "Lord Leech, you can't go out onto the ice without the proper supplies and equipment. Come to the caravanserai where we can outfit you."

As impatient as they were to be off, they had to concede that this was a better plan. Roxanna led them along another route until they came to the caravanserai.

They really couldn't have missed it, because the massive rectangular building dominated the wharf area, covering an entire city block and standing three stories high. It peered over the roofs of the other buildings as if watching them approach. Smoke rose from numerous chimneys, rising in the cold, still air like long locks of gray hair.

Lanterns shone on the caravanserai's sides so that, through the coating of ice, Scirye could make out blurred designs formed by different-colored bricks. The narrow windows were no more than slits. Scirye had been expecting some kind of princely palace, but this was a fortress that could have defied a thousand freebooters.

Cupping her hands around her mouth, Roxanna called out in Common, "Ho, the caravanserai! Open your gates."

The great wooden gates of the caravanserai had been kept clear of ice and a panel slid back on a little window, but no face appeared behind the grill.

"Oh, it's you, my girl," a woman replied in Common from behind the gates. Her voice was thin and wispy like the wind blowing sand across a beach. "We've been turning the place upside down looking for you." There followed a quick string of Common words that Scirye did not recognize, but she suspected from the annoyed look on Roxanna's face that they were an insult and one too rude for her own nursemaid to have used when Scirye was small.

Embarrassed, Roxanna glanced at Leech and then shouted to the unseen servant, "Mother worries too much. And anyway, why are you playing gatekeeper, Upach? You're usually huddling inside the house by a fire."

"I came to pass on a warning," Upach said surlily.

"Well, you've given it." Roxanna stamped a foot in vexation. "Now open the gates before I freeze outside."

"You might prefer that," Upach gloated, "to what your mother's going to do to you."

"Thank Nana you're with me," Roxanna whispered gratefully to Leech. "Mother can't do much too bad to me if I'm with guests."

Scirye heard heavy iron bolts groaning as they were thrown back and then the thick doors creaked open. She blinked when the little woman waddled out.

She was about four feet high and wore so many fur coats that she was almost as wide. Boots as thick as elephant legs protected her feet. On her head was a fur hat as large as a melon, and a thick muffler hid her face except for a small slit for her eyes.

"You can't just go traipsing off whenever you feel like it." Upach tried to wag a finger at Roxanna, but the glove on her hand was as big and clumsy as a baseball mitt. "You're off Nana knows where, and it's poor old Upach that has to take the blame."

Roxanna threw her arms around the woman in an attempt at a hug. "I've missed you too, Upach. What would I do without you?"

Upach stomped one booted foot. "Don't try to honey-talk me, my girl. I didn't leave my lovely, warm home for this sort of silliness. I won't stand for it, do you hear? I just won't!"

"I ordered a foot warmer for you," Roxanna wheedled. "That should leave your toes all nice and toasty. It should be somewhere in the caravan"—she indicated Leech—"that this hero and his friends saved."

Before Scirye could even open her mouth in protest, Kles's paw had clamped down on her shoulder for silence.

Upach dragged one boot across the snow. "Humph. How am I going to keep the rest of me warm?"

Roxanna looked over her shoulder at them. "Upach's an ifrit from the desert," she explained in English. "She's been my friend, my fussbudget and jailer, ever since I was born."

"And nothing but trouble from day one," Upach grumbled in thickly accented English. "I'm supposed to be the head housekeeper, not your nursemaid. Why, oh, why did I follow your mother here?"

"It was fate," Roxanna said with an impish shrug.

"I don't suppose"—in the layer of furs, Upach's arm moved as stiffly as a statue's while she tried to give Roxanna a friendly pat—"you'd tell your old nursemaid how you . . . ?"

Roxanna affectionately adjusted the servant's muffler. "I have to have some secrets, Upach. Otherwise, where would be the challenge for you?"

"I won't put up with this much longer," Upach said, but heaved a heavy sigh that suggested she was actually resigned to her fate.

"Father also brought a thermometer to replace the one you broke," Roxanna said mischievously.

"I did nothing of the kind," Upach snapped.

"You pounded it every day demanding to know when it was going to get hotter," Roxanna said. "Be kinder to this one."

They followed the Sogdian girl into a huge open cobblestone courtyard that could accommodate a dozen large wagons at one time. This hollow square, Roxanna explained, was the center of the caravanserai, with workshops for smiths and warehouses occupying the ground floor of all four sides. The two upper floors held the Sogdians' living quarters.

As porters and clerks streamed out of rooms on all sides to help, Kles murmured to Scirye, "They're all armed."

"If they don't have pistols, they at least have knives." The girl noticed the magical charms pasted on the walls and doors. "And there are magical wards all over. Do you think it's the freebooters?"

"Probably. The freebooters must be getting pretty daring with Roland backing them," Bayang said.

"Things have really gotten bad if the Sogdians don't feel safe from them in their own home," Kles observed.

At that moment, a thicker, older version of Roxanna emerged from a side door. She was wearing a fur robe with embroidered cuffs and hem.

"Do you know how much of a tizzy we've been in when we noticed you were gone?" the woman demanded in Common.

"At my age, Mother, you were racing camels in the desert with your friends," Roxanna replied sweetly in the same tongue.

Her mother glanced ruefully at the ifrit. "I see Upach has

been tattling on me again. I'll deal with her once I'm done with you."

Scirye felt a twinge, thinking about her own mother worrying about her. She decided she would ask the Sogdians to send a letter back to her.

Roxanna ran over to Leech and, grabbing his arm, she tugged him back to her mother. "Besides," Roxanna said, switching to English, "I was perfectly safe. I was with this hero. He saved the whole caravan."

"We all did," Leech said, turning red again.

Roxanna's mother studied the scrawny, undersized boy uncertainly and then the others. "Did you really?"

"Mother," Roxanna scolded, "don't embarrass our clan."

Remembering her manners, Roxanna's mother bowed to them. "Yes, I meant to say that we're honored."

"Extremely honored," Roxanna corrected, and then, after introducing each of them to her mother, waved a hand. "This is my mother, Lady Miunai."

"And a gray hair for every day since you were born," Lady Miunai said. "Where's your father?"

"Probably coming through the pass," Roxanna said. "He should be here in a short while."

"We'd better get ready to unload the wagons when they get here. See that our visitors are settled in the guest apartments," Lady Miunai instructed, and clapped her hands. Immediately, clerks and servants began to come into the courtyard, pulling on coats as they did so.

Roxanna led them through a wide doorway and into one of the clan's cavernous warehouses. From somewhere down the corridor came the faint tinking of hammers on metal.

Giving Leech a quick smile, she said, "You saved me with

your magic just like I hoped. I've seen the toughest drovers break down into tears when Mother scolds them."

A faint scent of spices and teas lingered in the air of the chamber. Many of its shelves, though, were empty because of the freebooters' siege, but there were still large containers scattered about: from huge ceramic jars to crates of medical supplies and books, baskets of woven twigs, and rolled-up straw mats that had been tied with thick ropes. All of them marked with the twin palm trees that Roxanna said were the family crest.

Leech pointed at a jar that was as tall as him. "What's in there?"

"Olive oil from the sun-kissed Italia," Roxanna said, and began to rattle off the original countries for the other objects. China, Azteca, Serendip—the whole world seemed to have sent something here for sale.

Scirye knew that the Silk Road was the name given to several routes that connected the East to the West. Goods and ideas passed back and forth along it, but it seemed that it now extended even to the Far North.

They followed Roxanna to a set of double doors at the foot of a broad staircase where they stamped the snow from their feet. Scirye had to blink when they reached the top of the stairs, for if the caravanserai appeared utilitarian down below, up here it burned hot and bright as flame. The rugs, wall tapestries, and ceiling murals were a riot of reds, yellows, and pinks showing hunters in forests, people feasting in fabulous gardens, and the strange creatures of the air and sea. The ground floor might be the commercial heart of the caravanserai, but the upper floor was its soul.

Here the air was pungent with the smell of incense and perfume—as if Scirye had stuck her head into the center of a bouquet of exotic flowers. Fat fire imps squatted in large orange glass bowls in wall sconces, burning as fiercely as desert suns.

When Roxanna took off her fur coat, her clothes were just as vibrant as her surroundings. She was wearing a crimson and gold brocade dress with a high collar over purple slacks that belled out above her boots. And Scirye caught a faint whiff of perfume as Roxanna handed her coat to Upach.

Roxanna led them down a hallway past rooms that seemed to be furnished and decorated with souvenirs from around the world. In one, a fountain with tile mosaics tinkled musically.

"Father calls this our little Chach," Roxanna explained. "Our clan came from that city in Sogdiana."

"Ah, it's as lovely as this," Kles said as he rode upon Scirye's shoulder.

"You've seen it?" Roxanna asked excitedly, and then sighed. "I've never been there myself."

"I spent a month in Chach with the princess," Kles said, looking around approvingly. "The temple to Nanaia—that's our name for your Nana—was magnificent."

"Then you must see our shrine," Roxanna said proudly. "It's small, but the statue has been with my family for generations."

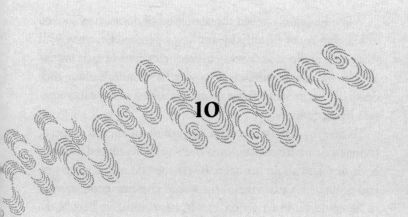

10

Scirye

They followed Roxanna through a maze of hallways to a small chamber. As befitted a busy place, they had heard some noise in the background wherever they had gone in the caravanserai, but it was strangely silent here. Perhaps it was some quirk of the construction or, Scirye wondered, it was the power of the goddess.

Actually, the statue of Nanaia was the last thing that Scirye wanted to see. In her grief and anger over Nishke's death, Scirye had rashly promised Nanaia that she would pay any cost in exchange for the goddess's help in recovering her people's treasure and avenging her sister's death. Scirye hadn't really expected the goddess to grant her wish, and now that Nanaia seemed to be, what price was Scirye going to have to pay? Scirye didn't want to be reminded of that hasty vow.

When Roxanna opened the double set of doors, they looked into a dim room lit only by fire imps perched in a few wall sconces. The floor here was covered with tiles of rich orange and the walls and ceilings were covered with murals of the goddess's life in the same bright colors as the rest of the caravanserai's living quarters.

To Scirye's right was a large picture of an ancient emperor trying to drink from a cup even as its contents turned into ribbons of steam about his head. It was the tale of the ruler who had promised Nanaia that if she would give him good weather so he could build irrigation canals, he would give part of the newly created fields to her temple. And when he had conveniently forgotten his oath, he found one day that liquid would hiss away as a steam whether it touched his lips or hands. It was said he had gone mad before he died of thirst.

On the opposite wall was the image of a man in gorgeous robes looking amazed as he stared at a mirror and fingered the huge horns growning from his head. That was the story of the wealthy man who had sworn to Nanaia that he would tithe a medical clinic if she would only save a very valuable breeding bull that was sick. When his animal recovered, this man, too, had had a lapse of memory—only to find one morning that a pair of horns had sprouted from his head. Everywhere in the shrine were reminders of what happened to those who did not keep their word to Nanaia.

How would Nanaia punish her if she failed to carry out her end of the bargain—even though the odds against success seemed so overwhelming?

Bayang had been watching her. "Just remember what I told you before: When Nanaia does something, she doesn't always take your interests into account."

It was on the tip of Scirye's tongue to ask to go someplace else.

But eager to show them her family shrine, Roxanna pulled at Scirye's wrist.

"Please, Lady, don't be shy. Come see the goddess."

It was either fall or follow Roxanna, so Scirye stumbled forward on stiff legs until she was standing before the four-foot-high statue of Nanaia astride her lion. Scirye shuddered. It was Nanaia the Avenger.

When they depicted Nanaia, the Kushans showed the gentler side of the goddess—the one who helped crops to grow and kept order among humans as if they were unruly children. But this Sogdian statue was the touchier Nanaia who punished those who broke the law or their oaths—like the one Scirye had made.

Scaled armor had replaced the soft gowns of the Kushans' statues and the heavenly flames about Nanaia's head and shoulders looked like swords and arrowheads. Gone was the elegant tiara. Instead, there was a helmet with a wide brim that curled downward. In one hand, She held a staff with a horse's head. In her other hands, She carried the spear, the bow, and the arrows that She used to carry out her vengeance.

Pressing her palms flat in front of her, Roxanna bowed formally three times as Kles fluttered down from Scirye's shoulder to the stones.

"Exquisite, simply exquisite," the griffin said softly. "I see the Persian influence in the carving of the face. It's so . . ."

"Stern," Scirye said, gazing upward. This was the face of a goddess who punished oath breakers like the thirsty emperor and the rich man with horns.

"Kushan art likes to depict the kindnesses that the goddess does, but the Sogdians worship another aspect of Nana," Kles murmured.

"You Kushans are secure in your power," Roxanna said sincerely, "but we Sogdians often live among strangers and far away from our own kind. We prosper because everyone knows we deal fairly."

"So your goddess reminds you to keep your word," Bayang murmured. "And She also serves as a warning to your customers of what will happen if they break a contract with you."

For a moment, it seemed the statue's blank eyes were gazing right at Scirye and she remembered how she had stood back at the museum with the dead and injured all about her, smelling the blood and looking through the dust wreathing that other statue of Nanaia and promisng Nanaia she would pay any cost if the goddess would make her into an Avenger too.

You're being silly, Scirye told herself. *After all, it's only a statue.*

Roxanna had extended her arms with her palms upward as a suppliant. "I ask thy patience with me, O Nana," she began in formal Sogdian. "Thou seizeth the lawbreaker like a lion, and that is Nana. Terrible is thy fury, and that is also Nana. Thou foldeth the babe and the old crone into thy dark embrace, and that, too, is still Nana...."

Scirye could not help closing her eyes and extending her arms just as Roxanna did before she began her own prayer. *I'm doing my best to get the ring back,* Scirye thought. *But don't you want someone else who's older and stronger and smarter?*

Suddenly there was a grinding noise. When Roxanna gave a gasp, Scirye opened her eyes. Nanaia was slowly extending the arrows toward her, triangular points first. At they drew nearer, the arrowheads seemed to swell larger and larger until they filled her field of vision.

The shrine had been very warm, but suddenly she was shivering in a cold, bitter wind. With a shock, she realized she was no longer in the shrine but upon the slope of a mountain. Below her was a strange city. The buildings were all in ruins, the roofs collapsed, the walls disintegrating. And far in the distance was a mountain roughly shaped like a lion's head.

She was standing in the middle of a large platform. Here and there through the layers of muck, the wind had exposed a bare patch of marble. A row of pillars flanked either side, their bases covered in accumulated dirt and the flowery capitals at the top cracked and weathered. They had supported ornate arches, a few of which still rested on top of some pillars, but most had fallen and lay in piles of rubble. There was no sign that there had ever been a roof, so perhaps this place had been left to the open air.

At the very end, three giant stone columns stood just beyond the platform's edge. They rose upward into the sky, their tops crumbled by time, but they looked vaguely like the dense branches of trees.

Before the three columns was a large bronze brazier on tripod legs, and she felt invisible strings tug her toward it. Despite the layer of soil, her soles felt the grooves worn into the floor by generations of feet.

As Scirye drew closer, she saw that the brazier was green with age and time had eaten small jagged holes into the side. The pillar closest to it was blackened from the smoke of past fires in the brazier. And there was just a trace of a sweet but stale odor of incense that still lingered in the bowl.

Then from her right a flute sounded high and sweet, and from her left a drum answered with cheerful thumps. From overhead she heard rustling sounds and saw living tree branches sprouting from the stone columns, and winding around the branches were flowered vines that cast down a heavy perfume.

The flautist, a man in a fur kilt, danced by with a high kicking step. From his head sprouted a pair of antlers. The drummer was a man in checkered pants and tunic. Little bells jingled on his cap, whose peak curled at the top. The musicians glided past her, playing their songs as they wove in and out among the columns and then disappeared.

Women in robes of brown and black and white feathers twirled after them, their capes flapping like wings as they pirouetted on bare feet. Rather than singing, they trilled like birds as they waved golden staffs with the heads of horses and other animals, some of which she did not recognize.

Next, women in dresses and caps of silver scales skipped after them, bending and straightening with a motion as fluid as dolphins swimming in the sea as they joined the dancers circling around the columns. A thin red line began to trickle from one column above the mulch at its base. Scirye knew the smell of blood by now. It reminded Scirye of the battle in the museum and it made her a bit queasy, but the little scarlet ribbon had the opposite effect on the dancers, sending them into a frantic pace.

Paws padded on the platform behind her and she turned in alarm to see a huge lion moving toward her. When she saw the rider, she felt even more scared.

It was Nanaia the Avenger, sitting upon a saddle of elephant hide. Her four hands were holding the same objects as her statue, and She was clad in armor of black scales held together with gold wire. On Her head was a helmet decorated with gilt and a wide down-turned metal brim. Tongues of fire danced around Her head like a tiara and down along Her cloaked shoulders, the flaming tips taking the shapes of swords, spears, and axes that swung back and forth.

Suddenly the pillars, the dancers, and the musicians vanished and Scirye was alone with the goddess and the lion. The great creature halted in front of her, so close that Scirye could see her reflection in his golden eyes and feel his warm breath.

Scirye knew she should bow, but she was frozen to the spot.

The flames on the goddess's shoulders and head began to stream along the goddess's scarlet cloak, and as it rose rippling in the air, Scirye could see the golden lining on the inside.

Slowly the cloak floated away from the goddess, rotating so that the colors had reversed—with the gold cloth now on the outside and the red cloth inside. Then the cloak drifted back to attach itself to Her, and the fire flowed upward again to become the holy, terrible flames anointing Her head and shoulders again.

When the goddess lifted Her lower left hand, the arrows rose from it and floated over to Scirye.

Scirye's eyes were as wide as they could get. "W-what do you want me to do?"

Nanaia was as silent as ever. Scirye tried to look at Her face, but all she could see was the sharp-pointing arrowheads.

Impulsively, the girl stretched out her hand and grasped the shafts of the arrows. At her touch, they began to shine with a silvery radiance, and she felt a cold fire burn painlessly against her palm. Then the arrows melted into her skin, filling her with a pale light as if she were an empty glass. Her hand and then her arm and her whole body glowed softly, but the goddess, the pillars, the city, and the mountains disappeared and the world was dark around her.

And Scirye fell into it.

11

Bayang

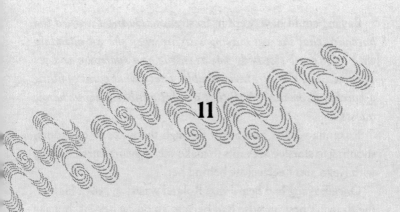

The fool! The silly little fool! Any hatchling ought to have had the sense to run out of the room when she saw a statue moving. Bayang revised that ruefully: *Make that any dragon hatchling—which perhaps was another reason why dragons lived so long and humans died so quickly.*

Leaning forward, Bayang scooped the unconscious girl from the floor. Her body glowed alarmingly like a lamp. "We need a doctor," Bayang said to Roxanna.

The stunned Sogdian girl recovered. "Yes, but first let me take you to the one of the guest rooms where she can lie down."

With the frightened Kles fluttering close by, Bayang followed Roxanna out of the room. Scirye felt as light as a moonbeam in the dragon's forelegs.

Bayang could have wept in frustration. *Hadn't I warned the hatchling that she was playing with fire when she got mixed up with a goddess? Her body was as fragile as a sparrow's and yet she acted as if she were invulnerable. That's what came of filling a hatchling's head with all that romantic rubbish about heroic quests.*

Roxanna settled into a trot through the maze of corridors, shouting to startled servants to make way. Bayang hurried along with Koko and Leech close behind her.

Once Bayang had heard that Roland wasn't in Nova Hafnia, the dragon's first impulse had been to go on by herself, but she knew the hatchlings would try to follow her. They would never have survived without her. She was not even sure they would *with* her.

Roxanna looked over her shoulder to stare in awe at Scirye. "I had no idea the Lady Scirye was the favorite of the goddess," she said in a hushed, awed voice.

Bayang adjusted her grip on the hatchling. "After what the goddess just did to Scirye, 'favorite' might not be the right word. Right now it seems more like it ought to be 'cursed.'"

Roxanna stopped before a yellow door. "In here," she said, opening it.

Bayang eased through the doorway into a large room that the whole world had furnished. Thick Persian rugs covered the floors, but the chairs were of some Brazilian purplish red wood and the tables of some hard, dark African wood. There were several northern Chinese beds built upon brick platforms with openings on the front. Niches along the wall held fire imps that gave it a warm, friendly light.

As Bayang headed to the nearest bed, Kles darted ahead, adjusting the cushions before she laid down the girl.

"I'll fetch the doctor," Roxanna said, and ran from the room.

A few minutes later, Upach herself waddled in with cloths and a basin of water.

Scirye's illuminated body did not seem to surprise the ifrit at all when she saw the hatchling. "The mistress sent me. Poor little chick," she said. Bending over clumsily because of her many coats, Upach set the basin down on a small table next to the divan.

Kles had been sitting on the cushions next to his mistress. With barely a nod of thanks, the griffin soaked a cloth and then laid it lovingly over his mistress's face. No nurse could have been more caring than Kles.

"Oceans that freeze, statues that move," Upach muttered. "I won't stand for it, you hear?"

At her whistle, lizards poked their heads out of the openings of the brick platform, tongues flicking out to test the new scents in the room. They seemed like smaller versions of the giant fire salamanders Leech had seen in Hawaii.

"Get to work, my lovelies," Upach urged.

The heads retreated inside the platform and a moment later the openings began to glow red. Quickly the room began to warm.

"Ah, that's more like it." The ifrit began to shed one coat after another until there was a small mound of them by her feet. With them off and her hat removed, Bayang could see that Upach's body and head were as thin as a rail and her skin was tan colored and smooth and unwrinkled. Without even eyebrows, her face had a new and unfinished look—like a statue that had just been sculpted out of wet clay. She was reduced to a robe of yellow gauze that seemed to float about her like a cloud above trousers of the same diaphanous material.

"Do you miss the desert much?" Leech asked.

"All the time." Upach sighed. Squatting, she held her hands

out toward the opening. "But without me to set things straight, they'd be running around like hens with the hawk diving."

Bayang curled her body along the divan and Leech perched on the edge of a divan near Scirye. "Will she be okay?" he asked.

Bayang shrugged. "Only Nanaia knows."

"Yeah," Koko said, plopping down onto a padded stool, "and after seeing what she just did to Scirye, I'm not about to ask Big N why."

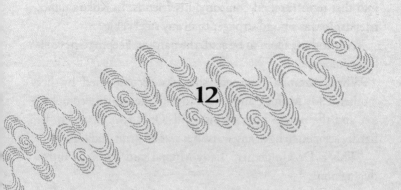

12

Leech

"We've seen some pretty weird stuff, but this one really gives me the creeps," Koko said with a shiver.

Leech scratched his head as he stared down at his unconscious friend. In the brutal world of San Francisco's streets, he'd learned there were few people whom you could trust, so when you met one you treasured him or her. "Me, too, but I know this much. She's a friend, so we have to help her."

Koko stuck his feet out in front of him and stared at the tips of his boots. "Yeah, she's not a bad kid—even if she's nobility and cheats at cards."

The badger was suspicious of everyone but Leech, so those few words meant that the cynical badger had admitted Scirye into that most rarefied company, his friends. In Koko's mind, friendship was a bond stronger than any steel cable.

With nothing more to be said, the pair sat, keeping Scirye silent company.

When Roxanna returned, she was accompanied by her mother, Lady Miunai, and a kobold with the swarthy complexion and the potato nose of his kind. Only two feet high, he hardly seemed to have any waist but was all arms and legs.

"This is Dr. Goldemar," Lady Miunai said, formally introducing him.

Stroking his red beard with one hand, the doctor waddled straight over to the bed. He tossed his medical bag up onto the bed and clambered after it. Kles, who had been sitting anxiously near Scirye's head, fluttered over to the back of a chair, where he perched.

Dr. Goldemar tugged his beard as he studied the unconscious girl for a moment. "From what I hear, you need a priestess and not me." Even so, he began to carry out a methodical examination.

While he did so, servants streamed in bearing silver trays heaped with food and drink, which they set down on tables.

"Upach," Roxanna asked sweetly, "would you please carry out that errand that I told you earlier you might have to?"

"This is the first time I've been warm in months!" the ifrit complained, but she quickly got back into all her Arctic gear. "Are you sure, my girl?"

Roxanna nodded. "It may not be necessary, but we should take care of it just in case."

With a heavy sigh, Upach stomped into the hallway.

With her typical competence, Roxanna oversaw the servants in filling plates with tidbits. She tried her best to interest the companions in eating, but even Koko was too worried to do more than nibble and Leech and Bayang had no appetite at all.

Finally, Prince Tarkhun strode into the room, snow melting on his boots and shedding his coat as he walked. He was sweaty, dirty, and tired, but he looked every inch the commanding prince. Two servants scuttled behind, one catching his coat while the other surreptitiously wiped up the little puddles the prince had left behind.

Prince Tarkhun stared in shock at the unconscious Scirye. "Why would Nana strike Lady Scirye down in our very own shrine?"

"It was a miracle, Father," Roxanna said. "The statue of Nana moved, and when Lady Scirye touched it she fainted."

"A miracle is when I've got twenty bucks in my pocket," Koko whispered to Leech, "not getting knocked out."

"Yeah, this seems like something else," Leech agreed.

"But what could Lady Scirye possibly have done?" Prince Tarkhun said, still puzzled.

Kles cleared his throat. "She asked Nanaia to help her recover the stolen treasure and avenge her sister's death."

"Oh," Lady Miunai cried, raising her fingertips to her lips.

With a sad shake of his head, Prince Tarkhun sat down in a chair. Somehow when he was on it, it seemed like a throne. "That was rash, indeed. We are always careful when we ask her for anything."

Leech didn't understand their uneasiness. "I thought Nanaia—I mean Nana helps people?"

"She does," Prince Tarkhun said heavily, "but sometimes not in the way you might expect."

"There is the story of the prince who lost his beloved wife," Lady Miunai said. "So he promised Nana anything if She would bring his wife back. That night he heard someone knock on the door of his bedchamber. And when he opened it, there was his wife alive again. But she had no sooner put her arms around him than the prince himself fell dead. You see, Nana's account books must always balance out."

"So you got to watch out for the fine print in one of Her contracts?" Koko asked with a worried glance at Scirye.

"Exactly." The prince sighed. "Heaven protect Lady Scirye if Nana is helping her."

They regarded the unfortunate Scirye in silence. Finally, Leech asked, "What should we do?"

Prince Tarkhun inclined his head toward Lady Miunai. "I count on my wife's counsel, so perhaps you should repeat your tale again."

As Bayang began their story, Lady Miunai listened intently, asking a shrewd question every now and then but otherwise letting the dragon go on.

Lady Miunai swung a worried, compassionate gaze toward Scirye. "Poor girl. It seems like the goddess really has chosen her."

"Ah, she's waking up," Dr. Goldemar suddenly interrupted, "and I have no idea why."

They all turned to see that Scirye's body was no longer shining. Instead, she was struggling to open her eyes.

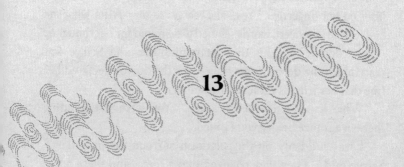

13

Scirye

At first when Scirye came to and heard the rumbling, she thought she was in the middle of a thunderstorm. She quickly realized that it was her friends talking. The conversation stopped as soon as she had opened her eyes.

"Water," a little kobold with a stethoscope said briskly. He placed his fingers on the underside of her wrist. "You had everyone worried for a little bit, my dear girl."

As he took her pulse, Scirye stared up at the ceiling and tried to collect her scattered thoughts. With a chill, she remembered Nanaia.

"Lady, are you feeling better?" Kles asked. He'd fetched a small silver cup of water and was holding it in his paws.

Scirye became aware of how thirsty she was. Sitting up, she

took the cup with her free hand, feeling the embossed decorations on her fingertips. "Yes," she reassured him. After what she had just experienced, words seemed too limited for her thoughts.

The doctor took his time examining her, and Scirye was grateful for the delay. It was only when the doctor declared her fine that her friends gathered around her.

"What happened?" Leech asked. "You were just standing there in a trance before you fainted."

"I was suddenly on this platform surrounded by pillars," Scirye said. "Then they changed into a forest and these musicians and dancers. Some were dressed like animals, but others were birds and fish."

"The creatures of the earth, the sky, and the sea," Lady Miunai murmured thoughtfully.

Beside her, Kles stirred, but he let Scirye go on. "And Nanaia was riding her lion."

"So it was the goddess who sent you a vision." Lady Miunai made a sign, and Roxanna glanced at Scirye uneasily.

"Or you were just tired from your trip," Prince Tarkhun said skeptically.

Scirye raised a hand to rub her forehead and noticed a dim light. She looked uneasily at her palm. The number "3" glowed there faintly.

"The goddess has marked you," Lady Miunai said in a hushed voice.

"But what does it mean?" Bayang asked.

Scirye cradled her hand in her lap. "She tried to hand me some arrows. There were three of them."

"I think a superbow would need special arrows," Prince Tarkhun observed.

Kles gave a cough. "Lady, was there any clue in the vision about where the arrows might be?"

"Well, the goddess had these flames around her shoulders and head and they got real long and formed this kind of cape that turned inside out." Scirye looked around, but everyone was as puzzled by it as she was.

"Was there anything else?" Leech prompted.

Scirye bit her lip a moment and then said, "Across from me was this mountain shaped like a lion."

"Ah, that sounds like Riye Srukalleyis, the City of Death," Kles said. He explained to the others, "It's part of ancient Kushan where Yi battled a monster. A temple was built on the site to commemorate his heroics, and there were so many pilgrims that used to visit it that a city eventually grew up there, and a fair place it was until the Huns invaded many centuries later. The defenders destroyed the enemy host but died in the effort."

"If it was a vision," Scirye asked, rubbing her temple, "why didn't She just tell me what I'm supposed to do?" She punched the sofa helplessly. "In the legends, gods and goddesses always make things clear to people."

Lady Miunai pantomimed scribbling something. "Legends are written down long after what happened, so they give ideal-ized versions of events. The real situations may have been more difficult." She pursed her lips sympathetically. "At any rate, perhaps Nanaia wants you to go there."

"I think it would be wiser," the prince urged. "It won't matter to Roland what he finds here if he can't get Yi's arrows. And in your homeland, your father can aid you."

"Another trip with that windbag Naue?" Koko groaned, slap-ping his forehead. "You got any earplugs for sale?"

Bayang drummed her claws on her chair. "But where are the arrows buried in that city? We could dig for years and never find them. If we can stop Roland here, we won't have to go to this City of Death."

"What if Roland has gone there while this Badik has come here?" the prince asked.

"I don't think Roland would trust anyone else with the parts of the superweapon," Scirye reasoned. "He wants to collect them personally. So if Badik is here so is he." She swung her legs off the bed. She was still a little woozy. "How long have I been out?"

"About an hour," Bayang said.

"Should you ignore Nana's command to go to the City of Death?" the prince inquired.

Scirye, though, was feeling annoyed with the goddess's riddles. "Who knows what the goddess means for me to do in that city? I'm sure that Roland is here, and that's what's important at the moment. Once we get him, I'll go wherever the goddess wants."

Her legs wobbled a little when she tried to stand up and Kles rose into the air, grabbing hold of one arm with all four paws to hold her up. As valiant an effort as it was, the lap griffin wasn't strong enough and Scirye would have fallen if the kobold doctor hadn't caught hold of her the next moment. Though no taller than a child, he had the strength of a grown human.

With nods of thanks to her rescuers, Scirye straightened up. "I'm all right now."

Prince Tarkhun rubbed his temples as if he suddenly had a headache. "Ai! Why did I promise to help you no matter what?"

Roxanna stiffened, switching from English to Common to scold him like some little nun: "If you gave your word, Father, you have to keep it."

"That was before I heard they were fighting Roland and his dragon," Prince Tarkhun argued in the same tongue as his daughter. "To destroy an island, to steal a treasure from a goddess—Roland's scheme is on a scale so grand that I cannot even picture it. Lady Scirye should go to the Kushan Empire, where she'll have powerful allies. She shouldn't challenge the ocean in winter where the Arctic is as deadly an enemy as Roland. I would never have made my vow if it meant helping them go to their deaths."

Roxanna pointed at her face. "I saw Nana's statue move with my own two eyes. Lady Scirye is special to the goddess. So if Lady Scirye says she has to chase Roland onto the ice, then we have to help her."

Concerned, Lady Miunai put her hand on her husband's arm. "Yes, we have to give all the aid we can to Lady Scirye and her friends."

"To refuse to help them is against all laws of honor and hospitality," Roxanna protested.

Prince Tarkhun squirmed as he looked from his wife to his daughter, annoyed that the pair was ganging up on him. "If I have guests who want to jump from the roof, should I let them? The philosophers can debate what's right and what's wrong. I have to follow what my conscience tells me."

"But Father—"

"Enough," Prince Tarkhun commanded in Common to his wife and daughter. "I've made my judgment. What happened in the shrine is a sign that Lady Scirye is precious to the goddess. We must protect her, not help her commit suicide."

He slipped back into English when he spoke to Scirye and the others: "I'm sorry, but I have to adjust my promise. I will assist you on your way to the Kushan Empire, where your father can help you, but I will not give you aid in this reckless pursuit of Roland. Until I can make travel arrangements, I must insist you stay here as our honored guests. We will give you every courtesy within our walls, but you will not be allowed to leave them."

Turning, he beckoned to the nearest servant. "Fetch the chakar."

14

Bayang

I was a fool, a fool! The only humans she could trust were the hatchlings, but because she had let her guard down with these treacherous Sogdians, they had trapped her.

But she would show them that it is not so simple to capture a warrior of the Moonglow clan.

"Let's go!" Bayang snarled as she worked her transformation spell. The world blurred around her as her form changed, and through the magical sparks swirling around her she heard Koko wail, "But I haven't eaten yet."

Once again in her dragon perfection, Bayang picked up the tanuki by the scruff of his neck and dragged him from a divan. "Can't you think of anything more than your belly, you furball?"

Koko squinted at Bayang. "Don't you call me names, you walking handbag!" The next moment, he had changed into a pudgy badger.

"That's more like it," Bayang said, and flung him down. Catlike, he landed on all fours.

When a servant tried to stop her, Scirye hit him over the head with a silver platter, scattering chunks of meat in all directions. In the meantime, Kles had risen into the air and was using his paws to pummel another servant who tried to intervene.

Leech had pulled off his weapon armband and had expanded it into a ring to use as a weapon, but the other servants didn't seem in any hurry to attack.

Bayang knocked over a table, goblets and plates crashing to the floor. "It's now or never," she called, and worked the expansion spell.

The next moment her body began to feel tight, almost painfully so. The air shimmered and whirled as the spell gathered matter from the surrounding area to add the needed mass. Then the people and furnishings seemed to be shrinking as she swelled in height, stopping before she wouldn't fit through the doorway.

As soon as Bayang sat on her haunches, Leech helped Scirye scramble onto her back and then followed.

"I'm coming too," Roxanna cried, hitching up her robe to reveal warm trousers of reindeer hide. Clambering over the debris, she ran straight up Bayang's spine to join the other hatchlings.

"Roxanna, come down here this instant!" Prince Tarkhun jabbed his finger imperiously at the floor.

Defiantly, Roxanna straddled the dragon and wrapped her arms around Leech's waist. "I'm sorry, Father. Someone in our family has to remember our duty to Nana and our honor."

There wasn't time to order Roxanna to listen to her father. Already Bayang could see some of the servants gathering by the large door to thwart their escape.

"Heads down," the dragon instructed, and sprang forward, gathering speed as she went. The human barricade lost their nerve at the sight of a ton of scales and fangs and scattered before her like straw.

They would lose too much precious time if she had to stop and open the door, so closing her eyes, she lowered her head like a battering ram. The impact on her skull made her fangs clack together, but the door fell off its hinges and its lock mechanism spun through the air with a cloud of splinters.

Bayang skidded as she tried to stop and smashed into the tapestry-covered wall opposite the doorway. She thought the bricks behind the woven cloth gave way as if she had dented the hallway. "Everybody still there?"

"To your left," Roxanna said.

I've seen how Roxanna bosses the Sogdian adults around, but now she's telling a dragon what to do, Bayang thought exasperatedly.

Bayang turned in that direction, paws skittering along the floor and demolishing a cabinet as she tried to recover speed.

Kles shot ahead like a tawny arrow. "You're leaving an easy trail for them to follow."

"You try being stealthy when you're learning how to be a ferryboat," Bayang puffed.

Koko's paws scrabbled on the floor as he followed them. "Hey, wait for baby."

Behind them, Bayang could hear people shouting the alarm, but it would take a while for word to spread through a place as vast as the caravanserai and the dragon intended to take advantage of that.

Then she heard an all too familiar hum. Curling her neck around for a moment, she saw the flying disks spinning under Leech's feet. Roxanna sat goggle-eyed, watching.

Leech was smiling self-consciously at having a new audience. "Kles can't guard your rear if he's scouting in front of you," he said, and hopped into the air.

"Kles is an experienced flier and you're"—Bayang could have gnashed her teeth with exasperation as the hatchling almost collided with a hanging chandelier—"still a beginner."

Leech left it swinging back and forth behind him, the fire imps flaring angrily.

"Then don't distract me," he insisted, rubbing his head as he zipped backward out of reach.

The elders should never have worried about him, sending her to kill him. The little idiot was quite capable of doing it on his own. Well, she'd save him despite his recklessness—in a purely professional sense, of course, and not because she was a spinster dragon trying to pretend she finally had a hatchling.

She'd treat this like a job, acting logically and without emotion. There was no question that their relationship could ever be more than client and bodyguard. Even if she carried out the task successfully, there was no way she could make up for assassinating those earlier selves.

But first things first. "Help us get outside and we'll leave you there," Bayang said to Roxanna.

Any other species would not have dared to defy a dragon. But human hatchlings, as Bayang was discovering, were different.

"Do you know how to survive out on the ice?" Roxanna challenged the dragon.

"Do you?" Scirye asked. "I thought you were cooped up inside the caravanserai."

Roxanna's voice instantly became respectful. "No, Lady. The freebooters have only been a big problem the last few years. Before that, they weren't organized and wouldn't tackle a large group."

"I bet that's Roland's doing," Koko said.

Roxanna sounded wistful. "I used to go out regularly with Father and my brothers on trading runs to the Inuit villages. So I'm as good as they are at camping out in the snow and hunting. I know this land as well as you do yours."

"I left Kushan when I was small," Scirye confessed. "I'm afraid I don't know it at all."

"That's all right," Kles shouted back to her. "That's why you have me."

Roxanna seemed puzzled by that. "Then where do you call home, Lady?"

"Everywhere," Scirye said, "and nowhere. My mother was stationed in Istanbul and then Paris before being assigned to San Francisco," she explained. "But her missions took her all over Europe and Turkey and around the Mediterranean. And when our ship landed in New York, we toured the eastern coast of the United States before catching the train to San Francisco."

"I'd die to see even one of those places you've been," Roxanna said, and then called out to Bayang, "Up those stairs."

As she galloped toward the stairs a hundred yards away, Bayang suspected that there was more to Roxanna's devotion to her family's honor and the goddess. They also seemed like convenient excuses for finally having an adventure of her own.

Unfortunately, Bayang knew the Sogdian hatchling was probably right. The Arctic wilderness would be as deadly a foe as Roland and Badik. In fact, the dragon wasn't even sure she could find her way out of the caravanserai without a guide.

"How come I keep attracting all these willful human hatchlings?" Bayang sighed. "It it some curse?"

"Hey, slow down, Stretch," Koko panted. "My legs are shorter than yours."

Bayang felt a sudden weight on her tail. Glancing behind her, she saw that Koko had leapt onto the appendage. Leech had flown in close and was helping the badger to wriggle to a higher perch on Bayang's tail.

"If you ate less and exercised more, you could keep up," Bayang scolded.

She depended on her tail to help her balance when she was on the ground, so the sudden weight there made it harder to keep on a straight line. She winced not with pain but with chagrin as her swinging tail smashed a table into kindling.

"Watch it. You got a passenger on the caboose," Koko protested as he shook some large splinters from his fur.

"If you don't pay your fare, you don't get to complain," Bayang snapped. But she was being so careful not to knock Koko off that she stumbled on the bottom step, barely managing to stay on her paws as she clattered up the staircase, which groaned under the combined weight.

Fortunately, the stairs proved sturdy enough, and at Roxanna's instruction Bayang opened the door at the top. An icy wind blew into their faces as Bayang stepped onto the roof. The long night had claimed Nova Hafnia.

Upach was waiting for them, wearing all her furs and with the muffler wound around her head and an imp burning fiercely in a lantern by her thick, furry boots. Next to her were various bundles and lengths of rope. Clutched in her arms was a rifle in a long holster.

"When you told me you were going to chase Roland," Roxanna explained smugly, "I suspected what Father would say. But

I also saw the omen and knew she wanted you to leave. So I took some precautions for our escape."

Bayang had never seen an ifrit with a rifle before, so as she pulled up beside the servant she nodded to the weapon. "Is that really necessary?"

"The rifle's mine," the Sogdian hatchling said. "I used to go hunting regularly, so I know how to handle it properly."

Bayang frowned. "In my experience, humans and guns are an accident waiting to happen."

"While you may not have to worry about getting eaten by bears," Roxanna countered, "the rest of us do."

Koko raised a hand but didn't wait for an acknowledgment. "D-do they include badgers on their dinner menu?"

Roxanna's teeth flashed in a savage smile. "I think your fur would get in their teeth, but otherwise they'd manage."

They could hear shouting from the central courtyard as if their pursuers were guarding all the doors, not realizing that Bayang was a dragon in disguise. It wouldn't take long, though, before Prince Tarkhun and Lady Miunai directed their followers to the roof.

"What if Roland heads into the Wastes? Aren't you scared of the phantoms?" Scirye asked.

"A good caravan leader has to look at the facts," Roxanna declared. "I don't think there are phantoms. Those stories have been around for centuries. Sure, people have disappeared, but they were hunters who probably had accidents."

"So it's just rumors?" Leech asked.

Roxanna bit her lip for a moment. "Um, no." She straightened her shoulders. "There's something there, but I don't think it will harm us. I talked to an Inuit who wandered into the Wastes because he'd become lost. Though he heard howls and weird noises, he never saw anything, and whenever he turned in the wrong direction something nipped at his heels to head him the right way. He said it was more like whatever was there was herding him out of the Wastes like a reindeer."

"Well, you've had your fun." Bayang snagged Leech from the air and dragged him down. "But you're going to ride on my back when we leave here. I'll have enough to do without worrying about you flying solo."

The hatchling looked stubborn. "I've done all right so far."

"Lord Leech, you'll have to take off your disks anyway." Roxanna pointed to a row of boots in different sizes. "Your feet will freeze in just shoes." Then she said to the others, "Better put on the furs." Upach had fetched new fur coats, hats, and gloves. "I don't think even your charms will keep out the cold where we're going.

"I think I may need more than fur," Koko said.

As the others dismounted and Leech reluctantly returned to the ground and restored the flying disks to his armband, Bayang began another expansion spell so she could carry their supplies.

Koko yanked on a coat with satisfaction. "There. A double layer of fur ought to keep the heat in and bear fangs out."

Roxanna changed her clothing with the other hatchlings, but when she caught sight of Scirye's feet she began chewing her lip.

"What's wrong, Roxanna?" Scirye asked.

The Sogdian girl bowed from the waist, keeping her eyes on the floor. "I beg your forgiveness, Lady Scirye. But your boots look as flimsy as Lord Leech's shoes." She paused. "Unless you think the goddess will protect you from the cold."

"Let's not test it." Scirye stood on one leg like a stork as she tried to remove the first boot. "I'll just put them in the baggage."

"No extra freight," Bayang declared. "I think it'll be all I can do to carry our supplies and all of you."

Scirye was hopping on one leg as she tried to remove the first boot. "Can't you grow just a few more inches?"

"More mass requires more fuel to move it," the dragon explained.

"Eh? In English?" Koko asked. He was putting on a pair of boots himself.

"Every extra inch means I need to eat more food so I can fly," Bayang said. "Which then means I have to carry more supplies and that means becoming even larger."

Roxanna had fetched a pair of thickly padded boots from the pile of clothes that Upach had brought. Clutching them to her, she came over and knelt. "If Your Ladyship will permit, I'll leave a note that the boots are to be saved for you. No one would dare touch them if they know they're yours."

The Sogdian girl shrank back when Scirye tried to support herself by putting a hand on Roxanna's shoulder. So, looking a bit put out, Scirye sat down on the cold floor instead. As Kles fluttered down to help tug the boots off, Roxanna prostrated herself.

"Are you feeling faint?" Scirye asked.

"It would be disrespectful to be taller than you," the girl answered humbly.

"There are a lot of people taller than me," Scirye said. "You don't expect me to cut off their heads, do you? Get up."

Roxanna straightened up again and timidly extended her hands. "If I may help . . . ?"

"Sure," Scirye said.

Looking as if she were afraid she would burst into flame at any moment, the Sogdian girl gripped the heel of the boot and began to yank.

"Why are you acting so funny?" Scirye asked.

Roxanna dipped her head respectfully. "You're the chosen of the goddess. I saw the miracle with my own eyes."

"That doesn't make me some kind of holy relic," Scirye said, annoyed.

"I'm sorry, Lady. I didn't mean to make you mad," Roxanna said. Between the three of them, they got off both of Scirye's boots. The Sogdian girl picked up the new boots and held them out in both hands as if they were an offering. "Do these please you?"

Scirye snatched the boots from her. "All I care about now is keeping my feet warm."

These were easier to put on by herself, and when she was done Roxanna held out a scarf. "You'll also need to wrap this about your head, Lady."

Uncomfortably, Scirye accepted it. "Thank you."

Kles fussed over the scarf's arrangement and then noticed Koko had already swathed his head in a gray muffler. "It's definitely an improvement on your appearance," Kles said.

The badger's snout was shoving the wool cloth outward.

"Yeah? Well, the only way to improve your looks is to cover you up completely," the badger shot back.

When the hatchlings and badger were dressed for outside, they climbed up Bayang's tail again and onto her back.

Then Upach hefted up a basket, thrusting it into the air. "Hurry up and take it. I haven't got all day."

Leech leaned forward so far that Koko grabbed his coat to keep him from falling. Even so, the basket was just out of his reach. "You've got to hold it closer," the boy said.

"Right you are then," Upach said, and shifted the basket over so Leech could grasp it, but it was still several feet away.

"Upach, can you see at all?" Bayang asked.

"I lost my eyesight long ago in a fight with an impertinent

roc," Upach said. Rocs were gigantic birds even larger than the clipper seaplane. "But Prince Tarkhun took me in."

"And you've never stopped nagging us from that day on," Roxanna teased. She'd torn a page from a little notebook and, after scribbling a note on it, left the page on Scirye's boots. Then Roxanna started to help her servant lift the baskets and boxes up for the children to secure.

"And where would you be without old Upach, my little chick?" the servant grunted as she made another effort to get the basket into Leech's hands. It wound up even farther away.

"Let me help you," Leech said, getting ready to spring back down.

"Don't feel sorry for old Upach," the ifrit said. "I manage better with my ears and nose than you do with your eyes. I know where you are now." She thrust the basket into Leech's hands.

Then, having located Leech and Koko, she handed up the boxes as efficiently as a robot.

"Nothing escapes Upach," Roxanna said as she scuttled up Bayang's tail and onto the dragon's back.

"Except my little chick," Upach sniffed.

When the last box had been secured, Scirye looked at the blind old servant with some concern. "Upach, I hope you don't get into much trouble after we leave," Scirye said.

"Oh, I'm not sticking around," Upach said, straddling Bayang's tail and then shinnying up it.

Concerned, Roxanna commanded, "Stay here, Upach. You can barely stand the temperature inside here. How can you handle the cold out there?"

"Don't you worry about old Upach," the ifrit snorted. "Do you think I'll let my little chick wander off without me?"

Roxanna put out a hand and tried to shove Upach back. "No. I order you to stay."

Lowering her head like a stubborn goat, Upach tried to shove forward. "And I say that I'm going."

Now Roxanna knows how I feel about unwanted passengers, Bayang thought to herself, but she tried to help the Sogdian hatchling: "I can hear the fear in your voice, Upach. Don't think you have to go from loyalty."

"She's going out of love," Kles said as he looked out from inside Scirye's coat. "This is something I understand better than the rest of you. She's more scared of what will happen to her mistress than she is for herself."

"I couldn't stand it if something harmed my little chick while I sat safe here," Upach admitted. "Do you hear me? I couldn't stand it."

"Don't mourn for me yet." Roxanna relented and took the loyal servant's arm. "You can come, but no nagging."

"That's one promise I can't keep, my little chick," Upach said. "You need a firm hand."

"Halt!" Randian shouted as he stumbled onto the roof.

"What if you miss them and hit me, Randian?" Roxanna demanded.

Bayang took advantage of Randian's confusion to spread her great wings. With a beat that sent the loose snow swirling across the rooftop, she sprang into the air. With rapid flaps, she flew above the central courtyard, where surprised faces were staring at her, and then out over the street. And for the moment the skies were empty of Mounties.

She found herself smiling as delightedly at Leech when he was soaring through the air. Nothing beat the joy of flying with one's own wings.

"I'm riding a dragon!" Roxanna yelled to the wind.

"Humph," Koko grumbled. "My idea of a good time is twenty

bucks and a sunny afternoon in Frisco—neither of which happens very often."

"I know how you feel, Roxanna." Leech laughed. "The next best thing to flying with my disks is riding on Bayang."

It was a compliment of sorts, but one that her dignity could have done without. "Which way?" the dragon asked.

"Follow the coastline for now," Roxanna said.

15

Leech

The coastline ran along the ocean's edge like a broken zipper with teethlike headlands and then gaplike bays, which were several miles in length.

Leech was looking skyward, yearning to be soaring among the stars. "How about I take a load off your back and go for a spin on my own?" he suggested.

"Yes, it seems calm enough right now," Roxanna observed. "I'd love to see you fly in the open sky."

Bayang was flying with her head thrust out ahead of her. Her words floated back to him: "Will you stick close to me?"

It's a trap, stupid, jeered that strange, savage voice.

The boy wrinkled his forehead almost in pain as he tried to understand where the malevolent words were coming from.

No, he said to himself, *she gave me her word and honor is every-thing to a dragon. She's trying to protect me.*

She's pretending to baby you and you're falling for it, the voice mocked. *She's just keeping you near her so she can kill you any moment she likes—just like she did all those other times.*

The voice vanished as soon as it had come, but it had left Leech feeling shaken, because those ugly things could only have come from some part of his mind—some secret, dark part.

It made him feel guilty to have such notions. Hadn't Bayang proved she'd had a change of heart? And after all these years of being picked on in the orphanage, it was nice to have someone on his side for a change. Primo had made him feel the same way, but Primo was gone. And Koko was . . . well . . . Koko was as likely to get him into some scrape as get him out.

Scirye broke into his thoughts: "Leech?"

"Uh . . . okay," he said absently. "I'll fly."

Bayang frowned. "What's the matter now? Isn't that what you wanted?"

He would have been ashamed to tell Bayang what he had been thinking, so instead he said, "Of course." Then, because he thought he owed her more, he added, "And thanks."

She turned her face forward again. "Bah, I shouldn't spoil you this way."

Leech grinned. Once he was off, he intended to stay out there as long as he could. In the caravanserai, Roxanna had been too busy orchestrating their escape to pay attention to the transfor-mation, but now she could give him her full attention. Aware of a fascinated Roxanna watching him, he pulled the disks off his armband and spat on them. "Change," he said.

Carefully he strapped them on and rose into the air and in-stantly began to swerve from side to side in the strong, chill winds.

Bayang was keeping an eye on him. "It's trickier than it looks, isn't it?"

Cheeks reddening, he managed to regain his balance. "I'll get the hang of it."

"Amazing," Roxanna said raptly.

Cautiously he drew level with the dragon's head, proud to be flying side by side with her.

Bayang glanced at him. "Not bad," she conceded.

But the constant adjusting for the wind soon tired him out, and in five minutes, despite Pele's charm, he could feel his arms and legs growing stiff with the cold.

The whisper crept into his consciousness like a trickle of ice water: *Finish her now while her guard's down.*

It surprised him so much that he dipped suddenly.

"That's enough," Bayang declared, and her paw caught his collar.

Are you going to let her boss you around like that? the voice demanded.

Shut up, shut up, shut up, Leech said to that inner voice as Bayang hoisted him toward her back.

He looked down at Koko and Scirye, who were holding up their hands to help him re-mount. What would they say if he told them about that strange wicked voice? More than likely they'd call him crazy. He knew what he would think if the situation was reversed. Worse, they'd be horrified to discover just what sort of person he was. He was shocked himself.

When he had resumed his seat on the dragon, he sat in silence for a long time.

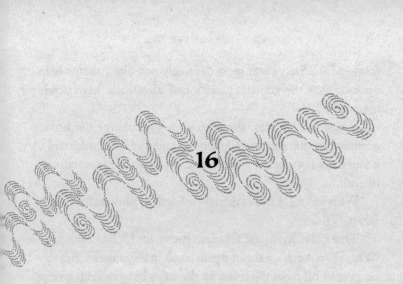

16

Scirye

Scirye was still so haunted by what had happened in the caravanserai shrine that she barely took in the scenery. She felt less like the goddess's chosen one and more like a plaything whom the goddess teased as if she were a pet kitten. She had heard of the City of Death, of course.

It was the site of a famous battle where Kushan defenders had delayed their enemies long enough for the emperor to gather an army and destroy the invaders. But why did she have to go there?

She glanced at her gloved hand. Was it her imagination or was the "3" glowing faintly through the material?

And as if that weren't bad enough, the magical sideshow at the shrine had convinced Roxanna that Scirye was some kind of saint—which Scirye was most definitely not. She couldn't help noticing that the goddess's mark had also made her friends uneasy.

Despite her worries, she couldn't help watching the broad promontory that gleamed like a porcelain tray. Two miles wide, it jutted out into the sea and reached deep into the mountainous interior.

"What's that?" Leech asked their Sogdian guide as he flew by Bayang's side.

"That's the Kristiana Glacier, young lord," Roxanna said. "There's so much ice that it doesn't melt in the summer. But icebergs split off from the front, so the ships have to keep an eye out for those."

"I see two fliers," Roxanna said, jolting Scirye from her thoughts.

Leech squinted, trying to see them. "Freebooters?"

Tensing, Scirye scolded herself. She had gotten quite a few bruises from Nishke during training bouts because she had let her mind wander. After each hit, Nishke had certainly lectured her enough that a Pippal, one of the elite guards of the empire, was alert at all times. So if Scirye wanted to join them, she had to stay focused.

Scirye's eyes were sharpest of the friends', so she stared hard. "No, they're riding owls, so it's probably Mounties."

"Your father calls the cops faster than a bill collector," Koko said. "How's the chow in a Mountie hoosegow?"

"I don't think you have to worry," Scirye said. "They're coming in from the ocean, so they were probably searching for Roland. They couldn't have heard about us yet."

"Still, we'd better hide." Banking, Bayang glided gracefully down to the surface of the glacier, landing with a puff of snow from the flakes covering the ice.

"There's a large crevice to our left," Roxanna said. "Upach, cover our tracks."

Some geological quirk had thrust up a shelf of ice from the glacier's top and something else had cracked its surface, forming an opening at the base of the upthrust shelf.

"Just when I was getting used to riding on that hard hide," Upach grumbled. "Go here, go there. I won't stand for it, you hear? I just won't." But she slid off anyway with a sack in her hand. Once she was standing on the glacier, she took items from the sack and stowed them in the pockets of her multiple layers of clothing so that she bulged even wider. Then she began to back up, dusting Bayang and her tracks so that the snow became smooth again.

The crevice was wide enough to fit Bayang with all the gear once her riders had dismounted, but it quickly narrowed at the top to cover them. The crevice also tapered quickly at the rear, so that Bayang was forced to coil her tail around herself.

Scirye and the others stood in front of her.

"Father's bound to tell the Mounties," Roxanna said. "So we'll have to keep an eye out for them as well as Roland."

They waited awhile, their breath misting before them in streamers where Upach joined them. "Sit up here. Let your feet get warm," Bayang said kindly, patting her tail.

Upach stared up at her warily. "Are you keeping me handy as a snack?"

"Naw, ifrits give her gas," Koko said, starting to climb up on Bayang's tail too.

"Do I look like a sofa?" Bayang said, and shoved the badger off with her muzzle. "The invitation was just for Upach."

Koko stood up, dusting the snow from himself. "Aw, who wants to sit on you anyway. You're hard as a rock."

"Quiet," Kles snapped.

Scirye felt her shoulders tightening, wondering if they were going to be discovered. The others were too scared to move—except for Koko. The enforced silence was hard on the talkative badger, and he fidgeted and tapped a hind paw until Bayang wrapped a big forepaw around him so he couldn't move.

Finally, Bayang flicked a claw to the griffin and Kles slipped out of Scirye's coat and fluttered outside. He returned a moment later, shaking his head. "There's no sign of them."

"Then we better get going," Bayang said, releasing Koko.

"I hope that paw was clean before you grabbed me," Koko said sourly as he padded outside.

Scirye caught her friend in her arms. Kles's body felt cold despite the charm, his fur, and his feathers and she slipped him quickly inside her coat, wrapping her arms around him as another layer of insulation.

Once they were outside the crevice, they quickly mounted Bayang and took off again.

Scirye looked at the vast wilderness, wondering where Roland was. Even a thousand searchers might not be able to find him.

"So where do we go from here?" Koko asked.

"We might as well follow his route and aim for the Wastes," Bayang said. "He'll have to re-fuel his plane, and if he didn't stop in Nova Hafnia he must have some fuel stashed along the way."

"Maybe that's one of the reasons why he didn't want anyone snooping around," Leech suggested.

"Then we're going to ruin his plans," Roxanna said, and at her instructions Bayang altered their course out onto the ice.

Beyond the glacier, the land retreated from the ocean, leaving them heading out into the vast expanse of frozen, empty sea.

Scirye had expected it to be as flat as a skating rink and it was at first, but then it became rather lumpy until they came to a zigzagging line of ice boulders that wandered for miles in each direction. It looked like the broken wall of a vanished ancient city. Some of the irregularly shaped ice blocks were as big as hills. "What made those?" she asked, pointing.

"It's a pressure ridge, Lady," Roxanna explained. "The ice isn't one sheet. It's really thousands of ice floes, some many kilometers across, that jam together. When the temperature thaws a little, the edges where the ice floes meet are the first to melt and also the first to freeze again when the temperature drops. But that new ice gets squeezed between the original floes and rises in a ridge."

Ahead, the frozen sea slid on to the horizon and Scirye could see line after line of pressure ridges dividing the surface. Salene the Moon cast shadows that seemed to limn the mounds with stark, black lines, and the ocean resembled a vast quilt of white patches sewn together with ragged, clumsy stitches, but each patch was the size of a county and the stitches ran for kilometers and were as high as a two-story house.

The Arctic is so overwhelming, Scirye thought, and then added to herself, *just like Nanaia.*

Roxanna took it upon herself then to explain the rules for survival in her homeland: "You must be careful, Lady, and listen to me. You've never been in a land as hostile as this. It will make you pay for any mistake."

Scirye had always disliked know-it-alls because their advice was usually the first step before they tried to bully her. "We've been inside a volcano, remember?"

"Yes, of course, Lady," Roxanna said, chastised.

Scirye was sorry she had said anything, but then, to her surprise and annoyance, Leech came to Roxanna's support: "Yes, but there we had a goddess's help."

"How hot was it?" Upach asked wistfully as she clung to the dragon.

"Too hot even for you." Leech laughed.

"Yes, well, you've jumped from the frying pan into the icebox," Roxanna said to Leech. "It can get below minus sixty-eight degrees centigrade. So even your magical charms might not protect you for a long time, and if you take off your gloves or hat you could lose your ears and fingers."

"Ouch," Koko said, putting a paw under his hat to check for any damage.

The snowy wilderness seemed so vast and lifeless and hostile that Scirye was glad to be flying above it.

"I think you could call the whole place the Wastes," Koko observed. "It's all dead down there."

"You're wrong," Roxanna said. "There's plenty of life below the ice in the ocean and above it; you just have to know where to look."

"I don't see anything," Koko stubbornly insisted.

"There, see the tracks?" Roxanna pointed to a line of paw prints that looked like twin lines of stitches across a white handkerchief. "It's an Arctic fox." It looked like a ball of ivory-colored fluff. "Often they trail polar bears, hoping the bears will leave some scraps for the foxes' next meals."

"See, Koko," Leech said. "There is life down there and Roxanna can show it to us. I mean, there's not a lot of it, but you got to hand it to the critters. They're real survivors."

Suddenly, Scirye was beginning to get an inkling of what Roxanna meant. "Yes," she agreed, "sort of like when you see a flower coming up through a crack in the sidewalk."

She tried to see the harsh landscape through Roxanna's eyes: the huge white expanse that dwarfed humans, their ships, and their cities. It took a certain type of creature, or person, one who could take pleasure in meeting its challenges, one who felt good at meeting this hostile, merciless land on its terms. In the countries to the south, humans boasted about taming rivers and jungles, but any idea of conquest up here was nonsense.

And when Scirye adjusted her attitude that way, she began to glimpse the loveliness of the Arctic—the grand sweep of the ocean, the long curtains of snow drifting like the veils of a dancer, the delight in seeing the tracks of another creature because one was no longer so lonely.

Koko, however, was unconvinced. "Humph, a Frisco pigeon'd take any of the critters apart in a minute." He tried to snap his claws, but his glove only made a whuffing sound.

"Perhaps we should have taken one of them along instead of you," Bayang observed, and flew on into the darkness and the cold.

17

Bayang

They had been flying toward the Wastes for several hours when their luck with the weather ran out. Bayang had been congratulating herself that if they hadn't spotted Roland, at least they hadn't seen Mounties or Sogdians chasing them either.

Suddenly the winds picked up in speed and force so that she felt as if giant invisible hands were trying to shove her backward. Bayang brought her wings down in rapid, strong strokes that made her shoulder muscles ripple beneath the hide.

Soon she was fighting for every foot forward. She doubted if Roland's airplane could stay in the air during this windstorm, so they might actually shorten the distance between them. For that matter, she didn't think the Mounties' owls were up to this either, so their pursuers wouldn't be gaining on them.

The winds began to blow so fast that even Pele's charm could not keep the ice from forming on Bayang's wings. Each downbeat sent showers of frozen pellets through the air. She'd badly misjudged the weather and her own strength. Not even a dragon could conquer the Arctic. Bitterly, she realized they wouldn't be able to gain as much ground on Roland as she'd hoped.

Bayang puffed, "My wings feel a hundred pounds heavier. I'm used to the cold of the seafloor, but it's nothing like this. I don't think I can take much more."

"Or m-m-me," Koko stammered.

"I think the charms are thawing out the moisture in the air for a moment," Kles piped up from within Scirye's coat, "but then the drops freeze right away again."

"And Roxanna and Upach don't even have magical charms to keep them warm," Leech pointed out.

Bayang had been so focused on the pursuit that she hadn't considered the hatchlings. If it was bad for her, it was even worse for them. And yet, as fragile as they were, they hadn't complained—and were willing to continue the flight if she hadn't spoken up. She had never thought she'd meet anyone braver and more dedicated than her, and it turned out to be hatchlings from another race. They needed to be cherished and nurtured rather than turned into icicles.

Guiltily, she began to dip toward the ground. "I'm sorry. I should have realized that sooner."

"But don't land right away," Roxanna ordered. "Let me off first so I can look for danger spots. Sometimes the snow forms a thin layer over a big crack. Step on it and you can fall right through."

Even though she had just met Roxanna, Bayang felt as protective of her as she was of the other hatchlings, so she would have liked to refuse. However, the Sogdian girl knew this wilderness and she did not. "All right. But I'll hover overhead and you hold on to my paw so I can pull you up if the snow gives way."

Bayang was tiring rapidly, each wingbeat becoming slower and more erratic as they dropped through the air. Roxanna leaned over the side, watching the white surface rise up toward them. When they were about a yard above the surface, she called out, "Hold it."

The draft created by Bayang's wings was raising clouds of snow, but Roxanna jumped into it fearlessly. Bayang's paw groped for her, but her shadowy silhouette had already stooped over and was picking up some of the snow and scrunching it in her hand. Then she high-stepped a yard away to repeat the test.

"I can't keep hovering much longer with the load I'm carrying," Bayang panted.

They all heard the loud grumblings and whiplike cracking sounds.

"What's that?" Koko asked nervously.

"I told you," Roxanna said as she moved on and stamped on the surface again in another spot. "The ice floes are always shifting and pressing against one another. And the full moon brings out the tides and makes them more restless than ever." She tested several more spots before she announced, "This is old ice, so it's pretty thick. It'll be about as stable as we find."

"I'd prefer something that's guaranteed for a hundred percent." Koko gulped.

"Don't be such a baby. She said it was safe, and anyway, you live in earthquake country, remember?" Leech teased.

Roxanna stepped up to Bayang and slipped her rifle from the large holster that hung in the netting. Then she turned in a slow circle, scanning the area warily and then beckoning to Bayang. "And no polar bears close to us. Come on down."

"Yikes, now it's polar bears!" Koko yelped.

"Thanks," Leech said to Roxanna. "It takes guts to be a guinea pig."

"You'll be all right as long as you're with me," Roxanna said, stepping back.

Bayang swung her head to make sure their guide was safely away from the landing spot and then plopped down, flinging up sprays of snow. She noticed that Leech was the first to slide off so he could pat her neck solicitously. "Are you all right?"

Ice fringed his eyebrows and scarf like crystal beads. He had to be worse off than her, but his main thought was of her and not himself.

When she'd first met him, he'd been so trusting and open, but lately he'd been more withdrawn, as if listening to someone else. She missed that earlier friendly Leech, so his solicitude now touched her. Bayang cut off those feelings quickly. *Don't get carried away again,* she reminded herself. *He's not your hatchling and he never will be.*

"Nothing that a rest and a thaw can't cure," she assured him.

When they had finished disembarking, Bayang saw that the others were as icy as Leech. In fact, there were so many little icicles on Koko that he tinkled when he moved.

"Upach," Roxanna commanded, "get a fire going. I think it's the third box on Bayang's right side."

The blind ifrit walked swiftly along Bayang's side, holding out her mittened hands until she found the box she wanted. From it she extracted a small portable stove and set it down. "Come now, my lovely. Wakey-wakey."

The fire imp began to burn hotter and Bayang lifted a great wing to hold it over the welcome warmth. As Scirye and her companions slipped under the wing to crouch around the stove, it hung overhead like a leathery roof. However, when the ice began to melt and drip upon them Roxanna told them it was time to work on the dragon's wings.

"Break off the ice gently," Roxanna instructed the others.

Her scales slithering on the snow, Bayang shifted, lowering the wing so the others could pick off bits of ice. None was more concerned than Leech.

Then they repeated the process with the other wing. She could feel nothing through her numb scales, and yet as they fussed over her she began to relax. It made her think of manta rays in the warm, sunny tropical seas as little fish picked parasites off their hide.

The companions were all too glad to take a short break after that.

With a minimum of words—as if she had guided her blind servant to something many times before—Roxanna directed Upach to the basket with the tea, the kettle, and the wooden mugs with a large bowl for Bayang.

Bayang could only admire how efficiently Roxanna made them comfortable—as if this icy wasteland was her parlor. Her clan may have come from Sogdiana, but she was a child of the Arctic and well adapted to the land. Perhaps that was a trait that had helped Sogdians spread their trade network across the world.

In no time, Upach brewed a pot of tea for them. Though the bowl had been boiling hot when the ifrit had given it to Bayang, it had already cooled so much that there were little bits of ice bumping one another in it. *How long before it turned into a solid block?* she wondered.

About fifty yards ahead was another pressure ridge. The ice blocks rose like giant teeth from the snowy landscape. The winds had carved them into strange fantastic statues. One looked like an inverted cone. Another looked like a disk on a stem—as if it were a flower all of whose petals had been pulled. Others looked vaguely like people hunching over.

All about them, the breeze whipped the snow along like wriggling snakes so the landscape seemed to be constantly moving and the shifting ice beneath them cracked and groaned . . . as if, Bayang thought, the Arctic was a giant living creature.

"It's almost like the pack ice is alive and talking to itself," she said.

"Father calls it the Song of the North. No opera house has a stage this big," Roxanna said with a patronizing smile. "And no opera troupe has as many singers." She turned her head abruptly, sniffing the air. "We're not alone," she whispered, and put a finger to her lips. Then, with hand motions, she gathered them about a nearby small hole in the ice. A moment later, Bayang felt a slight but noticeable moisture on her face and caught a faint whiff of fish.

As they were all puzzling over the mysterious mist, Roxanna beckoned them to step away.

"It's almost impossible to see it, but it's a breathing hole for a ringed seal," she explained softly. "Listen."

They all strained their ears and heard a faint bubbly chuffing noise.

"What is it?" Leech asked, staring all around.

"Seals spend most of their time hunting in the sea," Roxanna explained, "but then they have to come up to breathe, so they claw a hole through the ice up to the surface so they can breathe, but I think this is an actual lair because it's staying so long."

"And I thought we were alone here," Leech said admiringly.

Roxanna smiled, pleased. "I told you this was no wasteland. But while we're here, we'll really have to keep an eye for polar bears now. Seals are polar bears' favorite meal and they can sniff them from thirty-two kilometers away."

Koko jumped and twisted around, looking for any bears charging out of the darkness. "Give me a city sidewalk where you're bumping elbows with everyone and not dodging bears." He moved a few steps closer to Bayang.

"What are you doing?" the dragon asked.

"I figure a hungry bear will want meaty you rather than stringy little old me," the badger said before he sat down. He jumped up just as suddenly with a yelp. "Something bit me."

Leech got up and inspected the spot. "It's a piece of metal sticking up from the snow." Crouching, he dug for a moment to clear more of it. When he tried to pick it up, he found it was attached to a leather belt. "It's a belt buckle with some sort of design. There's three cats—"

Bayang leaned over to look over his shoulder. "No, those are three lions. And there's nine hearts. That's the coat of arms of Denmark. It must have belonged to a freebooter."

Leech let go. "But what's it doing here?"

"Who cares? Maybe he left behind his watch too," Koko said. Curious, he swept a hind paw back and forth like a broom. "There's something." His voice fell. "It's a boot." He held up the long thigh-high boot like the kind the freebooters wore.

Below the ice, they heard a splash as the seal dove for safety into the water. Roxanna threw away the rest of her tea. The liquid froze in the air, falling in tan-colored beads of ice.

Then she gripped her rifle in both hands as she scanned the area. "A bear might have gotten him."

Suddenly the tranquil spot didn't seem so peaceful anymore. By common consent, they all threw away the remainder of their tea and mounted Bayang.

As she rose into the air again, she was relieved to see that the winds had died down to a breeze. And Bayang resumed the chase with even more determination than before.

18

Scirye

As they flew in the direction of the Wastes, they kept an eye out for Roland, but so far there had been no sign.

With the long night, Scirye lost track of time, so she felt as if they had been chasing their enemy forever over the frozen ocean. Nor was each break very restful after their discovery of the freebooter's belt and boot. It seemed to her that there was always someone or something watching them.

It made all of them jumpy so that the slightest sound made them whirl around to look, and it seemed to Scirye that she even saw something flitting behind a boulder or another time a small creature dipping into a crack in the ice—both moving much faster than a seal could have.

"What else could we see up here besides bears and seals?" she asked Roxanna.

"There are Arctic foxes," their guide replied. "They feed off the scraps that bears leave. And there are wolves."

"But whose side are they on?" Scirye wanted to know.

"Their own side," Roxanna answered.

It didn't help Scirye's peace of mind that she was always cold despite her furs and Pele's charm. Nestled inside her coat, Kles had settled into a torpor, and Koko's teeth were chattering constantly. Scirye could not imagine how Roxanna was coping, since she only had her furs to protect her. Instinctively, the riders had pressed closer together for warmth.

After every stop, they took turns acting as a shield against the wind for the others as they rode on the dragon. And it happened that it was Roxanna in front when she announced, "There's a storm brewing. We should build a shelter. That must be an island up ahead."

Scirye leaned to the side so she could look past Roxanna. Perhaps when the ocean unfroze it would be an island in the middle of the water, but right now it looked like a giant mountain of soap flakes rising out of the chunky landscape.

"I don't see any signs of a storm," Scirye objected. "It's important to keep after Roland, not stop. How far are we from the Wastes?"

"About three days' flight," Roxanna replied, and then added humbly, "I don't want to go against your wishes, Lady, but I have to. A good caravan leader senses the hazards ahead of her. And I can feel it in my bones. There's a storm coming and it'd be bad to be caught in it. The correct conditions can make a whiteout. That's when there's so much snow in the air that you can't tell up from down or your left from your right. We ought to be on the ground preparing for it."

"I'm just as much in a rush as you, Scirye," Leech said, "but we ought to listen to our guide."

"I concur," Bayang said, and began to descend.

The dragon brought her wings down in roaring strokes that sent them shooting on ahead—though the great effort made her pant raggedly. When they were over the island, the dragon folded her wings over them so that they were almost enclosed in a leathery tent.

Scirye's stomach did flip-flops as they dropped through the air with sickening speed. Just as she was ready to scream, she felt Bayang's powerful shoulder muscles ripple as she beat her wings clumsily.

Snow flew up about them in a cloud as they landed with a thump. Wearily the dragon laid her head in the snow. "Dropping was easy. Stopping was hard. Next time let's take the train," she moaned.

Koko squirmed and then groaned as he swung a leg up. "I was afraid I was frozen to your hide."

"I don't need a hood ornament," Bayang snapped.

"The island should help protect us," Roxanna said, "but it would be better to build an igloo too. Only I don't think we can make one big enough for your size at the moment. Could you shrink again?"

"I'll shrink to whatever size you need," Bayang said, laying her head on her paws and closing her eyes. "But for the moment I need to rest."

Roxanna slid off the dragon's back with the others. Then the Sogdian girl tried to fetch something from one of the baskets hanging on the dragon's back, but she was having a hard time because her fingers were so stiff with cold. Scirye got off and walked over to her awkwardly. "What are you looking for?"

Roxanna had put her hands under her arms to try to warm

them. "There should be several long knives to cut the snow with."

Scirye pulled out what looked like a short sword in a sheath. "Is this it?"

"Yes, Lady, thank you." Roxanna started to reach for it, but Scirye waved her back.

"Warm your hands," Scirye ordered. She pulled out three more, as well as a small collapsible shovel.

Even though her fingers were still stiff and clumsy, Roxanna insisted on putting the shovel together. Then she knelt and began to feel the snow. "It's not as tight as I'd like, but I think it will do." She looked up. "And thank Nana we found the island," she said. "We're so numb with cold and the winds are so strong that we might have had trouble building it out in the open, but the island should help protect us."

They high-stepped after Roxanna with Scirye and Kles straggling behind. The snow crunched beneath Roxanna's boots, but the short walk loosened up her muscles.

Using the shovel, Roxanna traced a wide circle on the surface. "We need to dig a shallow pit here, say about a yard down."

Leech had taken the shovel and he began to empty the snow from the drawn circle. In one spot, they all heard a grating sound. "Hey, there's a rock here."

"I told you it was an island," Roxanna said.

Leech had lifted out five more shovelfuls before his shovel clinked against something. "That sounds like metal, not rock."

They all stood around as he cleared the snow away from a fuel can. Scirye lifted out the frozen container. It was so light it had to be empty. "What's this doing here?"

Kles poked his head and sniffed with his sensitive nostrils. "I smell airplane fuel." They all could. The stink of petrol was unmistakable.

Leech stabbed his shovel experimentally into the snow until they heard another metallic clink. "Here's another one." He went on checking until they had found six in all.

Koko scratched his head. "I bet if we went on digging, we'd find even more."

Roxanna brushed snow away near one of the cans. "There's a hole in the rock." It was about an inch in diameter, and with a pencil she probed into it. "And about eight inches long. Like a tent peg."

Scirye glanced at the resting Bayang, but she had her eyes closed. "Maybe we found Roland's fuel depot."

Roxanna nodded. "The island would provide a good landmark for a pilot."

"I wonder how far ahead Roland is?" Leech asked excitedly.

Scirye felt adrenaline surge through her as well. The chase was still on! She turned to the dragon. "Bayang, we found where Roland re-fueled."

Bayang opened an eye. "At least we know we're on the right track."

They moved a few yards away until they found an area where there were no cans.

Leech began digging, and when he had emptied an area deep enough for Roxanna she used one of the knives to cut the first block from the side of the pit. When she was done, she had a block about a yard long and fifteen inches high and eight inches deep. The hole continued to widen and deepen as she removed more blocks.

The other children's first tries crumbled for one reason or another and they would never have had enough building material without Roxanna's dogged efforts. "Don't worry," she encouraged them. "When my Inuit friends were showing me how to do this, I kept making mistakes too."

Then the Sogdian girl laid out the first blocks in a wide ring, tilting them inward slightly and then shaping them with the knife so they pressed together snugly.

Slowly the rings of snow blocks grew around the pit created by taking out the blocks. With more practice, the children got better at making them, so the construction went faster. Soon Roxanna was setting the last blocks in place over the dome and carving them into a smooth curve.

Roxanna nodded to the inert Bayang. "She has to be small enough to fit through the door." Roxanna waved her gloved hand at the entrance.

Scirye started toward the resting dragon, but Koko said, "Let me."

His short legs wouldn't let him high-step through the snow like the others. Rather, the badger threw his large stomach forward like an icebreaker's prow, waddled forward on his stumpy legs so that he caught up with his belly, and then repeated the process until he was leaning right next to one of the dragon's ears.

"You know," the badger shouted, "I bet I could make a million purses out of this alligator's hide."

Bayang's head shot up so fast that her skull flipped Koko hindquarters over forequarters. He tumbled across the snow several times before he flopped onto his back.

"You just try that," the dragon growled, "and I'll turn your mangy fur into a diaper bag."

"The igloo's ready," Scirye called. "We need you to shrink to about my height."

"Is my tail still there?" the dragon asked, and twisted her head around on her long neck to make sure. "I couldn't feel it for a moment."

Too tired to get up, the dragon shrank herself right where she lay, giving off a shimmering glow, leaving the harness with its cargo lying on the surface about her like a net.

Bayang tried to rise but only managed a half crouch. Scirye moved across the snow to her friend. Leech followed a moment later. With them pulling and her crawling, the dragon managed to reach the igloo.

Bayang's jaws cracked in a huge yawn. "It must be my reptile blood. We get torpid in extreme cold." Closing her eyes, she slumped back down.

"Ahem," Koko called. They saw his paw rise above the surface of the snow and wave. "Don't mind me. I'll just sleep out here. Is that the plan?"

"I'll get him." Leech grinned.

Roxanna, Scirye, and Upach followed him, and it wound up taking their combined effort to get the grumbling badger back on his hind paws.

"I'm going to sue that dragon for all she's worth," Koko complained. "I'm all one big bruise."

"You look fine to me," Leech said.

"The fur covers it up," Koko said, beginning to limp toward the igloo. "Oh, the pain. The pain."

Leech caught him by the tail. "Save it for acting class. We've got all that stuff to move." He jerked a thumb at Bayang's load.

"But—," Koko began to protest.

Scirye gave him a playful shove. "But nothing. If you don't help, we really will leave you out here to turn into a badger-cicle."

"You shouldn't pal around with that dragon," Koko said, floundering over to the boxes and baskets. "You're getting a real nasty streak."

As the children, Upach, and Koko retrieved their parcels, the sun disappeared and they all looked at the darkening clouds that were beginning to cover it up.

"I'm sorry, Roxanna," Scirye said. "You were right. We finished the igloo just in time. It's just like you said, one mistake out here could have cost us our lives—and I was the one who wouldn't have made it if it hadn't been for you."

Roxanna beamed at the praise. "Thank you, Lady. I'm trying my best."

With a greater sense of urgency, they carried the containers over to the igloo, piling them up near the entrance. They repeated this several times while from a set of marked boxes Upach took furs and covered the snow inside for ground cover.

This time Koko let Scirye rouse Bayang, though truthfully the dragon only half woke up and crept on her belly inside, where she promptly fell asleep again.

The others had to step around her as they shifted their gear inside, stacking it against the walls. Then Upach hung a leather hide over the entrance to keep out the worst of the wind.

From one of the baskets Roxanna produced a tiny fire imp in a lantern. It gave off only a dim light, but they were grateful for it.

Kles had been quiet since they had landed, but Roxanna had assumed he was napping. However, when she opened her coat to let him out he barely stirred. "Hey, time to get up," she said, prodding him with a finger.

He mumbled something about fish eggs and rolled over. "Kles?" she asked, now worried.

Raising the griffin in both hands, she pressed him against her cheek. "Kles, you have to wake up. Kles, Kles?" After a minute of calling, her friend's eyes finally fluttered open—to everyone's immense relief.

"This should help warm him," Upach said. She'd already taken out the portable stove and filled a kettle of snow. She soon had wheeled the stove's imp into flame, and the sweet scent of tea was filling the interior.

Holding the cup next to Kles's beak, she urged, "Come on, Kles. This is good for you." The feathery head turned drowsily, but he began to sip from her cup. As the hot fluid drove away the cold from his body, she was glad to see him sit up.

"Goodness gracious," he said. "What happened?"

"The cold gets to some creatures faster than others," Roxanna said, rummaging around in another basket until she found a tin of broth cubes and more of the little cakes that were frozen by now.

With Kles snuggling on her lap and with Leech holding up Bayang's head, Scirye then poured hot tea down the dragon's throat.

After that, Upach thawed out tasty little cakes made from berries and honey and made a pot of soup from reindeer jerky. By that time, both the dragon and griffin were sitting up alertly. And by the end of their meal, the igloo had begun to warm from the heat of their bodies as well as the stove and lantern.

Koko looked wistfully at the boxes. "That was good for a snack, but what's the main course?"

"That's it," Roxanna said. "Since we don't know how long we'll be out here, we have to make our supplies last."

Koko plopped his plump haunches into the snow onto a bed of furs. "A badger's belly is his pride." His paw pantomimed a swelling as large as a watermelon. "Pretty soon folks are going to mistake me for a lamppost."

"At least you'll finally be good for something." Kles sniffed.

Scirye had a soft spot for the conniving badger. "Don't worry," she said, patting him comfortingly on the paw. "When we get home, we'll feed you so well that every other badger will be jealous of your shape."

"And you'll weigh half a ton," Leech teased. "You'll never be able to fly on Bayang again."

"Great," the badger and dragon both said with equal fervor.

19

Scirye

They decided that one of them should keep watch while the others rested, and Scirye volunteered for the first shift. She was weary to her very bones, and she was afraid that once she went to sleep it would be nearly impossible to rouse her.

The others were rolled up in sleeping furs and on her lap Kles was making the loud humming sound that was his snore. The noise blended with the howling winds into an odd sort of tune.

As she sat there, the tune began to curl about sensuously within her mind like a ribbon of incense smoke, coiling about her thoughts and twisting them into meaningless shapes.

Before she knew it, Scirye had drifted off into sleep.

————

Scirye had the pleasantest dream. Her father had flown in from Bactra to San Francisco. He tried to join them wherever her mother was posted—though lately he'd been so busy that he hadn't been able to.

Her mother, her sister Nishke, and she were showing him the sights on a cable car. Far away on a hilltop were the three stone columns that were their destination. They would have a wonderful view from there.

It was a warm, sunny day in the city and her father was laughing as he stood on the outside step. And Scirye was laughing with him. It was rare when the family was together, and she felt safe and happy for the first time she could remember.

Ahead at the next corner, several people had crowded into the street, waiting to board the cable car. Something glinted on the head of a waiting woman. It was a lion's head, shining as intensely as the sun.

Frightened, Scirye called to the uniformed conductor and the brakeman, "Don't stop! Go faster!"

Without arguing, they released the cable so that the cable car sped along, clacking over the rails, bell ringing. The prospective passengers in the street whizzed past in a blur.

When the cable car slowed again, it was rattling through Honolulu. Scirye knew they had to get off the cable car and hide among the gaudily clad tourists swarming the city.

Scirye herded her sister and parents off the car onto the sidewalk, where they slipped through the mob and found themselves by a small fence with pickets made from bamboo. Opening the gate, they stepped into a luxurious garden of plants with leaves broad as emerald sails and strange-shaped flowers of every color. The air was thick with scents and sniffing them made Scirye feel almost dizzy.

The huge leaves closed overhead like a canopy so that they walked the path in green shadow. Just when Scirye began to hope they were safe, the ground itself began to rise, became the palms of brown hands and the trees the fingers. Shining down upon them was a huge moon that filled half the sky, and etched with diamond sharpness upon the moon was the face of Nanaia.

"Akshe!" her sister, Nishke, said in the Old Tongue. "Wake up!"

Scirye ran across one hand and leapt . . . into snow. It clung to her ankles and swirled all about her—as if the whole world had dissolved into a million billion bits of white snowflakes.

And yet through the snow she saw a figure trudging past her in short, gliding steps that made it look as if she were shuffling on roller skates. Unlike Scirye, the figure moved across the surface.

The traveler was in shaggy fur trousers that went *whuff-whuff* as the legs rubbed against one another. It wore a jacket of the same fur with a hood that hid the person's face. Over one shoulder and hanging limply down the person's back was a brown leather sack.

Around the traveler's waist hung a belt woven from leather strings, and dangling from the belt on thongs were all sorts of beads, charms, pebbles, carvings, shells, and feathers. They bounced against the person's legs as the traveler walked, making a *click-clack-click* in counterpoint to the noise made by the trouser legs rubbing together.

The figure stopped and turned slowly, snorting sounds coming from within the hood as it tested the scents in the air.

"Shh. Don't talk," Nishke warned. "Or the hag will hear you."

Scirye was standing right out in the open, and even with the swirling snow, the hag could not miss her. She wanted to run, to scream, but she could not move.

Her heart skipped as the hag seemed to look directly at her. In the shadows deep within the hood, two eyes glared at her. At least, they were where eyes should be on a face, but they were really more like holes behind which a bilious green fire burned—a fire so malevolent that Scirye found herself shuddering.

But then the hag faced forward, away from the girl, and began her peculiar sliding walk.

Whuff-whuff. Click-clack-click. Whuff-whuff.

The strange, ominous noises dwindled as the hag disappeared into the storm.

"Remember," Nishke whispered, "the otter will show you the way."

Her hand felt hot as if she were holding a boiling cup of tea. Scirye became aware that she was lying on her back inside the igloo. Outside the winds tore at the snow blocks with airy claws and howled in fury when they would not budge.

Scirye tried to open her eyes, but the lids felt as heavy as iron. Kles's familiar weight was still in her arms.

Whuff-whuff. Click-clack-click.

When she heard the noises, she was so terrified that she almost didn't want to raise her eyelids. But she knew she had to.

It was a great struggle, but she finally managed to squeeze one eye slightly open. The "3" on her hand was glowing as if that was causing the sensation of heat.

There was barely any light at all from the fire imp asleep in the lantern. But she managed to make out the hag standing in the middle of the igloo and shoving something into her leather bag.

It was starting to swell outward like a giant brown toad squatting on the floor.

When Scirye glimpsed the pear-shaped body disappearing into the bag, she realized it was Koko up to his shoulders inside the sack.

As the impatient hag shoved more of the badger inside, the bag expanded. In horror, Scirye watched the sides of the bag ripple like the muscles of a jaw chewing a meal.

The hag's right hand became stuck inside it. Her shoulders shook back and forth as she tried to tug free, but the bag drew her in steadily until she was in up to her elbow.

Then she darted her left hand to her waist and gripped one of the objects hanging from her belt. Suddenly she was straightening up, easily drawing her right arm out free as if it had been greased.

That's it! Scirye thought to herself. *It wouldn't do the hag any good just to be able to put her hand in and out if she lost her prey inside. There had to be some magical object on the belt that let her elude the bag's grasp.*

From the corner of her eye, Scirye saw the others lying asleep, oblivious to the badger's abduction.

Scirye tried to cry out a warning, but her vocal cords were as paralyzed as her body and no sound came out.

Even so, the hag whirled around so that she was facing Scirye.

20

Scirye

The hag's head jerked up when she saw that one of her victims was awake and she began to sway back and forth and hiss like a teakettle about to explode.

Setting one foot on Koko's body, the hag put one hand on the object on her belt. Stooping, she grabbed the bottom of the bag with the other hand and jerked it upward so that the unconscious badger plopped out onto the igloo's floor.

Then the hag began to shuffle a little quicker toward Scirye, pulling the bag behind her.

Whuff-whuff. Click-clack-clack.

Scirye fought to move her arms, her legs, her vocal cords, but they felt like stone. All she could do was lie there helplessly as the hag shuffled right next to her, looming over her like a greasy, furry shadow. The hag stunk of sweat and rancid fat and . . . blood. Scirye was all too familiar with that smell by now.

When the hag set the bag down, it tilted its mouth expectantly toward the girl. Looking into the sack was like gazing into a huge, dark cavern, and Scirye even thought she heard faint cries for help echoing from within.

The hag bent, her eyes glowing evilly as she reached down—not for Scirye but for Kles.

Fear for her friend gave Scirye extra strength. Finally, she found her voice. "Kles, wake up!" she screamed.

The little griffin did not stir. Only his buzzing snore told her that he was still alive.

Within the hood, the hag's eyes glowed brighter and angrier.

She hates me, the girl thought.

"What did I ever do to you?" Scirye demanded.

When the eyes narrowed to slits, the fire behind them blazed hotter and fiercer.

I think she hates me just for being alive, Scirye decided. *She hates everyone*. It was that hatred that fed the fire behind the eyes. A hatred so deep and mindless that it had consumed everything inside her, only leaving those sickly green flames.

Her friends gone or dead, isolated in a hostile land and facing a horrible monster by herself, the girl had never felt more alone in her whole life. What chance did she have? She was as small and insignificant and helpless as a bug on a glacier.

Then she heard Nishke again: "Yashe! Yashe!" Honor! Honor!

Scirye's sister and mother had shouted that as they had fought Badik the dragon. It was the battle cry that thousands of Pippalanta had yelled through the centuries.

It was as if Scirye's mind had been cloaked by darkness and now someone had thrown open a window so that the light could stream inside again.

The voice was compelling, forceful, like a hand shoving her forward, but instead of her body, it was her soul.

The hag must have cast some spell of despair over her.

So, yes, it was true that Scirye was now all alone. But this was no time to wallow in self-pity or use it as an excuse to do nothing. She was the last defender. It was up to her.

Scirye surged from the ground, anger fueling her to move with extra speed. Her hand reached for her knife, but it was gone from her belt. From the corner of her eye, she saw it on top of the pile of weapons that the hag had taken from them while they were unconscious.

The girl's mind raced desperately through the lessons that her sister, Nishke, had taught her about hand-to-hand combat, but they'd only had time to cover some basics of self-defense.

"Did you ever have anyone fight back?" Scirye demanded, and raised her fist. The hag whirled around, seizing the mouth of the bag in both hands and lifting it to her chest. The bag's mouth wriggled like a starving beast's lips waiting to be served its supper. All the hag needed to do was trap Scirye's hand inside and she'd have the rest of the girl soon after that.

Scirye slipped to the left, hoping to land a punch on the side of the hag's head, but the hag pivoted, holding the open bag between them like a dark shield.

Scirye feinted again and the hag thrust the bag out to capture her fist. Over the years, Scirye had developed agile hands to play her pranks—so agile in fact that she was adept at picking pockets—so she had no trouble pulling her arms out of the way as she darted back.

They shifted in an odd sort of dance about the igloo, Scirye trying to find an opening and the hag to trap her with the bag. As they wove their way around, Scirye realized that they were both the same height, for their heads were just brushing the ceiling.

Scirye had been so intent on watching the hag that she had not kept an eye on her friends on the floor. Suddenly, she stumbled over Koko. To her horror, she fell backward.

As the girl lay momentarily stunned, the hag shrieked in triumph and started toward her.

Desperate, Scirye rolled on her side, pivoting on her hip as she swung her leg in a wide kick. But she had misjudged the distance and made her move too soon. Rather than knocking the hag down, Scirye kicked the bottom of the bag. Since it contained her friends, Scirye had assumed that it was heavy, so she was surprised when the bag was as light as a feather pillow.

The bag flew from the hag's startled grasp, but instead of falling, it somersaulted in the air like a bird celebrating its freedom. And then it spiraled slowly through the air like a bird of prey selecting its next victim—which was the upright hag.

As the bag swooped toward her, the hag panicked and instinctively thrust both arms up to fend it off, but the bag stretched its mouth so wide that Scirye thought it would tear. The next instant, the sack had swallowed both the hag's hands.

Scirye seized her chance as she sprang from the floor. Her quick hands shot out now to snag the hag's belt. When Scirye yanked, there was a twang like a dozen guitar strings snapping. The leather thongs finally broke and Scirye fell on her back, the belt in her hands.

The hag screeched in fury and terror. Twitching and jerking, she tried to pull a hand free, but the bag had her ensnared. The edges of its mouth fluttering, the bag nibbled relentlessly along her wrists, her elbows, and beyond.

Desperately, the hag twisted her head this way and that to elude the bag, but it managed to stretch over that part of the hag anyway. Sides rippling, the bag swallowed the hag up to her shoulders.

The hag stumbled about madly, knocking over crates and baskets and even trying to brush the bag off by rubbing against the sides of the igloo. Every frantic effort was in vain, though. Finally, she tripped over some furs and as soon as she had fallen the monstrous bag engulfed her to her hips.

The hag fought the bag hard, but the result was inevitable. Inch by inch, the sack choked down its prey until the tips of the hag's boots slipped inside and she was gone.

Scirye almost felt guilty when she heard the faint wail echo from inside the bag. But then through the opening she saw a pair of eyes, blazing with hate.

The hag would show no mercy and neither could Scirye.

The bag's drawstrings wriggled along like worms, and the bag shut itself up tight.

Scirye sat exhausted as the bag rolled about as if the hag was tearing at its sides trying to break free. But gradually the movements subsided until the sack was still. And then, as if it were alive, the bag rose on its own so it was resting on its base now.

"Wha— What happened?" Kles mumbled, his beak opening and then snapping shut in an immense yawn. "I had the most awful nightmare about this horrible thing trying to catch me."

"It wasn't a nightmare," Scirye said, nodding wearily toward the bag. "And it was all my fault."

21

Scirye

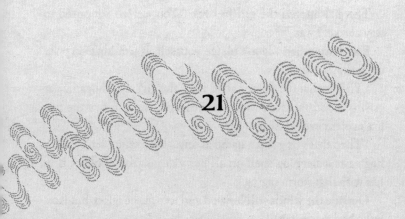 Face flushed with shame, Scirye told how she had fallen asleep and the strange dream she had that had saved them.

"Perhaps Nanaia sent you that dream," Kles suggested.

Scirye squirmed, rubbing her hand where the "3" was. It wasn't glowing now, but it still felt a little warm. "She always expects something in return for a favor. Do you think this will add to the cost?"

"What choice do we have?" Kles shrugged with both his shoulders and his wings. "She'll present the bill when She's ready. For now, I just want to know what happened when you woke up."

When Scirye was finished telling Kles about the battle, he crept onto her lap and wrapped his paws around her. "And you fought her alone. I'm sorry that I slept through it all."

The girl hugged the griffin back. "You weren't supposed to stay awake. I was."

Kles patted her. "Don't blame yourself. It wouldn't surprise me if the . . . hag?"

"That's what the voice called her," the girl said, hugging the griffin in return. Even with her eyes shut, she still saw the two malevolent eyes glaring at her.

"Then that's as good a name as any," Kles said. "I'm sure the hag casts a sleeping spell on all her victims. You couldn't hear her with that storm raging."

Outside the winds still howled and tore at the igloo, but Roxanna had made it well.

Scirye took comfort in the griffin's words, hoping they were true as she went to wake the others up.

The others were still a little groggy from the hag's spell, but the devoted Upach had already filled the kettle with snow so she could make tea.

"Who was that old biddy anyway?" Koko asked with a shudder. "Her grip was worse than any bill collector who ever chased me."

Roxanna lay where she had fallen, too exhausted to move. "The Inuit call her Amagjat. She ambushed"—she corrected herself—"or, rather, used to ambush stray travelers and take them back to her lair to eat them."

"Well, Bayang would have given her indigestion for sure," Koko said, careful to roll beyond the reach of the dragon's tail. "So I guess that would've been some consolation."

"I don't think it's any accident that Amagjat found us," Leech said. "Roland could have hired her as a kind of guard to take care of snoopers."

Roxanna gave a snuffle and wiped her nose. "This is Amagjat's hunting territory. I should have told you, but I didn't."

"No, Lady Roxanna," Scirye said, trying to comfort the Sogdian girl. "The fault's mine. I'm the one who fell asleep and let Amagjat invade the igloo. I should have been outside instead keeping watch."

"Hey," Leech said, "don't be so hard on yourself either. What could you see in a storm at night? You might as well have been inside. And the storm was so loud I could barely hear myself snore. You couldn't have heard her sneaking up on us."

"Yes," Roxanna said. "Amagjat has all sorts of spells to make her victims helpless. When she picks out her prey, she's relentless. Few escape her."

Scirye refused to accept that as an excuse. "I failed in Tumarg. Sentries have been hung for falling asleep."

Roxanna stared disconsolately at the ceiling. "And I failed in common sense. I warned you that one error would get you killed, and it turns out that I'm the one who made the mistake."

Koko's nostrils twitched. "Then it might have been nice if you'd warned us about her."

Scirye sprang to Roxanna's defense. "If Roxanna tried to tell us about everything, we'd still be back in the caravanserai."

The Sogdian girl was subdued, though. "No, Lady Scirye. The badger-badger-badger is right. Once the storm forced us to stay put, Amagjat became a real danger. She's clever enough to counteract guns." Roxanna seemed on the point of tears. "Lord Leech is a hero, and you are the chosen of the goddess. Here I was trying to show all of you that I'm worthy to be in your company, and I failed so, so miserably."

Was that why she'd been acting like so much of a know-it-all? Scirye wondered. Out loud she insisted, "Please don't say that.

I'm just like you." She was so upset that her voice trembled. Kles, who was sitting upon her lap, tried to comfort her by rubbing his head against her stomach and chirruping reassuringly.

Roxanna was too intent on confessing her own flaws to notice how she was disturbing Scirye. "Nana does not perform miracles for me," she said humbly. "Nor could I beat Amagjat. You just keep adding to your legend, Lady."

The last thing that Scirye wanted was to have Roxanna place her upon an even higher pedestal. "I just happened to get lucky," she insisted as she tightened her arms around Kles. "After all, if I really was as special as you claim, how come I nearly got us buried by that storm? You were the one who told us we had to stop. You knew there was a blizzard coming though there wasn't any hint of it yet. Now that's special."

Kles tapped a paw against Scirye's hand as a sign to be released. When she eased her grip, he shifted to face the Sogdian girl. He had been taught that the first rule of diplomacy was always to look presentable, so he smoothed his tousled fur before he spoke. "Upach, wouldn't you agree that a lady's entourage knows her the best?"

"Certainly," Upach said. "Our chicks would be lost without us."

Kles went on. "And wouldn't you also agree that what makes them special is their talents? My lady happens to be very clever and resourceful. Nor does she know when she's beaten."

"Maybe that's because I'm too dumb to realize that," Scirye admitted.

Kles regarded the Sogdian girl. "Lady Roxanna, you're leading this expedition admirably."

"Yeah," Leech agreed. "You read the land and sky as if they were both pages in a book."

"Sure, without your savvy, we'd have been icicles now," Koko contributed.

"And you've always guided us to a good landing spot," Bayang added.

Roxanna refused to be consoled, though. "They're such little things, though. And there are many people up here who could have done the same."

The ifrit sidled in close to her. Upach's hand groped through the air until she found Roxanna's arm and could pat it. "Not as well as you, chick."

"Lady Roxanna, I think you try to be too perfect," Kles observed. "That's why you're so hard on yourself."

Upach punched her palm with her other fist. "The birdie's right. You're your own worst enemy."

Roxanna turned her back on them and then lay on her side, curling up into a ball. "And I was nearly everyone else's."

22

Bayang

Bayang liked the Sogdian hatchling, so she hated to see Roxanna wallowing in self-pity and doubt. The Sogdian hatchling was insecure and brash, but she shouldn't be punishing herself the way she was. However, Bayang also had a more selfish reason to see Roxanna cheer up: If Roxanna did not act more like her old self, they might never survive. Indecisiveness would kill them as surely as a storm would.

Bayang wracked her brains to come up with something that would comfort Roxanna, but unfortunately she drew a blank.

It was Upach who knew how to take her mistress's mind off her faults. "What happened, Lady Scirye?"

Bayang was glad to see that Roxanna listened as attentively as the others while the Kushan girl told them about her battle with the hag.

Bayang shook her head admiringly. The more time she spent with the human hatchlings, the more she had to admire their courage. They didn't seem to know when they were defeated. "You not only beat her, but you captured her as well."

Roxanna regarded Scirye with awe. "Many brave people have tried to defeat Amagjat over the centuries, but you're the one who did it. Now I see why Nana chose you."

"And she did it all on her own. It's worthy of an epic," Kles almost crowed as he sat on his mistress's lap.

Scirye hugged her griffin to her. "It's nothing like that. I was scared the whole time."

Bayang curled into a tight ball for warmth so that she resembled a coil of scaly rope. "If you could take any epic hero and ask him or her, they would tell you they were terrified too."

Scirye shifted uneasily. "And I was lucky."

"Here, let some of that good fortune rub off on me," Koko teased as he leaned forward and brushed his paw against the sole of Scirye's boot. "I could sure use it."

"You're hiding something," Leech challenged.

Still on Scirye's lap, Kles looked up at her. "They need to hear the rest."

Scirye shifted uncomfortably, glancing at her hand where Nanaia's mark was. "I think She sent my sister to warn me while I was asleep." And she told them about the dream.

"To wake from a dream and find yourself facing Amagjat." Roxanna gave a shudder. "I would have been shaking in my boots."

Scirye tried to deflect the Sogdian girl's admiration: "Well, maybe you can help us figure out what Amagjat was using on this belt. When her hand got stuck in the bag, she touched something on this and pulled free."

Setting down Kles, Scirye fetched the belt and laid it among them.

Leech looked at all the beads, charms, pebbles, carvings, shells, and feathers tied to it. "But which one? There must fifty of these things."

Hair, scales, and feathers touched as the friends bent over to examine it together. Some of the carvings were from bone, others from ivory, ranging in style from elaborate to simple.

Bayang tapped a claw against her muzzle as she studied the belt. "Some of these might be trophies rather than real magical charms."

"But how can we tell?" Scirye wondered.

Kles glanced at her. "Did Nanaia say anything about them?"

Scirye drew her eyebrows together, screwing up her face in concentration as she tried to bring up every detail from the dream. Searching through her memories was like trying to catch hold of smoke . . . when suddenly she found something.

"It's hard to recall everything in the dream," she admitted. "But there was something about an otter."

They carefully inspected the belt again, but though there were plenty of bears, foxes, and seals, they didn't see an otter.

"You know how dreams are," Bayang said charitably. "It's impossible to remember everything accurately."

Scirye's shoulders slumped. The moment she had said it, she had been so sure it was the otter.

"All right," Bayang said. "What area of the belt did the hag try to touch when she was reaching into the bag?"

Now that the belt was lying flat on the rug instead of around the hag, it took Scirye a moment to orient herself. Biting her lip, she tapped a patch on the right side. "There, I think."

"Hmm," Kles said. "Let's assume that the hag has had the bag a long time; then she would have had the charm too."

Leech nodded. "Otherwise, the bag would have been worthless to her because it would be too deadly."

"And let's assume there's some wear on the charm she uses all the time." Bayang indicated the more-or-less realistic carvings. "So, for instance, these seem too new."

Scirye ran her eyes along the charms and then back again, squinting at a small oblong quartz. She had taken it for just another bit of stone, but when she examined it by imp light she could see faint markings on the sides. Even when it was new, she might not have recognized it as an otter . . . and yet the more she looked at it, the more it suggested the sleek body of an otter in motion.

"What about this?" she asked, pointing. Her fingertip brushed it and briefly she was swimming through the sea, the water breaking around her head and fanning out behind her in a V like a sketch of wings. Nothing could hold her, not the waves, not the seaweed, not the sharks. Untouchable. Absolutely free. "It's this one," she said with more confidence.

The griffin touched it gingerly and snatched his claw back. "Yes, I think you're right."

"It's animal magic. Sometimes otters have to hunt in dark waters," Bayang declared. She used a paw to pantomime a creature sliding along. "A bear charm might give you the strength of a bear. So maybe an otter charm gives you some of its elusiveness. Spells can't hold you and at the same time you have some of an otter's ability to hunt in the dark." The dragon stroked her muzzle. "Hmm, I wonder if some of the other belt charms let you cast spells too," she mused. "Like the one that let her put us to sleep?"

"When she saw I was awake, she had some sort of magic that made me almost give up fighting," Scirye remembered.

"Which one did it, though?" Bayang wondered as she scrutinized the belt. "Maybe if we recognized what animal a charm was, we could figure out the magic behind it."

"But which ones have power and which are just decorations?" Roxanna asked. "Some of the carvings might be ornaments taken from her victims like trophies."

"It's too risky to experiment on our own," Leech warned. "We should leave it until we can ask a wizard."

"Good luck finding an honest one. Most of them would take a powder with it." Koko raised a paw. "I vote to sell it. I bet it's worth more if we broke up the belt and sold each of the thingamabobs separately."

Kles launched himself into the air and then pounced upon the belt, his hind paws gripping it firmly. "It's the Lady Scirye's by right of conquest."

"I don't know if I can handle that thing on top of having the goddess hovering over me," Scirye confessed nervously.

"Do you have a pouch, Lady Roxanna?" Kles asked politely.

Upach got up and began limping over to a basket. "That's right; that's right," the ifrit grumbled. "Make me run around when the cold's got my rheumatizz acting up." After rummaging around inside, she produced a leather pouch that Scirye could hang around her neck.

Scirye took the precaution of pulling on her leather gauntlet before she picked up the belt's leather thongs. Even then, she was careful not to touch any of the charms as she slid it into the pouch that Upach held open for her. "Thank you."

"I think a little bitty thing like you is already carrying too much of a burden to add something more," Upach said gently as

Scirye slipped the pouch's strap over her head and around her neck.

After tea and a brief meal, they debated what to do with the hag. The problem as Bayang saw it was that they did not dare destroy the bag and possibly release the hag again. Koko, with an eye on being able to store an infinite amount of loot, wondered if there was a way to destroy the hag so they could keep the bag for later use.

"Well, I suppose we could give you an axe and send you in to take care of her," Bayang said.

Koko waved his paws back and forth. "No thanks."

Scirye glanced uncomfortably at the bag. Had it twitched? "I don't think I want to share the igloo with Amagjat either," she said.

As it turned out, no one did, so they decided to drag the bag outside.

"If you still trust me," Roxanna said humbly, "I'll go first."

"Of course we do," Scirye said.

Getting down on all fours, Roxanna crawled to the igloo's opening, where a fringe of icicles now hung. Many of them had been broken off and lay half-buried in the snow. The ones that remained were long and slender like crystal knitting needles.

"The moisture from our breathing must have condensed here," Roxanna said, indicating the fringe and then pointing at the stumps. "And these were broken off by Amagjat when she entered."

When they threw back the fur flap and emerged from the igloo, they discovered that the winds were dying down. Since the frozen ground made it too hard to bury the bag, they set it in the shelter of a boulder, and began to stack rocks all around it. Then, at Upach's suggestion, they heaped snow on top so that it was indistinguishable from the surface.

After that, they returned inside to wait out the storm and get what rest they could, but with the memory of Amagjat still fresh in their minds, that proved impossible.

No one was able to sleep for fear of the hag just outside the igloo, and Scirye was afraid the creature would haunt her dreams for a long time.

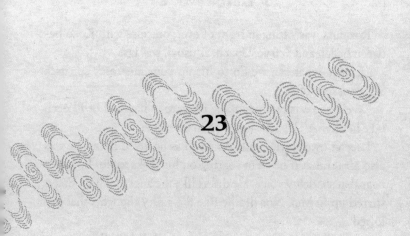

23

Leech

As they flew on, gray clouds scudded across the night sky like torn, dirty strands of cotton—the remnants of the storm. And the moon played hide-and-seek behind them so that the landscape alternated between dim light and gloomy darkness.

Leech eagerly scanned the horizon for some sign of the airplane, but he knew the sharp-eyed Scirye was more likely to glimpse Roland first.

Though before their encounter with the hag Roxanna had chatted away, she was unusually quiet now. Scirye had tried many times to convince the Sogdian girl that they needed her, but Roxanna treated the attempts as acts of mercy rather than the truth.

Roxanna was sitting in front of everyone else with Koko between Leech and Scirye. Upach, as usual, was last.

"Upach, what can we do to lift up your mistress's spirits?"
Scirye asked softly.

"Well, she was really looking forward to having Lord Leech
take her flying," Upach suggested in a whisper.

Leech's own spirits sank. As much as he loved flying, he was
also afraid that if he went soaring on his disks again, he might
hear that shadowy voice. He didn't like the angry feelings that it
stirred up in him. Nor did he like the guilty thoughts that followed.

After all, in giving up her mission to kill him Bayang was
willing to turn her back on her own clan. He owed the dragon
some trust for that sacrifice, not hatred.

"It's calm now," Scirye said. "I bet Bayang would let you take
Roxanna for a ride."

Leech hesitated. "I'm not sure. Things change so fast here."

"Don't be silly," Scirye said, and then she called to Bayang
before Leech could stop her: "Bayang, could Leech take Roxanna for a flight?"

Bayang gave in reluctantly. "Only for a little while and stick
close."

However, it was Roxanna who balked. "Thank you, Lord
Leech, for your kindness," she mumbled. "But I don't want to
bother you."

"Oh, go on, girl," Upach urged. "You know you've been
dying to."

Feeling reassured when he hadn't heard that inner voice,
Leech changed the armband's decorations into flying disks.
He tensed, waiting to hear that malicious whisper again, but
when there was nothing he tried to tough it out. "I won't take
'no' for an answer," Leech said. Plucking one of them from the

air, he put it on his ankle and repeated the same process with the other.

The others all but forced Roxanna onto his back. With no other choice, she wrapped her arms and legs around him tight, squeezing him even harder when they lurched into the air. He would have preferred a more elegant entry into the sky, but the extra weight threw off his balance and he lurched into the air.

Roxanna stiffened behind him and her arms and legs tightened. "I'm ready to go back now."

"Let me get used to the load—I mean, the shift in my center of gravity," he corrected himself hastily.

Bayang swung her head to check on them. "Don't go too far," she cautioned.

It was good to have a physical problem because he had to focus on that rather than cringe, waiting for that strange voice. When he had made the adjustment, he began to move slowly in a circle, taking care to stay at the same level. When Roxanna didn't scream, he dipped below Bayang, coming up on the other side and then slipping overhead.

Bayang smiled encouragingly at them. "There's nothing like flying, is there?"

"It's so scary," Roxanna admitted, "but I've never felt so free."

Leech could feel his own spirits rising. "Then I think you're ready for this." He soared upward into a loop.

"Hey, hey, no fancy stuff," Bayang said.

"You take care of my lady," Upach warned.

Roxanna had been holding her breath in and let it out in a rush. "I was so frightened that I forgot to scream."

"I won't do it again," Leech promised contritely.

Roxanna hesitated for a moment and then said, "I didn't exactly say not to."

That was a little like her old self. Encouraged, Leech said,

"We're your friends, Lady Roxanna—mistakes or no mistakes. After all, you're one of us now."

"Really?" Roxanna asked.

"And we're not going to survive without your know-how," Leech said.

Before Roxanna could reply, Scirye was pointing above them. "Look!"

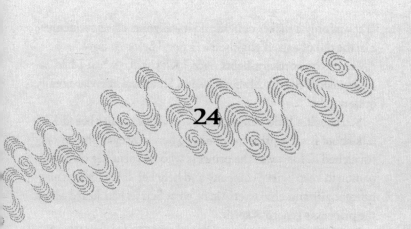

24

Scirye

Scirye was glad she had helped make Leech take Roxanna for a ride. It seemed to be picking up not only Roxanna's spirits but Leech's as well. Even if the weather had been poor, Scirye had expected him at least to try to fly. Instead, he had seemed tense and distracted, as if he was listening for something.

She craned her head back to look above them for some sign of Roland's plane. Instead, she saw a green glow above them.

"Look!" she cried.

"It's the northern lights," Roxanna explained. "I never get tired of it, though I've seen it many times. The Inuit say they're the spirits of the dead playing a game or hunting. But I like to think they're dancing."

It was only a flicker of light and it was gone just as suddenly—like the tail of a trout glimpsed in a pond before it dove.

"I saw the northern lights once," Kles said, "when I had accompanied Princess Maimantstse to Siberia. They were really quite a sight."

Scirye felt a little pang of jealousy whenever she heard Kles talk about his life prior to coming to her. However, she quickly squelched it, for it was the princess who had sent her own companion to keep Scirye company and help her. It had been a magnificent gift and characteristic of what Scirye had heard about the princess's generous spirit.

Suddenly it seemed like a patch of the sky folded itself back to reveal the soft green gauze that served as the backing to the black velvet of the night.

More and more of the sky unraveled and green light flowed slowly across the darkness until it was a river miles long. Like water in slow motion, it twisted and curled into waves that crested and crashed, splitting into currents that flowed in opposite directions or gathered momentarily in eddies and then swirled on.

"Oh, Kles, it's beautiful." Scirye sighed.

"But I hear San Francisco has everything," Roxanna said.

"They have neon signs and street lamps, but they can't hold a candle to this," Leech said with his mouth open in awe.

"The reds and purples are amazing," Bayang said breathlessly.

"I only see green," Leech said.

"Dragon eyes see more of the light spectrum than humans," Bayang explained.

Scirye would have loved to have traded her eyes for those of the dragon, though the green lights were spectacular enough.

She gave a gasp of delight as the northern lights began to spill downward in stages like a series of waterfalls. Lower and lower they cascaded.

"Yikes," Koko squealed. "They're coming to haunt us."

"I've never heard them coming down this close to the earth," Roxanna said uneasily.

Bayang made a quick decision. "I'll dive so we can take cover on the ground."

But it was already too late. As stately as the northern lights had appeared at a distance, they could drop as swiftly as an arrow. The dragon had barely folded her wings when they were surrounded by creatures with bodies like long wispy veils that drifted back and forth in the wind.

Once, while Nishke and Scirye had been exploring San Francisco's Chinatown, they had wandered into a laundry's drying room, where they had found themselves surrounded by lines of drying sheets. It was like that now, except the room extended across the entire sky.

"Down," Kles cried. "Go down!"

As Bayang and Leech began to drop, the nearest lights stretched into narrow ribbons a hundred yards long toward Bayang.

"They're going to electrocute us," Koko yelped.

When Scirye felt the ribbons drape themselves over her, though, there wasn't any shock but rather a pleasant tingle as if every pore were alive. The lights wound themselves around Bayang's limbs and wings, holding her suspended in mid-air even though the ribbons looked no stronger than ones wrapping a birthday gift.

Beneath them they could feel Bayang's mighty body struggle to break free. "I . . . I can't move!" she panted. Scirye and the others on Bayang's back were trapped as well.

Even more ribbons had enveloped Leech and Roxanna, who were wrestling the lights with equal uselessness.

For every northern light that held them prisoner there seemed to be a dozen more wheeling around them, as playful as dolphins. Occasionally, one would brush Scirye's face in passing like a silken tassel.

"What do you want?" Scirye asked, trying to keep the fear out of her voice.

Sparkles ran across all the northern lights and then a tendril cautiously slid downward from one of them, twisting and wriggling around each of them.

"I don't think they mean us any harm. They're just curious about us," Leech said, growing still. "They act like they've never seen a dragon."

"Or humans flying by themselves in the air," Bayang added, and ceased fighting. "You humans usually need to ride in airplanes or on the backs of giant birds."

As a light examined Leech's face, Roxanna said thoughtfully, "But some ghost would have to know about humans and airplanes. So I don't think they're the dead at all. I think they're alive."

"Yes," Bayang agreed, "a unique species of living creatures. But because they usually keep so high in the sky, no one knew, so they made wild guesses instead. We might as well call them Dancers for want of a better name."

The Dancers pulsed irregularly, some curling into cylinders, others into spinning wheels.

Scirye had lived in several countries, so every few years she'd had to learn a new language. As a matter of survival, she'd developed not only an accurate ear but also eyes adept at deciphering body language.

As the flickering Dancers cast strange shadows across her friends' faces, Scirye was sure in her bones that they were trying to speak to them.

If that was the case, how did creatures who communicated with sounds speak to creatures who spoke with light and shape?

"Please let us go," Leech implored.

There was something familiar about the way the Dancers flashed. Then Scirye understood. The light throbbed in the same rhythm as Leech's words.

"I wish I had a flashlight." Scirye sighed.

"We have a lantern, Lady," the ifrit said. "Do you want me to fetch it?"

"If you can," Scirye replied. "But do it slowly and try not to be threatening."

A few moments later, Scirye was surprised to hear Upach rummaging around in the boxes and baskets on Bayang's back. Scirye was tempted to see how the ifrit had managed to get free. But then the Dancers tightened slightly and she said, "Please. We're just getting something so we can talk." She was alert for any signs of anger, but again, they imitated the rhythm to her speech.

The next moment, Upach was murmuring to the fire imp within the lantern, "Time to wake up, Sleepyhead."

And the next moment light flared behind her. "Can you make the imp grow bright and then dim?" Scirye asked.

"Listen to me, my pretty," Upach said sweetly to the imp. "Two taps mean shine strong. One tap means glow soft. Got me?" She tapped on the lantern and the light increased. A single tap and it lessened.

"Then imitate my words by tapping on the lantern," Scirye said.

Upach immediately copied the rhythm, as did the Dancers.

Scirye held her breath. There was always the risk with something so primitive that they might be insulting them instead, but the Dancers only shifted around as if observing her intently.

Scirye could not move her arms, but she was able to hold her palms out to show they were empty—though she doubted that creatures with no hands would understand it as a symbol of peace. "We're sorry if we trespassed in your territory. We didn't know and we'll leave if you let us."

The light vibrated from a dozen Dancers again in the same pattern she had used. She spoke to them soothingly, trying her best to show every sign that they were harmless. Finally, after flashing in imitation of her words, the Dancers began to scintillate in a new pattern.

"Tap like I say," Scirye said. She had a good memory for such things. "Bright, dim. Bright, brighter, dim."

For ten minutes each group tried to copy the others' responses. Scirye doubted that she could have understood ten of the Dancers' words in a year of study. She was sure that the motion and shape of their bodies added subtle nuances—a little like the inflection of a human voice. However, she interpreted the Dancers' attempt at communication as a hopeful sign that the Dancers were as intrigued with the new flying creatures as Scirye and her friends were with them.

Suddenly the Dancers holding Bayang and Leech slid away, returning to the others. The dragon and the boy dropped for a couple of yards before they recovered.

Above them, the Dancers began swirling and coiling excitedly, some of them spiraling around others, some forming bubbles like water boiling in a pot. Light vibrated in patterns too quick to follow.

Scirye wondered if they were debating about what to do with their visitors.

One of them blazed like lightning and one after another the Dancers began to shine with the same intensity, bodies flattening and lengthening into elegant ribbons that wove in and out among one another as if on a giant loom. Perhaps they had agreed on what to do.

They hung in the air like that for a moment and then slipped away until they were once again restless banners dangling from the rafters of the night sky.

However, one Dancer lingered, spreading itself instead like a delicate curtain of green fire. The fringes along its edges twirled. About a yard away from Leech and Roxanna, one of the ribbons became a thread as slender as a hair and then drifted leisurely through the air toward Leech, where it slipped under his glove.

"Hey," Koko protested, "get your mitts off him."

"It tingled for a bit at first," Leech said, glancing down at it, "but now it's okay."

The thread snapped and the Dancer floated upward, whirling away as delicately as the down from a dandelion, leaving behind a slender ribbon glowing like cold fire around Leech's wrist.

25

Scirye

As they flew on, blind Upach was hungry for details about their encounter with the Dancers. They took turns telling her while she punctuated their remarks every now and then with an "Imagine that" or "I never."

When they were done, Leech pulled back his sleeve to reveal the glowing ribbon around his wrist. "Why do you think they gave this to me?"

Koko leaned over to peer at it, his eyes reflecting sparks of green light. "You'll never need a flashlight again, buddy."

Leech gave it a little experimental shake. The light stayed steady. "It's not that bright."

"A small flashlight then." The badger rubbed his paws together greedily. "Boy, if you could slice up one of those guys, you could maybe get a thousand ribbons. We could sell them at a buck a pop. No, make that twenty."

"Don't you ever think about anything except money?" Bayang snapped.

Koko rubbed his belly. "Sure, I think about food and how little of it I get."

Leech ran a finger along the ribbon. It seemed to pulse in response, casting faint shadows upon his features. "I think it's alive, though." Smiling at it, he asked, "How are you, little fellow?"

"It's not a pet," Koko said.

Leech looked sheepish. "Maybe not, but then what is it?"

Fascinated, Kles slipped out of Scirye's coat for a moment. "Perhaps the Dancer is curious and wants to share our adventure," he speculated. "Maybe the Dancer can sense what's happening through it. Or perhaps it will keep a record in its memory and then return to the Dancer sometime. Who knows?"

Leech raised his wrist so it was close to his lips. "Hello, can you hear me?"

Koko laughed. "It's not a telephone either."

"No," Leech said firmly, "it's a gift from that Dancer." He held his wrist up and turned it. "This is where we are. Can you see all right?"

"If it can, then it would be an excellent way to spy on us," Bayang said.

Leech, though, was enjoying his "gift" too much to be suspicious. Instead, he began trying to communicate with the strip the way Scirye had. Though he experimented with the lantern, he didn't have much success.

After listening to Leech for a bit, Upach chided her mistress. "And here you are, wanting to trot around the globe when you have marvels like this right in your own backyard."

"And once you leave, it won't be the same when you return home again," Bayang said. "I'm speaking from my own experience. There will be just enough changes so things won't seem familiar—both in places and in people."

Scirye gave the dragon a sympathetic glance. Perhaps that's the way Bayang felt after a long mission, but right now Scirye was going to seize the opportunity to build up Roxanna's confidence a little more. "Even though you say you're bored, you must love this place deep down inside your heart. Otherwise, you wouldn't bother learning so much about it. I envy you."

Perplexed, Roxanna drew her eyebrows together. "Me?"

"I've never felt like that about any place where I lived. I don't have any roots," Scirye confessed, and felt Kles brush her cheek sympathetically.

"If that's true," Roxanna said cautiously, "I could almost feel sorry for you."

"It is," Scirye said, feeling a little pang of regret.

"I've never seen so many stars," Leech admitted. "The city lights drown them out in San Francisco."

Roxanna looked up at the blaze of stars in an opening in the clouds. "I'd miss the stars."

"I think you'd miss more than the stars," Bayang said. "Even though you say you want to leave, you seem so much a part of this land and sea."

"Are you saying I'm as boring as this place?" Roxanna demanded.

Roxanna's attitude reminded Scirye of a diplomat she had met once at a reception in Paris. He'd been a well-dressed little man with a chip on his shoulder. He took anything anyone said to him as an insult, and yet he was soon chatting with her mother as if they were old friends.

Scirye had asked her mother if she had used some sort of

spell, and she had laughed. "There wasn't any magic involved. I just found a way to get him talking about himself. Most people have something interesting about them. As it turns out, he's a champion archer and makes his own bows and arrows. He was just afraid of having people make fun of him for being a throwback, but when he found out I could shoot arrows from horseback he was more than happy to speak to me. We're to visit his archery range next week."

Scirye had gone with her mother and it had been a fascinating time because she'd gotten a chance to shoot at targets. When she'd even broken some of his expensive arrows, he'd just laughed it off.

Feeling she was doing a clumsy imitation of her mother, Scirye said, "Your whole life seems like one big adventure. Did your family teach you everything?"

"No," Roxanna said shyly, "a lot of what I know comes from my Inuit friends, but that was before the freebooters made it too risky to leave the city." The Sogdian girl spoke wistfully about the good old days before the freebooter raids had increased and when she could travel into the wilderness. A little urging from Scirye got Roxanna to tell them about her adventures, from saving a moose trapped in a bog to fighting off packs of wolves.

Scirye leaned back on her hands. "Up until now, the most dangerous thing I had to face was riding a bicycle when a taxi lost control and came at me."

"Bicycles aren't very practical up here," Roxanna said. "There's either too much snow or too much mud." She leaned in close. "When I want to go for a ride, I get on a reindeer." She laughed and that pleased Scirye. "But the first time I tried, I thought the antlers were like bicycle handlebars, so I tried to hold those instead of the reins. I wound up being pitched into a bog. I was glad to land in something soft, but it was messy."

"I'd like to try that." Scirye smiled. "Would you teach me?"

"It's not very dignified," Roxanna warned cautiously.

"That hasn't stopped her yet," Kles announced.

"And it never will." Scirye laughed, glad to see Roxanna smiling again.

"What's that, Roxanna?" Bayang asked, and banked in a circle until they could retrace their flight path. Bayang went into a gentle downward glide, leveling off several hundred feet above the surface until they saw the pair of furrows.

"Don't go any lower," Roxanna ordered, sounding more like her old self. "The downdraft from your wings might raise enough snow to cover the tracks."

Careful to keep level, Bayang followed the tracks undulating over the surface until they met a tangle of more tracks. It made as much sense to Scirye as a ball of yarn that had unwound. Roxanna studied it alertly, leaning to first one side and then the other.

Even at this distance, Scirye caught the whiff of airplane fuel and saw the dark spots on the snow that might be oil. "Roland's plane landed."

"But where did the airplane go next?" Koko asked.

"I don't know." Roxanna pointed to numerous lines of small ovals that stitched across the landscape as if in some complicated knot. "But reindeer and sleds came here."

"Freebooters?" Leech asked.

Roxanna nodded. "More than likely." She waved a hand toward their right. "Put me down there and I'll walk back here to examine the other tracks."

Bayang set down where their guide directed, and Roxanna took her rifle. "Upach, you stay here and protect our guests."

The ifrit paced back and forth restlessly as her mistress trekked back to the rendezvous spot.

"Your mistress is beginning to sound more like her old self," Scirye observed to Upach.

Upach sighed in the barest of audible whispers. "Being the youngest and a girl, she's always felt like she's been in her brothers' shadows, you see."

Remembering the confident, capable girl they had first met, Leech said, "You could have fooled me."

"My chick's good at fooling everyone—so good she almost fooled herself. But old Upach, she knows," the ifrit said.

They waited impatiently while Roxanna moved around the site, sometimes crouching to examine something left behind. Then she returned to them, high-stepping as fast as she could.

"Two people left the airplane and didn't go back to it," she said confidently. She swung her arm up and indicated the west. "I'd bet anything that Roland and Badik left the airplane and joined up with the freebooters. The freshest tracks go that way, both reindeer and sleds, and there's a lot of them."

"Then hop on, because that's where we're going too." Bayang crouched against the snow. "And welcome back, Roxanna."

26

Bayang

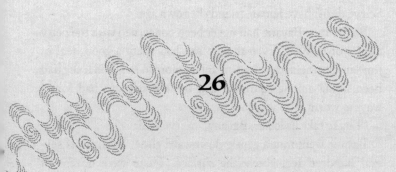

The sun was just creeping into the sky when they spotted the sled trails. "Roxanna, do you think that might be Roland?"

Scirye had been making a point of asking Roxanna questions, though up until now she had asked their guide to explain some feature in the landscape or about some aspect of Arctic life.

"Where, Lady Scirye?" Roxanna asked. "I think your eyes are playing tricks on you." Though Roxanna continued to treat Scirye with a respectful deference, she had relaxed enough with Nanaia's chosen to tease her a little.

Bayang could see nothing herself, but she was pleased to hear the female hatchlings chatting together like ... well ... hatchlings should. It was good for Roxanna, and it was also good for Scirye.

From what little she and Kles had said, the dragon gathered that Scirye didn't have female friends her own age.

Before this, Bayang had never been concerned with the petty affairs of humans. Even though she had spent a good deal of time among them, they had meant no more to her than if she had been living among squirrels. But these hatchlings had found ways to worm their way into her life.

"Please take us lower, Bayang," Scirye said.

Bayang went into a gentle downward glide, leveling off several hundred feet above the surface. There were dozens of tracks, but all were hardly more than scratches on the surface. A breeze was blowing wisps of snow along like ghostly brooms. It wouldn't be long before the tracks were obliterated.

"You have sharp eyes, Lady," Roxanna observed. "I missed them." It was a good sign that Roxanna no longer berated herself over a mistake.

Scirye had also been making a point to defer to Roxanna's judgment. "Or could it be your father looking for us?"

"I don't see how he could get ahead of us," Roxanna said. "The tracks have to be fairly recent or the storm would have wiped them away."

Bayang rose again into a bank of clouds. As she slipped into them, the moisture pelted her face in a steady drizzle. Then she began to skim along near the clouds' belly, low enough to be able to see the ground as if through a gauzy curtain but far enough away that she hoped to appear like a darker patch of the clouds.

The faster she flew, though, the more the water vapor would condense and strike them like raindrops. She would have been able to stand it longer than her passengers, so for their sake she kept at a slow pace.

As they went on, it became easier to see the sled tracks because they were fresher and deeper. After a half hour, the ground became more irregular, with dips and rises everywhere, and the tracks split off in three directions as the group separated into smaller parties.

"Which one do you think has Roland?" Leech asked.

Bayang circled uncertainly. "Scirye, any hints from Nanaia?"

"Sorry. It's not like I can call Her on a telephone," Scirye said.

Bayang chose the middle set. "We might as well try these tracks as any."

Farther on, the large chunks of ice began to litter the flat surface of the frozen sea. It was as if someone had broken a giant white vase on the floor and never bothered to pick up the pieces.

"W-we've come to the Wastes," Roxanna said. Their guide was shivering so badly that it made her voice tremble. "For some r-r-reason, it's a strange place where lots of pressure ridges got all crumpled together. Some say it's the phantoms' doing."

The Wastes spread over an area that must have been at least a hundred square miles, if not more. Here the boulders of ice were the size of hills and so crammed together that they looked like buildings and the valleys between them like the crooked lanes of a city.

"I w-w-wouldn't be in such a hurry to meet the ghosts," Koko stammered between chilled lips.

Apparently the cold and moisture were getting to her passengers as well. Bayang's own wings and body were feeling sluggish, so she was sure the hatchlings were suffering worse than she was. But they would all forget their suffering if they could catch Roland and Badik.

The sled tracks zigged and zagged around the obstacles. One wind sled, as large as one of Prince Tarkhun's, had not turned in time and lay on its side, its mast broken. There was no sign of its crew, who, perhaps, had been picked up by one of the other sleds.

"I wonder if the freebooters raided the caravans to get the sleds as well as the plunder," Bayang said.

"They have a lot to pay for, then," Roxanna said.

As they flew over the labyrinth that was the Wastes, she noticed that snow had filled the gaps between the ice boulders, lying in drifts several meters high. Footing could be especially treacherous there, Roxanna informed them, because the drifts would mask any hazards like ice bridges too thin to support a person's weight, or holes.

Eventually, they came to a clearing where all the sleds had been parked, their sails taken down. Bayang checked to make sure no one was around before she dropped lower to inspect the area. Numerous smaller tracks indicated that the freebooters had set off on foot into the maze itself.

Suddenly they heard a growl from the right, followed by shots and snarling sounds. Banking sharply, Bayang sped toward the noise of battle.

In a clearing surrounded by thirty-foot-high ice cliffs was the largest polar bear the dragon had ever seen. The giant bear had turned at bay, trapped by five freebooters.

Though they had their rifles up, none of them could get a clear shot without hitting the dozen horrible allies prowling restlessly in front of them. The monsters had the bodies of humans but the heads of dogs. Though they wore coats and trousers, their heads, feet, and hands were bare.

"*Ajumaq!*" Roxanna made it sound like a curse word. "This R-Roland must b-be truly evil if he would hire their k-kind. They poison everything they t-t-touch so that it d-decays quickly. All living th-th-things shun them because when Ajumaq t-touch actual flesh it w-will begin to rot away."

"Does f-fur count?" Koko asked.

"I'm not s-sure," Roxanna admitted, "but if you're l-lucky, the first touch will only rot the hair away."

"Oh, great," the badger groaned. "I've been l-losing fur from worry. Now I got a new way to go b-bald."

"R-relax," Leech said. "Don't you remember what R-Roxanna told us earlier about the temperature? Your exposed skin will freeze over long before it decays."

"The bunch of you are just a b-bundle of j-joy, you know that?" Koko grumbled.

Suddenly one of the Ajumaq rushed in with an outstretched hand as if in a deadly game of tag while the freebooters cheered it on.

With amazing speed for an animal so big, the bear side-stepped and swung his paw, knocking the Ajumaq against the frozen wall. The monster lay very still in the snow.

Bayang began to back away. "Well, Roland's not here, so we should keep searching."

"We can't just leave the bear to die," Scirye objected.

"This Tumarg thing of yours can be very inconvenient some-times," grumbled Bayang. "We need to keep our minds on our objective." The excitement had gotten her blood flowing so she wasn't stammering anymore. Perhaps the same thing would happen to the others.

From her early training on, the dragon had learned that her mission came before everything else. If it meant burying her scruples, then that's what she did—even if she hadn't liked it. By now, she couldn't recall how many times she'd had to look the other way when she saw some crime being committed so she could maintain her disguise.

Maybe, she reflected, *it's not Scirye's code but my own con-science being inconvenient now. Perhaps the hatchlings are helping me to remember a part of me that I thought had died a long time ago.*

"The enemy of my enemy is my friend," Scirye observed.

"I want to get even with the freebooters finally," Roxanna agreed.

"Yeah," Leech said, "every one of Roland's gang that we take out now is one less we have to face later."

"That's as good an excuse as any other," Bayang said. Feeling lighter of heart than she had in centuries, she landed on a cliff and crouched immediately. "Get off so I can help. The rest of you stay here. It's my job to risk my life, not yours."

"I can cover you from up here at least," Roxanna said, and then told her servant, "Upach, fetch my rifle. And then cut the netting that holds our supplies. We don't have time to undo it. Lady Bayang needs to be free to fly and fight."

Bayang was relieved to see the Sogdian girl acting like her old self, but she said, "You should stay out of sight."

"I may not know about goddesses or flying," Roxanna observed, "but I'm very good at shooting a rifle. I've been in fire-fights before. Even when things were safer and I used to go with the caravans, there were occasional bandit raids."

Bayang was not sure if it was a good thing Roxanna had gotten back *this* much of her old confidence. *Human hatchlings are so rash! It's a wonder that any of them survive into adulthood.*

When they were still a few feet from the ground and with snow spraying up beneath Bayang's wingbeats, the intrepid little ifrit was already leaping down and positioning herself. As soon as the dragon landed, Upach slid out the rifle in its long holster along with several ammunition clips. Roxanna jumped off Bayang before the others, took her weapon and ammuntion, and strode toward the cliff's edge.

As Bayang's other passengers dismounted, Upach began slicing several key ropes of the netting with a curved dagger. Soon baskets and boxes began thudding onto the snow.

When Roxanna reached the lip of the clearing, she hoisted her rifle to her shoulder and commanded with all of her old authority, "Throw down your weapons."

The officer in charge of the freebooters recovered from his surprise quickly enough. Raising his pistol, he commanded, "Get her."

As his men obediently swung their rifles up, Roxanna dropped to her stomach to make herself less of a target. However, to shoot the freebooters she would have to risk being shot herself. And all just to prove she belonged with them.

And then, as if trying to outdo Roxanna's boldness, Leech said, "I better go with you, Bayang."

She whipped her head around in time to see Leech taking the flying disks off his armband. Her paw shot out like lightning and snatched them from him. "No, it's too dangerous for you to fly."

27

Leech

See, see! the voice cried. *She was just waiting for this excuse to leave you helpless.*

"Those are mine!" he said angrily, and began to pound and kick at her, even though the blows against her armored hide hurt him more than her.

Even Koko seemed startled at Leech's fury. "Take it easy, buddy."

All Leech could think about was getting back the disks. "Why do you keep holding me back?" he demanded. "Wouldn't it make your life easier if someone else killed me?" He snatched the disks from Bayang's startled claws.

Bayang quivered with hurt and fury. "Haven't I proved I've changed?"

Scirye put a hand on Leech. "Yes, you shouldn't talk to her

like that. Remember, she's turned her back on her whole clan for you."

Kles was squirming out of Scirye's coat. "Maybe she's a little overprotective, but that's guilt making her go too much in the other direction."

"And in this case, I think Bayang's right," Koko said. "You're not bulletproof."

Leech pouted. "That's right, gang up on me. Take the side of the big green lizard! She wants me helpless so she can kill me anytime she wants."

Bayang sucked in the cold air sharply with a hiss like a steam pipe leaking. "I gave you my word. I'd no more lie than . . . than Scirye."

Leech cringed, wrapping his arms around his belly as if in pain. He could feel the hatred and anger roiling around in him like a pot of boiling water about to overflow. But this time he wasn't sure if the words had come from the voice or from himself. What was wrong with him?

28

Bayang

Scirye tried to play the peacemaker. "This is no time to fight with one another. Maybe you shouldn't have tried to take the magic away from him," she said, inclining her head to the dragon and then to Leech. "And maybe you shouldn't have doubted Bayang."

Bayang said stiffly, "Perhaps not."

"Sorry," Leech mumbled.

Despite his apology, the hatchling had made it clear enough that they would never really be friends. There were too many wrongs between them and she'd been a fool to think otherwise. Well, she would safeguard him whether he trusted her or not.

"It seems, after all, that we can't erase the past as easily as a chalk drawing," Bayang said coldly.

As she unfurled her wings, she was sure he was glowering at

her still. She felt sad at that, but she refused to feel sorry for herself. *It's like any other wound. Ignore it and it will heal eventually.*

"Yashe!" she shouted, but there was as much despair as defiance in her cry. And then she swooped down between the riflemen and the hatchlings.

29

Leech

Great. Let those guys kill her for you, the voice exulted smugly.

Shut up, Leech said.

He'd been so ashamed of the ugly insults that had tumbled out of his mouth earlier, and he was shocked by the even uglier things that he had wanted to add. But this selfish thought was even worse.

No, I won't shut up, the voice said. *You're going to get us killed.*

Leech fought to shove the voice back into the darkness inside his mind, concentrating inside on all the sacrifices that the dragon had made. He should be grateful, not angry with her. All right. She might be overbearing at times, but she was also the bravest and most reliable companion.

And what if Kles was right? Maybe she'd been so overprotective not as part of some conniving scheme but because she was trying to make up for past crimes.

He wasn't without blame either—at least not that first Lee No Cha—so who was he to judge her? He wanted to ask her if she'd try to be his friend again, but before he could speak the dragon had plunged straight into the fire, more concerned with their safety than hers.

Most of the bullets ricocheted off the scaly armor of Bayang's chest, but there was suddenly a much louder report.

The dragon jerked from the projectile's impact like a marionette being yanked backward. And then spun downward.

Sitting on Scirye's shoulder, Kles jabbed a claw downward. "They've got an anti-tank rifle. If it can punch a hole through a tank, it can do the same to a dragon."

Leech looked down to see a much larger rifle with its bipod resting on an ice boulder for better elevation. The freebooter was sliding to the side in the snow, shifting the angle of the heavy rifle as he tried to track the plummeting dragon.

Bayang crashed into the clearing, sending up sheets of snow as she plowed forward, bowling over the freebooters, including the officer, as if they were mere pins. Blood was spurting from one leathery wing.

She lay stunned on the ground as the anti-tank man took his time trying to find a vital spot.

Leech wouldn't be able to live with himself if the last words she heard from him were those ugly ones. She'd looked so hurt and angry.

Leech pulled the flying disks from his armband, and he frantically began the conversion spell even as Roxanna fired. The force of the gases released from the shot lifted her rifle upward as the shot hit the anti-tank man with such force that it knocked him onto his side.

"Throw your weapons away and lie down with your arms in front of you," Roxanna commanded. When they didn't comply immediately, she fired again, sending the snow spraying upward inches from the freebooters' officer. Reluctantly, he tossed his revolver into the snow and ordered his men to do the same. When his troops had tossed their guns aside, Roxanna ordered them to lie down on their stomachs. And they reluctantly obeyed as the Ajumaq scampered off.

Leech could see the blood spreading across the unconscious dragon's wing. He had only one thought in his head and that was to help her. The anger, the hatred, the voice, were gone. All he could think of was that she needed him. "We've got to stop Bayang's bleeding."

"Upach, the medical kit," Roxanna ordered.

The ifrit made her way quickly to the discarded cargo, feeling among the boxes and baskets until she found the right one. Opening the lid of the basket, she took out a small leather satchel. "Here. There are bandages and compresses."

She held it out, letting Leech fly over to her to get it.

"Kles, help him," Scirye said, and the griffin slipped out of her coat and fluttered into the air.

In his anxiety, the boy hadn't waited for the griffin but was already darting toward the dragon. When Leech got close, he was relieved to see that it looked worse from a distance than up close. The wound itself was small, but he saw blood bubbling up from it.

One great eyelid went up. "You came," the dragon grunted in surprise. "Why?"

"To save you, and you're welcome," Leech said, opening the satchel.

"Ah, well, yes, thank you," the dragon said awkwardly, "but I repeat, 'Why?'"

Leech knew all about surviving on the mean streets of San Francisco, but he didn't know how to tell her how scared he had been when she'd gotten shot. So, instead, he grinned insolently.

"For once, I get to boss you around."

"Humph, I think you're enjoying this far too much." Bayang sniffed, but she fell silent.

By now, he had seen injured people and blood, but it sickened him to see it was a friend who was suffering. He tried to keep his hands from shaking as the griffin directed him in cleaning out the wound.

He hesitated, though, when Kles told him to use some medical thread and a needle to stitch up the tear. "But it'll hurt."

"It hurts anyway," Bayang said. "Go on."

Leech threaded the needle but had to take several deep breaths to steady his hands. Bayang sucked in her breath when the needle pierced her, and the boy stopped. He hated to cause pain to the dragon.

"Get it over with," the dragon insisted.

The leather hide resisted the needle, which made the process even slower, but the dragon endured it uncomplaining. Both of them, though, seemed relieved when Leech was able to tie off the stitches.

He was so busy concentrating on the task at hand that he was only vaguely aware of more shots followed by panicked yelps. It was only when he had applied a bandage that he looked up. Four of the Ajumaq lay still in the snow while the others had run away through a gap in the cliff walls, frightened of Roxanna's deadly rifle.

"Upach, tie up the prisoners," Roxanna ordered her servant. As the ifrit got a coil of rope from their supplies, Leech felt something tickle his wrist. When he peeked at the ribbon under his glove, he saw it was wriggling and pulsing. Guessing that it wanted to see, he rose into the air and exposed his wrist as he spiraled upward. "I bet you want to look at more than my sleeve and my glove."

Suddenly the ifrit's clothes fell in a pile while a cloud of tan-colored smoke rose from them. Leech wondered if the clothing had given Upach a shape as well as kept her warm.

Upach flowed off the rim and poured herself down the side, her misty tentacle having no trouble holding the rope. Without any direction from Roxanna, she flew over the prone humans—perhaps finding them by their breathing. She quickly began to tie them up.

All this time, the bear stood erect, eyes moving from the ifrit to the boy, the dragon, and the griffin.

Koko took the precaution of shouting to the bear, "Don't eat the kid. He'll taste lousy. If you got to eat someone, start with the dragon."

Before the astonished Leech could tell his friend to shut up, part of the southern ice wall near him exploded into softball-size fragments.

"Fasolt! Fasolt!" A frost giant stood there in the ruins of snow and ice, brandishing a hammer with a head the size of Leech's own skull.

With a deafening roar, the polar bear pivoted and charged.

Repeating his war cry, the frost giant moved forward to meet the bear, but he could only plod through the snow that covered the frozen sea while the bear's wide paws let him move easily and swiftly over the surface.

The frost giant brought his hammer down in a crushing stroke, but he was nearly a yard taller than the bear and the bear was able to duck under the mighty swing. Lifting a paw, the bear raked the giant's stomach. The claws gashed through the giant's fur coat but screeched over the iron armor beneath it.

With a shout, the frost giant swung his massive hammer but only managed to clip the bear, who was ducking. Even that glancing blow was enough to drop the bear to his knees, and the giant readied himself for a deadly backhanded swing.

Kles's paw tapped Leech's arm. There was a strange wild glint in the griffin's eye; his small chest was heaving, a hollow growl reverberating in his beak. The boy would have sworn that every fur and every hair was bristling. "Is that other ring just for decoration, or can you really use it?" Kles demanded.

Leech felt a wild, giddy fire race through his blood. "You'll see." Pulling the other armband from his wrist, he spat on it and said, "Change." Then he made the fiery sign in the air.

Suddenly the dense iron ring expanded, becoming a ring some twenty inches in diameter, thin as paper, stronger than steel, and yet so light that he was hardly aware that he was holding it. It seemed made for him, just like the flight disks. The ring hummed when he waved it in the air as if it were alive and excited.

Bayang had taught him a little about how to handle it while they had been traveling on the wing. Unfortunately, the dragon had emphasized defensive rather than offensive tactics. Still, he thought he could use it like a club if he had to.

Suddenly he heard the voice from the shadows in his mind, but this time it was a shout, not a whisper: *Yes, yes, we are free in the sky again! No one can stop us.*

Leech lurched involuntarily when he heard a scream loud enough for one of the giant falcons. Before he could scan the sky, the griffin swooped past him shrieking as if he'd gone mad. And Leech dove, wanting to shout as well, so he copied Scirye's war cry as the dragon had done. "Yashe! Yashe!" he hollered as he plunged toward the ground.

In his excitement, he was barely aware of Roxanna yelling at them in exasperation. "You're blocking my shot."

Screeching "Tarkär!" Kles slashed at the giant's face with his claws and beak and struck with his wings. With a bellow, the giant began waving his hammer back and forth frantically, trying to drive the feathery tornado away.

"No, Kles," Scirye shouted from the cliff top. "You can't fight him by yourself!"

The griffin was paying no heed to his mistress, for he'd gone berserk, shouting his war cry over and over as he attacked,

The ring vibrated in Leech's fingers, the energy surging up through his arm as he sped toward the giant's wide back.

He's got a helmet, so aim for the side of the head, the voice urged. *Now strike! Strike!*

Leech swung his ring against the thick tangle of hair at the giant's right temple. The impact jarred Leech's arm, but the giant's knees buckled and then, like a majestic redwood, he toppled forward.

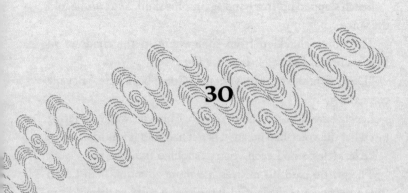

30

Leech

Leech was shocked when the frost giant fell, suddenly feeling like a spectator in his own body. The flying disks sent vibrations through his legs so that they felt like charged batteries and the ring hummed a joyful battle chant. He was so alive, so strong. Nothing could stand in his way. Ahead of him was the injured Bayang, still lying before him.

Yes, the inner voice exulted. *I was born to win. Now take care of the dragon and then the bear.*

Leech was bewildered by the anger that thrummed through those savage words. "No!" he said in a fierce whisper, and forced his body to tilt so that he banked away instead toward the growling bear behind him.

Right. Right. First take on the enemy still standing. Then do the dragon, the voice said.

Leech slapped his free hand against his skull. *Shut up,* he told the voice.

The voice chuckled from somewhere in the shadows in Leech's brain. *I can't . . . because I'm you.*

"Don't fight the bear by yourself! Come back here," Bayang was calling.

Leech barely heard the dragon because he was wondering just what the voice had meant when it had said it was him.

"Kles, Kles, stop Leech," Scirye shouted frantically.

The griffin paid his mistress no more attention than Leech did to Bayang. Leech glanced at the griffin and saw the wild fire was still in his eyes and his fur and feathers still bristled. *He's gone mad,* Leech thought to himself. *I wonder if I look like that?*

Suddenly Leech heard a hissing sound and then a dusky cloud rose up from underneath the griffin, enveloping him and shooting misty tentacles out toward Leech. He started to bank away but could not avoid them. They were cool to the touch but gritty rather than moist the way a cloud in the sky would have been. It was like having cold water flung in his face.

"You've pushed your luck far enough," Upach said in a thin, hollow voice.

He glimpsed Upach's eyes, nostrils, and mouth as they shifted constantly upon the restless surface of the cloud.

Leech forced his mouth and tongue to move. "Y-yes," he said. He became aware of something squeezing his wrist. Through a narrow gap between his glove and sleeve he could see the Dancer flashing as it constricted. Had he scared it?

He stroked it soothingly. "It's all right," he assured, and felt it relax.

"What happened to you?" Bayang called.

"Young warriors get reckless," Upach explained for him. "They think they'll live forever."

"Yes, I suppose it might be the heat of battle," Bayang said.

The griffin nodded as he floated inside of her. "How . . . how unseemly of me."

"Then let's withdraw," she said, tugging them backward. All three of them were careful to keep their faces toward the bear, who was studying them curiously.

"Sometimes the battle rage takes me over," Kles said shakily. "Thank you for bringing me out of it, Upach. I'm glad you move so fast."

"This is nothing," the ifrit said. "The cold makes my body stiff, so it slows down. But on sand, ah, I move like the wind."

Leech wanted to ask if the battle rage wanted to make you kill even your friends but was too ashamed to. He didn't think he would ever work up enough courage to talk to the griffin about it.

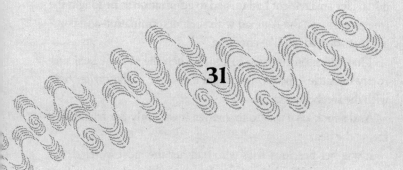

31

Scirye

Scirye had seen bears before, but they had always been dull creatures caged in a zoo, with no more animation than furry cushions. So it had been a thrill at first to see a bear in his natural home, running and leaping with such power and grace—perhaps moving with less grace than the dragon but with more vitality.

As lithe as Bayang was, there was never any wasted motion in what she did. Whether fighting or flying, she never seemed to move without some intelligent calculation beforehand.

The bear, on the other hand, was as restless as an Arctic wind, prowling about, testing the air, glancing about. And when he attacked, he struck with the violence and force of a hurricane.

Though Scirye and her friends had taken many risks while they were pursuing Roland, nothing had seemed quite as brave or foolhardy to her as the bear's battle against overwhelming odds. Her amazement had turned to admiration as he fought the freebooters and the Ajumaq with such determination and courage that she had felt like cheering.

That had soon changed to shock when she saw the bear's ferocity in battle—she'd only caught a glimpse of the earlier fight with the freebooters.

And shock gave way to fear when it was only her friends left facing the bear.

It was her precious Kles who had her the most worried, because when the battle madness had seized him he would fight creatures a hundred times his size. So she was grateful when Upach managed to get Kles to withdraw with Leech to Bayang's side as she lay in the snow.

When the ifrit flowed back up the cliff and onto the top, Scirye thanked her.

Upach's smoky form floated by her mistress, her dusky shape vibrating as if she were shivering. "I could smell their madness."

Their? Did she mean Leech? Scirye wondered. She hadn't seen any outward signs like with Kles. Leech had fought hard, of course, but that was to survive. Upach must be mistaken.

The bear was pacing back and forth at one end of the clearing, staring at her friends as if he were at a buffet and deciding which one he was going to have first for dinner.

"This could go on for forever," Scirye said.

"You're right." Roxanna leaned her rifle against some baskets and held up her empty hands as she called, "We greet you, Lord of the North."

The bear only growled menacingly.

"Humph, that's gratitude for you," Koko grumbled.

"After encountering Roland's troops, can you blame him for mistrusting humans?" Scirye asked.

"Well, what do we do?" Roxanna asked, frustrated.

Scirye had hated to be a spectator while her friends battled for their lives, but perhaps, as she was the daughter of a diplomat, there was something she could do now. Her mother often said sometimes it was harder to end a battle than to fight one.

"Leech," Scirye shouted, beckoning him over, "take me down there so I can talk."

"Leech, you'll do no such thing," Bayang ordered.

"I can't negotiate when I'm yelling at the top of my lungs," Scirye replied. "It's dumb for us to fight with one another instead of against our real enemy Roland."

"But Lady—," Kles tried to protest.

Scirye cut him off with a gesture. "I'm going and that's that, Kles—even if I have to jump off the cliff to get there."

The griffin knew that tone all too well. It had gotten them into more trouble than he liked to think. "Please, Lady. Stay up there. Let me handle the bear."

"He eyed you like you were a flying snack," Scirye said, and beckoned to Leech. "Please, Leech."

As the boy began to fly up toward the cliff top, Bayang said, "Leech, do what I say."

Leech shrugged. "I think she's right. Why should we fight the bear?"

Roxanna picked up her rifle again, ready to set the butt against her shoulder and snap off a shot. "I'll keep an eye on him from up here, or for any more of Roland's men sneaking up on us."

The battle seemed to have finished restoring her confidence, because she sounded as sure and capable as ever.

"Then I know I'll be safe," Scirye said.

Roxanna smiled her pleased acknowledgment and then went back to surveying the landscape for threats.

When Leech reached the cliff's edge, he swung around, presenting his back to her. "Here's the taxi, Lady. Hop on. The meter's running." As she climbed on, he wobbled immediately at the change in weight.

Alarmed, Kles darted in to steady them with his forepaws, but he wound up overcompensating so that Leech and Scirye tilted even more to the side.

"Aim for the snowbank," was Koko's advice.

Somehow Leech managed to regain his balance, and then, with the persistent little griffin helping, they descended like a leaf in a hurricane.

Scirye swayed a bit when she got off, and the ever-attentive Kles flew about her, brushing stray snowflakes from her clothing.

Leech glanced at the bear. "I don't think he cares how neat and tidy his dinner is."

Down in the clearing, the scent of blood was much thicker than on the cliff, and she did her best to hide the fact that it was making her a little sick. Waving her hand, Scirye shooed Leech and Kles away. "We don't want to make him more nervous. You can keep an eye on me from the air."

Leech rose, hovering several yards above her, but Kles settled on her shoulder and sank his claws lightly into her clothes. "My place is with you," he insisted.

In the snow, Bayang struggled to her feet, wincing as she folded her injured wing against her back, and then moved to block Scirye's progress.

Her friend's concern touched Scirye and she put a hand affectionately against the dragon's armored cheek. "Does it hurt much?"

"Some," Bayang admitted. She glanced at her back, wincing as she tested her injured wing. "But I don't think I'll be flying until that heals."

As soon as the dragon had turned away, Scirye had started to run—or more like jog, because the snow slowed her.

"Come back here!" Bayang said, reaching out with a paw.

Scirye jumped to the side and then continued to head straight toward the bear.

When he snarled at her, exposing wickedly sharp fangs, Scirye's legs went all wobbly so that she stumbled.

"You'll get yourself killed!" Bayang yelled, the worry plain in her voice, but that only spurred Scirye on.

Throwing out her arms to the sides, Scirye managed to get her balance as she staggered on. As she righted herself, she tugged the stiletto and axe from her belt and threw them down. Then she held up her empty palms. "We . . . we come in peace," she panted.

She gave a jump when the bear reared up to his full height. There was so much of him! He had looked imposing enough when seen from above. Up close, he was downright terrifying. He towered over her like a white furry mountain. A growling furry mountain . . . with big claws.

Her legs suddenly turned to jelly, and she plopped backward onto the snow. As she sat on her rump gazing up at him, the bear seemed even more gigantic. When people saw bears in the zoo, it was easy to think that humans had tamed Nature, but they were only fooling themselves. Away from their cities, humans were lunches who very considerately delivered themselves to the animal diners.

Kles had instinctively flown into the air when Scirye had fallen. He hovered overhead now, his claws aimed at the bear, prepared to leap to her defense. There wasn't an ounce of fear in his small body.

"Why," the bear rumbled in a voice like boulders rumbling down a hill, "have you invaded my territory?"

The bear exuded a massive sense of power. Pele had been as quick, loud, and explosive as the volcanoes she ruled, a strength that was rooted in the fiery heart of the earth. The bear's temper was as deep, slow, and relentless as a glacier grinding mountains into pebbles.

Pele was quick to fight, but she had no patience. Draw out the struggle and she might lose interest. The bear, on the other hand, would be slow to quarrel, but once he did he would not stop until he had crushed his enemies.

Though she was frightened, Scirye made herself concentrate on his eyes. She didn't see the all-consuming hate that had been in the hag's eyes, but she didn't see any friendliness either.

"Gee, sorry, mister. We didn't know this was your front yard," Koko yelled. "Come on, kids," the badger said, waving urgently for them to retreat. "Let's not annoy the nice critter."

"Critter, am I?" the bear roared.

When she felt the violent energy radiating from him, Scirye wished that she had listened to Bayang and hidden behind the dragon. It was as if that terrible Arctic storm had condensed into the shape of the bear—and that furry hide could barely contain the rage of its destructive force.

But then Scirye saw Kles's fur beginning to fluff outward—not to be cute but as a sign of anger—and she heard the faint hum of Leech's rings as he spiraled close, ready to snatch her up and escape.

Her friends' presence reassured her and she bowed her head respectfully to the bear, finding it a relief not to look at him. Then she did her best to imitate her mother when she was calming down hostile foreign officials—or French waiters, whom she said were even more dangerous.

"We mean you no disrespect, Lord," Scirye said, her voice

sounding strained and shrill to her own ears. "We are hunting our enemies, a human called Roland and a dragon."

"Don't be a worm. Stand up on your hind legs," the bear commanded.

Though Scirye's legs were still trembling, she rose, but the difference in their heights was so great that she was already getting a stiff neck from tilting her head back to face the bear.

"How did you get here?" the bear demanded.

"In Hawaii, we fought the enemies of the goddess Pele. In return, she helped us to get to the Arctic," Scirye said nervously. "She'll vouch for us."

The bear growled menacingly. "You and a goddess? I hate liars."

Scirye's protective charm was hanging around her neck. Opening her coat, she pulled out the black flower that Pele had shaped from molten lava as if it were child's clay. "The goddess gave each of us one of these to keep us warm."

The bear stretched out a broad forepaw, the claws looking like daggers, and Scirye could not keep from flinching.

"Stay where you are, dragon," the bear growled to Bayang, who was trying to advance to Scirye's side. "This conversation is between me and this human cub." Then he addressed the Kushan girl again, the amusement . . . and the challenge . . . plain in his voice. "When you're shaking like a lemming, it's hard to see how you could help a goddess."

Scirye's eyes were focused on the large talons hovering before her face. "Um, no," she said in a quavery voice. "But who *wouldn't* be scared of you if they had any sense?"

She was puzzled when she heard a chugging sound like an old truck motor and even more confused when she realized it was the bear's laughter. Setting his paws on his hips, he conceded,

"Yes, I guess I'd be frightened of me too." And then he actually winked. "In fact, I quake in terror every time I see my reflection on the ice."

His broad, round jowls stretched in a good-natured smile. At the moment, he seemed less like a dangerous beast and more like a large teddy bear with extra padding around his middle.

"Please, Lord, examine the charm." Despite the claws in front of her, Scirye extended the charm toward them.

The bear held his forepaw a few inches above it. "Yes," he said in surprise, "I feel the magic coming from it, but not who put it there." He lifted the paw up and scratched a jowl. "How can I be sure that the trinket came from Pele and not Roland?"

The injustice stung the girl. "My friend got hurt trying to help you."

The bear dismissed that fact with a clack of his claws. "How do I know that you're not more of Roland's worms and this whole battle was staged to gain my gratitude?"

That was a deadly insult to Scirye and to Tumarg itself.

"We're no friends of Roland," she protested. "He killed my sister and this boy's friend." She motioned toward Leech. "We're here to get even with him and to get back the treasures he stole from my people and from Pele."

Kles dipped his head politely as he hovered. "They are the ring and bowstring of the archer Yi. We think Roland may have come up here seeking a third treasure that once belonged to him."

The bear's head jerked up, startled, and for a moment Scirye thought he knew something. In a low voice so the freebooter prisoners wouldn't hear, she said, "Have you heard of such a thing up here?"

The bear swung his head to the side so abruptly that it was Scirye's turn to be surprised. His black, moist nostrils widened as he tested the breeze and then his body stiffened. "I can smell more of Roland's lice coming." The bear curled his lip scornfully. "There are always some fools who hear that phantoms are protecting an ancient treasure in the Wastes and come here to find it."

Kles added, "Whether Yi's relic is here or not, Roland thinks it is. And he won't stop looking for it."

"We have to stop them from getting any more of Yi's artifacts," she urged, hoping that the powerful creature would side with them. "You have to believe me."

The bear regarded her and then leaned forward and took a good whiff of her. "I smell your fear, and I smell your worry. But is that because your foes might catch you or because your allies may not get here in time?"

That was just too much for Scirye. She chucked diplomacy out the window. "It's not my fault that I haven't been able to take a bath in a while," she snapped. "If you're going to be *that* sort of . . ."—she hunted for the right word—"of bear, we don't want your help."

He swung his head back indignantly. "And just what kind of bear is that?"

She was so annoyed by the bear that she didn't stop to think. "You know, suspicious, snotty, ungrateful . . ." She was ready to enumerate his flaws at length, but she felt Kles give a cough that warned her to be more discreet. "And . . . and stuff like that," she finished lamely.

Perplexed, the bear roughed up the fur on his head with both paws. "What do I do? Should I believe a lie and betray my people, or should I doubt the truth and betray my rescuers?"

Apparently, Roxanna had put up with just as much of this as Scirye. Lifting her head proudly, she declared, "Prince Tarkhun's clan do not beg anyone for help. Go. We'll manage on our own and no thanks to you."

The bear whirled around to glower up at the Sogdian girl on the wall. "Prince Tarkhun! Are you really his daughter?"

"Don't tell me you have a grudge against him too?" Scirye asked, wondering just how many feuds the bear was conducting.

The bear lowered his voice so their prisoners would not overhear: "The prince has done me many favors. Argh!" His paw rubbed the back of his neck almost hard enough to scrape the fur away. "This is getting worse and worse. If she's truly who she says, I can't let that scum kill *both* my rescuers *and* Prince Tarkhun's child. But if I take her and the rest of you with me and you're lying, then I reveal the location of our home to my enemies. My people have survived all these centuries because we've kept it hidden."

Kles cleared his throat. "If you can work some kind of magic, might I suggest a conditional curse, my lord? Perhaps if any of us break our oaths, dire things will happen to us. That should help remove any uncertainties about taking us."

The bear thumped one paw against another. "I guess that will have to do. I'll bind you with a spell that will make you sorry if you don't keep our secret."

Scirye lifted her hand and gave a little admiring nod to Kles for being such a clever griffin.

Finally, the bear's eyes found Scirye again. "So, let's begin with you. You talk bold enough to be a bear. Can you act like one? Do you swear not to reveal my secret in any manner or have death take you?"

"Yes," Scirye said bravely.

As the bear muttered a spell and his claws traced mystic signs in the air, Scirye felt a tingling along her scalp. She was sure if she could have looked under her coat, she would have seen goose bumps break out on her arms. And the air felt as thick as honey to breathe. The bear was making a powerful enchantment.

The bear tapped a hind paw impatiently while Leech went up to ferry Roxanna and Koko down to the clearing. Having tossed her clothes below first, Upach returned on her own. Then the smoke flowed into the garments and they filled out as she took her regular shape again—the process happening in the wink of an eye. By the time that Roxanna set her feet on the snow, Upach was already pulling on the outermost coat.

One by one, the others made the same vow, with Koko the last and most reluctant.

"What happens if I talk in my sleep?" Koko asked cautiously.

"Something bad." The bear tapped a claw on his muzzle in a humanlike gesture. "Like having your head explode."

"What?" Koko shrilled in alarm. "I kind of like my head where it is." He clamped his paws to his cheeks as if he were trying to hold his skull in place.

The bear folded his forelegs across his broad chest. "All of you must take an oath, or none of you will go with me."

"Well, I like playing a game of tag with Roland even less than having my head go boom." Koko sighed, throwing up his paws. "So, okay."

"So be it," the bear grunted, and worked his spell. When he was finished, he added, "Tell anyone about my people and it will become quite messy. Understand?"

The badger drew a paw across his muzzle as if closing a zipper. "Right. Mum's the word, Lord Boss, sir."

"You might as well call me Lord Resak." The bear motioned for Scirye to pick up her weapons again.

"What do we do with the prisoners?" Bayang asked.

"Leave them for their master," the bear said.

Roxanna protested, "But Lord, we can't let them loose to commit more crimes."

"We don't have time to kill them all and we can't take them with us either." Pivoting, he began to lope away on all fours. "Keep up with me. I won't wait for stragglers."

And he disappeared into the maze.

32

Scirye

As they entered the twisting passages, Kles flew above them to keep an eye out for any more of Roland's creatures.

Leech would have followed on his flying disks, but Bayang said to him, "It'd be better to walk. If Roland does have men around, they might mistake Kles for some bird, but you'll stick out."

Scirye felt sorry for her friend, because he looked a little disappointed. She knew how much he loved flying, but he still wasn't as polished and skillful a flier as the griffin or the dragon.

In the maze, Lord Resak moved with an easy, fearless stride—as if he knew that he was the fiercest and deadliest creature in this dangerous land. It was sometimes difficult, though, to pick out the bear's white fur.

It seemed to blend into the snowy walls, and the bear jinked through the turns so quickly that Kles lost sight of him and they were reduced to following his tracks, jogging along until they caught up with him.

Lord Resak had stopped and was shoving at a large ice boulder, the powerful muscles of his body rippling on his back and shoulders.

Trusting that he had a purpose, Bayang stretched her long body and joined him. With the dragon's help, the boulder slid across the snow, revealing an opening about a yard wide and three yards deep.

"The ring seals are used to digging breathing holes through the ice and carving out lairs for their pups," Lord Resak explained. "I just expanded it a bit."

Scirye peered down into the hole, realizing that it was the mouth of a tunnel connecting the top of the frozen surface to the Arctic Ocean. At the bottom of the shaft, chips of ice floated on the dark water like pieces of broken glass as the ice pack tried to solidify and heal itself.

The bear looked up at the sky where the clouds were beginning to thicken again, reducing the sun to a dull glow as it began to sink toward the horizon.

"There's going to be another storm soon. The snow should cover up our tracks and the drag marks when we pull the boulder back over the hole. Dragon, I think you should come last so you can do that," he instructed. Then he studied the rest of them. "I don't think you can swim very far or fast with those scrawny arms and legs even if the water wasn't freezing. We'd better get you some help."

He gave a couple of coughs to clear his throat and then began to growl in a deep rhythmic monotone that made the friends instinctively draw closer to one another. Raising his forepaws, he stamped his right hind paw rhythmically while he dragged his left as if he were lame in that paw, dancing sometimes faster and sometimes slower while he created patterns upon the snow.

As he turned his head from side to side and up and down in time to the beat, his jowls drew back in his teddy bear smile. Despite the hostile land and his enemies closing in, he was happy to be alive, to see the sky and snow and ice, to feel the frozen ocean beneath his paws, to have the cold wind riffle his fur, to draw the crisp, chilly air into his lungs and nostrils, for all the wonderful scents in the world . . . for, well, everything.

All of the sea's frozen surface seemed like his drum. The staccato rhythm of his paws traveled joyfully through the snow and ice and up through the soles of Scirye's boots and into her body, and she found herself tapping her feet in time with him.

As Lord Resak celebrated, he seemed to grow larger—not in size but in power. And she realized he was not just that "sort" of a bear. He wasn't a bear at all but some spirit of the North. And perhaps not just any spirit either but the spirit of every Arctic creature, from the smallest to the largest, who lived in this harsh but beautiful place.

Suddenly the sea began to roil, the ripples sending the ice chips floating away from the center. Scirye started when a horn thrust up from the sea. Water trickled from the sharp tip and along the grooves of the spiraling pattern on its sides. Scirye waited to see the creature that owned the horn . . . and waited and waited, for the horn kept on shoving into the air until it was some nine feet long.

Ringed by foam, a glistening, speckled head finally emerged with small eyes and mouth but with a large bulbous dome on the forehead. The horn itself seemed to extend outward through the left upper lip of the milky white creature.

The horn tilted as the creature bent its head momentarily so it could shoot a fine spray of mist from what must have been its blowhole on its back. And then it began to wave its horn in time to Lord Resak's drumming paw.

"A narwhal," Roxanna gasped. "I've only seen pictures of them."

"I thought it might be some kind of unicorn at first," Scirye said.

"Long ago their horns used to be sold as that," Roxanna explained. "But narwhals usually winter farther south."

The narwhal gave a brief series of clicks, whistles, and squeals that made Lord Resak chuckle as he got down on three legs and extended a foreleg. And that paw that had knocked down freebooters and Ajumaq stroked the slick domed forehead of the creature as gently as if it were a kitten. Then he spoke to the narwhal in its strange language in a loving, soothing voice.

Which will we see next, Scirye wondered, *the fighting machine or more of the teddy bear?*

Suddenly there came the patter of many paws and then Scirye saw the largest otters she had ever seen. They were about a yard long, with sleek brown fur dusted with snow. When the surface was level, they pulled in their short forelegs and slid along, letting their hind paws trail behind them. There were over a dozen of them—she was never sure how many because they kept moving about restlessly.

A sea otter with a brindled muzzle rose on his hind legs in front of Lord Resak. "We are the last group, Uncle. The others have already used the seal doorways to retreat into the ocean. We've trapped many of the humans, including the group that was after them." The otter indicated Scirye and her friends.

"If you sent them to help us, we thank you, Lord," Scirye said with a bow.

Lord Resak waved a paw. "I didn't know who you were until you introduced yourselves just now."

The otter twisted around. "We figured if the freebooters were after you, you had to be all right."

"We understand the principle." Bayang laughed. "That's why we interfered with your personal battle, Lord Resak."

"What are sea otters doing in the middle Wastes?" Roxanna asked.

"I believe you humans call them the phantoms." Lord Resak chuckled and motioned to the otters. "Now go home for a well-deserved rest."

The otters slid down the snow and ice, splashing into the water and then disappearing.

Lord Resak turned to the friends. "Hold still. I need to cast a spell so the cold water won't affect you and yet you'll be able to breathe."

Once again, Scirye felt the tingling sensation as his claws sketched a quick design and he muttered the secret words. Then he gestured. "Come. One of you climb onto this one. You'll find paw-holds along the walls of the hole." He indicated the side where they started.

Scirye was going to step forward, but Roxanna beat her to it. The Sogdian girl lowered herself into the shaft, feeling around with her boot until she found the first niche. She descended rapidly after that until the sea was lapping at her boots.

The narwhal watched her descent with eyes shiny as pebbles and then lowered its head, exposing the long, white and gray dappled expanse of its back. As it slid forward across the water, its fins looked small compared to its body.

Shoving herself from the wall, Roxanna dropped onto the narwhal. The impact submerged them both for a moment. When they re-surfaced, she was clinging awkwardly to the slick, glistening skin.

"Sit forward and hold on to the horn," Lord Resak instructed.

Roxanna had trouble climbing toward the head until the narwhal bent its body even more so that she slid over the moist skin, grabbing desperately onto the horn. Instantly, the narwhal began to buck.

"Not so hard," Lord Resak snapped, and then spoke a series of clicks and whistles so that the narwhal calmed down.

When Roxanna loosened her grip on the horn, she spluttered as she spat out a mouthful of seawater. "Well, I wanted to do something my brothers haven't. But now I can't tell anyone about it."

Before she could even cry out, the narwhal submerged into the water so that all that was left was the ice fragments tossing up and down on the surface.

Roxanna's head had barely disappeared before another narwhal rose to the surface, sending up a spray of mist from its blowhole. This time Lord Resak said something and the creature adjusted its position, perhaps so it would be easier to climb on.

Peeking out of Scirye's fur, Kles said, "I'm not so sure about this. Griffins were born with wings, not fins."

Scirye stuffed his head back inside the coat. "You're my entourage, remember? You're supposed to go where I go."

Kles's voice came muffled from inside the coat. "In the sky and on the land, but not underwater."

"And I belong on good old terra firma," Koko insisted. "My mother never raised her baby boy to be a submarine."

"Then you can wait here and say hello to Roland," Bayang said.

Koko gulped. "I didn't volunteer to be a monster's chew toy either."

"Actually," Leech said, "you did when you got on that carpet in the museum."

Koko flung up his paws. "Okay, okay, but"—he eyed Leech defiantly—"I don't have to like it."

Ignoring Kles's complaints, Scirye clambered down the shaft until she was just above the restless ocean. As she tried to gather up the nerve to push away from the side and jump onto the narwhal, Lord Resak gave another order in the narwhal tongue. The creature slid through the water, curling its body to fit against the curving wall of the opening. Apparently, Lord Resak had learned from Roxanna's difficulties.

Lord Resak said something else to the narwhal and it twisted its body so that she slid down the slippery hide toward the horn. The temptation, of course, was to seize it and hold on for dear life, but she made herself hold it loosely. She was surprised at how smooth the spiral-grooved horn was.

Before she could even blink her eyes, her narwhal, eager to escape the hostile air, sank into the ocean. The winter sea was dark as ink, but the bottom of the tunnel, lit by the intermittent moonlight, shone like a huge silver disk. There was just enough dim light to make out the underbelly of the Wastes. If the top half was rugged, the bottom half was even more jagged where there were no winds to wear the edges away. Even though there were water currents, the temperature was so cold that they replaced as much as they took away.

Scirye almost panicked. Within her coat, she could feel Kles squirming in alarm. This was no visit to the seashore on a vacation. She could not tell up from down anymore in the gloomy void and her lungs were on fire.

She held her breath as long as she could before it exploded outward from her aching lungs in a stream of bubbles. She stiffened as she took in a mouthful of salty water, but to her surprise she wasn't suffocating. It was as if her lungs were taking air from the water like a fish. Her breath rose like a chain of silvery beads to where they splattered into a flat oval like a misshapen pancake of air.

She took a few more experimental breaths, grateful to learn that Lord Resak's spell was indeed working. Nor did her clothes feel heavy and soggy with water—as if the traveling spell kept them dry as well.

It was almost as if she weren't swimming underwater but instead was drifting through a twilit world.

Another narwhal churned past her, its body almost a silhouette against the opening above. As her eyes adjusted to the faint light, she vaguely became aware of other shapes about her, sensing them as much by the slight currents that their bodies made as they circled slowly as by sight. But she could certainly hear them, for there was a constant chatter of buzzes and clicks. She assumed they were other narwhals and that Roxanna was somewhere on one of them.

A third narwhal returned, followed by a fourth and fifth, and then someone heavy plunged into the water, creating a column of bubbles. Lord Resak emerged, his paws propelling him along.

A moment later, they were plunged into momentary darkness as Bayang filled the tunnel. It stayed black even after she entered the ocean, having covered up the hole in the ice as Lord Resak had ordered. Now the only illumination came through the opaque ice itself.

Though the dragon had tried to go gently into the water, the sheer bulk of her body created a wake that tossed Scirye's mount about. For a brief moment, she almost lost her grip on the horn, but then her narwhal adjusted to the turbulent water that Bayang created and surged forward with a powerful twist of its tail.

Scirye felt like screaming in protest, but no sound came from her—as if the dusky ocean had taken her voice away. The gloom seemed to close around her so that there was only her and the wild narwhal, who would probably be relieved if she floated away. The isolation crushed her like an invisible hand. Just as she began to pant in fear, she felt a large leathery paw touch her arm.

"Don't worry," Bayang's voice reassured her. "I'm keeping an eye on all of you."

Yes, of course, not only would the dragon be used to the sea, but her large eyes would be able to see in what was darkness to a human also. Scirye wasn't alone at all. She had friends who had already fought to protect her. Suddenly her terrors began to evaporate like mist before the sun.

She tried to ask about their other companions, but her words came out as gurglings. Bayang, though, could guess what she wanted to know: "Yes, everyone's all right."

For a while, the powerful dragon swam beside Scirye, keeping her comforting touch upon the girl's arm until Scirye managed a grateful smile at Bayang.

When Bayang finally left Scirye, she didn't feel afraid because she sensed now that the dragon was nearby, her sleek body easily keeping up with the speeding narwhals.

When they left the Wastes, the frozen ceiling flattened out like translucent glass. Scirye could see bubbles of air trapped within the ice now and how the surface itself was pitted.

Around her the narwhals moved with a fluid grace, swimming with swift beats of their tails while they used their small fins like steering rudders. The ones who were carrying passengers were careful to keep level as they dipped and then rose through the ocean, but the ones without were playfully corkscrewing through the water.

They all seemed to move in time to a pattern of clicks and squeals in a rhythm that reminded her of Lord Resak's drumming. Could the narwhals be singing?

Still they swam on with the sea and ice darkening as the sun set until the water was inky black. Scirye fought her panic by trying to think of other things. Beneath her, the narwhal sped on, its powerful body moving with efficient twists.

Her narwhal whipped through the sea like a spiked torpedo. *It's like being on a roller-coaster ride,* she decided. *It's scary and exciting all at the same time. First the volcano and now this.* And so she even began to enjoy herself.

She actually regretted it when her narwhal finally slowed down. Slim, shadowy creatures about a yard long darted around her, moving in a spiral path. High-pitched voices squeaked and squealed, and their tone made it plain they were challenging the intruders.

Then, from somewhere nearby, she heard Lord Resak answering, and she almost giggled, because his deep voice was not really designed for such sounds and the words came out more like the noise a rusty hinge would make.

Then they were moving forward again. The water grew stiller—as if there were only the currents made by swimmers and not by the ocean about her. She guessed they were entering some underwater gate in a wall.

Suddenly there was a shimmering brightness—though it took her a moment to orient herself and realize it came from above her. The surface glittered in restless, ever-changing patterns, but she could make out blurry fires that must be lights.

She could make out figures around her now. There must be a dozen narwhals surrounding her, and after counting she was glad that her friends had all made it.

Something zipped in front of her, creating a cloud of bubbles, and as they dissipated she found herself staring into the muzzle of another sea otter. The creature was about a yard long and her black eyes regarded Scirye with friendly curiosity—which was reassuring, because the otter's forepaws held a spear and there was a flint dagger tucked into a belt around her waist. Then the sea otter flipped onto her back and kicked backward—in motion looking as sleek as her charm.

The otter waited respectfully as Lord Resak came into view. The large bear had to be drawn by two narwhals, keeping a paw on the horn of each.

Releasing his twin mounts, the bear motioned for Scirye to get off and then pointed to their right. She made out the outline of steps carved into ice that led into the water.

Scirye patted the narwhal gratefully upon the head and swam toward the steps, moving through more sea otters and narwhals. From the corner of her eye, she saw her friends heading in the same direction.

Lord Resak moved beside her until he was sure she was going to the steps, and then with a sudden powerful kick he burst upward, shattering the brilliant surface in a storm of bubbles.

For a moment, Scirye lost her orientation in the cloud of bubbles that enveloped her when Lord Resak rose out of the water, but Bayang took her arm, guiding her along until she could feel the steps beneath her feet.

She saw Roxanna's blurry shape next to her and together they climbed out of the water. Little beads of salt water clung to the tips of their furs, but otherwise they were as dry as when they entered the ocean.

The dock upon which they were standing had been carved from ice just like the huge cavern that surrounded them—though the cave walls were rough-hewn while the dock was worn smooth as concrete. Here and there the ice had a beautiful blue tint, and the whole cavern glowed with a golden light as if the very sunlight had been trapped within it.

A squad of guards was standing at attention, two bears, a seal with a mottled pattern of irregular rings, a walrus, a white wolf almost as big as the walrus, and, to Scirye's surprise, two humans.

Lord Resak's fur was now matted to his skull and made him look sleek and yet powerful at the same time. He shook his head joyfully, as if he were taking a hot bath, and the drops splattered everywhere.

"Taqqiq." Lord Resak signed to an old brindle-colored wolf with huge muscular shoulders and scars on one jowl and barked some commands to him. Spinning about, the wolf loped on all fours in a kind of half-walking, half-skating gait, his nails clicking along the hard surface through a door on the left. Then Lord Resak listened intently to the walrus, whose jowls and whiskers twitched as he made his report in a whuffing voice.

"Hey, easy on the merchandise," Koko complained as he dangled upside down by one hind leg. Bayang had used her tail to lift him out of the water.

"Quit wriggling, you idiot, or you'll make me lose my grip." Bayang harrumphed. "If it weren't for me, you'd still be swimming around searching for the stairs."

"Well, for future reference," Koko said, and pointed at his head, "this end always goes on top."

Kles had poked his head out of Scirye's coat. "I think you ought to throw him back until he grows more."

"I'm tempted," Bayang said, but she lowered the badger down gently on the dock before she let go.

Koko barely had time to hop upright on his hind paws when the walrus and seal waddled past him to the edge of the dock and plunged in.

"The narwhals said that they spotted a Tizheruk, so I'm sending them out and expanding the patrols," Lord Resak explained.

"Tizheruks are giant snakelike amphibians that can come out

of the water," Roxanna whispered to the friends. "They don't move very fast on land, so they try to snatch some careless person on a beach, but they're deadly in the water."

At that moment, one of the doors on the right opened and out came a group of Arctic foxes using the same gait that Taqqiq had used as they walked upright on their hind legs. The foxes' winter fur was a shining white, and around their necks were crude gold chains that suggested they were officials rather than servants. In their paws was an old wooden staff as thick as Scirye's wrist. Others carried a cape of pure white fur. There didn't seem to be anything special about the staff, which looked like a plain old wooden pole, but the cape gleamed like newly fallen snow. A tortoise with a long neck had been sewn upon it with gold thread.

The foxes waited respectfully until the walrus had finished his report and waddled backward.

"Give Lord Resak room," one of the foxes intoned in a shrill but solemn voice, and Scirye and the others imitated the walrus's example.

Looking about to make sure he had enough space, Lord Resak held his head up high and started a different dance, stamping first his right hind paw and then his left, turning slowly as he did so.

Stomp, stomp, stomp, his feet went in a slow, steady rhythm.

Closing his eyes, he began to murmur a chant, picking up the beat so that he was whirling around rapidly like a toy top.

Stomp, stomp, stomp. The bear was spinning now faster and faster until the drumming of his paws was as quick as Scirye's heartbeats and he himself was a blur

It seemed to the girl that his silhouette was changing, but he was so quick that she couldn't be sure.

And then he was slowing down so that Scirye could see he was no longer a bear but a man in a white fur coat and trousers with furry mittens over his hands. A silvery white beard covered his jaw and a thick, bushy eyebrow formed a thick, solid line across his forehead. Clothes and hair contrasted to his dark skin, which was almost black. Her mother would have called him ruggedly handsome.

He was now about six feet tall but thick and wide as a boulder and gave off the impression that he was just as solid and permanent as one.

Scirye glanced at the humans and bears and wondered if they had the same power.

The foxes moved forward then, raising the cape respectfully to Lord Resak. As Lord Resak took the cape and tied it about his shoulders, the foxes reverently lifted up the staff. Taking it, he turned to Scirye and her friends and thumped his staff against the ice. "Welcome," he boomed, "to my palace"—his voice dropped ominously—"and your prison until I can send a messenger to Prince Tarkhun and learn the truth about your identities."

33

Scirye

"Hey, I'm a shape-shifter too," Koko said, thrusting out a paw as he strolled forward. "That makes us sort of cousins, so you don't need to suspect me. Want me to show you the secret paw shake?"

The guards growled and burbled ominously. Lord Resak, though, stilled them with a gesture and then scolded them sternly. Turning back to Koko, he said, "I told my children that you are a fool and until we hear from Prince Tarkhun we will tolerate you."

Koko gave a nervous laugh as he rubbed his head. "Heh, heh, that's me all right: just one big happy idiot."

Curling her tail, Bayang poked Koko with the tip as if he were a billiard ball. "Right now you're being an exceptional jerk."

However, Leech was more direct. "Ut-shay up-quay," he warned, and dragged Koko backward.

"We are careful whom we claim as kin." Lord Resak inclined his staff toward the still-snarling guards. "They have proved over and over that I can depend on them. Wolves, foxes, walruses, seals, otters, and narwhals, they are all my children."

"So that's how the narwhals and otters could stay up here during the winter," Roxanna explained to the others. "He makes sure they have everything they need."

"Yes," Lord Resak said. "Now give that rifle to my child here." He indicated a wolf. "You'll get it back if you truly are Prince Tarkhun's daughter."

Reluctantly, the Sogdian girl unstrapped her rifle and held it out so the wolf could clamp his jaws around it.

"Do you want these, Lord?" Scirye asked, taking out her stiletto and axe.

Lord Resak waved a paw. "No, against my warriors, those toy fangs and claws won't give you any unfair disadvantage in a fight."

Kles had crept back out of Scirye's coat and onto her shoulder, where he had just finished grooming himself. "You have a remarkable clan then, Lord. In many other places, they would be natural enemies."

"After the First Dawn, it's true that their ancestors hunted and killed one another," Lord Resak agreed. "However, when humans came to this land, some of the creatures of the North came to me and asked for my protection. I said I would, but only if they agreed there was more to kinship than blood: That worth is measured not by how many legs or fins you have, but by the size of your heart."

His guards growled their assent.

Koko gazed at their surroundings. "So you all live in this big ice cube?"

They heard his chugging laugh again.

"In a way," Lord Resak said. "Originally, the clan just carved out barrows and dens within the glacier. But over the generations, it's grown into our palace."

Kles gave a polite bow. "And may I compliment you on its magnificence, Lord Resak. So innovative. So unique . . ."

As she listened to her friend sing the palace's praises, there were times when Scirye regretted that her friend had learned the art of flattery at the imperial court.

"The glacier will melt before you're done talking." Lord Resak frowned and Kles snapped his beak shut with a clack.

"If you don't live in the Wastes, Lord Resak, why were you there?" Bayang asked.

"It's our hunting and training preserve," Lord Resak said, "where the young ones learn the old ways and we old ones keep up our skills. Lately, a large band of vermin had come to the Wastes, so I went to see for myself."

"And got ambushed," Leech said.

"Inconvenienced," Lord Resak corrected the boy.

"And the phantoms?" Roxanna asked.

Lord Resak seemed to be weighing how much to tell them, but, Scirye guessed, he figured that since they would never leave unless he decided they were telling the truth about themselves, it would do no harm to give them more information.

"Yes," he said. "No one sees the foxes when they don't want to be seen. And the otters and seals dig all sorts of tunnels and hiding holes in the ice so they can pop out and play their tricks when they want. They excel at it. Harmless travelers were guided out of the Wastes. And hunters . . ." He shrugged. "Well, we did to them what they would have done to us."

"Couldn't you have just made those people do what you want?" Scirye asked.

"My magic is the magic of Nature," Lord Resak said. "I can't make humans go against their own wills, because that would be unnatural."

"But you . . ." Scirye paused. It seemed impolite to say the word "kill," though it was the truth.

"Killed some of them? Yes. Dying is as much a part of Nature as living," Lord Resak explained gently. "But I neither enjoyed nor regretted their deaths—no more than the blizzard that slays a mother reindeer and leaves the calf bawling. It is simply something that I do."

Bayang had once warned Scirye that powerful beings like Pele had a different perspective than humans. If Lord Resak's perspectives were just as inhuman, what about Nanaia?

Roxanna bit her lip as she looked around. "Wait. I just realized something. There's no glacier in the Wastes." She paused as she thought a moment. "But the Kristiana Glacier is twenty miles to the north of Nova Hafnia."

"Is it?" Lord Resak said.

"Very sly misdirection," Bayang said. "If someone suspected that the phantoms were real, they would think their homes were in the Wastes rather than here."

"Especially the treasure hunters." Lord Resak chuckled.

At that moment, Taqqiq trotted back into view with a half-dozen more wolves. Behind them were large trays piled high with salted fish, which seemed to float over the ice. Then Scirye noticed all the tiny furry bodies carrying them.

"Ah, time to repay my debt," Lord Resak said.

Scirye could see about a dozen shadowy shapes circling about in the water below. At Lord Resak's call, a familiar ivory horn broke the surface and a pale narwhal twisted its upper torso backward so its eyes could look up at the bear-man.

In clicks, whistles, and squeals Lord Resak seemed to be thanking their rescuers, and then he bent and picked up the nearest tray, revealing a platoon of lemmings who had been supporting it. With a quick toss, he sent the fish sailing overhead to splash into the water. The narwhals swam about furiously as they found and ate their reward.

Tray after tray followed until the same white narwhal rose halfway out of the water and bowed. Then he dove again and disappeared.

Scirye called out, "Good-bye. Thank you." But whether they heard her before they disappeared back through the gate she couldn't say.

"The least I can do as your host—or warden—is show you your new quarters," Lord Resak said. "We have no need of jail cells here, but we'll house you in a secure part of the palace."

He began to move easily across the slippery floor with the same walk that Taqqiq and the foxes had used. A fox accompanied him. He slowed down when he saw that Scirye and the others were picking their way gingerly across the ice, taking small quick shuffling steps like a penguin's waddle.

They left the dock area through a large doorway into a hallway. The icy floor had been worn smooth by countless paws and flippers, and the walls, though a little rougher, glowed with the same faint glow as the dock—though now that they were close they could see that it was thousands of tiny stripes gradually moving along like tiny neon signs so that the light seemed to scintillate.

Intrigued, Leech ran a hand over the bumps of one wall. "Lord Resak, where do the lights come from? Is it some sort of spell?"

The bear-man seemed to be relaxing now that he was at home. "Yes," he explained, "it's magic in the way that all Nature is enchanted. There's a type of ice worm that gives off light. We've even bred them for special colors. They feed off tiny creatures—I think your word is 'bacteria'—in the ice itself."

A group of bears and otters was busy by one wall. Fire imps on stone hearths kept buckets of water from freezing. A team of otters brought one of the buckets of warm water over to the wall, where a bear poured it down the surface. It froze as it ran downward forming rippling layers. Then another bear with a blowtorch carefully smoothed it.

"The ice needs to be repaired constantly and the ice worms renewed," Lord Resak said with a wave of his paw. "We take great pride in maintaining our home."

"You mentioned that my father had done you some favors," Roxanna ventured, "and yet this is the first I've heard of it."

"A secret is more likely to stay a secret if fewer people know about it," Lord Resak commented.

"No wonder he was trying to keep us from going into the Wastes," Bayang mused.

"Yes, he's been very helpful perpetuating tales of the horrors that wait in the Wastes," Lord Resak said. "But here, see how else he's aided us." They were passing by an open doorway showing a chamber as huge as a warehouse. It was filled with crates, gear and food and medical supplies.

Roxanna pointed at the twin palms stamped on a stack of boxes. "Those are my clan's markings."

Lord Resak nodded. "Your father has protected our secret ever since he settled here and we made contact with him. We take our human forms and go about the city as yet another group come to trade." He added proudly, "With your people's help, we have a hospital and even our own library now."

"You can't fight your enemies if you don't understand them, is that it?" Bayang asked.

"That's part of it," Lord Resak said, "but there's also much about the world we would simply like to know."

Scirye read the label on another crate. "These are tins of corned beef." She glanced at another stack. "And those are peaches. Don't you hunt for your own food?" she asked, somehow feeling a little disappointed that they shopped for groceries like anyone else.

Bayang shook her head. "If I may make a guess, my Lord, I would say that you cannot have this many wolves and bears together in the same area without exhausting the local game or calling attention to yourselves. That's why you use the Wastes for your hunting preserve."

"Just so. We like to keep up the Old Ways." Lord Resak nodded to Scirye. "Life is hard up here, but we have our little amusements."

With a sudden kick, he glided along the slippery floor, holding up his arms for balance, his bulky frame moving as if it weighed no more than a feather. Twisting his head, he looked over his shoulder at Scirye. "If you're brave enough to insult me, surely you're brave enough to try this."

Scirye was not about to lose the challenge and, digging in the toes of one boot, she kicked herself forward.

"Wait!" Kles cautioned as the walls slid by. "You'll break a leg, my Lady."

"I've skated before without getting hurt," Scirye announced, and grinned at Leech and Roxanna. "Race you." As she started to glide after Lord Resak, her griffin fled to the air.

"You were only on skates once," he squawked in protest.

The walls whizzed by as she sped along the ice with her arms spread out for balance.

"This is a little like flying," Leech said. He'd already caught up with her.

"Turtles!" Roxanna cried as she raced past them.

Scirye went down at about the same time as Leech, both of them skidding along the floor. Fortunately, Lord Resak had been keeping an eye on them, so he halted to form a backstop and they bumped into his stumplike legs.

Kles settled down now on Scirye's stomach, looking—or so Scirye thought—more smug than anybody had a right to be. However, like a true courtier, he also knew enough not to remind her that he had warned her. Instead, he asked her as he tidied up her clothes, "Is my Lady all right?" He almost fell off as Scirye rose up on her elbows.

"I guess I'm just a little out of practice," she admitted.

"Well, that was fun while it lasted," Leech said enthusiastically as he also sat up. "Let's try it again." When he tried to rise, he plopped back down again.

"But will you knock our palace down in the process?" Lord Resak chuckled, and he barked a command to the fox, who immediately trotted away.

When Lord Resak closed his large hands around their small ones and helped them to their feet, and as long as he had a grip on them, she was sure she would not fall down again.

As her boot soles made shushing sounds, Roxanna skated back to them. "It looks like this corridor goes on forever."

"If you keep going, you'll find the communal kitchen as well as dining rooms." Lord Resak jerked his head in that direction. "And beyond those are lockers for fish and game—refrigeration isn't a problem here—as well as nurseries where we breed the ice worms. We also have a sewage treatment room that converts waste into food for them."

"So you use magic to recycle everything in a closed loop," Bayang said, her claws clicking on ice as she and Koko caught up with them.

"It's natural magic again," Lord Resak said. "We use different little creatures, the bacteria, to transform the waste."

Scirye wondered just how much of the vast glacier Lord

Resak and his clan occupied. "This isn't a palace," she whispered to Kles. "It's a city."

At that moment, the fox returned, dragging along a large hide bag in his fangs.

Dipping his hand into it, Lord Resak took out some frizzy green balls. "This moss will help you walk," he explained. He stretched a ball flat so that it was like a slipper and the sticky moss clung to the soles of Scirye's boots. Then he carefully fitted the others with gear for their feet and paws. Only Bayang declined, because her talons bit into the ice enough for her to keep her footing.

Putting a mitten against the wall for support, Scirye eased back onto her feet and took a tentative step, expecting her foot to fly out from underneath her again. Next to her head, she felt the flapping of Kles's wings and the tug of his claws on her collar as he tried to help her stay upright. To her relief, she found herself walking. It was a bit like trying to move through molasses, but at least she wasn't going to take a tumble again. Though she wouldn't admit it to Kles, the fall had left her with a few bruises.

When Lord Resak was sure his guests could follow him, he led them down another large hallway to a wide staircase carved from ice. More moss had been attached to each step to prevent spills.

Suddenly Scirye heard high-pitched cries of excitement from above.

"Not again," Lord Resak grumbled, but he hurried over to the bottom of the banister. The next moment a human and two bear cubs, little more than balls of white fur, hurtled down the banister on burlap rags.

The child knocked Lord Resak to the floor and Scirye noticed that she had the same hair and skin color as Lord Resak, so perhaps she was also a young shape-shifter. For that matter, the two bear cubs, who bounced off his stomach, could have been shape-shifters as well.

Lord Resak gathered them in his arms. "How many times do I have to tell you that you are not to slide down the banister?" With a menacing growl, he lifted the little girl toward his out-stretched mouth.

34

Scirye

The girl was squealing as she wriggled her limbs, and a horrified Scirye was sure Lord Resak's fangs were going to take a bite out of her, but instead Lord Resak blew a loud raspberry against the cub's belly. The girl had been squealing not with terror but with laughter. "Stop, stop, Uncle!" she screamed gleefully.

Giggling, the girl and the cubs tried to wrestle Lord Resak as if he were not some mighty spirit of the Arctic but simply a large cuddly toy. He held them tight, though, until he gave the other two the same punishment as the first.

When he lifted his arms, they scampered away, the girl running on all fours like the cubs. He smiled as he sat up. "They never listen to me." He picked up their abandoned burlap rags and set them to the side, where the girl and cubs could find them again. When he straightened up, he looked at Scirye and her friends. "Now you know why I fight so hard. I'm protecting them and all our families."

"And well worth it," Bayang said fervently.

Scirye could not help smiling. They all were. Lord Resak took such obvious pleasure in his people and his home—in contrast to Scirye, who had wandered from one city to the next, never staying long enough in one place to sink down roots or find friends.

By the time that Scirye reached the top steps, she heard the noise from the next level. She could make out high-pitched squeals to bubbling rumbles. It reminded her of the collective sound that all the creatures in a zoo might make—though far more cheery and relaxed—and there was the strong smell of wet fur and fish, but it wasn't unpleasant because it seemed so natural.

Here the Arctic foxes, shape-shifting bears, wolves, and otters lived according to their own taste, so it felt as if she were visiting different worlds all jammed together. The bear-men and bear-women preferred spherical rooms large enough for families of three or four that, Lord Resak explained, reminded them of the dens a mother would dig in the snow for her cubs.

The walls of their section were also all curved, billowing inward or outward like sails so that the corridors themselves seemed to be alternately expanding and contracting.

"Oog," Koko whispered, "I feel like I'm in a glass intestine."

"I can't say I've ever had the pleasure," Kles said, and held a claw to his beak. "Now to use Leech's patois, ut-shay up-quay."

The Arctic foxes lived in warrens of tunnels and rooms that were smaller versions of the bears', but the foxes' hallways looked like cake batter had been poured down the walls and floors in folded layers. It made the footing precarious even with the walking moss on the companions' boots, and they were continually bumping their heads on protruding ceilings and walls.

The wolves' section was all angles, so parts of it made Scirye feel as if she were within a crystal while other parts widened into open ice fields where the wolves could run—or more likely skate.

In contrast, the otters' corridors had undulating floors that curled back on themselves and reminded her of fun-house slides. Instead of living in separate homes, the otters stayed all together in a large communal cavern where, despite all the space, they tended to cluster together in one rowdy, sociable superraft and with no regard for privacy at all. It reminded Scirye of school cafeterias at lunchtime.

As the companions passed through it, they noticed some of the otters had wrapped themselves in long pieces of green felt, which they wound around them so they resembled green caterpillars with fuzzy heads and feet.

"Why are they doing that?" Leech asked.

"In the ocean, otters would wrap themselves in the leaves of a bull kelp," Lord Resak said. "Even here, some habits die hard."

The decorations carved into the ice varied according to the group. Bears cut deep parallel grooves in patterns that swirled and spiraled across walls, floor, and ceiling. Wolves embellished their homes with carved rows of triangles like distant mountain ranges—or, Koko suggested with a shudder, like fangs. Different-colored ice worms added to the beauty of the carvings. The foxes' taste ran to circles while the otters' ornamentation was so chaotic that it gave Scirye a headache to look at it.

Scirye and her friends' progress through the palace was slow. As the news of Lord Resak's return spread through the level, creatures of all kinds came to greet him. They treated him not as

a powerful spirit but as a favorite relative, even calling him
Uncle. For his part, he had a friendly word for everyone—from
elderly lemmings to wolf cubs that nipped at his legs.

And he always had a patient ear for their grievances. Scirye
watched as Lord Resak calmed an elderly otter who had been
complaining about his cousin's snoring. "Well, I could crush his
head for you." There was a mischievous twinkle in his eye.

The otter's whiskers twitched violently. "I want him to stop
snoring, Uncle, not breathing."

"Then I suggest you turn him over on his side when he
snores," Lord Resak suggested.

The whiskers wriggled in horror. "But that's not natural.
Otters always sleep on their backs."

"And otters snore," Lord Resak said. "So perhaps you might
try putting moss in your ears and sleep farther away from him if
you can."

"Well," the otter said, scratching his shoulder, "he's only a
nuisance when he's asleep, so I'll see what we can work out." And
he went away still grumbling but apparently resigned to his fate.

35

Scirye

 Though the palace was as cold as the surface, it didn't feel hostile at all. Perhaps it was because she was so close to Lord Resak. In his own home, the angry energy she had felt in the Wastes had been replaced by a sense of peace—a calmness brought about by Lord Resak's presence: He made everyone feel safe.

His spirit was large and generous enough to match his body—which made Scirye's own soul feel small and shriveled in comparison. How often had she been unselfish enough to do some kindness for her own family, let alone for others? *No,* she thought to herself, *I just complain all the time and feel sorry for myself.*

Scirye took advantage of one of the rare lulls when Lord

Resak was not speaking to someone: "You must really love your clan. Not only do you protect them, but you're so patient listening to their silly demands."

"I take them as they are," Lord Resak said, "including all their faults."

"I could never handle so much responsibility," Scirye said.

Lord Resak spread his hands. "And yet you're here. You didn't leave the thieves for someone else to catch."

"I . . . I don't have any choice," Scirye confessed. "I know this sounds crazy, but I made a promise to a goddess and She expects me to keep it. I asked Her to help me get revenge for my sister's death and recover the ring. It was a present from the Emperor Yü. It's said to have belonged to the archer Yi."

"Yü? I met him long ago in his travels." Lord Resak smiled as he remembered. "An amazing wizard. But so restless. He never could stay in one place for long. Still, he was as kind as he was powerful. His ring would truly be a treasure." Lord Resak's bushy eyebrow helped intensify his gaze. "And what makes you think the goddess is behind all this?"

"She's under the goddess's special protection," Roxanna supplied. "She warned Lady Scirye in a dream that Amagjat was attacking."

"Wa! Amagjat?" Lord Resak clapped his hands in surprise. "And you escaped?"

"We captured her," Scirye said. "If you don't believe me, you can see for yourself. And anyway, I'd feel better if I knew she was in your hands."

"She's been my enemy ever since the First Dawn"—Lord Resak bowed—"so I thank you. We'll lock her away for good in the ice."

Roxanna gave the approximate location of the sack that held her and then added, "And before She helped Lady Scirye fight

Amagjat, the goddess sent an earlier sign of her favor: Her statue came to life and marked Lady Scirye. Show him, Lady," Roxanna urged Scirye.

Reluctantly, Scirye pulled back her glove to show the "3" marking her hand.

"Many would call you fortunate to be so chosen," Lord Resak said, and leaned his head to the side as he studied Scirye. "And yet I sense something is troubling you."

Though she had not known Lord Resak long, he seemed so kind and wise that Scirye found herself blurting out, "She sent this strange vision too when she made the statue move." After briefly describing it, the girl asked hopefully, "We're to go to the City of Death in the Kushan Empire, but do you know what the '3' means?"

Lord Resak's eyebrow twisted as he pondered the matter. "Many special things come in threes. The only way is to go there and find out what it means."

"Oh, thanks," Scirye said softly in disappointment.

He bent his shaggy head, gazing down at her compassionately. "And yet you're such a little cub. Why does she burden such small shoulders with such a great load?" Wanting to comfort Scirye, he wrapped his arms around her.

As soon as he had enveloped her, Scirye felt as warm, safe, and snug as if she were under her quilt at home, warm. She was willing to bet he made his whole clan feel this way. "I wish She'd get someone else," Scirye muttered.

"I understand, little cub. You walk a path that would frighten even me." Since they were touching, his deep voice seemed to rumble right through her.

Scirye bit her lip. "Then what do I do?"

"No one would blame you if you gave up and went home," Lord Resak suggested kindly.

"My sister didn't run away. She fought a dragon and died," Scirye said. "I can't do anything less."

Lord Resak held her at arm's length, eyes intent on her face. "Then let me put your duty in perspective. Do you like your friends, little cub?" he asked.

"Of course, Lord," Scirye said, wondering what that had to do with this.

"But there must be times when they wanted to do something that you didn't," Lord Resak said.

Scirye nodded, remembering when she had wanted to push on while her companions voted to make camp.

"Did you leave them?" Lord Resak asked.

Scirye needed only the briefest moment to think about it. "Of course not, Lord."

Lord Resak nodded. "To have friends means giving up some of your freedom. Duty asks the same of you, only its demands are greater and the sacrifices larger. And there may be no reward except the satisfaction of having performed it. Have I scared you enough to quit?"

Selflessness was Tumarg, the code by which her sister had fought and died. "No," Scirye said.

There was an approving twinkle in his eye that was worth more to her than a volume of praise from someone else. "I didn't think I could." With a pat on her back, he stepped away.

His tone reminded her of the way parents spoke when they were encouraging a child to walk—they knew the child could do it and that the child needed to do it and that they would be so happy for him or her when the child did.

Scirye would have liked to ask Lord Resak more, but at that moment a group of foxes trotted up to complain about some wolf cubs and he was busy playing peacemaker and lawgiver again.

It wasn't until much later that Lord Resak was able to lead Scirye and the others to what he said was the clan's true treasure.

"So you do have one after all," Koko said with avid interest.

"Yes, a very old one." The bear-man indicated two wolves pacing in front of a side corridor. "Which is why we always guard it. We'll put you in some side rooms there."

Koko was all but rubbing his paws in glee. "Great idea."

It was, Scirye thought, like leaving a cat in a goldfish store.

The wolves padded to either side to make way for Lord Resak, their eyes boring into Scirye and her friends.

The bear-man led them through a wide doorway into a round chamber from the center of which rose a tree carved from ice, spiraling toward the ceiling like a frozen explosion. The tree's three trunks rose from a common base, but instead of being solid, each trunk was a column of intricate icy lace that twisted and undulated like a serpent coiling playfully upon itself as it rose upward. The branches stretched upward as gracefully as dancers trying to touch Heaven. Red ice worms pulsed like fiery blood within the lace, and up above the ice had been shaped into broad, thin ovals in which had been embedded bits of quartz, which made Scirye think of shining leaves.

"Long ago, before the clan had books, a sculptor heard about trees, but she didn't know what one looked like. So she imagined one." Lord Resak patted the trunk lovingly and the tree flickered in response. "I like to think it's what a tree is even if it doesn't resemble any real one."

"It's the essence of trees," Kles suggested helpfully.

Openmouthed, Koko pointed at a rayed disk nesting high up in the leaves like a bird. "Is that gold?"

"What else would you make a sun out of?" Lord Resak laughed.

"And...and diamonds?" Koko gestured toward the lumps that Scirye had thought were quartz.

"Yes, I like them in their original raw shapes myself," Lord Resak said. "But the ones we want to sell we send to Prince Tarkhun and he has specialists cut and shape the diamonds."

Suddenly Koko dropped to his knees, caressing the floor. "All this gold and all these jewels."

Scirye looked at her feet for the first time. Beneath several inches of ice was a vast mosaic of gold and diamonds in the silhouettes of the different members of the clan: walruses and seals, whales and bear-people, otters and wolves and foxes.

Lord Resak regarded the fortune under his feet and then shrugged in resignation. "The otters like shiny things, so every spring they search the rivers for the gold washing down from the mountains. And the lemmings are worse. They dig for the diamonds. I keep telling the otters and lemmings that the storerooms are full, but I can't get them to stop. So we just have to carve out new places for storage."

"So that's how you pay for all those supplies," Leech said.

Lord Resak seemed almost embarrassed. "Yes, at least the gold and diamonds have one use. Oh no, wait. They also make good toys for the little ones."

"Toys?" Koko squeaked. When he had recovered his breath, he hinted, "You know, I'm really a big kid at heart."

Lord Resak waved a paw in dismissal. "You're welcome to some of them and good riddance."

Koko looked ready to burst into tears. "You're a pal, a real pal."

Lord Resak gestured to the glittering objects. "Could these trinkets be what Roland really wants?"

"No, Lord," Bayang said politely. "He's gone to too much trouble for the other possessions of Yi."

Before Lord Resak could reply, they heard an explosion in the distance. It shook the whole palace so badly that Scirye almost fell.

Then from overhead she heard a thunderous cracking like the spine of Heaven was breaking.

"Duck!" Leech shouted.

Scirye had just enough time to look up and see a twenty-foot section of the ceiling fall. Her openmouthed reflection on the mirrorlike surface stared back at her, a reflection that swelled in size as a ton of death dropped down straight upon her head.

36

Bayang

As soon as she had heard the ceiling breaking, Bayang said the growth spell the fastest she ever had. Seen through the shimmering air, the tree seemed to shrink as she expanded in size. Bracing her legs, she arched forward, knocking Lord Resak and the children to the floor. Like a living shield, she stretched herself over them just in time. Her knees buckled as the ice crashed against her back, but by sheer will she held her legs rigid enough to keep from flattening her friends.

But she couldn't help groaning at the new pain in her injured wing. The fallen ice had probably set her recovery back another week. Near her, she heard a noise like the shattering of a hundred glass bells.

Dazed, she glanced toward the tree and saw that it been smashed by the ice slab.

Lord Resak crawled out from underneath her and shook his head groggily. "The tree," he gasped.

"I'm sorry," Bayang panted. "It was beautiful, Lord Resak."

"After saving me twice," the bear-man said, smiling, "I think you've earned the right to call me Uncle Resak."

Scirye and the other children crept out from underneath the dragon and stared in dismay at the destruction. "Can you make another?" Leech asked.

"We can try," Uncle Resak said, putting his hands beneath the edge of the giant flat chunk. "Now help me free your friend."

Immediately the others sprang to help. The effort was sincere enough, but they were more likely to crush their hands and paws. They didn't seem to understand that she would rather that they take care of themselves than her.

"I can do it," she said. She took several breaths of the cold air and then set her forepaws against the belly of the ice chunk. Carefully, she walked in a squat, easing herself from underneath the crushing weight. The agony renewed itself in her wing as she slipped out from underneath the huge chunk. Now there was only her right forepaw supporting the edge.

"Step back," she warned them. When she was sure they were in the clear, she yanked her right foreleg away and the ice smashed down.

She collapsed then, panting as she tried to recover.

"What blew up?" Koko asked.

"I don't know," Uncle Resak said, shaking like a dog to get the ice chips off him. "But I'm going to find out."

Suddenly a gong began to sound, the reverberations traveling through the ice so that the dragon felt them through her paws.

Uncle Resak's head whipped around. "Invaders," he said grimly. "They must have followed us somehow."

Scirye put a hand over her mouth in horror. "It's all our fault."

Uncle Resak shook his head. "Whether you were with me or not, they would have followed me. I think that was the real purpose of the ambush. This Roland is a clever fellow. He knew that I would come to see why there were so many vermin up there. And when I did, he was prepared."

With one last regretful look at what had been the tree, Uncle Resak walked toward the doorway. Shrinking in size to fit through the doorway, Bayang followed him with the children. They were just in time to see a fox scurrying as fast as she could over the ice. A few paces behind were the guard wolves. All three looked grim.

"Tizheruks, Lord," the fox panted. "At least a dozen came up at the docks."

"They find their prey miles away in the sea." Uncle Resak growled. "They're how Roland tracked me."

"I thought they were solitary creatures," Roxanna said. "You can't have two together except at mating time."

"Roland must be a truly foul but very skilled master to bring so many together." Uncle Resak grunted, and then jerked his head at the fox. "What about the narwhals and our sentries?"

"I don't know, Lord," the fox confessed. "But behind the Tizheruks were dozens of humans with guns."

Bayang assumed Roland's men were protected by breathing spells similar to the ones that Uncle Resak had cast on them.

Uncle Resak gestured toward the dragon and her friends. "Take our guests to one of the hiding places."

Bayang remembered when she had been a hatchling cowering in her room while Badik destroyed her city. Her whole life had been preparing for this moment. "I'm staying to fight."

Uncle Resak's chin rested against his chest for a moment as he thought. Then he slapped a hand on the dragon's scaly leg. "I'll welcome your help, but the cubs will go."

"No!" Roxanna blurted out. "This fight is as much mine as it is yours. Roland is served by awful monsters who are a danger to my clan too. And his freebooters have put Nova Hafnia under siege. That makes him my enemy too."

Scirye folded her arms defiantly. "And we're not going to let Roland wreck your wonderful palace either."

"Lord—I mean, Uncle Resak is right," Leech agreed, pulling the axes from his belt. "This is worth defending."

She'd been so surprised and pleased when he had come to her rescue during that battle in the Wastes. But she hadn't known how to tell him at the time.

Of course, she'd felt a small twinge of worry when she'd seen how well he had fought in the Wastes. She'd wondered if that original, murderous self, Lee No Cha, was surfacing. But then she'd told herself that Leech had only been defending her and that was hardly something the dragon-hating Lee No Cha would have done.

Leech had shown he was someone she could trust to protect her back in a fight. So were Scirye and Roxanna for that matter.

Bayang smiled. "I can always count on you three *not* to do the sensible thing."

"Can we take a vote on that?" Koko asked hopefully.

"For once, I agree with the badger," Kles said. "It would be prudent to retreat."

"No." Scirye had taken out her stiletto and axe. "We came to stop Roland."

"Besides, there are families here," Leech added.

"Yes," Roxanna said. "His mercenaries show no mercy even to the harmless."

Resigned to his fate, Koko covered his eyes with a paw. "Here we go again."

Uncle Resak pointed down the corridor sternly. "You will leave."

Scirye drew herself up stubbornly. "With all due respect, Uncle, we won't."

Bayang couldn't help admiring the hatchlings who had matured into fledglings in so short a time.

"You're wasting time arguing with them, Uncle," Bayang said. "I've tried that many times already, but their heads are harder than stone."

"And hearts bigger than their bodies," Uncle Resak said with a grudging grin.

Bayang shrugged. "You've seen what they can do in battle." She faced the hatchlings. "You can stay, but during the fight you have to follow orders, just as I'll be obeying Uncle Resak's commanders." She jerked her head at Leech. "Especially you. Don't disobey me like you did in the Wastes. It was very foolhardy."

"I was just trying to protect you," the hatchling protested.

She relented a little. She couldn't treat him as if he were a helpless hatchling anymore. He deserved some respect. "Yes, and you fought well. But"—she thrust her head forward so they were eye to eye—"don't do it again."

"Uncle, there's no place for them in the defense plans," a fox objected.

Uncle Resak held up a paw. "No, the dragon's right. I've seen these cubs in action. We can use this bloodthirsty little pack. Take them straight to Taqqiq. Tell him they'll be part of our reserve."

"Reserve?" Leech asked suspiciously. "Is that a fancy word for hiding?"

"You don't know the palace like my clan does." Uncle Resak tweaked Leech's ear playfully. "Our defense won't be a regular battle line. We'll pick them off one by one and drive them into a trap. I'll use the reserve when we can destroy them. Will that satisfy your pride?"

"But—," Leech began to protest.

Uncle Resak was already stomping in his transformation dance. In a moment, his shape blurred and he became a huge bear again, though he held his staff in one paw. "Now join the reserve." When the hatchlings still looked like they were going to argue, he held up his staff. Somehow it added to his already considerable authority. "Against my better judgment, I'll let you fight. But how and when I say. Understood?"

The hatchlings reluctantly nodded their heads and followed the impatient fox into a side tunnel. Only Koko seemed glad about the momentary reprieve. As a precaution, Bayang brought up the rear, glancing behind her for invading monsters.

"Hurry, hurry," the fox yipped at them. "We don't have much time."

With the moss on their feet, though, it was hard to run.

"I'm taking mine off," Roxanna said impatiently. Putting a hand on Upach for support, she pulled the moss from her feet.

Impulsively, Leech, Koko, and Scirye did the same, but while Roxanna was able to skate along smoothly, they skidded and thumped against one another and the walls, to the growing impatience of their guide.

A family of foxes trotted past, bundles tied to the adults' backs. The kits, who were almost as big as their parents, had their own smaller packs.

"You've done evacuation drills," Bayang noted.

Their guide nodded, stepping to the side as a mother led a group of young wolves after the foxes. "There are hiding places with plenty of supplies deeper in the palace, as well as escape tunnels."

Eventually, they entered a large auditorium-size room where about a hundred foxes, wolves, and bears waited. Strangely, most of them had their eyes closed.

Taqqiq growled irritably when the fox told him it was Uncle Resak's orders that Bayang and the others were to join his force. Glancing from the hatchlings to Bayang, the wolf snarled, "I like dragons even less than humans."

Koko put up a paw timidly. "Uh, how do you feel about badgers?"

"Oh, I like them fine," Taqqiq said, and licked his lips pointedly. "The fat makes them so succulent, you see."

"Heh, heh." Koko laughed nervously. "Good thing I went on a diet." And he folded his forepaws over his stomach, trying to squeeze himself so he would look slimmer.

As they made their way over to an empty spot, they heard a bear complain loudly to his neighbor, "Everything was fine until these strangers showed up. Then the next thing you know we were being invaded."

Scirye was about to reply hotly, but the griffin quieted her with a touch as he always did. Leech's shoulders slumped guiltily.

Suddenly the chamber went dark. Not just the dark of night, because the stars give off a faint light even when there is no moon. The darkness now was the complete absence of light. It was impossible for Bayang to see her paw in front of her face.

"Yee-owch," Koko screamed.

Taqqiq barked loudly, "What's going on?"

"I . . . I think I sat on an icicle," the badger said.

There was harsh laughter from around the chamber. They heard the high voice of a fox: "How are you going to help us if you can't even see what you're sitting on?"

Darkness held neither terror nor confusion for Bayang, who was used to swimming in the sea depths where no sunlight ever reached. But it still took a moment for her eyes to adjust. *That's why the defenders had their eyes closed,* she realized. *They wanted to be able to see in the dark sooner.*

"You always planned to shut off the light from the ice worms," she said.

"In our drills, we practice moving in pitch-blackness," a fox said grimly.

A bear gave a deep, ominous laugh. "We hunt best in the dark."

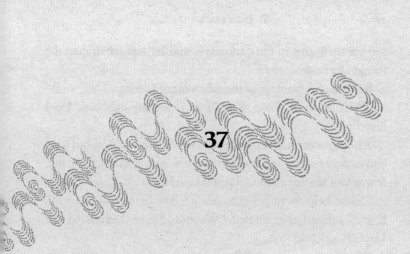

37

Leech

Leech stood, unsure of what to do next, when he felt Bayang's paw pat his shoulder. "It's safe to sit where you are."

It was reassuring to feel the dragon's bulk next to him. He eased himself down on his haunches in the place where he had been standing. Despite his harsh words, she was still trying to take care of him.

He sat guiltily while Bayang helped Scirye, Upach, and Roxanna in the same way.

He had said such mean things to Bayang before. Ashamed, he cleared his throat. "Bayang, I want to apologize again for what I said in the Wastes."

"They were just words," the dragon said—he could almost

see her shrugging in the darkness—"and far less harsh than the things I've done to you."

Koko took advantage of the momentary silence.

"Psst, Bayang," Koko said. "I can't see my caboose. Am I bleeding?"

After a moment, the dragon said distastefully, "No, but trust you to find the only spot where there was an icicle sticking out. Step a foot to your right and you'll be fine."

"Some help we're going to be. It's like being inside an ink bottle," the badger grumbled. "We should have skedaddled like Uncle Resak said to do."

"Too late for that now," Bayang said in a low voice. "Just stay close to me."

As he sat there with his knees up against his chest and his arms wrapped around his legs, Leech knew that he would do just that. He'd find a way to show her that he trusted her.

He'd been so lost in thought that it was only now that he noticed that his eyes had gradually become adjusted to the darkness. All around them were glowing eyes, the highest pairs belonging to the bears and the lowest to the foxes.

He hated combat, beginning with the struggles in the nooks and crannies of the orphanage where the bullies took their victims because the staff never went there. And standing back-to-back with Koko in street brawls, he had swung his fists out of desperation rather than rage.

Even though Primo had been refining Leech's martial skills, he had always emphasized self-defense rather than attacking. Perhaps Primo had sensed that Leech's heart wasn't in fighting. So he didn't understand why he was suddenly hearing a voice that took such delight in battles.

Occasionally in the distance they heard a howl and a gigantic crashing noise from some battle, but all he could do was imagine what horrors were coming for him. He decided that waiting in the dark was worse than any battle itself.

He fingered the disks on the armband in frustration. If only he could fly. With the disks, he'd gone from being a gutter rat to someone special. When he was flying by himself, he felt as free and comfortable as Kles and Bayang. If he could have fought from the air, he would have had more confidence.

However, even when the corridors had been lit, they'd been too narrow and too twisting for him to fly. Now that they were in the dark he knew it would be impossible. And that dumped him right back in the gutter again, which made him increasingly uneasy.

His hand found the other band and he changed it into the weapon ring. It was as light as if it were made out of cotton candy and yet he knew it was as strong as steel.

As he felt the familiar hum in his palm, the inner voice whispered to him, *You have this. You don't have be scared of any bullies ever again—not humans, not dragons, not monsters, not Roland.*

Leech recalled that strange bloodthirsty battle rage that had seized him back among the Wastes. If he let it take him over again, he would be as dangerous to his friends as his enemies. He shut out the voice though it screamed in rage. Even if it put him at risk, he couldn't give in. He would rather have something happen to him than harm his companions.

So Leech fought a battle within the palace not against Roland but against himself. And even though Leech's friends were around him, it was a very lonely fight, but he won at last.

He became aware then of fur rustling and claws clicking on the ice as clan warriors stirred restlessly. Then came a screech that made him grit his teeth.

Szzz-eee.

It repeated in a slow, steady rhythm: *Szzz-eee. Szzz-eee.*

"What's that?" Leech pulled back his coat sleeve to expose the Dancer's ribbon so he could see.

Ever since he'd gotten the ribbon, he'd been studying it, but it was handiest for Koko's suggestion as a flashlight.

The ribbon glowed faintly at first but grew brighter when Leech touched it. All around him, he saw animals turning their heads in surprise at the intense light.

"Cover that thing," Taqqiq barked. "We don't want to lose our night vision."

Shamefaced, Leech yanked the coat sleeve back over the ribbon, and the room was instantly dark.

Scales rasped against one another as the dragon bent her neck and lowered her head. "I think they're using a stone to sharpen their claws," she said.

Leech spoke in a whisper, hoping no one else heard him: "Sorry. I guess I'm a little jumpy. Were . . . were you ever scared before a battle?"

"All the time," Bayang sympathized in a low voice. "Just like I am now. Being scared isn't cowardice. It's wisdom."

"Thanks," he said, but Bayang's words didn't really reassure him. The last thing he wanted to do was turn tail and leave his friends in the lurch.

Szzz-eee. Szzz-eee. Szzz-eee. The noise came from a different part of the room as the stone was passed on. Round and round.

The sound seemed to put everyone on edge, and the clan warriors around them stirred even more. So tense was the clan that they did not speak except to growl in low voices at the echoes of the distant struggle. They had only one thought, one desire—to defend their home. There was no place for idle conversation to pass the time. Even Koko, who normally talked your ear off, picked up on the mood of the room and stayed quiet.

Leech heard again the patter of a fox messenger and then Taqqiq barked out something short and harsh. Around them, the clan warriors rose as one, just as silently as they had waited. As scared as Leech was, it was almost a relief to stand back up.

Bayang spoke softly to each of the other friends in turn and then her paw took his wrist and guided it against her side. "Stay close to me. And no heroics when we get there."

He felt Koko's paw next to his hand. He was sure Scirye and Roxanna were holding on to Bayang the same as he. Upach would be staying protectively near his mistress, as would Kles.

Claws clicked against stone-hard ice, angry tails whispered as they whisked at the air, and a breeze brushed Leech's cheeks as the warriors surged out of the room.

Leech and his friends shuffled through the slippery corridors that had once been so filled with laughter and light and were now eerily silent and dark. Taqqiq had detailed a young wolf to make sure the human cubs stayed with the reserve, and she did so with a warning *whuff* or nudge of her muzzle like a dog guiding particularly stupid sheep.

The reserve padded along at about the same speed as a human walking fast, but even that pace was enough to leave Leech and the others behind. Without their nursemaid, they would have become hopelessly lost.

Fortunately, when the reserve halted they managed to catch up. Leech would have plowed into the warrior ahead of him, but their nursemaid turned sideways like a furry barricade. Somewhere up ahead, Taqqiq was talking with a fox—another messenger perhaps, because after a moment Taqqiq barked another set of commands and the clan swung around.

Moving back the way they had come, Leech and the others were suddenly at the head of the column, but not for long. The others slipped past them like shadows until they were again at the rear.

They caught up with the reserve once more only to have it march in a totally different direction after receiving orders from another fox messenger.

By the time they had repeated the process three more times, Leech was ready to scream. Sometimes it seemed to him that they were going downward rather than forward or backward. He was ready to take out his frustration on someone with his weapon ring.

"Why don't they make up their minds?" Koko grumbled.

Bayang's talons bit into the ice floor with crunching sounds. "Uncle Resak said their plan was to hit and then run," she explained, "which is smart against guns. The darkness takes away much of the freebooters' advantage in weapons. And the clan knows the layout of the palace and Roland's men don't. But that means the battlefield will keep shifting from place to place. When it does, we must be moving to catch up with the new struggle."

As they stood in the blackness, waiting yet again, Leech felt the mist wrap itself around his ankles like cold, damp snakes.

"Oh, great," Koko complained. "Now there's fog."

"The explosion must have heated up the air," Kles reasoned. "When that air came in contact with the ice it created the vapor, and it's drifting through the corridors now. That could help Uncle Resak's clan even more."

Leech almost jumped when he heard the noise from overhead, as if a herd of cattle were stampeding toward him from overhead. The icy roof began to glow with a weird purple light and there was a flash as bright as lightning and a roar like thunder. Was it a storm within the palace?

Bayang studied the ceiling. "We must be on a lower level."

"I thought we were moving downward for a while," Leech said.

Suddenly humans shouted and guns roared overhead. Through the ice above he saw their silhouettes as their weapons flashed. The humans seemed to be gathering in a defensive circle, but at its center was a strange tubelike shape that writhed. It seemed to be about twelve feet in length, with all sorts of bumps and rough patches along its side, like a giant worm with acne.

"What's that?" Scirye gasped.

"A Tizheruk, Lady," Roxanna said.

"It's sort of knobby, isn't it?" Scirye asked.

"The bumps are caused by parasites, or skin that grows over barnacles that latch on," Roxanna said. "Whales are the same way. The young ones are sleeker, so this must be one of the older ones."

The monster was big enough to crush a human with one blow of its body.

I hope the defenders have destroyed the others, Leech decided.

Shadowy beasts skated and danced on the edge of the humans' circle like angry clouds whipped about by a hurricane. They howled and growled defiantly. Every now and then a bullet found one of them and they went down, but the others didn't retreat. They kept on wheeling around the intruders.

With a shock Leech realized that the clan warriors were herding the surviving invaders together before they sprang the final ambush.

The faint light filtering down from above let him see the others now. With their comrades fighting and dying so near them, it was hard for the company to keep silent. They shifted restlessly from paw to paw. Next to him, a wolf spun in a circle as if impatiently chasing her tail.

A bear in the company, eager to join the struggle, began to rumble in sympathy until a sharp word from Taqqiq cut him off.

The veteran barked a series of low commands and in the overhead twilight he saw dozens of bears slipping from the company to gather a few paces away. There they reared up a little bit away. Scrambling up their backs were foxes who stood upon the bears' shoulders and heads so their forepaws could scrabble at the ice. Their limbs were a blur as their claws raked the ceiling, and the shavings swirled around them like snowflakes.

Leech heard a click and turned. In the dim light from overhead, he saw Scirye hand her axe over to Roxanna. Upach had taken out the curved dagger that was so deadly in her hand.

Scirye was wiping the sweat from her hands onto her coat before she pulled the gauntlet over one hand. Kles was perched on her shoulder, arching his back and fluttering his wings, stretching before the exertion of battle. And the boy couldn't see what protection the leather would provide against bullets. She smiled nervously at him as she took out the stiletto.

Leech put away the axes. He realized he had even less practice with them than with the armband weapon. Taking off the armband, he changed it into the weapon ring again. *Yes, this feels a lot better than the axes,* the boy thought.

Koko had taken out an axe and was eyeing the blade.

Bayang lowered her head and whispered to the badger. "Do you really know what to do with that?"

Koko shrugged. "What's to know? You swing it at something."

"Wouldn't it be more effective if you changed into a creature more deadly?" the dragon asked, and then added, "If you can?"

"I didn't miss every lesson," Koko said defensively, and changed into a miniature dragon. Unfortunately, he retained the same silhouette he had as a badger, so that unlike Bayang's body, with its sleek lines, Koko's was wide of hip, with stubby legs and short forelegs.

"That," Bayang sniffed, "is insulting."

"Picky, picky, picky," Koko said. In another instant, he became his lumpy version of a wolf. "Satisfied?"

Several wolves nearby swung around, pulling back their lips in a snarl.

"Change back," Leech warned, "before they take you apart."

"Everybody's a critic," Koko grumbled, and returned to being a badger.

Bayang scratched her snout. "I think we'll work on your transformation skills later."

"You could have saved me a lot of trouble," Koko complained. His belly rumbled. "All that shape-shifting makes a guy hungry too."

The blizzard of ice shavings stopped abruptly and a fox yipped something to Taqqiq. Taqqiq gave another low command and the foxes leapt down. The foxes dropped to all fours but stood up again, this time with small hammers in their paws. They swung the tools awkwardly as they began to rain blows at the weakened ice.

It was as if a giant crystal plate had broken overhead. Ice fell in splinters as sharp as Scirye's stiletto and some chunks as big as refrigerators. Fog billowed downward. And within the mist fell screaming freebooters. But then a huge serpentlike horror crashed on top of them and they fell silent.

Leech figured it must be a Tizheruk in the flesh. The monster was about ten feet long and four feet wide and it seemed to be mostly head attached to a large fluked tail. Its head was blunt like a moray eel's, with a long jaw filled with daggerlike teeth.

Even though its black eyes were as large as Leech's fist, they seemed too small for a creature that size.

Near the base of the skull were gill slits, and just behind them long, bony fins protruded. They were strong enough to support the Tizheruk's head, giving it rudimentary legs. Its body broadened into a forked tail as large as a sail. And from head to tail its skin was as knobby as the older one they had seen. So it must have had the same problem with parasites.

The Tizheruk thrashed about, wrapping itself in streamers of mist and throwing frozen rubble around like pieces of cardboard.

At a command from Taqqiq, a blade of bright flame stabbed through the dimness, licking against the Tizheruk's hide. With a roar, the monster drew back.

Leech saw a bear with a blowtorch driving the creature into a ring of wolves and foxes. At another order from Taqqiq, the squad sprang upon the monster from all directions, savaging it. The Tizheruk's head was so big it could only swing it and its end clumsily. As a result, it was always too late when it tried to bite one of its speedy attackers or club one with its tail. In a narrow tunnel, where you could only assault from the front, the Tizheruk would have a formidable advantage, but in a large room—like this one—its sides were vulnerable.

When the monster had fallen below, it had already been weakened by dozens of bleeding bite wounds, and now the clan warriors were tearing large chunks from its hide. After only a few moments, the monster was already moving slower.

Another squad of animals was taking away the freebooters' weapons and gathering them in a cluster. The humans stood, dazed and frightened, as if waiting to wake up from their nightmare.

Not all the bears and foxes had survived the collapse of the ceiling, but the remaining bears gathered side by side in a line just beneath the rim of the hole. Squatting, this time they lifted sturdy wolves up to their shoulders. The wolves in turn stretched upward, trying to grasp the edge and form living ladders, but their paws flailed in vain just a few inches short.

Above them, a few of the intruders were recovering from the shock. Shots began to ring down. A wolf howled and toppled backward off a bear.

"Stand back and don't go up until I do," Bayang instructed Leech and the others. Then she said to Taqqiq, "Wait. Let me help."

The dragon's outline blurred and the air around her began to sparkle as she drew in the elements she needed. When Bayang's shape sharpened again, she had swelled to twice her former size, knocking over the nearest animals who had not gotten out of the way like the children.

The sight of a giant dragon shooting upward through the opening threw off the freebooters, but only for a second. The next, shots were pinging off Bayang's scales.

Ignoring the bullets as if they were mosquitoes, Bayang stretched forward to form a sturdy highway for the clan warriors.

"Poor guys." Koko shook his head. "The first wave is going to get gunned down."

Leech had caught a glimpse of the floor above. It seemed to be a large chamber with a high domed ceiling.

"Not if I can help it," he said. He'd had enough of being on foot and slipping and sliding. If he tried that up above, he'd wind up on his rump in the middle of a battle. So he pulled the disks from his armband and spat on them. "Change," he said. As soon as his fingers had traced the magical sign, the wheels were whizzing in front of him.

"Bayang said to wait here," Scirye protested.

"I'm tired of doing nothing while the clan dies," Leech said, and stepped onto the whirling circles. His heart leapt as it always did when he sprang into the air.

"You're right," Roxanna said. Tucking the axe into her belt, she skated over to a fallen freebooter and removed a bandolier full of bullets before she headed toward the discarded rifles.

Scirye pointed overhead. "Kles, help Leech and Bayang."

"But Lady—," the griffin tried to protest.

"You can protect me best by distracting the freebooters up above," she said. "Now go!"

Kles bowed his head. "As you wish," the griffin said, and sprang into the air. With rapid beats of his wings, he caught up with Leech as he flew upward. They darted over Taqqiq, who was already climbing onto Bayang.

Leech took stock as soon as he popped out of the hole. Purple fire imps glowed in a handful of lanterns that the invaders had brought and which had now been set on the floor. By their light, he could see that he was in a vast circular chamber into which a dozen corridors led. The room was easily several hundred feet in diameter and eight stories high from the floor to the center of the dome. An ankle-deep layer of fog billowed around above the floor.

There were about fifty freebooters in a ring around the hole, some in fur coats, others in white parkas. Their uniform trousers were patched—as if the ex-soldiers had replaced their army-issued gear with whatever they could steal.

Most of them looked as stunned as their comrades who had been captured below. The raiders had formed a circle to make a last stand—only to have Taqqiq and the others erupt from below into the very middle of their formation. Sandwiched now between two sets of enraged defenders, most of the intruders had lost heart.

Five of them, though, were raising rifles toward Leech and Kles. A man with a pistol—most likely their officer—was hollering at the rest of his survivors to shoot.

Leech's first reaction was to cringe and duck, but suddenly he heard the voice: *Fool, you can't outfly a bullet, but you might be able to outfly the eyes aiming at you.*

Guessing that the only way he was going to survive was to let the voice take over, he gave in. Immediately, he found himself raising the ring over his head as he swooped down.

The griffin, wings half-folded against his body, raced past. "Tarkär, Tarkär!" Shrieking his war cry, Kles struck the officer's head with four sets of paws. It was as if a whirlwind of claws and a beak had engulfed the officer. Screaming, the man fell to his knees, his revolver thudding onto the ice and skidding away.

Then it was Leech's turn. He swept his arm in an arc that knocked the first rifle aside and by luck his backstroke struck the head of the second rifleman. Leech crossed his legs like a skater and twisted as he spun.

His forward swing with the ring missed the first rifleman's head, but Leech's momentum carried him into the freebooter so that he stumbled backward.

As Leech went on pirouetting through the riflemen, he glimpsed the remaining three turning around to shoot him. That was their last mistake.

Taqqiq struck one of those three, bowling him over. Bayang had stretched a foreleg and knocked over the remaining pair.

Now, the voice said, *knock out the dragon while she isn't looking.*

Leech had been waiting for something like this. "No," he said to himself. He spun sideways as he and the voice fought for control, the cavern whirling around crazily. And then he was himself again—though he was not sure how.

As he straightened up, the rest of the company were surging up Bayang's back and sweeping over their enemies like a fanged tidal wave.

Having taken care of his opponent, Taqqiq bounded toward the nearest freebooter and sprang into the air.

Horrified at the sight of the open jaws, the freebooter flung his rifle away and thrust his hands into the air. *"Jeg give efter!"* he cried.

In an amazing display of control, Taqqiq's jaws snapped shut and the wolf thumped against the freebooter instead, knocking him over. As the man cowered beneath the wolf, Taqqiq's legs trembled as he fought to contain his rage.

All around them, guns and knives were clattering on the floor as the remaining freebooters shouted the same thing in Danish—Leech assumed they were surrendering because they were also putting their hands over their heads.

"Leech, Kles," Bayang called. "Watch over Scirye and Roxanna."

The griffin's eyes were glittering with a mad battle fury, but Leech called to him, "Kles, Scirye needs you."

The griffin's head jerked up straight as he fought to control himself. "Yes, thank you," he said in a ragged voice.

Leech circled back with Kles next to him. He was glad to see a squad of bears and wolves that had formed a wall in front of his friends as they climbed up from the lower level. Upach led the way, followed by Roxanna with her borrowed rifle with the bandolier hanging from one shoulder. Scirye came next and finally Koko, both moving with shuffling steps on the ice.

"Is the fighting over?" the badger asked Leech nervously.

"All but the cheering," the boy said, hovering overhead.

"Aw, shucks," Koko said, trying to sound disappointed but not doing a very good job of acting.

Sinking her claws into the rim of the hole, Bayang flapped her good wing and managed to haul herself upward to join her friends.

By that time, the prisoners were on their knees, with their hands clasped on top of their heads. Uncle Resak, bleeding from several wounds, was leaning on his staff as he spoke Danish to one of them.

When Uncle Resak growled something at him, the freebooter started to rise angrily but sank back down on his knees when he saw Taqqiq slinking toward him, ready to leap.

With the help of his staff, the bear-man turned his back on the invader. "This worm," Uncle Resak said contemptuously, "claims that he is a patriot who is fighting to protect Danish territory and wants his company to be treated as prisoners of war. I told him that the war was over, so that even if he was a soldier once, he's nothing more than a bandit now."

Roxanna looked ready to spit at the Dane. "This scum gives no quarter. They shoot anyone they capture. You ought to do to them what you do to the hunters in the Wastes."

"The time for that kind of thing is over. I'm afraid more that these fellows know about the location of my home now." Uncle Resak nodded to Roxanna. "I'm going to ask Prince Tarkhun to act as our liaison to the other humans."

"I'm sure he'll be only too happy to help," Roxanna promised.

"As the first friendly act, we'll turn these humans over to him for trial." Uncle Resak gestured toward his prisoners.

Roxanna glared at the freebooters. "This scum is lucky that you're more civilized than they are." Her angry eyes made it plain what she would have done to them.

Despite everything, Uncle Resak had to chuckle. "I suppose you could say we're more humane than humans." He waved his good paw. "I release you from your promise to me. Soon it won't matter who you tell."

Bayang looked around, worried. "But where's Roland?"

"Slinking away if he knows what's good for him," Koko snorted.

"Uncle, his freebooters would have invaded only if you had something he wanted," Bayang said urgently.

Uncle Resak hesitated and at that moment a scarred dragon rumbled out of a distant tunnel. Iron bands armored his chest.

"Aren't we ever going to get rid of you pests?" Badik called.

Behind him lumbered the biggest Tizheruk that Leech had seen. The head was easily fifteen feet long. Just beyond its gill was a bulge about six feet long. *That*, Leech decided, *must be some parasite*.

The Tizheruk was moving too slow and was too far away to worry about now. But Badik soared into the air. "You haven't won yet, beast," he cried.

And then he swooped down, straight at Uncle Resak.

38

Bayang

Howling in rage and fear, the clan warriors raced to protect Uncle Resak, but the plunging Badik was already a green blur. Bayang knew they would never reach their leader in time.

Roxanna, standing as coolly as if she were at a target range, fired methodically, working the rifle's bolt each time to eject the old cartridge and put in a new one from the magazine, re-aiming, and pulling the trigger again.

Three shots missed and the fourth pinged off Badik's armored hide harmlessly.

Bayang knew it was up to her, dragon to dragon, as it should be. Crouching, she unfurled her wings, feeling the pain already in the injured one. She would need to time her spring just right to intercept Badik. . . .

Now!

She ignored the agony as she brought her wings down in a great stroke, hurtling into the air at a point barely a dozen feet above and away from Uncle Resak. She crashed into Badik with the noise of two locomotives colliding.

Her momentum carried him backward several yards, and rearing upward, she brought up all her legs and tried to rake him with her claws. Metal screeched as her claws scored his armor, and then his paws were able to grab hers. The two dragons twisted chest to chest, grappling with one another in an aerial wrestling match. Bayang, though, knew her injured wing would not allow her to stay aloft for very for long. She had to bring the combat to the ground as quickly as possible.

Whipping her head around on her long neck, she tried to use her skull like a club, hoping to stun him so that he would fall to the floor. However, Badik ducked; at the same time he swept his long tail with a whoosh against Bayang and flung Bayang tumbling toward her right.

Scirye gave a cry as Badik darted forward, with talons ready to gut Bayang. But Bayang had pulled her injured wing in tight against her body while flapping her good one. The motion sent her rolling to the side so that her enemy hurtled past.

Badik nearly hit the far wall before he was able to halt. He did a swift loop so he could face her again. "You'll hound me no more, Bayang of the Moonglow," he puffed, "because today I'm going to crush you as I have so many of your miserable clan."

"And today I'll pay you back for some of the misery you've caused, Badik of the Fire Rings," Bayang panted. Even though her wing pained her, she tried to fly normally because she didn't dare reveal the weakness to her foe.

Screaming their war cries, they clashed beneath the domed ceiling, swooping and circling as graceful as hawks but far more deadly. Claws clacked together in blow and counterblow. Heads darted and ducked as they tried to tear at each other's throats.

Bayang could see that trying to fly and fight in the cold was getting to the both of them. Their chests heaved already and their breath fountained from their nostrils in steamy plumes that wreathed their heads. They could not continue fighting in the air for long.

Badik must have realized it too. With a sudden motion of his wings he bolted toward the ceiling, trying to gain some height.

Bayang's own wounded wing was sending jagged bolts of fire through her with every stroke now. *You've waited all your life for this moment,* she thought to herself. *You can't give up now.* So she drove herself upward in a spiral.

Despite her best efforts, though, she could not get ahead of him, nor could he gain the advantage either. Her wing was a constant torture now and she was growing very tired.

Then Bayang heard Leech cry out, "Don't die, Bayang. I need you. We need you."

"Yes," Scirye shouted encouragingly. "Yashe, yashe!"

Kles, Leech, and Koko joined their voices to hers and soon Roxanna was copying them, echoing the ancient battle cry.

They were Bayang's friends, her true clan. She was fighting for them now and not just the folk of the Moonglow.

They're depending on you, she told herself. She felt the energy surge through her.

Then the clan warriors, ringing Uncle Resak protectively, began to bay and roar their approval.

She re-doubled her efforts so that she rose a few precious yards above Badik, but her wing was now a sheet of fire.

This will have to do, she said to herself. In a few seconds, she would not be able to bear the pain any longer and the wing would become useless.

When she was young, her old instructor, Sergeant Pandai, had pounded the same lesson over and over into Bayang's skull. She could hear the raspy voice even now: "Always control your speed and direction. A reckless dragon is a dead dragon."

Bayang was desperate. So she did something that would have fetched her a cuff on the ear from the sergeant: She snapped her wings against her sides so that she plummeted like a steel tank. She felt Badik's fangs gash her neck—but fortunately not near a major artery or vein. And then she thudded into him, an instant later, using the claws of all four paws to slash whatever she could reach—wing, chest, leg, or head.

Badik screeched in agony. There was no song that could have sounded sweeter to Bayang. As he fell, she plunged with him, her claws continuing to tear and gash.

They crashed hard against the ice, throwing up crystalline shards. Badik was beneath her and she heard his wing bones snap and he let out a groan.

In torment herself, Bayang raised her head, trying to focus her bleary eyes. When she saw his exposed throat, she opened her jaws wide.

But just as she was about to seize his windpipe and choke the life from him, she heard Roland shout, "I'm here."

Bayang started to raise her head to look for him and Badik shoved her off.

The next moment, there was an explosion and Badik and the room disappeared in a blinding sheet of white light.

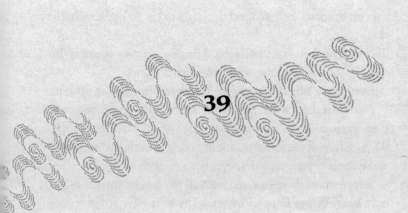

39

Scirye

Scirye's hands had flown to her mouth to stifle her cry of alarm as Bayang lay sprawled on top of the inert Badik. Then Badik gave a moan and Bayang reared her head, jaws stretching open, fangs ready to bite Badik's exposed throat.

The next moment, Scirye caught the motion from the corner of her eye. She whirled around in time to see Roland emerging from the huge bulge on the giant Tisheruk's side. Roland had squirmed out past his shoulders and in one hand was a knife and in the other was a golden sphere the size of a softball.

Too late, she realized how he had fooled them. Roland had hidden inside the bump instead of a parasite, perhaps using some spells to force his way under the monster's hide and let him breathe. While they had been distracted by the battle between the two dragons, he had used the knife to rip an opening in the skin.

"I'm here," Roland hollered. Flinging an arm up over his eyes, he tossed the globe toward the two dragons.

Even as the object descended, Badik heaved Bayang off him.

And then there was a flash as brilliant as the sun. Everyone's eyes, especially the animals', would have adjusted for the dim illumination of the lanterns. Light as bright as that would blind and daze everyone temporarily.

Scirye stood there stunned with all the others, unable to see, only hear. Wings flapped overhead as Kles flew about wildly. She heard a thump as Leech crashed against the floor.

There was the sound of flesh ripping as Roland widened the opening with his knife. "You've given me a lot of trouble for a beast, Resak," he announced. "So I'll take your head as well as your staff. And then I'll take care of the dragon and her brats."

"To me, children, to me," Resak roared, attempting to rally his warriors. "Use your noses and not your eyes."

Growling and snarling, the clan warriors began to sniff the air loudly as they tried to protect their lord.

Amid the frantic noises, she barely heard Roland's knife clatter on the ice. Straining her ears in that direction, she just made out the ominous click of a hammer being drawn back on a revolver. She could have cried in frustration. Roland would kill Uncle Resak before anyone could stop him.

Then Scirye heard Roxanna shout, "Upach, stop him!"

There was only one of Scirye's companions who would not have been dazzled by the light, and that was the ifrit who never depended on her eyes.

The scent of smoke tickled Scirye's nostrils as the ifrit raced past to intercept Roland. Scirye was just starting to cheer the ifrit on when she heard the crack of a revolver and Upach cried out.

"Do you think I'd use ordinary bullets?" Roland's mocking tone turned to incredulity. "What?" He fired a second and then a third. "Why won't you die?"

Apparently, the ifrit was still trying to obey Roxanna's orders.

Two more shots followed.

"I'm sorry, mis—," Upach began, but her voice faded away.

Roxanna's voice was full of rage and grief: "Upach!"

Roland's revolver cracked a sixth time, and this time it was Uncle Resak grunting in pain. A moment later there was a heavy thud. Despite the clan warriors encircling their lord, Roland had been able to hit Resak after finishing off the loyal ifrit.

Rage overcame all else and claws clacked on the ice as the clan warriors charged toward the spot where Roland had fired his pistol. Even Scirye ignored the danger to herself and stumbled toward where she had heard Uncle Resak fall.

She was nearly knocked off her feet by one furry body. Just as she was regaining her balance, a paw swished by her ear. Desperate to avenge Uncle Resak, the clan warriors were mindlessly attacking whoever was next to them. She was in danger of being trampled or clawed to death.

All around her were howls of rage and pain as the warriors cuffed and bit one another, more of a threat to one another than to Roland.

Scirye's heart sank when she heard him shout in triumph, "I've got it." In the confusion, Roland had slipped through the warriors and taken his prize. Already his voice was moving away as he fled. "Badik," he panted, "turn eighty degrees. The tunnel will be straight ahead. Clear the way for me."

The next instant came the noise of Badik's body crushing

anyone who got in his way, whether they were his human allies or the warriors of the clan. The thumps of colliding bodies mixed with yelps and yells of pain.

Roland's boots scraped the ice as he followed the dragon. Scirye pivoted and raced toward the sound. "He's getting away," she hollered.

"Badik, duck your head," Roland instructed his dragon. "The tunnel mouth's almost in front of you."

"Don't leave us, Mr. Roland," a freebooter hollered in English.

"You've outlived your usefulness," Roland taunted, his voice reverberating already from the tunnel.

"But you promised to help us take back Nova Hafnia," the freebooter protested.

There was a thunderous blast, and Scirye felt the burst of warm air and thought she could smell an even heavier whiff of gunpowder than that from the gunshots as ice crashed and tumbled onto the floor. Roland must have used a grenade to block pursuit.

"Kles, Kles," Scirye called urgently.

She heard the flutter of wings. "Here," Kles said, and when she raised an arm she felt the griffin's welcome weight. "But I can't see."

Kles crawled up her arm tentatively, testing each inch before he moved on. When she put a hand out to steady him, she could feel how he was trembling. He was her brave one, the smart one, the dignified one. However, the sudden loss of his sight had scared him, so she stroked him as she would a frightened kitten. His tiny tongue tickled when he licked her palm in gratitude.

When his small body had stilled a little, she shouted out again, "Bayang? Uncle Resak? Upach?"

"I'm all right," the dragon panted in pain, "but Badik got away while my eyes were dazzled by that flash of light."

"Calm yourself, little cub," Uncle Resak reassured her as well. But his words were strained. "He only hit me in the shoulder, but it hurt enough to make me lose my grip on my staff. It's really Yi's bow. Lord Yü himself gave it to me."

"So you did have part of Yi's weapon," Bayang said.

"But your staff was straight up and down," Leech said. "And it was so thick."

Remembering her archery lesson in Paris, Scirye said, "Maybe the ring makes the archer strong enough to bend it. Roland could string it then."

"I wish you'd told us," Bayang said in an accusing tone.

"I've guarded that secret even more than the location of my palace," Uncle Resak gruffed. "Not even my children knew. Do you expect me to tell strangers?"

"Upach?" Roxanna called out suddenly. The fear and worry were plain. Scirye had felt those same emotions when she hadn't known what had happened to Kles.

But Upach made no answer.

"Will someone help me find my servant?" Roxanna pleaded so plaintively that it nearly broke Scirye's heart.

Tears running freely down her cheeks, Scirye began to shuffle forward, hands groping for . . . what? The ifrit was smoke. Still Scirye stumbled on, adding her voice to Roxanna's: "Upach?"

"No hollering." Upach's voice was as thin as a wisp as she strained to talk. "It's undignified. I won't stand for it, you hear?"

As Scirye headed toward the sound, she heard the noise of another muffled explosion. Roland must have detonated another grenade to block the tunnel farther along the route. He was taking no chances. Despite their best efforts, he had escaped.

And with each second he was getting farther and farther away from justice.

Scirye moved toward the location of the ifrit's voice. First she'd take care of her friends. Then she'd take care of Roland.

And at their next encounter, she wouldn't underestimate him.

40

Leech

It took several minutes before Leech could make out blurred shapes, but once that happened his vision seemed to clear rapidly. He was grateful that the ice worms had begun glowing once more, though as yet the light in the chamber was still a soft twilight, but the Dancer was flashing and squeezing his wrist. Was it frightened again?

He slipped his fingers under his glove so he could pet it soothingly as he called out, "Koko?"

"Right here, buddy." Koko was shuffling toward him. "So that's what it's like to see lightning up close and personal," Koko said, blinking his eyes rapidly as he tried to clear them. "It's hard on the peepers."

With Koko's help, Leech stood up. He was relieved to see that

Uncle Resak was breathing. Bayang was sitting up on her haunches as she waited for her vision to come back, but except for her damaged wing, she seemed to be all right.

Kles was blinking his eyes rapidly as if trying to clear his vision while he sat upon Scirye's shoulder, but Scirye herself seemed to have already recovered some of her eyesight and so had Roxanna—enough of it anyway to try to help Upach, who was a couple of yards away from the bear-man.

The two girls knelt, patting at the ifrit's smoky body, trying to keep the small tan-colored cloud from dissipating. Within it were five dark blunt shapes that might have been the bullets.

Upach extended a smoky ribbon and feebly tried to push Roxanna's hands away. "I won't stand for this fuss, you hear? You know how upset your tummy gets when you worry like this. And then who is it who has to clean up the mess?"

"Oh, be quiet, you old worrywart. You're more important than my digestion," Roxanna scolded, trying to blink back her tears. "I'm going to take care of you for a change. So don't you die. I won't stand for it, you hear. I won't."

The ifrit appealed to Leech, who had stumbled over to the two girls. "Sir, she'll listen to you. Make her stop. I won't have my little chick sad."

Leech shook his head. "I'm sorry, but I have to agree with Roxanna. You're like her right hand." And he joined them in trying to keep the smoke together. A moment later, his joints popping, Koko added his paws to the rescue attempt.

"I won't put up with it," Upach grumbled, and tried again to shove Roxanna away, but she was even weaker now. Fast losing her ability to stay together, the ribbon broke apart.

"I think she kept trying to get Roland even after she was

hurt," Roxanna said tearfully. "That's why she's so close
to Uncle Resak. Because she kept coming, Roland rushed
things. His shot missed any vital spot on Uncle Resak, but
Roland didn't dare wait long enough to finish killing Uncle.
He just wanted to steal his treasure and leave." She twisted
around suddenly. "Please, Lady Scirye. Ask Nana to save
Upach."

Scirye's hands paused in mid-air and Leech saw his friend
break out in a cold sweat. She must have been scared of asking
the goddess for anything else. "I would if I could, but Nanaia
doesn't listen to me. I'm just her tool. You wouldn't care what a
pair of pliers thinks."

"You're her chosen one," Roxanna begged. "I saw her statue
move. And she warned you in the dream."

"Yes," Scirye said, "but I never know when she's going to do
something like that." She saw the wretched expression on Roxanna's face. "Well, if she won't do it as a favor to me, maybe I can
make her see that it's in her own interests."

Closing her eyes, she screwed her eyebrows together in intense concentration and held out her hands.

"Please don't get annoyed," she pleaded. "Roxanna and
Upach are your faithful servants and my friends. They're helping me in my quest. I need them if you want me to carry out your
plan."

When nothing happened, she opened her eyes again. "I'm
sorry. She does what she wants."

Leech's eyes cleared just in time to see despair replace hope
on Roxanna's face.

Her shoulders slumped. "I don't understand. I saw the miracle.
And then she saved us from Amagjat."

"I don't understand either," Scirye confessed helplessly. Tears squeezed out of the corners of her eyes and froze midway down her cheeks.

Roxanna turned back to Upach. While she had been distracted begging Scirye's help, her servant's body began to thin out and dissipate. Frantically, Roxanna tried to gather the escaping streamers and fan them together. "Then Upach..." Her voice broke.

Leech gave a start when he felt something extra cold and wet wrapping itself around his leg. Had Roland left behind one more bit of mischief, some sort of monster with tentacles? Puzzled, Leech glanced down and saw the streamer of mist that snaked across the floor from the blocked tunnel. A team of bears was working frantically there to clear it, heaving blocks of ice recklessly in every direction. Heat from the explosion had created a pool of water.

"Upach, could you hold your shape in water?" Leech asked.

"Better than in air," she said. The voice was barely above a whisper now.

"There's a puddle over there," Leech pointed.

The girls glanced toward it.

"What if it freezes?" Roxanna asked. "What would happen to you then?"

"I don't know," Upach confessed.

"You won't be any worse off than you are now," Koko argued. "And maybe you'll go into hibernation until Dr. Goldemar comes to help."

Together the badger and children guided the ifrit forward with gentle waves of their hands, but the cloud was much smaller by the time they reached the pool.

A large chunk of ice crashed nearby, smashing into bits. A startled bear waved an apologetic paw and then gestured for them to leave.

Roxanna ignored him, flapping her hands to create a breeze that blew Upach right over the wide, shallow pool. Small wedges of ice were already forming on the surface, but Upach slipped through the cracks and flowed like dark milk through the water. A moment later, they saw the flattened shape of the ifrit. She was now about six feet long and four feet wide but only a few inches thick.

Bubbles rose above the mouth. "Ah, that feels good," the ifrit burbled.

"Let me see the bullets," Roxanna said. "Forgive me, Upach." Reaching into the pool, Roxanna thrust her hand into her servant. She hesitated for only a second when Upach moaned. "I'm sorry," the girl said, and carefully extracted one. "It's silver and enchanted," she said, holding it up so they could all see the tiny runes and magical signs scratched into its sides.

Roxanna repeated the operation, blinking back tears as her faithful Upach groaned in pain. She did this three more times before she sat back, shoulders sagging.

"Oh, much better." Upach sighed in relief. Her voice had already grown stronger again. "Thank you, my girl. I think I'll be all right in a little bit."

Roxanna tapped the nearest bear, who turned impatiently. "My friend is in there. Please don't throw any ice into the pool."

He glanced downward, and when he understood he nodded. Then he said something to the other bears, who also bobbed their heads in comprehension.

On the way to the pool, Leech had noticed a discarded blowtorch—perhaps one of those that had been used to drive another of the Tizheruks. Leech fetched it and a small waterproof tin of matches next to it. When he handed it to Roxanna, the girl lit the blowtorch and kept it at a low flame, moving it carefully so it just brushed the surface and did not touch Upach.

"I think we'll be all right now." She even managed to smile. "See to Bayang. And thank you."

When the children approached the dragon, she was alternately wiping her eyes and blinking them as she tried to focus.

"How are you feeling?" Scirye asked.

Bayang turned her head toward the girl. "Better."

"If you don't," Koko teased, "I can always get you a great job as a carousel animal."

Bayang held up her paw in warning. "Koko, I insist that you stay on my left." Then she nodded to her right. "And Scirye, Leech, stand over here. I don't want that fuzzbag to be the first thing I see."

If the dragon could joke—at least Leech thought she was making one—then she was probably going to survive. Though her scales were scored in a dozen places, her cuts were already beginning to scab over. Bayang was one tough old dragon. She'd soon be ready for the next round.

After a short while, she squeezed her eyelids tight and then opened them. "Yes, I can see shapes now. What about Uncle Resak?"

Leech looked over to where the clan warriors huddled about their leader. An elderly woman was shaving a patch of fur from Uncle Resak's shoulder by the bright light shed from a big ice block filled with worms. The healer had both an open modern medical kit as well as the friendly but no-nonsense attitude of any doctor in San Francisco. Leech realized that one of the first human things the clan would embrace was modern medicine, especially when it came to treating gunshot wounds.

Leech didn't know if the healer knew how to treat ifrits, but maybe she would try later.

Uncle Resak was growling to Taqqiq, who was sitting faithfully next to his lord. "We must go after the thieves."

"Quiet, if you please, Lord." The healer wiped the bare patch on Uncle Resak with cotton that she had dipped in alcohol.

"It can't wait," Uncle Resak said.

With a grunt, the doctor plunged a hypodermic into Uncle Resak.

Taqqiq dipped his head submissively, but he insisted, "You are in no shape to chase them, Uncle. And the ways to the gate are blocked. It will take a while to clear the tunnel."

Uncle Resak tried to slam a paw against the ice, but the drug was already taking effect, so he merely slapped the surface. "But he stole Yi's bow," Uncle Resak protested sleepily.

Bayang winced as she struggled upright on her paws. "Even if Roland has the bow and string and the archer's ring, he doesn't have the arrows yet."

"We should have gone to the City of Death in the first place," Scirye said regretfully. "He'll get there ahead of us in his airplane."

Bayang padded across the ice, moving slowly at first but picking up speed. "But he still has to get to it. He couldn't have it land too close before the attack because that might tip us off. And if it comes to flying, we have that straw wing from the Cloud Folk."

"Well, Roland might have radioed it just before the attack began," Kles reasoned. "He could have set up a time and place to meet that way. But he still needs to swim out of here and then break through the ice. And after that, he'll have to get to the rendezvous."

Uncle Resak jerked upward as the doctor probed the wound for the bullet. When he settled back, he kept his eyes closed. "So we have a chance to stop them," Uncle Resak said, hissing with the pain. "There are other routes to the surface."

"Those are only for the fox scouts." Taqqiq's tail thumped on the ice as he thought out loud. "It's possible that wolf cubs might make it through, but it would take as long to widen them for adult wolves as it would to clear the main tunnels."

Bayang tapped her talons together as she scanned the ceiling. "Could human children get through the escape tunnels?"

Uncle Resak fought to keep his eyes open. "Yes—though it might be a tight squeeze in parts. You're way too big, dragon."

"I can shrink to their size," Bayang replied.

Koko groaned and wriggled his shoulders as if trying to shake off the soreness. "Have a heart. I ache in muscles I never knew I had. We've done our part. Let someone else take up the chase."

Bayang regarded the badger. "For most of my life, I never got to ask if what I did was good or bad. But I know it would be wrong to let Roland have his way."

Leech had never liked the dragon more than at that moment. In a way, Bayang reminded Leech of himself in the orphanage. All the children were supposed to do chores, but the others had usually skipped the unpleasant ones—so Leech had done them. It wasn't because someone had bullied him into performing someone else's work either. He had seen that the tasks were necessary ones, so he had done them, ignoring his own feelings. Bayang had been cut from the same cloth. So had Scirye, in fact, which was why he liked her as well.

Of course, the cut had not been perfect with all of his friends. Koko squinted at the dragon. "Life's a lot easier when you ignore your conscience, you know." When the others just looked at him, the badger said, "Okay, okay. I give up. But when they build statues to us, there'd better be someone keeping the pigeons off me."

"I wouldn't worry," Kles sniffed. "Even pigeons have their standards."

"Show them the tun—," Lord Resak began, and fell unconscious.

Taqqiq waved a forepaw and called an Arctic fox scout over with a sharp bark.

As the wolf gave the fox concise directions, Bayang worked the spell that shrank her to the size of the children. Even though she had been that same height on the straw wing, it still seemed strange to Leech to be at eye level with her.

The dragon looked away quickly as if she, too, found her change in perspective odd. "Now let's go."

"Wait," Taqqiq commanded. "There may still be some of Roland's vermin skulking about. We're going to check the entire palace and make sure it's clear. Let a search party go ahead of you in case there are any surprises along the route."

The clan warriors were circling among one another and baying and yelping, working themselves up before they began the search. The bears, who had been assigned to the hunt, were roaring, standing on their hind legs, and rocking from one paw to another.

Leaving Koko to see to Bayang, Leech and Scirye sidled through the warriors and back to Roxanna. "There's a healer tending to Uncle Resak. She might be able to do something for Upach," Leech suggested.

Roxanna nodded gratefully at the suggestion. "At least, until I get word to my father to send Dr. Goldemar."

Behind them, Taqqiq barked an order and the chamber cleared as the clan warriors began to fan out through the tunnels that were available.

"We're going to go after Roland now," Leech said.

Roxanna spoke as if she were biting out the words: "Get him."

The smoke swirled within the pool. "Yes, hearing he's dead would be the best cure for me," Upach burbled.

"And come back safe," Roxanna urged.

"We will," Leech promised, and returned with Scirye to Bayang and Koko.

The fox guide waited until the soldiers had gone ahead and then took them through a corridor on one side of the chamber. Three wolves and a bear accompanied them just in case. As they walked, their escorts continued to turn their heads, checking corners and testing the air. Their presence comforted Leech, who had seen how well the clan fought.

The party moved through a series of tunnels, which grew progressively smaller. In some places, the ice worms had not roused yet, so Leech pulled back his glove so the Dancer could cast its faint light.

Eventually, they had to leave the bear behind when they were reduced to crawling on their hands and knees. As the roughly finished walls closed in, they scraped their shoulders and bumped their heads. The passage began to tilt upward, and their progress slowed because they kept slipping, for they didn't have the moss on their gloves and knees.

They finally came to a passage that tapered so much the wolves had to stop. Here they had to wriggle upward on their bellies like snakes.

But the fit was so tight that Bayang's scales rasped against the ice and she gave a gasp, as the tunnel must have pressed against her injured wing.

The last thirty feet, the passage had deliberately been left free of worms so there would be no telltale glow on the surface, and Leech was told to keep the Dancer hidden as a precaution. The darkness made the boy feel as if the glacier would crush him at any moment. He heard the howling winds outside dimly now, sounding like dying ghosts.

Bayang, who was just behind their guide, stopped and flicked her tail as she whispered a warning: "We're near the entrance. Pass the word."

Leech was next and had not realized she had halted and got a slap in the face with the tail tip. "Careful with the caboose," he said, and then sent the word to Scirye, who was the fourth in line.

The clan had left a thin sheet of ice covering the entrance so it would look the same as the rest of the glacier. That meant that they had to lie still now while they waited for the lead fox to dig through the ice. Their guide's claws scraped rapidly against the surface.

That was the hardest part of their journey. As long as Leech had been moving, he hadn't thought about the darkness, but now that he could only lie there with the confining walls squeezing his arms against his sides, he felt as if he were suffocating, as if he were being buried alive in a coffin of ice. He could barely keep himself from screaming at the fox to hurry.

It seemed to take forever until the first wisp of cold air slipped through the tunnel from the opening the fox had made. Leech waited with growing impatience as their guide widened the hole.

Trying to distract himself, he made himself think about his friend Primo. Brave, kind Primo. When they had first met, Leech felt as if he had known Primo all his life. He had died all too soon, but Leech treasured their friendship. He'd been happy and, more important, he'd felt safe for the first time in a very difficult and insecure life.

Finally Bayang whispered, "It's open. Let's go."

Her hide grated on the ice as she slid upward, and Leech scrabbled eagerly after her. Since it was night up above, his eyes couldn't tell him when he had reached the surface. He was just suddenly aware that he was no longer being tightly gripped by tunnel walls. And then he crawled out of a hole in the front of the glacier and slid onto the frozen Arctic Ocean itself.

It was nighttime again. The tunnel led to a spot in the glacier a few yards above the sea surface. The face of the glacier rose a hundred yards above them like a crystal cliff, gleaming in the moonlight.

"Up you go," Scirye said, helping to pull him out of the tunnel.

Despite the magical charm protecting him, the first blast of cold made him gasp. Winds howled all around him, tearing at his clothes. Against the snow and in the dimness, he barely saw the fox scout casting about for a trace of Roland's trail. And the shimmering cloud around Bayang meant she was already swelling to a size capable of taking on Badik again.

Even though Koko was panting when he emerged, he still had enough breath to complain. "If Heaven wanted me to live in a burrow, it wouldn't have made Frisco." He collapsed on the snow-covered ice. "Give me cement and asphalt any day."

Leech stood, stretching the kinks out of his legs, anxious to be on the go after their icy confinement. "A little fresh air won't kill you."

"Yeah, it's the other critters breathing it that will," Kles griped.

Bayang stretched her forelegs in front of her like a cat. "Ah, this is a much more proper size." She turned to Scirye. "While we're waiting for a report, let's unfold the wing. We ought to be ready before we summon Naue."

Scirye took out the bundle, removed the covering, and stowed that back inside her clothes before she handed the wing to the dragon.

As Bayang unfolded it efficiently, Leech felt the irresistible desire to be up in the air away from the glacier. "I'll scout around too," he said as he pulled the disks off the iron ring.

"You should wait here," the dragon said, and then sighed. "But I don't suppose I can stop you."

Leech couldn't help noticing the change in phrasing. In the past, she would have ordered him to stay put. But now she seemed to be treating him more like an equal. "I only promised to follow your orders inside the palace. We're outside now." He grinned as he worked the spell on the disks.

"Don't take any unnecessary risks," Bayang said. "If you see Roland and Badik, come back and fetch us."

Leech could feel the sky pulling him. "Will you quit fussing like a wet hen?" The need to escape the ice and be free was irresistible. He jumped upon the rings and began to rise.

He didn't care how cold the winds were, he felt like laughing now. The sky was where he belonged, not plodding through the snow, not trapped in ice. His body instinctively adjusted for the pushing and pulling of the air currents.

He circled over his friends below. He felt the Dancer tickling his wrist, and when he looked at it he saw the ribbon was wriggling—as if it was as happy to be in the air as he was.

"I'll come back as soon as I spot them," he promised Bayang. Then, with a cheery wave, he swooped down to skim along the surface, rising and falling to its undulations.

In the moonlight, a fox's tracks looked like rows of neat little stitches on a white shirt and Leech followed them until he saw the fuzzy fox. Because the newly fallen snow was loosely packed and her legs were short, she moved along in a bobbing motion.

"Which way to Nova Hafnia?" Leech asked, reasoning that Roland was most likely going to take a direct route there.

The fox rose on her haunches and pointed.

"Thanks," Leech said, and headed that way, feeling almost as if he were drunk as he zipped along.

His eyes were scanning his surroundings for any sign of Roland when the ice ahead of Leech suddenly exploded. Crouching, he weaved and dodged the falling lumps of ice. He was still thirty feet away from the opening when Badik's head thrust out of the water and he flung himself toward the jagged edge of the hole. About a foot of the crust broke under his weight, but the rest of it held and he crawled out of the water.

Roland was clinging to his back and water rilled downward from the pair.

Leech remembered his promise to Bayang, but as he circled, getting ready to return to the glacier, he saw Roland frantically re-loading his revolver. Maybe this was their chance to knock him out while he couldn't fire.

Don't wait, the voice urged. *You'll never have a better chance.*

Taking off his other armband, Leech changed it into a weapon as he executed a loop and headed back. As he picked up speed, he felt a fierce exultation.

Yes, take care of them first and then the dragon, the voice whispered to him.

Who are you? Leech asked the voice. *What did you mean when you said that you were me?*

I'm you, the first Lee No Cha, the voice snickered.

Startled, Leech lurched, almost piling into the snow, but

righted himself in time. He remembered what Bayang had told him about that Lee No Cha: how he had killed a dragon prince and then skinned him and turned part of his hide into a belt.

Did you really murder a dragon? Leech asked.

He had it coming, the voice said defiantly.

Leech felt his horror and revulsion grow. *And then you skinned him.*

I needed a present for my father, the voice answered defensively.

Well, I'm not that way now, Leech told the voice. *So go away.*

I'm just trying to save you, you fool, the voice told him petulantly.

Well, if you don't shut up now, you'll get us killed, Leech ordered the voice. Gratefully, the whispering stopped.

Roland hadn't seen him yet. Instead, Roland twisted around and pointed his pistol at the ocean. A second later, a narwhal horn stabbed out of the choppy water and a slick, domed head peered out. The narwhal disappeared before Roland fired. The bullet sent spray upward. Another horn rose and a different narwhal bobbed to the surface. Again Roland missed.

A sea otter scrabbled out of the hole. Then a second and a third. However, their short legs floundered in the snow that covered the ice. Still more came in a determined dark, furry wave—far more little warriors than Roland had bullets for. So wheeling around, Badik began to gallop away. There was no way the otters could keep up with a dragon on their stubby legs.

So Leech would have to fight in the otters' place. Lifting the ring above his head, legs crouching, muscles tensing for a blow, he sped to intercept them. Badik saw him and snarled, "It's one of those brats again."

"We'll get rid of one of them at least," Roland snapped.

When he saw Roland raise his pistol, Leech jinked back and forth through the air, wondering just how many shots Roland had. The boy had heard of some guns that held as many as eight shots.

A shot whizzed by his ear. He banked sharply to his left and the next missed him by a wide margin. He executed a roll that now had him charging toward Badik's flank.

Roland took aim. He was smiling.

Leech rocked from side to side like a pendulum, making himself a more difficult target.

Roland's bullet zipped past him a little closer than the boy would have liked.

If only it were snowing, he could use that as cover.

Fool, make your own snow, the voice said to him.

The last thing he wanted to do was listen to the voice, but he had no choice. And at least this suggestion from it was practical rather than bloodthirsty.

He darted downward, skimming just inches above the surface. *Faster,* he told himself. *Faster.* He heard the hiss behind him and saw snow spraying upward in his wake.

He zigged and zagged crazily, keeping one eye out for any rises and raising a white curtain that hung in the air. He could barely see his enemies as silhouettes, and if that was so, they would be having the same trouble. A shot went wide of its mark. So his artificial snowfall was working.

He tried to be unpredictable when he changed directions, but he always kept narrowing the gap toward the faint outlines of dragon and rider until he was on them and swinging the ring. The Dancer was squeezing his wrist tight with fright now.

In the last moment, though, Badik swerved to his left, at the same time whipping his tail around.

It was like being hit by a scale-covered club the size of a tree. The frozen sea whirled around Leech as he spun out of control through the air and into the snow.

And into the darkness.

41

Bayang

They all gave a jump when they heard the explosion several miles away. Spray and ice rose into the night as fluffy and delicate as a waving feather.

Bayang started to rise when she remembered she was anchoring the unfolded straw wing. "Roland's surfaced," she said excitedly.

Koko scanned the horizon anxiously. "But where's Leech?"

Bayang had been uneasy the moment he had flown off, and her apprehensions had only increased with every second he was gone. It would be just like the overconfident little fool to take on Roland and Badik by himself instead of retreating.

She thought of Leech, alone and outmatched, facing their enemies without her, and she felt a terrible fear twisting her insides. Why? It wasn't her fault. She'd tried to warn him, but the little idiot would break his promise to her. And yet her anxiety had made her as taut as a bowstring.

The sooner they got to him the better. "It's time to call Naue."

Scirye scanned the heavens as she scratched her head. "Did he tell us how?"

Too late, Bayang realized it too. "No, he didn't. He rushed off in such a hurry that I forgot to ask."

Koko shook his clenched paw at the sky. "You big, worthless airbag! Why didn't you tell us something important like that?"

"We could try calling his name." Tilting her head back, Bayang began shouting to Naue. The others joined in.

When nothing happened after several minutes, Koko stamped a hind paw. "Aw, we can't wait for that blowhard. We got to get to Leech on our own."

The top of the glacier seemed so very far away to Bayang. "We need some height to launch the wing ourselves." She tried to unfurl her injured wing, and the agony lanced through her.

Concerned, Scirye said, "You can't fly with that bad wing of yours." She tried to get a grip on the icy surface and could not. "But you and Koko might be able to climb up there with your claws. And maybe I could hold on to your back."

Time was the problem. They never seemed to have enough. "Climbing would take too long." Even as they discussed what to do, Leech might be dying. Wincing, Bayang forced her bad wing to open. "I think I can stand the pain long enough to carry you and the wing up there."

Kles coughed. "You'll pardon me for saying this, but I beg to differ. At the moment, you look dreadful, and you haven't even tried to use your wings yet."

"I can't sit around while Leech could be in trouble." Bayang crouched, hooking her claws into the straw surface. "Hop on."

Fear for his friend had overcome his usual fear of danger, so

Koko was the first to scramble up on the dragon's back. Scirye followed while Kles rose into the air, circling a little to the side.

Bayang brought her wings down and tried not to gasp at the stabbing pain. With every beat after that, the ache spread from her wing through her shoulder. The top of the glacier seemed an impossibly long way off, but she told herself not to think like that. Instead, she concentrated on the next wing stroke, the next breath.

A worried Kles fluttered near her head. "Go back while you can."

The foot of the glacier looked just as far away as the top, and Bayang was not sure she could break her descent once she started. "I think it's already too late for that," the dragon puffed.

"Of course you can reach it," Scirye urged, and then scolded her griffin. "Don't distract her, Kles."

Yes, this is my penance for all the harm I've done Leech, Bayang told herself. Faces flashed through her memory of his other lives, young faces, frightened faces. And they merged into Leech's face as he was now in this life. Scared not of her but of Roland and Badik. Alone. A novice at flying and fighting with a ring he barely knew how to use. Battling with more courage than sense or skill. They would make short work of him unless she could stop them.

She had to go on. It didn't matter that they were of two different species. And so what if he insulted her? Or if he eventually despised her one day. She had to protect him. It would not make up for everything in the past, but it would be a start. She would save his silly little hide no matter what the cost.

Clenching her teeth, Bayang drove herself upward yard by yard until her eyes were level with the glacier's top. By now, her back and chest were hurting as well.

Another yard. She had already asked too much of her tortured wing. She couldn't keep from giving a little groan.

Through the red cloud of agony that filled her mind, she heard Scirye say, "Leech needs us."

She thought of Badik looming over a helpless Leech, and she forced herself up another yard, her body on fire.

Suddenly there was no shining crystal wall in front of her, only open air. She had reached the top. Through the haze, she dropped the straw wing onto the snow-covered ice. As much as she wanted to collapse, she had to move farther on or she might crush the wing. Somehow she managed ten more yards before she skidded along the glacier, piling up the snow in front of her and exposing a wide strip of ice behind her.

42

Scirye

Scirye slid off Bayang's back. With her wings still spread, the dragon lay like a sinking sailing ship. If it were not for the heaving of the dragon's sides, Scirye would have thought her friend was dead.

Scirye knelt and brushed the stray snowflakes from Bayang's head. She had never seen any creature as beautiful as the dragon. Even now, the dark green scales, moistened by some melting flakes, gleamed like jewels.

Scirye had felt how Bayang's sides had heaved with the effort, seen the labored strokes of her wings, and guessed at the cost in pain. Leech meant so much to the dragon. Whatever had happened between them in the past was ... well ... in the past.

"Is there anything I can do for you?" Scirye asked.

The dragon just moaned, her warm breath steaming the air as

it left her nostrils. Scirye was so worried that she became reckless.

I don't care what it costs me, Scirye silently said to Nanaia. *Please help my friend. She's suffering so much.*

Scirye remembered how Roxanna had pleaded with her to help Upach, because every word had been etched into Scirye's heart. The Kushan girl understood Roxanna's despair when nothing had happened.

Scirye had been unable to aid Upach then. She was unable to aid Bayang now.

"We need Bayang. What's the point of saving us from the hag," the frustrated girl demanded, "if you're going to let us fail now? Don't you care? Why play these games?"

Scirye listened to the whisper of snow as a breeze blew the light coating away from the glacier's top. She pulled back her glove long enough to look at her palm, but the mark wasn't glowing. There was no sign of acknowledgment.

Scirye was sure some philosopher could come up with reasons why Nanaia came at the oddest times and yet was absent when Scirye really needed her. However, Scirye was like Prince Tarkhun. Deep thoughts were for other people. What she cared about was deeds. And she was now feeling very exasperated with the goddess.

Timidly, the girl stroked a scaled cheek, wondering how dragon nurses comforted their patients.

Kles poked his head out of the coat. "I don't think she can feel that through her armored hide. That gesture is more for you than for her."

"I have to let her know we care," Scirye said, and tried a harder slap, hoping that it might be the dragon equivalent of a love pat.

An eyelid fluttered open. "Don't," the dragon warned in

measured tones, "ever do that again if you want to keep your fingers."

Scirye snatched back the offending hand and hid it behind her back. So much for trying to take care of the crusty old dragon. Bayang's attitude seemed to be recovering faster than her injured body. "Right, sorry. Can I do anything to make you comfortable?"

"Yes, stop babbling," Bayang murmured. "I'm trying to master the pain. In the meantime, make yourself useful and anchor down that wing somehow before it blows away."

Scirye noticed how the dragon's jaw worked and the tension lines furrowed her scaled forehead. Bayang was now performing as heroic a mental feat as the physical one she had just performed.

By then, Koko had scrambled off the dragon to join Scirye. "We ought to be getting after my buddy." He was practically hopping from one paw to the other with anxiety.

Scirye pulled Koko away. "Didn't you see her fighting to get us up here? She understands that, but look at her face. She's in agony and needs to control it first. She wants to rescue Leech as much as you do."

Koko scratched his jowl. "Yeah, I guess I really knew that. But I'm anxious about my buddy."

Scirye motioned between herself and Bayang. "He's our friend too." She noticed a breeze lift one side of the wing. "We can't help him if the wing drifts away. Help me find some rocks."

It wasn't as easy a task as it sounded, for though the glacier had picked up stones of all sizes, they were wedged tightly into the ice. When the friends located one and began to chip it out of the ice with the axes, they had no idea if it would be too big to move or possibly damage the weaving of the wing. It was simpler to act as their own weights and sit on the wing them-selves.

Scirye had left Kles to keep an eye on the dragon while she worked, and the griffin had perched on Bayang's paw as the most convenient sentry post. When she heaved herself up abruptly, he fell off, skidding through the snow.

"Hey!" he said.

"Do I look like a piece of furniture?" Bayang huffed.

"You must be feeling better if you're back to being an old grump," Koko said.

The lines of pain had not left Bayang's face, though. "You're still hurting," the girl said, worried that the dragon would drive herself until she was nearly dead.

"I'll have plenty of time to rest after we catch Roland. And anyway, dragons heal a lot faster than humans." Bayang cautiously furled her wings tight against her back. "At least, Badik is as bad off as I am, so the fight will still be equal."

Together, the three of them turned the wing around so that it was pointed forward like an arrowhead. "You and I will push, Koko," she said to the badger. "That means we'll have to time our leaps for the moment when momentum is carrying the wing off the glacier." Then, at the dragon's direction, Scirye got on, with the girl at the steering loops.

"Just try to keep the nose up," Badik said. The air began to shimmer around the dragon as she shrank.

The girl nodded and tightened her grip on the straw loops woven into the wing. Kles hovered overhead anxiously, though it was unclear how he could keep her aloft if something went wrong.

The straw wing itself weighed nothing at all, but its size made it awkward to shove. Digging their paws into the snow coating the glacier, Bayang and Koko began to push. The wing began to move forward, slowly at first and then faster, and suddenly its point was tipping over the lip of the glacier.

The frozen ocean looked very close and very hard and Scirye swallowed.

"Jump," Bayang told Koko, and the two hopped onto the wing as it glided downward.

The sudden addition of weight at the rear made the straw wing buck, and Scirye could hear Koko yelp and scratch at the straw, trying to find a hold. And then she was too busy to think about anything but hauling back on the loops with all her strength, because the nose was heading downward.

Bayang, though, let herself slither forward over the wing, letting gravity carry her to the girl's side. Hind paws dug into the straw to stop Bayang's slide while her forepaws gripped the steering loops as well.

The ocean was perilously close when the nose of the wing finally went up and they were gliding along. Scirye slid back to her usual spot, all too glad to surrender the controls to the dragon.

"Are we dead yet?" Koko asked. He was splayed across the straw with all his claws dug in, and his eyes were shut tight.

Scirye couldn't help feeling exhilarated that their plan had worked. "Where's your sense of fun?"

"Back there with my stomach," Koko grumbled. He sat up and then, still on his haunches, slid onto the opposite side to balance the wing.

"Kles," Scirye called to the griffin, "scout ahead of us."

With a nod, her friend folded in his wings partway and swooped downward at first to pick up speed. His forelegs were tucked against his chest, hind legs stretched out straight behind him and tight against his tail to make as streamlined a silhouette as possible.

Her heart caught as it always did whenever she saw her griffin in action. In full dive, he was the epitome of grace and speed.

A yard above the ocean, he slid his wings out so that his flight path became a curve with him shooting forward. A confident stroke of his wings sent him rocketing on, a small dot against the white expanse.

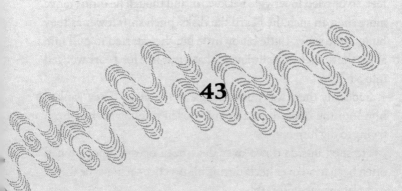

43

Leech

Leech spat snow from his mouth, but when he tried to breathe he took in more flakes of it. He tried to wipe the snow away, but his arms were pinned to his sides by cold white stuff. He was buried alive.

He fought down the panic. Lying still, he shifted his eyes from side to side. There was a little space around his head, but the slightest movement caused snow to drop on him.

When he had fallen after Badik's blow, the disks must have driven Leech deep into the snow. And as the snowflakes in the air settled, they had lightly covered the tunnel he was in now. That was probably the only reason why he was alive. Roland and Badik hadn't wanted to delay long enough to search for Leech's location.

He could still feel the disks vibrating against the soles of his feet, so he tried to wriggle backward, and though he didn't move more than an inch, he heard the disks' pitch shift lower as they bit into the snow. Little bit by little bit, they started to pull him along the tunnel. Now he knew what it was like for a cork wedged into a bottle.

Suddenly there was no resistance to the disks. They yanked him into the open, past a couple dozen otters who had been trying to dig him out.

He sped upside down over the frozen ocean. Since he had often been head over heels during his practice sessions, he wasn't completely uncomfortable.

Aching all over, he moved his arms experimentally and was relieved to see that they weren't broken. Putting his hands flat against the snow, he shoved himself cautiously upward so that he was squatting. With just as much care, he pulled his legs against his chest and then swung his feet downward so that he was right side up, adjusting for the way his feet bounced up and down during the activity.

Roland and Badik were gone, but they would have left tracks. It was one thing to fight a dragon when you had another dragon at your side and quite another to take one on by yourself. Even injured, Badik had looked very big and very deadly. Besides, Roland had a gun and Leech had . . . nothing.

He realized he had lost his weapon ring. He didn't feel whole without it. He sped back to the otters. "I've lost a large iron ring." He held his hands apart to indicate the size. "Could you look into the tunnel?" He pointed at the spot where he'd been embedded in the snow.

Obligingly, one of the otters disappeared down the hole, but he returned a moment later to shake his head.

"I was afraid of that," Leech said, biting his lip. He wasn't proficient enough to miss the ring as a weapon, but it had been with him since he'd been left at the orphanage. With the flight disks, it was the only link he had back to his past.

His eyes scanned the snow as he began to circle outward in an ever-extending spiral. At the same time, the otters started to search the area as well, but with their short legs they floundered about slowly.

Leech gave a cry of relief when he saw the dark circle lying on the snow.

He executed a loop, picking up speed at the bottom of the circle, and crouched, stretching out his hand to snatch up the ring, and then sped back toward the otters.

"Thank you for your help," he said. "Will you go back to Uncle Resak and tell him what's happening?"

Bobbing their heads, the otters began to make their way with difficulty back to the opening Roland had made in the ice. As Leech watched them leave, he heard Kles call, "Did you find them?"

Crossing his legs, Leech twisted around. He was relieved to see the griffin speeding toward him. "Yes, but I didn't do a very good job of stopping them."

"If they were easy to catch, they'd have been in jail a long time ago," the griffin said, curving around the boy. "You seem to be intact after tangling with Roland and Badik. You're lucky."

"I know it," Leech admitted.

Kles pointed his tail behind him. "The others are coming on the straw wing."

Leech listened hard for his boastful racing partner. "So Naue came?"

"No," the griffin said. "Bayang almost killed herself flying the straw wing up to the top of the glacier so we could launch it."

Leech shook his head. "It's hard to believe she could fly with those wounds. She must want to catch Badik a lot."

Kles somersaulted in exasperation. "She did it for you, you ungrateful little numbskull. I suspect she considers it part of her penance for her past sins."

"Oh," Leech said. He tensed, waiting for that inner voice to find something sinister in Bayang's sacrifice, but the voice was silent. Was it as stunned as he felt? "So she really wants to pay me back?"

Kles clacked his beak together. "And more than that. You don't fight like that to get up that cliff just because your conscience is bothering you."

"What was it then?" Leech asked, puzzled.

Kles darted in so close that Leech flinched. "She loves you like a mother!"

"That's impossible," Leech blurted out.

Kles spread both paws and wings apart resignedly. "The sad part is that I don't think she realizes it any more than you do." His eyes regarded the boy compassionately. "But maybe this is what happens when two people who have never been loved before suddenly get together."

"What do you mean? I've got Koko," Leech countered.

"Don't fool yourself. Money is a tanuki's only real love," Kles said, and then gestured with a paw. "But first things first: Roland and Badik are getting farther away. We should try to find their trail so we won't waste any more time when the wing arrives."

While Kles took the left, Leech took the right, but his mind was only partly on the task. He was thinking over what the griffin had said. Bayang would sacrifice anything for him. But what would she do if she found out he was hearing Lee No Cha? He didn't want to lose her friendship. He musn't let her know about the voice.

After a few minutes he heard the griffin shout, "I found it."

Leech followed Kles's voice until he could see it himself.

Badik's footprints were deep ovals in the snow with grooves at the top that his claws had made. Every now and then between the paw prints was a short trench when he had brought his tail down.

Kles darted back to direct the wing in the right direction while Leech soared upward until the tracks looked like stitch marks on the snow. He glided along, waiting for the others to catch up and keeping an eye out for Roland and his dragon.

"You okay, buddy?" Koko yelled up to Leech. Kles and the wing were following the marks that Badik had left in the snow.

Leech swooped downward, waving his arm. "I've had worse tumbles. Remember when that gang was chasing us over the roof-tops and I jumped?"

It was good to see the homely furry face peering up at him. "You would have needed a grasshopper's legs to make it. Lucky you landed on that shed."

"Luck had nothing to do with it," Leech insisted as he paralleled the straw wing's course. "It was skill."

Koko dismissed his words with a skeptical wave of his paw. "Yeah, right."

"You broke your promise, didn't you, and tried to stop them on your own?" Bayang demanded from the control loops.

The dragon seemed more annoyed than affectionate. Leech wondered if the meddling griffin had misinterpreted everything.

"I thought I could sneak up on them." Leech hesitated and then added, "Kles told me how hard it was to launch the wing. Thank you for what you did."

Bayang shot an annoyed glance at the griffin and then looked again at Leech. "Scirye was worried."

"Me?" the Kushan girl said. "You were just as anxious."

"Now that Bayang knows he's safe, she can afford to scold him." Kles laughed.

"I think a certain griffin should keep his little beak shut," Bayang snapped.

Leech was puzzled and a little hurt as they flew along. Was Kles making up stuff or was he telling the truth?

He needed time to think about everything, but that would have to come later—after they caught Badik and Roland. Leech wouldn't survive if he let himself be distracted by other matters.

"I'll scout ahead," he said.

"Don't go too far," Bayang warned. "We should hit them together, not separately."

After his last encounter with Badik and Roland, Leech could see the wisdom of that strategy. "Okay," he said, and flew a hundred yards in front.

If they had not been pursuing their enemies, the boy would have enjoyed racing over the frozen ocean with his friends. But they weren't here for pleasure.

He was skimming over the surface so fast that he barely noticed the long yellow strip of paper with the red writing. He circled and came around again, seeing that a lead fisherman's weight had been tied to it so it would stay in one spot.

He angled lower so that he was only inches above the snow and slowed to pick it up. The words looked like Chinese but not the modern words he'd seen in Chinatown. These looked like pictures and above them was a caricature of some demon.

What was it? Had Roland left some insult?

Compared to the guns and monsters, this seemed harmless, so Leech brought it back to the wing. "Look what I found," he said, holding it up.

"Throw it away," Bayang and Kles shouted at the same time.

"But it might be a clue if you can read it," Leech protested.

Bayang jabbed a claw at it. "It's a magical charm."

"Get rid of it," Kles added, waving his paws frantically.

Balling the paper up, Leech flung it away.

And not a moment too soon.

The paper burst with a bang and a cloud of smoke as fluffy as a cotton ball. But instead of dissipating, the smoke began to spin with a hissing noise until it was a globe. The air was filled with a howling noise as the sphere flattened suddenly into an oval.

Fierce winds began to tug Leech this way and that.

"Get away if you can!" Bayang ordered as the straw wing tilted crazily.

As Leech twisted around in the air, the snow rose in streamers like a tangled skein of white yarn to engulf him.

And then the boy was tumbling about in a howling world of white.

44

Bayang

It was all Bayang could do to stay with the wing, let alone steer it in the turbulent air. Despite Pele's charm, the wind-driven snow stabbed against her eyelids like needles. She could only imagine the pain that the hatchlings were going through.

"Hold on," she shouted. But there was no answer from any of her passengers. "Scirye? Koko? Kles?"

Through the screaming wind, Bayang thought she heard a muffled cry, but even her eyes, which could see just as well in the sea darkness as in daylight on the land, could find nothing in the swirling snow. She could not even tell if she was right side up or upside down. This must have been the whiteout that Roxanna had warned them about.

Roland had set a trap with a spell that would activate after a set period, creating an obstacle for his pursuers, and allow him to escape. The winds would suck up the snow covering the frozen ocean, creating a confusing white tempest. Stay in one place and you risked being buried and yet keep moving and you risked wandering in circles until you froze.

And the hatchling had been right at the center of the spell.

What was this terrible sense of loss, this agony? She and the hatchlings were of two different species, and as dragons measure time they had only been together for the blink of an eye. And yet she felt such pain. Such emptiness.

"Leech?" she wailed. "Scirye!"

Was it her imagination or did she see a flicker of green light in answer?

A sudden gust plucked her from the wing like an invisible hand and flung her away, the helpless plaything of the storm.

45

Leech

Unable to tell up from down, Leech was hugging his knees tight against his chest to form himself into a protective ball as the winds tossed him about. It was all he could do to breathe, for every intake of air clogged his nose and mouth with snowflakes. It was like being buried alive.

He had never seen snow before this trip and he'd be happy if he never encountered it again. He had seen, felt, and eaten more than his fill of it.

His eyes, starved for anything beside snowflakes, noticed the faint glow coming from his wrist. Suddenly he was desperate for company and he pulled his glove back to expose the Dancer's ribbon. It slipped onto his palm, where it pulsed like green flame. Snowflakes sizzled against its sides, but it did not go out or even shrink.

In the short time they'd been together, he'd come to think of the ribbon as a friend or—maybe Koko had been right—as a kind of pet. "Can you help me?" he asked desperately. "My friends and I are trapped in the storm."

The ribbon pulsed in response, but Leech wasn't sure what it meant. Leech pleaded with it for several minutes, growing as frustrated as Scirye had when she'd been asking Nanaia to aid Upach.

Then, even with the wind screaming in his ears, he thought he heard Bayang.

As hope surged through him, the voice urged, *Keep quiet. This is the perfect time to kill you and no one would ever know.*

He thought of what Kles had said. Sure, Bayang could be an awful grump, but she had never raised a paw against him personally. Instead, she had sacrificed and suffered for his sake.

No, he told the voice, *she's my friend.* And then he began to shout out loud, "Bayang? Help, Bayang!"

Suddenly he felt something tickle his wrist. It was the ribbon wriggling away and forming a compact sphere the size of a marble that suddenly flew upward, whipped about by the winds.

"Wait, come back," he called, feeling even more alone than before. Even the Dancer's ribbon had deserted him.

His back hit the frozen ocean surface so abruptly that it knocked the wind from him. Instantly, snow began to pile up around him and he fought to rise into the air again. Better to die in the sky than be buried on the land.

He wheeled through the air, as helpless as a leaf in a hurricane. All of a sudden there was a green glow to his right and he heard a sizzling sound like a giant frying pan cooking bacon. The noise increased so that the roaring wind seemed to fade into the background, and he could see stars peeking through a gap in the clouds.

He realized then that he'd been turned sideways and righted himself so the sky was now above him again and the sea below.

The hole continued to widen, green fire eating along its rim. Leech felt the elation rise inside him as he saw the Dancers flooding downward toward him. They formed a seething tunnel in the shape of a corkscrew that the pounding winds could bend but not break. As they grew closer, he heard sizzling sounds whenever the whirling snowflakes came into contact with them.

And then he was standing at the bottom of a glowing tube that stretched through the storm to the stars above.

The wispy glowing body of a Dancer spiraled around him like a twirling veil, and Leech wondered if the ribbon had rejoined it. He felt a bit of regret that it had merged with its fellows.

"Thank you for rescuing me," Leech said, "but how did you know I was in trouble?"

The Dancer pulsed in response as it circled him.

Leech would never really know. Had the Dancer understood him once the ribbon returned to its host? Or had the Dancer actually seen his predicament by means of the ribbon? Either way, he was grateful.

The Dancer wound part of itself around his wrist and tried to tug him toward the stars, but Leech twisted away, heading in the direction of Bayang's voice. "I have to find my friends."

His hands tingled as he tried to shove through the glowing wall, but as fragile as the delicate Dancers appeared, their bodies were as tough and elastic as rubber bands. They bent under the pressure but did not give way. If the winds were not strong enough to push them aside, Leech knew he could not.

The Dancers began to flash up and down the tunnel until Leech felt like he was inside a neon lightbulb.

The flashing stopped abruptly and the tunnel began to unravel, each Dancer slanting toward the frozen ocean, burning the snow as it went. Other Dancers joined with his savior to form a sheltering sphere around him.

"Bayang?" he called again.

"Here." He heard her faint cry. "Are you all right?"

Now's your chance, the voice said. *You can get away while you leave her to freeze to death.*

Leech ignored the voice again as he felt the relief wash over him. As he flew at a slant toward her, the sphere rolled through the air, keeping him in its shelter while other Dancers shot ahead to clear the way. "I'm coming. I'm okay," he called. "What about you?"

"I'm fine too," she said. "Keep talking."

"The Dancers are helping us," he said.

"Where did the Dancers come from?"she wondered.

"The ribbon brought them," Leech said. He was hovering a yard above the surface now.

"Have you seen the others?" Bayang asked anxiously. "The wind snatched us right off the wing and I couldn't catch them."

"No," Leech confessed, moving forward.

"Can you ask the Dancers?" the dragon inquired desperately.

"I'll try," Leech said, "but first let's get together."

He almost bumped into her. One moment there was a wall of swirling snow, and the next the dragon was there, head lowered against the savage winds and snow, a paw raised to plod along.

He was glad that he had not given in to that savage inner voice.

Dancers flitted around her, forming a dome large enough to hold them both. Though the dome constantly changed shape under the pounding winds, the sides held firm.

As Bayang lifted her head, surprised and grateful for the respite, Leech flung his arms around her neck.

"Am I glad to see you," he said.

To Leech's surprise, he felt her head nuzzling against him. "Not more than I am to see you. Thank Heaven. I thought I'd lost you."

After the first delightful thrill, Leech didn't know what to say and Bayang seemed to feel just as awkward. Now that they had finally acknowledged the bond that had grown between them, neither of them had a clue about what to do next. There was nothing in his abused childhood to use as a measuring stick. And he suspected that the dragon had a similar problem.

"You were right when you said words can't erase our past," Leech said.

Bayang pulled her neck up, looking uncomfortable. "Yes, unfortunately."

Desperately Leech tried to put his thoughts into words. "But I figure you and me are in the same boat. We both did bad things that we'd like to forget but can't. What's really important is that we're both trying to change."

"Yes," Bayang said slowly as if savoring the notion. "Yes, I guess we are. But I imagine there are always going to be some bumps in our way."

"But if we keep reminding ourselves that we're friends, we can get over them," Leech said hopefully.

Bayang smiled. "Words of wisdom from a mere hatchling."

Leech tried to cover up his embarrassment by saying lamely, "Well, we shouldn't be resting like this while they're in trouble. We've got to find the others."

He looked around the globe of Dancers, wondering how to find the savior Dancer among all the others. He noticed that more Dancers were arriving, tunneling through the snow in this area so that it quickly resembled pale Swiss cheese.

"What's that?" Bayang pointed to a bright green hemisphere flashing to their right.

Dancers were already clearing a path for them. "Let me go first," Bayang said. Her legs floundered through the layer of loose, newly fallen snow, but her paws trampled it so that Leech had no trouble.

They found Scirye huddled with her face against the snow, arms wrapped around Kles inside her coat. She was just looking up in amazement at the shielding Dancers.

"Am I happy to see you." She grinned. The Dancers slipped away as she stood up.

"Are you all right?" Bayang asked.

"Yes, but I'm as sick of snow as Upach." Opening her coat, she nudged the griffin with a finger. "Kles?"

He poked his head out, clacking his beak together in a yawn. "I was having such a good dream."

"Well, this could have been a deadly nightmare for all of us," Bayang said. She explained about how Roland had trapped them.

"We should go looking for Koko," Leech said.

At that moment, though, a Dancer snaked through the storm to them.

"I think they found him," the dragon said. She took the lead again while the children followed until they came to the delta-shaped wing.

"Thank you," Leech said to the Dancers, "but can you help us find our other friend?"

Together, he, Scirye, and Kles tried to ask about the badger. When words failed, the griffin resorted to pantomime, doing a credible job that would have had Leech laughing if he had not been so worried.

Even when Dancers started to serpentine away in all directions, the companions couldn't be certain their rescuers had understood. To distract themselves, the children helped Bayang fold up the wing. If she was right and the storm was localized, they could carry the wing to the border and try to launch it somehow.

The storm itself seemed to be lessening, as if the Dancers were winning the wrestling match with the winds.

Finally, a Dancer came to them. Leech could not be sure if it was his earlier savior. "Did you find him?"

The Dancer flared with a light so glaring that Leech had to squint. Then the Dancer repeated it at a rapid, staccato rate that was irritating to the nerves as well as the eyes.

"Whatever they found, it seems to be annoying them," Bayang observed.

"Well," Leech conceded, well aware of his friend's shortcomings, "that certainly sounds like Koko."

They found the badger rolling around in the snow with a Dancer wrapped around him like a glowing mummy.

Leech hurriedly high-stepped through the drifts and helped free his friend. Immediately, the Dancer zipped skyward, flashing and wriggling indignantly as it flew.

"Koko, what happened?" Leech asked as he helped the badger sit up.

"I was just trying to hitch a ride." Koko patted one side of his head as if trying to clear snow out of his ear. "And we sort of got tangled up. Where were you guys?"

"Maybe we ought to leave him here until he learns some manners," Kles said.

"He'll starve first." Leech laughed in relief and helped the badger stand up.

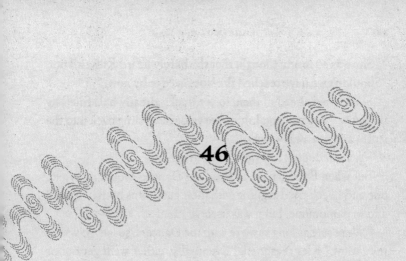

46

Bayang

Shielded by the Dancers, the friends slogged through snow covering the frozen ocean. It was as if the raging winds and whirling snowflakes were held in a giant glass cylinder, because beyond that was calm and still.

Bayang was trampling down a path for the others. Despite the growing numbness in her limbs, she was determined to save the hatchlings. Though she had known that they had become close to her, she was still surprised at the pain she had felt when she believed that she had lost them.

And she was not the only one who had changed. Leech had matured in the short time she had known him. But, she admitted ruefully, meeting your would-be killer might make anyone grow older. It certainly was altering her, the would-be killer.

She was so lost in thought that she barely heard Kles call out, "Shouldn't we have reached the storm's edge by now?"

She looked ahead of them to see tracks already half-filled by the snow. "You're right. I think we've been circling back into the storm and not away from it."

"Yeah, it doesn't feel right," Leech agreed.

But when Bayang tried to turn, the Dancers would not yield. She and Leech tried arguing with their guardians both in speech and in pantomime, but it was useless.

"We're safe as long as we're with the Dancers, so let's go where they want," Kles reasoned. "Eventually, either we'll get out or they'll listen to us."

"But we're wasting time," Scirye said.

"It can't be helped if they won't let us," the griffin said.

The others reluctantly had to admit there was no easy solution.

During the course of their trek, one or another of them would become convinced the Dancers were taking them in the wrong direction. However, the creatures of light either didn't understand or were too stubborn to give in. So the group, growing increasingly frustrated, was forced to continue on.

After an hour, Bayang stopped so suddenly that Leech bumped into her. "I can see clear air ahead," she said.

The children and badger squeezed past her to stare. There, at the mouth of the Dancers' living tunnel, was the lumpy plain, and not a single snowflake spinning about.

Leech scratched his head. "I was so sure that this wasn't the way."

"Roland must have added a confusion spell to the storm to make sure we never got out," Bayang said. "Somehow it didn't affect the Dancers." She had been feeling weary and paw sore just a moment ago, but her anger washed the fatigue away.

Scirye started to tramp forward. "He's got a lot to answer for."

47

Leech

They were all in need of a rest after the battering they had taken, but there was no time. With grim purpose, they unfolded the straw wing again as the Dancers circled curiously. After they had gotten on it, through pantomime the children and Kles politely requested aid in launching it.

The Dancers seemed to understand, because they raised the edges, more and more of them sliding underneath the exposed wing's belly and lifting it so even more Dancers could slip in and join the effort.

Leech grasped some straw loops as the wing rose jerkily, higher and higher. The Dancers seemed to think it was great sport, flocking in from all sides to add their strength until there were a hundred of them dangling from beneath the wing. All of them fluttering their tails excitedly.

Higher and higher the Dancers took them until they were looking down at the surface of the storm. It roiled like a pot of boiling milk, snowflakes slopping over the edges and cascading downward.

"I think this is high enough," Bayang said. "They can let go now."

Leech passed the message on to the Dancer rising beside them with both words and pantomime. However, when the wing still kept going up Scirye gave it a try and then Kles.

"How far are they going to carry us?" Scirye asked, glancing over the side.

"I'm not sure I want to find out," Kles said.

Koko drummed his heels on the straw mat. "Why can't anything ever go right?"

"Maybe if we rock from side to side, we can break their grip," Bayang suggested. She started to shift on her haunches. The others copied her, but though the wing tilted from left to right and back again, the Dancers' hold was unshakable.

Suddenly the clouds overhead began to shred as if puppies were tearing the stuffing out of a cushion, and the air turned choppy. The edges of the wings began to flap.

"Not another one of Roland's traps," Koko groaned.

"I am Naue, swiftest of winds, never tiring, always laughing," boomed Naue. He pounced on them with a roar like a locomotive thundering down the tracks.

"Oh, great Naue, kindest of winds," Bayang said, "we're very glad to see you."

"Brother Naue," said a wind in a voice like the bass pipes of an organ, "how do these lumplings know your name?"

"Ho, brothers and sisters, these little lumplings are my friends,"

Naue shouted. "We had so much fun on the way up here, for is not Naue the jolliest of winds?"

As the other winds joined Naue in circling around them, the sky became so turbulent that the wing swayed crazily and the Dancers not holding on to the wing were tumbled helplessly one way and then the other.

"This is w-worse than Roland's storm," Leech said, fighting desperately to hold on to the straps.

"Hey, you big blowhard, paws—I mean hands— Look, just back off," Koko hollered.

"And that lumpling is the noisy one," Naue added.

"I've heard noisier," another wind said in a loud but reedy voice.

"Listen to this, though," Naue said.

"Oof," the badger gasped as an invisible tentacle coiled around his waist and jerked him up from the wing. Kicking his hind paws, the badger desperately clung to the straw loops. "Let me go," he screamed.

"You can do better than that, Noisy Lumpling." Naue sounded disappointed. Koko's belly sagged inward as Naue squeezed the badger like a squeaky toy. "Come on; come on."

"Let's see who can make him squeal the loudest!" a third wind screeched, whose voice was like fingernails on a chalkboard. The badger began to jerk back and forth in mid-air as the third wind tried to pull him from Naue and Naue refused to let Koko go.

Afraid for his friend's life, Leech spoke up quickly: "Excuse me, great Naue and Naue's wonderful brothers and sisters, we need your help. We asked the Dancers to take us up into the sky and now they won't let go. We have to get to Nova Hafnia right away."

"Is that what you call them? Well, it's as good a name as any,"

Naue observed merrily. "I know them of old. Once they grab an idea, they don't always let go. Why didn't you ask Naue, kindest of winds?"

"You didn't tell us how to contact you," Bayang said.

"That is just like you, Naue, 'most forgetful of winds.'" A fourth wind laughed in a rumble like a kettledrum.

"True, true," Naue said proudly. As long as an insult was a superlative, the words didn't seem to hold any sting. He plopped Koko back on the wing. "But I am here now. And there is no thief craftier. Shall I steal you from the Dancers?"

"Let's make it a game," the second wind suggested. "Everyone must obey the one who can free your friends."

"Me first, me first," the second wind said, and tried to yank the wing away from the Dancers' grasp. To Leech's alarm, a foot-wide chunk of woven straw ripped off and whirled upward.

"No, no, no, not that way," the third wind objected. She tore the wing away from the second and began to twist the wing round and round as if it were the top of a screw.

The fourth shook the wing up and down so that Leech and the others bounced up and down like popcorn in a red-hot kettle.

"My silly brothers and sisters, the contest isn't about being the strongest," Naue mocked, "but the cleverest." Instead of attacking the Dancers gripping the wing, he began to swirl around, gathering up the loose Dancers like cards and packing the surprised creatures together into a dense gleaming ball. Then he hurled them away through the torn clouds.

Immediately, the other Dancers let go of the wing and swarmed up to attack Naue.

"I have won the bet, so you must pay the forfeit. And this is my command: The losers must keep the Dancers from bothering me," Naue ordered, and swept around the wing, lifting it in an upward diagonal.

Leech turned to see the Dancers flashing angrily as Naue's kin flung them back and forth to one another like a team of jugglers.

"Naue," Leech called guiltily to the wind, "will the Dancers be all right?"

"You can't kill them," Naue said. "They're just going to be held long enough to let us get away."

"Sorry about this," Leech shouted to the Dancers, "but we have to get going. Thank you for all your rescuing."

Koko was lying flat on his back on the wing, looking very sick. "Oog. I am swearing off roller coasters for good."

48

Scirye

Scirye felt crushed, her eyes tearing up in frustration. "We came all this way to catch Roland and he still got the treasure and then got away."

Koko threw up his paws. "Yeah, we might as well have saved ourselves the trip."

"The chase still isn't over," Leech said to them. "According to the goddess, he must be heading to the City of Death."

"What a lousy name," Koko said. "Why didn't the chamber of commerce change it?"

"Because it's a sacred site where a great battle took place," Kles snapped.

"Ah," Naue said, "you talk much about the Roland lumpling and his half lumpling of a dragon. Do we race them?"

"Yes," Leech said eagerly. "Let's go."

Within Scirye's coat, Kles murmured to her, "I wonder how much of the buffoon is just a pose?"

Scirye was beginning to wonder herself. "I'm not so sure myself," she whispered. "Naue *does* like to play games."

Bayang shook her head. "I'm sorry, Leech. I want to catch Roland as much as you, but we need to get help for Upach first and let Prince Tarkhun and Lady Miunai know where she and their daughter are. So it's Nova Hafnia first."

"I guess you're right," Leech said, "but I hate to see them get such a head start on us."

"Even with a lead, wondrous Naue can chase down any nasty, foul-smelling machine lumplings make," Naue said.

"And let's pick up some eats too," Koko said. "I can't eat just air like some windbags I know."

On Naue's back, they flew swiftly toward Nova Hafnia. The frozen harbor resembled a crescent moon as the ice gleamed in the moonlight. Scirye was glad to see that the Mounties on their owls were elsewhere.

"Oh, great and generous Naue, we have to leave for a short while," Bayang addressed the wind respectfully. "Will you wait here and pick us up when we come back?"

Naue swung in a lazy circle. "No one should expect a mighty wind such as Naue to make or keep promises," he guffawed. "Naue stays until he gets bored, and then he leaves."

"How do we ask you to get us?" Leech wanted to know.

"Ooh, send Naue stars," Naue shrilled. "Naue so loves them when they blossom."

"Do you mean some kind of flower?" Leech asked. "I could bring it up to you, but I don't think anything's growing in Nova Hafnia right now."

Naue spun the straw wing playfully about in a slow circle. "No, no, they twinkle; they sparkle. They're born, but then they die too soon. Humans are always throwing great heaps of them up into Naue's sky."

Scirye glanced at Kles, who was peeking out of her coat, but he shook his head. He was just as perplexed as she was. Then she twisted her head around and raised an eyebrow at Leech and Koko. Leech shook his head, but the badger seemed thoughtful.

"Do you mean fireworks?" Koko ventured.

"Yes, I think that's what lumplings call them." Naue made puffing sounds. "Whoosh, whoosh, whoosh."

"The caravanserai probably has them," Leech said to the others. "They seem to have everything."

"The question," Bayang said, "is whether they'll give them to us."

"Or even if they'll let us leave," Koko pointed out gloomily.

"We'll just make another daring escape," Leech said confidently. "We always have so far."

"There's a first time for a flop," Koko groaned. "And I'd rather not be part of it."

Despite the badger's misgivings, Bayang steered the wing away from the wind's embrace and spiraled down gently until they glided to a smooth landing on the harbor where the snow acted as a cushion.

A lone gnome mechanic was standing on a small ladder as he toiled beneath an airplane cowling. Near him a pair of humans in coveralls were bobbing up and down as they used a hand pump to re-fuel a different airplane from barrels on a sled. They both resembled Roxanna's Sogdians. Next to them several imps circled lazily inside a large glass jar, casting light and heat in the immediate area.

Suddenly one of the Sogdians noticed the companions. "It's Lady Roxanna's kidnappers! Tell Lady Miunai quick."

At his shout, the gnome hit his head against the cowling, but the humans' reaction was more hostile. The second Sogdian jumped down from the sled and, slipping and sliding over the ice, headed toward the city to sound the alarm.

"If we'd stolen her, do you think we'd come back so conspicuously?" Scirye snapped. "It was her own idea to help us find Roland. She's safe with friends. We'll tell Lady Miunai and Prince Tarkhun all about it."

The first Sogdian had picked up a wrench and was holding it, ready to throw it if they tried to escape. "Prince Tarkhun's out hunting for you in an airplane. And half the clan is out there too in sleds, and the Mounties as well. So there's no use trying to escape."

"We're not trying to run away," Scirye said, irritated. "We're trying to explain."

As they got off the wing, the human mechanic raised his wrench menacingly. "Stay where you are."

Bayang grew larger so she could carry everyone on her back again. "I wouldn't do that if I were you. I wouldn't feel that thing any more than I would a twig. And if you hit one of the hatchlings by mistake..." She paused, letting the mechanic's own imagination fill in the gap.

Scirye tried to play the peacemaker. "Besides, we're going to the caravanserai by our own choice. Whether we're friends or foes, that would be what Lady Miunai would want. You're welcome to come along and make sure we deliver ourselves into your mistress's hands."

The mechanic gulped as he gazed up at the dragon. "No, thanks," he said, lowering the wrench. "I got too much work here. So I'll take your word for it."

"I'm glad to see that you're smarter than you look," Bayang said as she folded up the wing.

Bayang set off at a slow, steady trot, her paws sometimes

skidding on the slippery surface, leaving the Sogdian behind scratching his head with the wrench.

After a few minutes, they overtook the other Sogdian who had left to warn Lady Miunai. He was plodding along and there was snow all over him as if he'd slipped and fallen several times.

"Can we give you a lift to the caravanserai?" Bayang asked.

The puffing mechanic shook his head. "My mother made me swear to avoid two things: strong liquor and dragons."

"Suit yourself," Bayang said, and moved away, leaving him to plod after them.

They couldn't miss the caravanserai, which dominated the wharf area. It peered over the roofs of the other buildings as if waiting vigilantly for them.

There were steps leading down from the dock into the ocean for rowboats when the thaw had come. Bayang did not bother with them but arched her long body so it could climb up onto the planks. She skidded at first on an icy patch but managed to pull herself up.

Some attempt had been made to shovel the streets and dockside, and the dragon made better time as she wound her way past all the boats hauled up out of the water.

As Prince Tarkhun had warned them when they had first entered the town, dragons were a rarity. As they turned onto a broad, crowded avenue, a dwarf stopped scraping the barnacles from a hull to stare and all along the street humans, trolls, and the city's other inhabitants gaped.

A frost giant, his hair and beard pale and pointed as icicles, was so stunned that he just stopped in the middle of the road with a barrel on either shoulder. "Is there a parade?"

"Yes, a short one." With the suppleness of an eel, Bayang slithered around the living roadblock, ducked under the sign hanging in front of a restaurant, and slogged on, dodging around other obstacles.

"The Sogdians must not have put a price on our heads yet," Kles observed. "Or someone would be taking potshots at us."

"Just as a matter of discussion," Koko speculated, "how much do you think we're worth?"

"The Lady Scirye is priceless." Kles sniffed. "You, on the other hand—well, I'd pay them to take you off my paws."

"Now, now, Kles," Scirye scolded mildly. She'd developed a soft spot for Koko. "A talented badger like you is worth his weight in gold."

"So my mama always said," Koko said smugly.

Bayang twisted to her left down a side street that led to the great gates of the caravanserai.

Without Roxanna by their side, the walls looked as high and forbidding as a prison's, and Bayang slowed. Suddenly dozens of rifles pointed at them from through the wall's slits and the huge gates began to swing open.

Scirye pressed an arm around Kles. "They're already expecting us."

"A lookout must have seen Bayang flying over the harbor," Kles reasoned.

Lady Miunai strode out with a bandolier strapped across her body and a rifle that looked large enough to put a hole even in a dragon. "Where is my daughter? Why didn't she come back with you?"

Over the years, Scirye had seen her mother calm the ruffled feathers of countless foreign diplomats. Scirye was not sure she could do the same, but she was determined to try.

She slid off Bayang. It was a small gesture that might help ease Lady Miunai's state of mind, since she wouldn't have to tilt her head back to see Scirye's face.

"She's staying with Upach, who was shot by Roland," Scirye explained quickly. "They're both safe with Uncle Resak."

Lady Miunai started at the third name, then glanced around the street and motioned them into the caravanserai. "I think you'd better come inside so we can talk," she said, shouldering her weapon.

"Is that a good idea?" Koko muttered.

"You can stay out here and get shot if one of the chakar gets trigger-happy," Bayang said as she trotted after Scirye and Lady Miunai.

"Naw, I'm tired of being in a shooting gallery," Koko said, and pressed himself flat against the dragon's back to make himself a smaller target.

After they had crossed the courtyard and entered one of the warehouses, Lady Miunai ordered all the workers to leave. "And close the doors behind you."

It took a few minutes for them to exit through the several doors. Each seemed to shut with the ominous thud of an executioner's axe.

Finally, except for the fire imps on the walls, they were alone in the cavernous room. Lady Miunai spoke in a low voice, her breath frosting the air in the vast, cold room: "So you survived the phantoms?"

"As I think you knew we would," Scirye said.

Lady Miunai folded her hands in front of her. "But we couldn't be sure."

Scirye told her about their encounter with Uncle Resak and the subsequent fight within his palace and their own adventure in returning to Nova Hafnia. "Uncle realizes that his secret is out, so he wants your husband and Roxanna to act as his go-betweens with the humans."

"It was only a matter of time before the truth came out," Lady

Miunai observed. "His secret was safe enough when hardly anyone lived up here, but every year brings more people, more ships, and more airplanes." Her fingers tapped the stock of her rifle as she considered the next step. "I'll send word to my husband so he can head to Uncle's."

"Upach will need Dr. Goldemar," Leech said, and explained about Upach's situation.

Lady Miunai nodded. "I've a man who has handled the supply route to Uncle. He can take the doctor. But what will you do now?"

"We'll head to the Kushan Empire," Bayang said.

Kles gave his purring chirp at the prospect of going home, but it only made Scirye uneasy. She had not seen the empire since she was a small child, and most of the Kushans she had met since then had never made her feel welcome. They usually looked down at her because she did not act like a proper Kushan girl—which made her decidedly inferior. In the small, self-contained world within the embassies that had been bad enough, but the Kushans there had never numbered more than a few hundred. There would be millions of them in the empire, and all of them would wear the same disapproving expression.

Still, she had already done a lot of things she didn't think she could, so she would treat this just like she had any other problem.

"Ah," Lady Miunai said, "if you ever need help when you are in the empire, find my husband's great-aunt, Princess Catisa, and she will give you whatever you wish."

If Princess Catisa was anything like her kinswoman, Scirye thought, they wouldn't have any worries. Lady Miunai was only too happy to supply them with more of the powdered emergency rations—Leech kept Koko's grumbling to a minimum. She also thoughtfully added a tiny water imp in a portable distillery.

She wanted to give them more equipment, but Bayang did not want to overload the straw wing, which was in need of repair.

However, Lady Miunai was amused when they asked for fireworks. "I think it'll take more than a flash and a bang to scare Roland."

"They're to summon Naue the wind, who'll take us into the air so we can catch him," Scirye explained.

Lady Miunai shook her head in amazement. "My husband said that meeting you was like wandering into a tale of marvels."

"Believe me. It's not all that wonderful when you're smack in the middle of it," Koko mumbled.

Lady Miunai set her palm upon Scirye's head in blessing and said in formal Sogdian, "May thou pounce upon thine enemy like the mighty griffin. And may Nana keep thee and thine safe."

Scirye answered her humbly in the same formal tongue: "I thank thee, Lady Miunai, for in thy kindness thou hast been like my own mother. Knowest thou that I will." *If I'm alive*, she added to herself.

The lines of worry on Lady Miunai's face and the sadness in her eyes suggested the opposite of her cheerful words. She obviously shared Scirye's own concerns.

That made Scirye think of her own mother. Even though there had been no time to do it, Scirye felt guilty that she hadn't written or called her. "And will you send a message to my mother that I'm all right and headed to Bactra? Her name is Lady Sudarshane and she's at the San Francisco Consulate."

"Of course. She must be as worried sick about her little chick as I am about Roxanna," sympathized Lady Miunai. "But that's what happens when your children become the stuff of wonders."

Not satisfied with having re-supplied them, Lady Miunai insisted on escorting them personally. Some of her men went along as porters for her gifts. Others carried the dogsled on their shoulders. The driver, a short, stocky man, was busy handling his dog team. Behind him waddled Dr. Goldemar wearing a derby hat, which he had secured with a long scarf knotted beneath his chin, his medical bag resting on his shoulder.

They marched out of the caravanserai and eventually down the broad street. The frost giant clapped his huge hands together with childish delight. "I knew there was going to be a parade." He fell into step behind them, windmilling his hand at the bystanders encouragingly. "Come on; come on. Join in."

There was not much in the way of entertainment in a small town in winter, and the news spread like lightning. People poured out of houses and stores so that soon they had a hundred people of all species, dogs, cats, and even a parrot trailing them along the avenue. A man with a concertina wheezed out a jaunty marching tune for everyone to step to.

Lady Miunai took the friends down a boat-launching ramp that they hadn't noticed before.

Bayang skidded a bit on the frozen harbor but recovered nicely to polite applause from the expectant crowd. Then, while the dogsled was assembled and the team harnessed to it, the dragon unfolded the wing again.

In the meantime, Lady Miunai put herself in charge of the pyrotechnics and oversaw her helpers as they unpacked the rockets, throwing excelsior all over. Several were propped against a now empty crate. The rockets were genuine Chinese ones, for Lady Miunai was determined to give them a grand and glorious send-off.

An enterprising tavern keeper had come out with a tray full of steaming reindeer sausages. Koko sniffed the air woefully. "If only I had some money," he hinted.

"Here, here." The keeper shuffled forward and pressed the badger to take one, no—two. "Oh, why not? Let's make it three?"

As Koko happily munched away, the keeper returned to the crowd shouting that the sausages had been endorsed by the strange wonder beast.

"Badger," Koko corrected the tavern keeper, but his mouth was so full of meat, the word came out garbled. Even if Koko had taken the time to swallow before he spoke, the keeper was so mobbed by customers that he wouldn't have heard anyway.

When Scirye and her friends had stowed their supplies carefully on the wing so it would balance right, they climbed onto it.

"Good-bye," Leech called. "Please thank Roxanna and Upach for us."

"I will, and fare thee well," Lady Miunai said, and gestured to one of her men.

Lighting a match, he lit the fuses as he walked along, retreating to safety when all of them started to fizz. The fuses were of different lengths so the rockets would go off at different times.

Whoosh! The first one soared up into the air in a plume of white smoke. A hundred feet above them it burst in a spray of paper scraps and more smoke. *Bang!* The little star of light spread petals of a shining red chrysanthemum across the sky. And the tingling smell of gunpowder descended thick around them.

Whoosh! Whoosh! Rockets sped upward and exploded and more flowers blossomed in the field of the night.

Below, the crowd oohed and aahed at the spectacle.

Even as more rockets went off, they heard the roar of Naue. "Ho, a garden, a garden!" the wind shouted, as thrilled as the audience below.

In the air the fireworks' smoke and light trailed after him in his wake, and on the harbor snow swirled in wispy streamers across the frozen surface.

"I am Naue, friend of heroes, dancer among flowers," Naue boasted as he darted in and out of the explosions, twisting the shapes of the fiery blossoms.

When the last rocket had gone off, Naue yelled, "Now *that* is how to greet Naue!" He circled far out to the mouth of the harbor and then slanted down toward them. Snow sprayed up in sheets as he sped toward them.

The wing, edges flapping, lifted into the air and rose swiftly on Naue as the townsfolk clapped and hollered good-bye in a dozen different languages.

Leech let out a long breath. "And I thought riding in a seaplane was exciting."

When Koko thumped his belly, he gave a satisfied burp. "I'd settle for a nice, boring evening reading a telephone book."

Below them, the dogs sped over the ice with the doctor tucked into the sled. Scirye hoped they could help Upach.

Leech poked Scirye's shoulder. "You okay? You're sitting so stiff. Don't worry about Roland. We'll get him the next time. Just think about going home."

"Home," Kles murmured happily as he snuggled inside Scirye's coat.

"Home," Scirye echoed softly but not with any pleasure. She hadn't even been thinking about Roland but about all the Kushans waiting to scold her in Bactra—just for the crime of not being what they wanted: a proper Kushan lady.

Now she couldn't help wondering uneasily what new surprises Roland had in store for them.

And then there was the pact with Nanaia. Could she really keep it, and if she did what would be the price?

Bayang, who was at the control loops, had twisted her long neck around so she could see what was wrong with Scirye. "Think about now and not the future," Bayang advised the girl.

"Otherwise, you'll get so scared that you'll be afraid to go on. We're still alive and that's the important thing."

Bayang was right. The more Scirye thought about Nanaia's mission, the more terrified she became. There were better people than Scirye for this quest, but for whatever reason it had fallen on her. As Uncle Resak had said, all she could do was follow the path that the goddess had set for her. At least she wasn't alone. She had friends—more friends than she'd ever had before in her life—and they had managed so far.

When Naue passed through the clouds, their moisture pattered against the travelers like a light drizzle. They burst out of the cover into a glorious black sky full of stars and a moon that hung like a large round lantern to light their way.

As she stared up at its face, the moon seemed to smile gently as Nishke would have. *Yes, you will,* her sister seemed to whisper to her reassuringly the way she had when Scirye was small.

And her heart soared upward as she flew on into the night.

Into the promise.

Into the future.

Afterword

Many years ago, I read about an opera troupe that was performing Humperdinck's *Hansel and Gretel* in small Alaskan towns near the Arctic Circle. The children of each town were asked to paint a backdrop of a forest. However, this was in the days before satellite dishes and the Internet, so one group of Inuit children had to imagine what a forest looked like. I've always wondered what they came up with. If they'd had gold and jewels instead of poster paints, perhaps they would have created a tree like Uncle Resak's.

I should also say a word about the general background of the novel. While everyone knows about the gold deposits in Canada, there are also diamond mines in the Far North. And centuries ago the Danish began to explore the Arctic territories. Jens Munck was a real explorer who died in 1628 trying to find the Northwest Passage for the ambitious King Christian of Denmark. The Thirty Years War, which began in 1618, drew his attentions and finances elsewhere, or perhaps the Danes would have claimed northern Canada just as they control Greenland to this day.

While this is an alternate history, I want to emphasize that the Sogdians are not an imaginary people. The beginnings of their city Afrasiab, which became known as Samarkand later, date back to the seventh century B.C. Clever and energetic, the Sogdians dominated the Silk Road for centuries, so that their tongue became the language everyone used for business transactions. Led by merchant princes, they established a network of trading posts that stretched all across Asia. And their music and dance became all the rage in medieval China, and these are often depicted in the art of the T'ang dynasty. Some of them even rose to high positions in the Chinese government, and one of them, An Lu-shan, nearly toppled the government when he raised a rebellion. As for the Arctic itself, I am fortunate to have a wife, Joanne Ryder, who not only took me up to the Arctic to see the Aurora Borealis firsthand but also has written several books about the environment and the creatures who live up there. The Wastes themselves are an exaggeration of the pressure ridges that were shown in a BBC Two program, *Top Gear: Polar Special*, which a friend kindly provided me. The narwhals are in the National Geographic special *Masters of the Arctic Ice*.

These are some of the sources consulted for this book:

Adams, Douglas Q. *A Dictionary of Tocharian B*. Amsterdam: Rodopi, 1999.

Asarpay, G. "Nana, the Sumero-Akkadian Goddess of Transoxiana." *Journal of the American Oriental Society* 96, no. 4 (October–December 1976): 536–542.

Bayliss, Clara Kern. *A Treasury of Eskimo Tales*. New York: Thomas Y. Crowell, 1922.

Cribb, Joe, and Georgina Herrmann, eds. *After Alexander: Central Asia before Islam*. Oxford: Oxford University Press, 2007.

Ghose, Madhuvanti. "Nana: The 'Original' Goddess on Lion." *Journal of Inner Asian Art and Archaeology* 1 (2006): 97–112.

Juliano, Annette L., Judith A. Lerner, and Michael Alram. *Monks and Merchants: Silk Road Treasures from Northwest China.* New York: Abrams, 2001.

Masters of the Arctic Ice. DVD. National Geographic, 2007.

Nuttall, Mark, and Terry Gallaghan, eds., *The Arctic: Environment, People, Policy.* Amsterdam: Harwood Academic Publishers, 2000.

Rasmussen, Knud. *Eskimo Folktales*, trans. W. Worster. London: Gyldendal, 1921.

Rink, Dr. Henry. *Tales and Traditions of the Eskimo.* Edinburgh and London: Blackwood and Sons, 1875.

Rosenfeld, John M. *The Dynastic Arts of the Kushans.* Berkeley: University of California Press, 1967.

Sims-Williams, Nicholas. *Bactrian Letters II.* London: Nour Foundation with the cooperation of Azimuth Editions, 2007.

Vaissière, Étienne de la. *Sogdian Traders: A History*, trans. James Ward. Leiden: Brill, 2005.

Turn the page for a
sneak peek at

City of Death,

Book 3

in the City Trilogy

"How fast do storms come in here?" Bayang the dragon asked. She was sitting at the apex, steering the giant triangular wing that had been magically woven from straw.

Dark gray clouds boiled rapidly through the sky toward them. A mile across and two miles long, the misty wave cast shadows that plunged the mountains beneath them into an ominous twilight.

The great wind, Naue, began to rise as he reassured them in his booming voice, "Ho, fear not, lumplings. No little drizzle can stop Naue the magnificent. He will just carry you above it."

Koko the badger rolled his eyes. "Or," he muttered, "you can talk it to death."

"It's following us," Leech said in alarm, for the storm cloud had arched upward to intercept them, its sides churning and writhing like a giant panting worm.

Bayang dug her claws into the interwoven straw and tightened her grip on the straps that steered the wing. "That's no normal storm cloud. Everyone sit down and grab hold of the wing. And that especially means you, Leech."

"But—," Leech began to protest.

"I don't want you hopping on your flying disks and going to check out the cloud," Bayang snapped.

Leech reluctantly plopped down and grabbed some straps that had been placed strategically about the wing.

Scirye sat down and took hold of another pair of straps. "Do you think this is Roland's work?"

Kles, her lap griffin, uncoiled from around her shoulders and slipped inside her coat. "He might have set patrols as a precaution. Or it could just be our bad luck. The mountains are very old and full of magic. And there are monsters here that go back to the creation of the world."

"Monster or Roland's slave, nothing can catch Naue," the wind bragged as he flew even faster and higher.

Thunk-a thunk-a-thunk.

"That sounds like a drum roll," Leech said.

A bolt of lightning shot from the cloud to blast the mountain beneath it, the light temporarily highlighting the curling mist of the storm.

Boom!

More and more lightning bolts crackled from the cloud's belly so that it resembled a giant centipede climbing after them on fiery legs. It was gaining on them very quickly.

"Ho, so you want to play tag with Naue? Then so be it," Naue boomed.

And the next moment Naue banked sharply until he was zooming toward the cloud.

"No, no, go away from it!" Bayang shouted.

But the wind ignored her, and as they rushed toward the roiling surface of the cloud, the inky strands writhed like charcoal snakes.

Naue roared with laughter as he plowed through the cloud, whipping it into smoky tendrils. Their straw wing bucked and rolled as Naue twisted and turned, tearing the storm to shreds.

And yet through Naue's merriment the drum roll deepened until it was a steady booming.

"Ha, that will show it," Naue announced as he finally circled away.

"Who's that?" Leech asked.

It was as if a huge ball of dark cotton had been ripped apart to reveal an inner core, a rough gray oval about ten feet long like a huge bar of soap. And upon the disk a creature danced on two stubby legs. He looked like a squat man but his skin was blue and tusks rose from his lower jaw. From his shoulders hung a wide strap of drums and in his hands were the bones he used to beat them.

Bayang swore an oath in an old dragon tongue. "What's a thunder lord doing here? He belongs in China."

The thunder lord brought both sticks down upon one drum, and the next instant there was a flash of light and a bolt streaked from the drum across the sky and through Naue.

Boom!

"Aiee," Naue cried out in agony and shock. "Naue hurts!"

The sudden flash made spots dance before Scirye's eyes, and the smell of ozone tickled her nose.

Boom! Boom! Boom!

Naue screamed as each beat of the drums shot lightning bolts through him. It was all they could do to hold on as the wind whirled about, trying to escape, but the lightning was relentless. Too late, Bayang realized that their wing marked where the invisible Naue was.

"Naue . . . can . . . not . . . keep . . . together," the wind gasped.

Though the lightning could not destroy the air that made up the wind, the energy was making it hard for Naue to keep his currents together. It was like unraveling the threads that make up a piece of string.

Naue bellowed in torment, and suddenly the wing was spinning earthward as they fell out of the injured wind's grasp.

With a ripping noise, a large scrap of the wing fluttered away and then more and more pieces. The wing was falling apart. The long trips and abuse had taken their toll upon the wing's woven straw. Through the numerous holes, Bayang could see the earth waiting for them three thousand feet below.

Bayang tried to test her injured wings to see if she could fly away with her friends, but pain shot instantly through her back.

Their only hope was to land the wing before it disintegrated. Her eyes searched the mountains below for a soft landing spot, but at first it was one fanglike mountain after another. And then she saw the silvery oval that must be some frozen lake in a bowl formed by the mountains.

She yanked at the left strap, trying to angle the wing toward it, only to have the strap tear off in her paw. Sometimes all you can do is trust your instincts, her old flying instructor, Sergeant Pandai, had told her. So she threw away the useless strap. Then she dug the claws of her left forepaw deep into the woven material itself and began to pull.

If she had used all her strength, she probably would have torn a whole section from the weakened wing, but instead she used a steady tugging. Bit by bit, the wing began to point toward the oval.

All Bayang could do was hope there was enough snow on the lake to cushion their landing and the ice was thick enough to take their weight.

Above them, Naue had stopped screaming. Bayang hoped that the wind was still alive and had gotten away.

The thunder lord could now direct his lightning bolts at them. A streak of dazzling light sizzled the air near them and her scales tingled with the electric charge.

Boom!

The lake rose toward them quickly. It looked about a mile long and about half that in width. Wisps of snow drifted across the top.

Even as she began to try to ease the nose up, something made her jink to the right. A lightning bolt shot past, just burning the port side.

Boom!

Her muzzle wriggled as smoke tickled her nostrils and she felt the warmth as the wing's edge caught fire.

What were they going to do now?

Reader's Guide

ABOUT THIS GUIDE
The information, activities, and discussion questions that follow
are intended to enhance your reading of *City of Ice*. Please feel
free to adapt these materials to suit your needs and interests.

WRITING AND RESEARCH ACTIVITIES
I. Friends and Family
A. Create a descriptive page for at least six *City of Ice* characters. Using information found in the novel, note each character's name, age, physical attributes, homeland, personality traits,
special talents, and goals. Compile the pages together into a
booklet entitled *Characters from* City of Ice.

B. In the character of Bayang, write a journal entry describing your feelings for Scirye or Leech. Explain how these
feelings have changed you and what you have learned from your
friendship.

C. Compare and contrast the characters of Scirye and
Roxanna in terms of their heritage, talents, goals, relationship to
their families, and sense of their obligations to their families,
friends, community, or future. Create a two-column chart or other
diagram to illustrate your comparisons.

D. Hold a class discussion as to which is more important:
loyalty to friends or loyalty to family. Are there circumstances,
such as war, that may alter your priorities? What are the most
important things you can learn from family? From friends? If
desired, take a class vote to determine what the majority thinks

about key questions. Write a newspaper-style article summarizing the outcome of your debate.

II. Worlds and Weather

A. The novel begins in 1941. Go to the library or online to research what was happening in real history in 1941. Create a month-by-month timeline of interesting events that occurred in the United States and around the world in 1941. Share your timeline with friends or classmates. Do you see any connections between the events in real history and the events taking place in Laurence Yep's alternative world? Make a list of the connections you observe.

B. Using clues from the novel, draw a map of Nova Hafnia, the Wastes, and other icy landmarks through which Scirye and her friends travel. Label natural formations, the homes of clans or groups, and other important landmarks on your map.

C. As they journey to the Wastes, Scirye and her friends experience brutal cold. Write a poem or song expressing their experience of nearly freezing.

D. Pele provided a charm to help keep the travelers warm on their icy journey. Use clay, paints, and/or other craft materials to create the charm you imagine the main characters wearing.

E. Imagine you are riding on the wing with Scirye, Bayang, and the others. Write two to three pages of dialogue in which you and other characters try to persuade Naue to slow down, speed up, or perform some other action. Include lines about how you feel riding the wing, where you want to go, and whether you think Naue can get you there.

F. Go to the library or online to learn more about the Aurora Borealis or Northern Lights, called "Dancers" in the novel. Create a painting, photo collage, or other visual artwork depicting the Northern Lights. Caption your work with information from your research.

III. Secrets and Promises

A. *Tumarg*, or honor, is an important Kushan principle for Scirye. Draw three to four graphic novel–style panels depicting a moment in the story when Scirye grapples with the need to keep *tumarg*. Then, write a paragraph describing why you chose this particular moment in the story as a good example to illustrate a crisis of honor.

B. Throughout the novel, Leech struggles with evil thoughts, particularly ones that suggest harm to Bayang. Write a letter to Leech, advising him on how to handle these troubling thoughts and whether or not you think he should reveal them to Bayang.

C. Koko, Upach, Lord Resak, and Bayang all have the capacity to change form. In the character of Dr. Goldemar, describe the forms these characters can take. Add details about these abilities based on information from the novel.

D. Nanaia is a goddess worshipped by many cultures in different ways. Write a short essay describing the "bargain" Scirye has made with Nanaia and how her journey from Kushan to Sogdian lands, with their different senses of Nanaia, has affected this promise.

DISCUSSION QUESTIONS

1. As the novel begins, of whom are Sciyre and her friends in pursuit? Why do they want to catch this character? What supernatural creatures are helping them on their journey? Through what type of landscape are they traveling? Does the landscape remind you of any real-world locations?

2. What aid does Prince Tarkhun provide the travelers? What country is he from? What is his relationship to Roland and Badik? To the freebooters? What is important about the types of language Tarkhun and Scirye use in their communication?

3. Who does Scirye come to know at the Sogdian caravan-serai? How do these Sogdians come to find themselves in the North? Does Roxanna consider herself more of a Sogdian or Arctic girl? Compare Roxanna's sense of nationality with Scirye's.

4. What is the relationship between Leech and Bayang? How does this relationship change in the course of the novel? What role does flying play in their relationship?

5. Compare the friendship between Leech and Koko with the friendship between Scirye and Kles. Do you think one friendship is stronger than the other? Why or why not?

6. Describe the strange experience Scirye has with the statue of Nanaia. What do you think is the meaning of this experience? How does the experience change other characters' understanding of Scirye?

7. How do Scirye's memories of her parents and her dead sister, Nishke, affect her thoughts and actions? How might you compare Scirye's sense of guilt over her lost sister to Roxanna's lost confidence when she feels she has failed Scirye?

8. Who is Lord Resak? In what form do Scirye, Bayang, and the others first meet him? Describe Lord Resak's secret home. Why do you think so many characters call Resak "Uncle"? How does this relate to Resak's relationship with nature?

9. What are the ring and bow string of the Archer Yi? What theories does Scirye advance to explain why Roland wants them? How does sharing this information with Lord Resak impact their relationship?

10. On page 246, Scirye recalls that Bayang once warned her "that powerful beings like Pele had a different perspective than humans." Do you think this statement is one of the central ideas of the novel? Explain your answer.

11. How does Naue help the characters in the course of the novel? How do Scirye's conversations with Naue reveal her talents at diplomacy?

12. What is the secret of the Wastes? What happens when the secret can no longer be kept? To what decisions does this lead Lord Resak and Scirye?

13. What happens to Upach during the battle with Roland's thugs? How does this affect Roxanna's actions? What does Roxanna's decision to stay with Upach, and not return to her father with Scirye, reveal about her character?

14. Describe Scirye's, Leech's, and the others' journey back to the caravanserai. How does Bayang deal with her injury? How are the friends greeted by Lady Miunai?

15. Where is the City of Death? What worries Scirye about making the journey to this city? Are you surprised by her greatest concerns? What do you think Scirye's greatest worry should be?

16. If you were describing *City of Ice* to a friend, would you call it foremost a story of power, of friendship, or of honor? Explain your answer, citing examples from the novel.

Starscape

*Award-Winning
Science Fiction and Fantasy
for Ages 10 and up*

STARSCAPE

www.tor-forge.com/starscape